The Kombinatsia Conspiracy

by

Robert T. Haller
Colonel, USAR (Ret.)

Leister & Sons Publishing Company
Pennsylvania

Copyright © 1990 Robert T. Haller
Leister & Sons Publishing Company
PO Box 758, Hamlin, PA 18427
(717) 689-3687

*This story is a work of fiction. While the events described here
are imaginary, this scenario may be "a tragedy waiting to happen."
All names, characters, settings and events are fictitious and not
intended to represent real people, living or deceased.*

ADVANCE EDITION: January 1997.

ISBN-0-9618234-1-0

Printed in the United States of America

This book is dedicated to:

my comrades-in-arms in the U.S. Army Reserve, both past and present. You know who you are.

To my son John ... pals forever,

And to my loving wife and editor, Charlotte.

ACKNOWLEDGMENTS:

Without mentioning names, I'd like to acknowledge the help I received from friends and colleagues in the U.S. Army Reserve, U.S. Navy, intelligence community, airport security, nursing, pharmacy, coroner, computer, and public relations professionals, who added to the authenticity of this novel and helped make it possible.

I also owe a debt of gratitude to my wife Charlotte, who endured this writer's temperament and work schedule, debated and edited many key points, and spent endless hours proof reading. Without her encouragement, this novel would still be on the "shelf."

And a special thanks to Bob Baisley, who helped retrieve my computer disks, reformat it to publisher standards, and get it to the printer on time.

My sincere thanks to all.

Prologue

March 6, 1988.

Murder. Deception. Disinformation. Treachery. The essential elements of a terrorist campaign. As the cold war ends and the world moves toward a new political equilibrium, the radical forces of espionage unleash a deadly mission on America's shores. Adversaries are hurled at each other in this last clandestine battle. To gain advantage. To catch the eagle asleep.

1

2330 hours, 6 March 1988.

The moonless night, shrouded with dark ominous clouds, sensed the intrusion of the Soviet trawler as it ploughed through the deep swells of the North Atlantic on a south by southeastward course. The sinister spy ship, bristling with a vast array of intelligence antennas, slowed down to four knots and rolled in the heavy seas, barely making steerage. Ahead, about twenty miles to the starboard lay Fire Island and the Hamptons. Beyond that, New York City, asleep and unsuspecting.

On deck, a heavy muscular figure, clad in a black skin-diver's suit, sat perched on the trawler's midship rail, his legs and flippers dangling over the side. The Soviet GRU agent slipped on his face mask and snorkel, his life support, and popped it for air to check for leakage one last time. With a glancing nod to the two seamen and captain standing nearby, the GRU agent jumped into the running sea, which was icy cold. He bobbed back to the surface. He signaled the seamen to toss a large floatation cylinder, measuring about five and a half feet long, fifteen inches in diameter. He checked the stabilizing fins of the waterproof container and pulled the eight-foot tow line taut, which was hooked up to him like an umbilical cord. Everything was in order. He kicked off, pointing toward the landfall, One powerful arm stroked out. Then the other ... in long deliberate pulls, propelling him and his deadly cargo toward a rendezvous before first light.

Looking over his shoulder, he saw the trawler turn north to rejoin the Soviet fishing fleet, monitoring the computer companies near Boston. Their intelligence mission was unending, just like his army career.

The GRU agent swam effortlessly on his back. He pointed his fins in and out in a frog kick, slowly, never making a splash. One and glide. Then push out again. He glided gracefully, pulling the tow line. He kept a steady pace, never missing a breath. Straight through the nose, out through the mouth. Deep breaths. Good and easy.

His intrusion into the veil of uncertainty met with no acknowledgment, the ocean current continuing its endless drift. He tried to concentrate on other matters, anything but swimming. It was the only way he could make the twenty mile swim in these heavy seas.

Colonel Yakov Petrovich was 47, a powerfully built man, five foot ten, one hundred eighty pounds, with a bull neck, massive shoulders, bulging biceps and a barrel chest. His penetrating green eyes peered out from the face mask, alert to the dangers of the deep.

How many wars must I fight? he wondered. How many men must I kill? Why must I live like animal? Cold war is over. Capitalist world, why does it keep resisting? Why is it barbaric? Imperialists will lose. It is inevitable. Yet, they do not yield. They do not surrender. There is no other way. Only bloodshed.

The killings in Germany, Czechoslovakia, Angola and Iraq had blended into one. Afghanistan was worst. A bloody forsaken mountainous land not worth fighting for. His comrades were dead, Killed by dreaded Mujahideen Moslem zealots, who wanted to die fighting as martyrs. How does one conquer such people?

Americans are to blame. Weapons and ammunition come from America. Stinger missiles cause our defeat. No MIG or helicopter is safe from its deadly accuracy. Gregorievich paid with his life. My son, my only son, such a fine pilot. To be blown out of sky, for what? Americans will pay dearly. Gregorievich's death will not go unanswered.

Petrovich looked back at the watertight container slicing through the water behind him. He remembered the night raid when he led a parachute team against a Mujahideen stronghold to capture the American-made Stinger. His men had been killed retreating down the mountain slope. He had been seriously wounded, barely making it to the helicopter landing zone and extraction. Now vengeance was near. To bring America to its knees. To shoot down an American jetliner with an American-made Stinger missile, so American Congress will stop its warmongering president from sending more weapons to Russia's enemies.

The ocean tide had changed, pushing him back to sea. The whitecaps were running about twelve knots, making headway difficult. Petrovich slowed his pace, feeling a twinge of fatigue. He rolled over onto his side. He continued to frog-kick, using the side stroke. He never changed pace. Kick out, grab ... sixteen feet. Kick out and grab ... sixteen feet. He cupped his hands, never bringing them out of the water, gaining five extra feet each time.

He thought about Russia. Mother Russia. And Anna. Beautiful, brazen, card-carrying Anna. After twenty years of boring marriage and long army separations, he wondered if she had remained faithful to him while he trained for this mission. Faith? Anna's only faith is to Communist Party.

She must be sleeping with Party bureaucrat. She makes one feel strong and superior. Then foolish. I spoke of love and she laughed. "Love is bourgeoisie slogan to make one weak and impotent. It is Party that counts. Nothing else!" To think, she criticized my ambition. Is it wrong to aspire to higher army rank? To become GRU general? He shook his head. Perhaps, she is right. Individual is nothing. Communist Party is everything.

Yet, he thought about *perestroika*. After fighting all these years to become superpower, why is Politburo talking disarmament? Did Gregorievich and all my comrades die for nothing? Or is Moscow playing a game of deception to consolidate our gains, telling West this is how real world will be, to live and let live? Petrovich recognized that living conditions needed to be changed. Russia's economy must be improved. Incompetence and special privileges must be stopped. He shut his eyes painfully, then reopened them. If everyone must now make sacrifices, I better not lose army pension. Perhaps army general staff is waging silent war with Politburo to keep large standing army intact. Now that cold war is over, west will drop its guard. When time is ripe, we attack and seize all of Europe's wealth. Then Russia's problems will be solved. But first, corrupt officials must be stopped before they emasculate Soviet army. My mission must destroy them.

Petrovich thought about his enemy. Rich, decadent America. If I was born in

America, I grow up to be stockbroker or gangster. Maybe colonel in Green Berets. I would not know better. He laughed derisively. He felt lucky he was born in Russia. Yet, buried deep within his self-conscious lay a recurring nightmarish dream that haunted him about his roots. He forced the secret nagging thoughts out of his head. "I find answer in New York."

He checked the luminous dial on his watch at 4:08 a.m. Fire Island lay three hundred yards away. He closed the distance, swimming another hundred yards toward shore. He treaded water smoothly, not splashing, his arms and fins the only movement. These were the moments he hated most. Waiting. He was on station early. He checked his bearing and drifted calmly with the tide. He pulled the Stinger container closer and adjusted its stabilizer fins so it could float upright just below the water's surface.

He waited patiently, treading water in the early morning fog. A sea swell rolled over his head. He tried to forget his anguish, focusing on the mission. Only five weeks before Stinger attack. At 4:25 a.m., he flashed his infrared light north by northeast. He flicked the light on at ten second intervals ... on, off, on, off ... signaling to those ahead.

Within minutes, a 36-foot white cabin cruiser surged out of the misty darkness, knifing through the water at high speed. Reversing its engines, it came to a churning stop fifteen yards away. Petrovich swam closer. He looked up at the faces staring down at him. He grimaced when he recognized Colonel Dmitri Kolchak, KGB controller. A political propagandist and assassin that GRU headquarters had warned about. I trust no one.

"Welcome to America, comrade!" Kolchak rasped in a patronizing tone. His delicate blond features blurred into a dark silhouette, obscuring the sardonic smile on his face. He leaned over the guardrail. "All is well?"

Petrovich pushed his face mask onto the top of his head, ignoring Kolchak's greeting. He grabbed the cargo sling thrown down to him and wrapped it around the Stinger capsule. He treaded water as the Stinger was hoisted aboard. Once it was secured, he swam to the ladder on the boat's stern and scrambled aboard.

He leaned against the gunwale and pulled off his flippers. He recognized two PLO Shiite terrorists, whom he had trained in Iraq as surrogates to fire the Stinger. They had flown from Iraq to Italy, then Brazil, Mexico, Chicago and New York under forged identities. He nodded. He unzipped his skin-diver's suit and caught a towel thrown to him by a crewman. Phase One of my mission is complete. Next comes personal reconnaissance. He glanced at the terrorists. Then suicide attack. And martyrdom ... theirs, not mine. He shrugged his shoulders callously and went below where dry clothes and hot tea awaited him.

The two PLO terrorists spread a canvas tarpaulin over the Stinger and tied it to the boat's deck. The KGB controller stood nearby, supervising their work. Kolchak kept a watchful eye on the cabin below. He distrusted all GRU agents, especially those designated as special forces. They are army first, Party second. They are too elitist, too independent. They show too much initiative like American Green Berets. They are difficult to control. *Perestroika* or not, GRU loyalty must be scrutinized at all times. Kolchak had received conflicting orders from KGB Central in Moscow. His operation orders for his deception plan were clear ... to force the Americans out of Europe while protecting Soviet reputation. But Petrovich, he choked, when reading the KGB secret message. "Watch from distance, but leave GRU agent alone."

Kolchak turned toward the two PLO terrorists, having no respect for them either. An angry sneer swept across his angular Slavic face. He pointed his finger in Petrovich's direction, spitting-out contemptuously the acronym for Russian special forces: "Spetsnaz-z!"

On Tuesday evening, the day after the Spetsnaz had infiltrated into the United States, the temperature dropped to freezing. Not prepared for the sudden cold front, New Yorkers pulled their collars up tightly around them and hurried home to the warmth and security of their apartments, oblivious to the danger that was about to descend upon them.

Uptown in his spacious four room apartment on East 87th Street, Kolchak readied himself for tonight's covert operation. He keyed a coded file into his IBM-PS/2 computer and scanned the list of names and addresses on the screen. His secret media network. Their modems would buzz with shocking news before they arrived at work the next morning.

Until tonight, Kolchak's undercover work as a KGB controller had been kept at low intensity. As the New York editor of *New World*, a Soviet foreign affairs magazine, Kolchak recruited agents of influence to build public opinion that supported the political goals desired by Moscow.

During his five years in Manhattan, Kolchak targeted on media influentials. Some of his agents were easy to manipulate, never knowing they were identified as Soviet agents. He kept others under rigid control. Kolchak liked to recruit people who responded to personal motivations, rather than ideology. People who wanted money, travel or sex. People who craved for power and prestige. Kolchak knew Moscow had a long range perspective. He was evaluated by the size of his network and quality of his agents, not by the effectiveness of a specific story.

Kolchak lit a Carlton and walked into the bathroom. He stood in front of his medicine cabinet and stared at the two day stubble of beard. His pale blue eyes were bloodshot, his thinning blond hair in disarray. High cheek bones and a tall, thin frame accentuated a raunchy appearance.

Nodding approval, he walked back to the living room of his apartment. He paced back and forth anxiously, stopping to empty a large ashtray on the marble coffee table that was littered with cigarette butts. He slumped into a black leather chair in the corner, hating the serenity of a seascape that adorned the far wall.

At 49, Kolchak was ambitious and wanted more recognition in the KGB. Having cultivated a pseudo-intellectual personality, he provided a constant flow of insider tips to his secret media network. Unlike his conservative Russian colleagues, Kolchak created a facade of *glasnost*, long before openness became official Soviet policy. He presented a portrait of candor that subtly supported the Soviet image, never revealing his true predatory character. He was accepted as a harmless Soviet functionary by American journalists and the FBI, who never suspected he was a KGB master spy.

Kolchak made every effort to protect his cover, to remain above suspicion. Tonight, he would risk it all. "I will work with Spetsnaz as Moscow orders, but watch him like hawk." He walked back into the den, his computer command post, and sat down in the center of the horseshoe, surrounded by state of the art technology. "I will orchestrate brilliant *kombinatsia*," he proclaimed, "a coordinated action. Phase II operation starts tonight. Then I unleash tremendous barrage of disinformation, deception, and terror. Dirty tricks make everybody's head spin."

Swiveling in his chair, Kolchak faced the computer. His fingers raced across the PC's keyboard. He typed a fact sheet, reporting the events of a major story before it happened. He leaned back in his chair, gloating, confident he was in full control. Every fact on the PC's screen would happen before the night ended. It would have been easier to send out a press release, but he wanted the journalists to write the story in their own style. He knew their headlines would scream with sensationalism. The TV news networks would pick-up the gauntlet and give the story maximum air time.

A smug look creased his face. "My credibility is firmly established. My tips are accurate and timely. My agents will not reveal their source of information. Freedom of the press. It's the American way. Their silence will protect my cover."

He merged the fact sheet and his mailing list into a secondary file. He keyed in special instructions, directing the computer to transmit the message by modem early Wednesday morning at 4:00 a.m..

He walked into the living room and turned on his TV set to NBC's evening news, but didn't pay attention to it. He thought about Moscow's new global strategy. General Secretary Gorbachev's summit meeting had been a public relations success. Congress and the liberal press had taken the bait, reacting like the Politburo had planned. A popular groundswell was rising to meet the Soviets halfway, to normalize relations, to negotiate a new peace treaty to assure a safe, nuclear-free, non-violent world.

"Timing is right!" he asserted. "America must pull back all its troops from Europe. We have tried to weaken NATO and force U.S. withdrawal from Europe for forty years. Now is the time to take advantage, when the U.S. relaxes and drops its guard." He knew his analysis was correct. He thought about his mission tonight. Each act of terror would be exploited like a chain reaction, climaxing with the Stinger attack. "After we blow-up jetliner, and blame it on PLO terrorists, there is no way they can stop my *kombinatsia*. No way, whatsoever."

He wet his lips. His pulse quickened, envisioning hundreds of dead bodies hurtling to earth in a ball of flame. "I will return to Moscow a hero. A KGB general. If mission fails ... No, I will not think of consequences. It is rogue operation. To act before General Secretary Gorbachev gets too strong. If I fail, Politburo will want more than pound of flesh. KGB will be scourged from top to bottom. They will hunt me down. They will kill me."

A foreboding fear swept through his body. He walked into the kitchen, puffing on another cigarette, inhaling deeply. He looked at a brown canvas totebag lying on the table. He patted the bag, subconsciously, rechecking its deadly contents. The totebag had been flown to New York from Moscow by Aeroflot Airlines and delivered to the embassy and then to his apartment by Soviet courier, its contents safeguarded by diplomatic immunity.

He reached for the wallphone and dialed his most effective agent of influence. He heard the phone ring three times before it was picked up.

"Hello, this is Gretchen speaking." She spoke curtly with a slight German inflection. "Who am I speaking to?"

5

Kolchak pulled the receiver away from his ear. He smiled, enjoying the silence. She asked again, emphasizing the second word. "Who is this?"

Kolchak smirked. He hung-up. "Good, Gretchen is home." You're the perfect unwitting agent, he thought. An opportunist. He knew her political column in the *Times* was syndicated in over fifty major newspapers in the country. "All you think about is your career. Wait, my lovely fraulein until you get my midnight call. Then let's see how well you influence the influentials ... and the great American public."

At 8:35 p.m., Kolchak slipped a tattered navy pea jacket over his shabby black sweater and baggy pants. He pulled a black wool watch cap down over his ears. Ten minutes later he walked rapidly out of the basement of his apartment building into the cold night air. He clutched the totebag tightly as he surveyed the empty street. A black 1986 Chevy van was parked at the curb. He climbed into the passenger side, nodding to the chauffeur, Boris Vladimir, a KGB lieutenant from the Soviet Mission to the United Nations. He turned and spoke to the French Canadian college student sitting in the back. "Bon soir, René." He winked and pushed back his wool cap, forcing a thin smile. "The night is cold. You got hot pants? You feel sex-x-x-y?"

The slender, effeminate student winked back. "Oui. I'm always ready, especially for you, comrade."

"That is good." The KGB colonel looked out the side window and didn't see anyone watching. The black Chevy van worked its way into traffic and headed south, downtown.

At 9:22 p.m., Dave Maccabee relaxed in the passenger seat of the red Porsche 944, as Brigadier General Andrew Palmer steered the sleek sports coupe out of the U.S. Army Reserve Center in the Bronx Heights. They edged past a maze of double-parked cars alongside the over-crowded tenements, doglegged onto Harlem River Parkway, heading south for Manhattan.

"It's hard to let go," Maccabee said, opening his tan safari jacket. "I looked forward to retiring. I didn't think I'd miss the reserves, but I do." Looking like an ex-jock, Maccabee was 41, a shade under six feet tall, his weight mellowing around one hundred ninety five pounds. He had close-cropped wavy brown hair, intense green eyes, a hawk-like nose and strong ruddy features. He rubbed a half-moon scar on the ridge of his chin, revealing a cleat mark from a football game long ago. "I don't miss the weekend training or these Tuesday night admin drills. I guess I miss the people, the camaraderie, being part of something important."

"I know," the general replied. "We're a big family." He turned and looked directly at Maccabee. "Nobody forced you to retire after twenty years. I tried to talk you out of it. You're a colonel. Green Beret. You developed the CIMIC concept. You could have served another ten years, maybe make general."

"I have to spend more time rebuilding my advertising agency. I've been ignoring it too long. My partner is getting madder than hell. We need to get back into the big leagues and land some blue chip accounts. It was a tough decision, the only one I could make. Somehow, the army reserve became my vocation, instead of my avocation. My priorities got all screwed-up."

The general smiled. Having come straight from his job at U.S. Chemical, he was dressed in a gray pinstriped business suit. Even in civvies, he looked like a general: tall, lean, professional; a commanding personality. "We're going to miss you overseas, Dave. Germany won't seem the same without you."

"Yeah, I know. Just when I'm at my highest level of productivity, I put myself on the shelf."

"You're never going to be on the shelf. We'll find some way to use you. You better believe it."

Maccabee laughed. "Andrew, you're just going to have to get along without me." He stared ahead.

The general wheeled the Porsche past the incoming traffic coming off the Willis Avenue Bridge. "I do appreciate your coming tonight. You're the best copywriter I know. You really fine tuned my NATO speech. It's right on target. We have one more month left before we go overseas. I hope everyone can adjust to the changing situation in Europe."

Maccabee had known Andrew Palmer since they were lieutenants in Vietnam. They had come up through the ranks together, attended the Army War College together, were close personal friends and tennis pals. Palmer had become one of the best commanders of the 38th Civil Affairs Command, gaining the respect of the U.S. Army active forces and NATO general staff. Maccabee knew the general was concerned about the new officers that had joined the unit. There hadn't been sufficient time to train them in the new CIMIC doctrine.

"Don't worry about the new people," Maccabee said. "They're fast learners. One overseas tour and they'll know what CIMIC is all about. There's no substitute for overseas training. Everything's different. The people, the language, the culture. You can't simulate a foreign environment. You have to be on the ground and get hands-on experience."

The yellow checkered taxi swerved into the Porsche's lane, barely missing it as it came off the Triboro Bridge ramp. Maccabee grabbed a hand-grip as the general geared down to avoid hitting the rear of the cab. "The last thing I need tonight is an accident!" the general said.

"Yeah," Maccabee agreed, shifting his body in the cramped seat. "That was a close one." He released his grip and sat back. CIMIC, Maccabee reflected, associating the acronym with its correct term, Civil Military Cooperation. "You have to get the message across to the active army that CIMIC's the glue that holds our NATO alliance together. Our troops depend upon logistical support from our NATO allies in a new form of coalition warfare. Their resources are limited. The 38th is the catalyst, the go-between unit that makes it happen."

"We're making believers out of them," the general reassured.

"The regular army knows they're so interlocked with the reserves logistically that they can't go to war without us. The one army concept really works."

"Before Washington calls up the reserves, it has to build public opinion and establish strong public support."

"We'll never go to war again unless the vital interests of the U.S. are threatened. That's why diplomacy is important, why NATO has served as a successful deterrent all these years." The general headed the Porsche onto the FDR Drive, maneuvering carefully through bumper to bumper traffic.

"Do you think the staff believed me when I told them it was a whole new ball game in Germany, that the days of ordering the Germans around is over?"

"You're right, Dave. We have to respect their sovereignty. We're guests in their country. West Germany has become an economic giant, much like Japan. I agree that there's been a tremendous resurgence of national pride."

"Can't blame them. World War II ended over forty years ago. The Germans want to put their Nazi past behind them. Half their population was born after the war."

"They're going to have a lot to say about how a future war will be fought on their soil. That's why CIMIC is so important." Maccabee knew that every German resource was accounted for: people, equipment, material, transportation, labor and public facilities. Everything was based on a series of parliamentary emergency laws, pre-planned in peacetime for execution in war.

You've left a fine legacy behind. I plan to use your CIMIC Network during OPERATION FALCON FLASH. Just think, our CIMIC teams from the 38th can now phone Top Secret intelligence directly to my headquarters at NATO and link-up with every other CIMIC team on the continent."

Maccabee smiled, proud of his accomplishment. The CIMIC Network had been his baby from start to finish. The CIMIC operator was a new breed of citizen soldier, a skilled generalist, logistician, linguist and diplomat-warrior.

They drove past the United Nations and stopped at the 34th Street exit before Maccabee realized it. The general became personal. "How about coming up to my apartment and having a nightcap with Beth and me?"

"Thanks, but I have to make a new business pitch in upstate New York tomorrow morning. I need to call it a night."

The general wheeled the Porsche onto Second Avenue and pulled up to the curb by the newsstand on the corner of East 28th Street. Maccabee unlimbered his body, got out, and waved. He bought a copy of the *Post*, flipped it open to the sports page, and headed home.

The general drove the Porsche back into traffic, turned cross-town, then uptown, finally turning into the GMH parking garage on East 38th Street in the Murray Hill section. His Park Avenue apartment was two blocks away.

He put on his overcoat and grabbed the black leather attaché case, which had his military reading file and memos his secretary at U.S. Chemical had typed for signature. He turned the Porsche over to the parking attendant. "I won't be needing the car until Saturday morning. Army reserve weekend. Zero six hundred hours, sharp. Okay?"

"You've got it," the attendant said, slipping behind the steering wheel.

With a wave good night, General Palmer walked briskly up the garage's steep incline. He reached the street and felt the bitter cold air stab at him. He turned left onto the dimly lit sidewalk.

A dark shape suddenly loomed out of the shadows, about six feet away. He looked like a New York homeless derelict, wearing a tattered Navy pea jacket and black watch cap. "Gotta quarter for cuppa coffee?" Kolchak asked with one hand outstretched. He pushed a shopping cart laden with empty soda bottles right at him.

"No, I haven't any change," the general said, trying to dodge the cart.

"Just a quarter," Kolchak implored gruffly. He pushed the wire cart deliberately into the general's legs.

"Watch-out!" The general felt the cart's wheels dig into his shins. Off balance, he glanced down at the cart, then up into the KGB colonel's menacing eyes. "What the hell are you trying to ..."

Kolchak lunged at him. He held what looked like a pocket flashlight in his left hand and pointed it at the general's neck. He was inches away.

The general jerked his attaché case up with both hands to fend off the attack, shouting: "Sto-p-p!" It was too late. He felt something sting his neck. It shocked every nerve in his body.

He wanted to shout for help, but couldn't. Everything froze in place. A heaviness overwhelmed him. He wanted to fight back, but couldn't. He sensed someone else near him. His vision blurred. A dark cloud of grayness rolled over him.

The KGB colonel heard the shower running in the bathroom. He looked across the dingy bedroom at General Palmer lying face down on the double bed, unconscious. His long, well-toned body was naked, spread-eagled across the rumpled sheets. A sofa bolster had been placed under his hips for elevation. René Lemoine washed himself, having sodomized the general, both rectally and orally.

Kolchak had taken eight Polaroid photos of the sex orgy. He had stage managed each position so the general's face could be recognized in each photo. He fanned the photos out on the night table next to the bed.

Time was moving fast. 11:02 p.m. An hour had rushed by since the kidnapping. Kolchak's technician had told him the drug would last a minimum of four hours before wearing off. Everything was moving according to schedule. After the kidnapping, they had been careful not to bruise the general's body, when they placed him in the van and carried him up five flights of stairs to Lemoine's apartment on East 11th Street, off Avenue B in the East Village.

The building was an old, dilapidated brownstone, which hadn't been painted in years. Kolchak didn't see any tenants when they carried the general into the grimy flat. Dusty bamboo partitions with faded cockatoos set each room apart. Chipped paint marred the ceiling and walls. The furniture looked like second-hand odds and ends. Kolchak stepped around the mound of dirty jeans, undershorts and socks that were heaped in the corner of the bedroom.

He was satisfied that his high velocity air gun had not caused any trouble. The miniature pellet of thorazine had immobilized his victim instantly. Kolchak tried to find the mark where the chemical agent had entered, but couldn't. The penetration was smaller than a pinhead and invisible to the naked eye.

The KGB controller pulled a pair of black surgical rubber gloves over his hands carefully, telling himself that he would not be contaminated. He reloaded the air gun through the flashlight casing, inserting a second micro capsule ... containing the deadly AIDS virus. He snapped the flashlight casing shut. He scowled, not liking what he had to do, but wanting to get it over quickly.

Kolchak climbed onto the edge of the bed between the general's long hairy legs. He pushed the air gun up against his rectum, and fired it. There was a fast puff. Nothing else. No wound, no discoloration. Only rapid absorption of the AIDS virus into the general's rectum, intestines and bloodstream.

9

Kolchak stepped back. He took a deep breath. 11:18 p.m. He picked-up his canvas totebag that was draped over a caneback chair and placed the air gun back into it. He took out a stack of lewd homosexual photos, and spilled them onto the floor, overlapping the erotic gay magazines lying there. One caught his fancy. He started to reach for it. Feeling an erection coming on, he thought better of it and kicked it aside. "Must concentrate on business."

Lemoine walked out of the bathroom, wearing a pink floral bath towel wrapped around his waist. A few droplets of water glistened on his slender arms. "How long before he wakes up?" he asked, nodding towards the bed.

"In about an hour, maybe two."

"What kind of drug did you use to knock him out?"

"It's none of your business." Kolchak leaned against the highboy, stepping aside as the litter spilled onto the floor.

"Ah, come on, Dmitri. Tell me." Lemoine cozied up to Kolchak, smiling coyly, flirting with him.

"You get under a person's skin, René. Do not irritate me!"

Lemoine shrugged his shoulders and pouted. He placed both his hands on his hips, daring Kolchak to touch him. "Do you want me to get dressed?"

"No, we're not through yet. There's time for business, time for play." He had recruited René in Montreal from the gay community, paying him well. The man had an insatiable sexual appetite that Kolchak put to good use. Lemoine was 31, looking more like 21, a professional student and communist courier. Kolchak had encouraged him to transfer to New York City College as an exchange student.

Lemoine saw the Polaroid photos on the edge of the night table. "Oh, let me see." His bath towel started to come loose. He hitched it tighter, skimming through the photos. "This one's magnificent. I love it!"

"Put them down, René. He will wake up before we are ready. We have no time to lose. Get back in bed. You pose for one more photo."

"Will you stay after he leaves?" There was a hint of anxiety in his voice. A blackmail scam was one thing. Sex, another.

"Yes, my friend. I will stay." He tried to sound convincing.

"You liked me before, Dmitri. I will please you again. I want you to seduce me, to make my body crave for your touch. You make me feel so good inside. I don't do this just for the money."

"I know," Kolchak answered, sighing. Male lovers, female lovers, he enjoyed them equally. "Now is not time. Get into bed and get rid of damn bolster." Lemoine let his bath towel drop to the floor. He climbed onto the bed on all fours. He tugged on the bolster and yanked it loose from under the general's limp body. He tossed it onto the floor, watching it tumble.

Kolchak strode to the highboy, brushing aside a bevy of crushed beer cans. He balanced a small stereo radio on the dresser's edge, switching frequencies until he found Z-100, a blaring rock station. "We need music." He flicked its volume to high, drowning out the shrill, bleating horn of an ambulance racing by on Avenue B.

He picked up his totebag and pulled out four forged documents, carrying them into the living room. He opened the general's attaché case lying on the coffee table and slipped three documents marked TOP SECRET onto the top of his reading file. He carried the fourth back into the bedroom and placed it onto the night table.

Kolchak pulled a Polaroid camera out of his totebag, and moved across the room, stopping three feet from the bed. "Turn him over. Get closer. Embrace."

Lemoine obeyed. He shut his eyes, hyping himself, getting into the mood. He felt another erection growing hard.

"Hug him tight and kiss. I get good shot."

Again, he obeyed. Yet, a sixth sense triggered a warning. He opened his eyes, raised up on an elbow and started to look back. His instincts were too slow.

The KGB controller pulled a snub-nosed black .38 caliber revolver from his totebag. He pointed it at Lemoine's right temple, only sixteen inches away. He squeezed the trigger as Lemoine looked back.

The shot rang out, piercing Lemoine's brain. His eyes widened in one last glimpse of horror. Blood spurted across the pillow case and splattered onto the general's face. Lemoine's body convulsed. Then lay still.

Kolchak reached over and placed the .38 into Lemoine's lifeless right hand, forcing his index finger around the trigger. He lifted the gun one more time. He placed it directly against the general's temple ... and fired.

Kolchak picked the forged document off the night table and smeared Lemoine's fingertips across its edges. He placed it back onto the night table. It wasn't a document. It was a farewell letter forged in Lemoine's handwriting. It said: "I cannot stand to see Andy Palmer die a slow death from AIDS. We both agree it is better this way to die in a lover's embrace and share an eternal love together. Farewell to all!" It was signed "René."

The cunning KGB controller looked around one last time, wiping away any last vestige of his fingerprints. 11:52 p.m. A complete night's work. He took one last look at the general. His body had been used and abused, violated shamefully. "Be grateful, my general, I let you die," he mocked, maliciously. "You could not live with humiliation."

Kolchak left the door unlocked and disappeared down the empty stairwell.

At 12:32 a.m., Kolchak sat in the security of his apartment on East 87th Street, chain smoking. He watched the haze of blue smoke curl up to the ceiling. He dialed Gretchen Lundstrom's private line, awakening her.

"I'm sorry to bother you at such late hour, but I receive hot tip from confidential source that will win you Pulitzer Prize."

"I'm all ears, Dmitri. What happened? Give me the facts quickly." Gretchen sat up in bed, rubbing the sleep out of her electric blue eyes. Her tawny blond hair fell loosely to her shoulders. She pulled a heavy white satin quilt tightly around her trim figure, her blue pastel silk negligee revealing a well-shaped bosom for a woman of 36. She propped her knees up, as she cradled her princess phone. She listened intently.

"It is real juicy story! American general and homosexual lover die in double suicide pact. Military secrets are involved. If you hurry to East Village with photographer, you beat police."

11

"And scoop the *Daily News* and *Post*," she added, as she pushed the button on the automatic redialer to rouse her best photographer.

"Yes" he repeated, excitedly, "and scoop every newspaper and TV network in the country if you act fast!"

"What is the general's name?"

"That you must find out for yourself."

"Who is the lover boy? Has he got a name?"

"Communist radical from Canada. Terrorist courier. That's all I know."

"A communist," she repeated in a hushed conspiratorial voice. "Dmitri, why are you telling me all this? If he's a communist, why isn't your embassy covering it up?"

"Maybe two years ago, but not now. We have nothing to hide. With *glasnost*, everything is out in open. Our country wishes to normalize relations with U.S. and put Cold War behind us permanently. Soviet position is absolutely clear."

Still cradling the phone to her ear, Gretchen stepped into the jumpsuit pulling it up under her negligee, which she tossed onto the bed. At five foot six, Gretchen had the look of a professional athlete, which came from years of pampered living and a strict regimen of aerobics, tennis and jogging.

She stood erect, zipping up the front of her jumpsuit. "Dmitri, I know you're using me," she said solemnly, "but I'll do anything to get a Pulitzer ... anything." I'm using you, too, she thought, as she slipped on her white Reebok jogging shoes. Even if I have to climb into bed with you some night. "Thank you for the scoop. I'm off and running."

They both laughed. He gave Gretchen the address and hung up.

An hour later, Kolchak dialed 911 and spoke in a disguised Puerto Rican accent. He reported a shooting at the East Village address. There were no witnesses, he thought. But what he didn't know was going to hurt him.

2

Dave Maccabee's new business pitch to Taconic Apple Orchards in Poughkeepsie moved into high gear. He paced back and forth in front of the conference table, pointer in hand, directing his comments to the marketing director and his staff. Maccabee felt fluid, dynamic, his persuasive best. He hammered home each point, dominating the meeting. Dressed in his tan safari jacket, white button-down oxford shirt and power red tie, he exuded confidence. "We've had our share of success. What you get from Maccabee and Martin is first class creativity ... plus the personal involvement and expertise you can only get when you work with the principals of an agency. We're smart enough to do it better. Small enough to do it faster. We're looking for quality companies, so we can grow as you grow."

An ash blond secretary stuck her head into the conference room. "Mr. Maccabee, there's an urgent call from your office. Said to interrupt you."

Maccabee forced a smile. He tried to mask his dismay. He had laid down the law to his people. An advertising presentation was sacrosanct, especially on a client's turf. Don't ever interrupt me, he had warned, unless it's an emergency. What could be so damn important? He glanced at his partner Bob Martin, a short, stocky art director with a shiny bald head, who nervously fingered a cassette of the agency television reel. "Bob will show you our award winning television commercials while I take the call."

Maccabee followed the secretary to an outside office. He picked-up the phone and was surprised to hear the familiar voice of Major Kathy Morgan, his former deputy when he was Chief of Public Affairs for the 77th U.S. Army Reserve Command. "Colonel Maccabee, I've been trying to track you down for hours. I missed you at your apartment and your office."

"I'm in the middle of a new business pitch, Kathy," he said in a reprimanding tone. He realized he hadn't spoken to her since his retirement party in December. "I wish you could have wait ..."

She cut him off in mid-sentence, her voice strained and emotional. She spoke rapidly with a slight Texas drawl. "Colonel Maccabee. Dave, I'm so upset. I'm beside myself. There's been a terrible tragedy. Didn't you read this morning's newspaper? Didn't you listen to your radio or watch TV?"

"Slow down, Kathy. What happened?" Maccabee knew he became single-tracked before he went into a new business presentation. No distractions. Total concentration. Do your homework. Anticipate. Plan ahead. Focus on key points. Then rehearse and rehearse some more. "Bob and I came straight from home."

"It's General Palmer. He's dead! They found his body early this morning. He's dead, Dave. Dead!" She began to sob, but brought her emotions under control. She had served on the general's staff as a captain. Professionally, they had been good

13

friends, just like she was with Maccabee.

"Dead ..." Maccabee repeated, his voice rising. "Andrew dead? I can't believe it. He was in perfect health. I was with him last night at the 38th, at their admin meeting. We car pooled together. Andrew wanted to drive." He paused, regaining his composure. "How did he die?"

"They say it was suicide, but I don't believe it! The newspaper photos are awful. Dave, the newspapers say he was gay."

"Suicide?" Maccabee's anger increased, his ruddy complexion becoming flushed. "A homosexual? No way, not Andrew. There has to be a mistake."

"Where did he drop you off last night?"

"At the corner newsstand on 28th Street, around ten. I saw him head south on Second Avenue, said he was going straight home."

Morgan's voice became somber. "They found his body in the East Village. You say he was heading downtown?"

"Yeah, Second Avenue is one-way. I'm sure he cut cross-town on the next block to head back to his apartment." He paused momentarily, thinking. "East Village ... It doesn't make sense." He shook his head. "Andrew asked me to come up to his apartment. To join Beth and him for a nightcap." The impact of the tragedy suddenly engulfed him. He gripped the back of his neck in anguish, his muscles tense. "If I'd only stayed with him, he might still be alive."

"Don't start blaming yourself. You might have been killed, too. It's all so bizarre!" She described what information she had. The sordid details were horrible.

Maccabee drove his black S-10 Blazer off of the Westside Highway into mid-Manhattan three hours later, exceeding the 55 mph speed limit most of the way down from Poughkeepsie. He left his disgruntled partner, asking him to finish the presentation, hoping they might still beat the other agencies competing for the business. He had listened to his car stereo all the way down the Taconic Parkway. The radio announcers were having a field day with the *"gay general"* as they now characterized him.

Maccabee's anger grew in intensity as he switched frequencies from one station to another. General Palmer had not only been his boss at the 38th, but had been his classmate at the U.S. Army War College, the top of the educational pyramid that developed mutual trust and bonding among senior army officers. The news story had to be a pack of lies! How could the radio stations slander the general's good name and reputation? The press made mistakes before. This time they've gone too far.

He drove cross-town on 23rd Street to avoid getting locked into a traffic jam on the side streets, where trucks were backed-up unloading heavy crates of merchandise. He dropped the Blazer off at the parking garage in the basement of his high-rise co-op apartment on East 28th Street.

He strode into the corner deli on Third Avenue and purchased copies of the *Times, Daily News* and *Post*, barely glancing at their headlines. He stuffed the newspapers under his arm. He hurried past two neighborhood toughs milling about, almost bumping into them. They took one glance at his flashing green eyes and gave him a wide berth. He charged into the lobby of his building, and stopped at the front desk.

"Tommy, any mail?"

The concierge, who was sorting the mail, pulled several letters out of the mail slots on the rear wall and handed them to him. "Have you seen the headlines?" he asked, discreetly.

"Just got back into town. Haven't had a chance to read a paper yet." Maccabee started walking toward the bank of elevators.

"Pretty heavy stuff, colonel. Shows you never know people. Never know what turns them on." He shrugged, apathetically.

"Don't believe everything you read in the papers," Maccabee shouted over his shoulder as he stepped into an open elevator. He rode it to the 16th floor, and walked to his apartment, which was furnished in a contemporary Scandinavian style. He sat on the edge of a deep cushioned, L-shaped beige couch in his living room that looked out onto his balcony and another luxury apartment building across the street. He unfolded the three newspapers and spread them out on the red Karastan carpet. "Damn!" he swore softly. "The bastards really did a hatchet job!"

He glared at each newspaper's headline:

TIMES: **"ARMY RESERVE GENERAL FOUND DEAD IN DOUBLE SUICIDE WITH HOMOSEXUAL LOVER IN EAST VILLAGE."**

DAILY NEWS: **"GAY GENERAL DIES IN LOVER'S EMBRACE."**

POST: **"FAG GENERAL HAD AIDS!"**

The photographs were worse, causing Maccabee's stomach to constrict painfully. He riveted his eyes on the *Times'* photo, which had been cropped tightly on the enlarged faces and upper torsos of the two dead men. He took a deep breath, then leaned over to scan the other two newspapers. The *Daily News* and the *Post* outdid each other, revealing what they should have concealed.

Maccabee winced. He grabbed the front page of the *Times* and read the caption under the photo of René Lemoine's "farewell" letter. "No way would Andrew take his own life," he murmured. "He had too many close calls in 'Nam to throw it away this way. He placed great value on the sanctity of life, on the safety of his men."

He questioned each line of copy, searching for an answer. "Die a slow death from AIDS?" It had to be someone else, not Andrew. "Die in a lover's embrace?" Who the hell are they kidding? He was a happily married man. "Share an eternal love together?" Bullshit! Pure, unadulterated bullshit. Maccabee stood up. "Who is this René Lemoine?" He threw the newspaper onto the carpet, watching the pages scatter. "Pure tripe!" He stepped over the two tabloids, their bad taste exceeded only by their zeal to build circulation and sell more newspapers. Even the police appeared to be acquiescent. They had written off the two deaths as "an obvious suicide pact with homosexual implications."

Maccabee walked the length of the living room to the wet bar in the corner. He poured himself a stiff J&B, filling the rocks glass to the rim. He sat on a bar stool and

15

downed the drink. Then another. His unlisted phone rang four times. His answering machine was on, recording the messages. He wanted to be alone. To sort things out.

He gazed at the silver army saber that hung prominently above the mantle over the fireplace. Below it, a small trophy case displayed his combat infantryman's badge, insignias from the Green Beret, 77th ARCOM and 38th Civil Affairs Command and four rows of medals, including the silver star and purple heart.

His eyes swept across to a walnut plaque, reading the words engraved on it. "Colonel David Helner Maccabee. In recognition of the twenty years of dedicated service in the U.S. Army Reserve in furtherance of this unit's mission as G-5. From the officers and enlisted soldiers of the 38th U.S. Civil Affairs Command." It was dated December 22, 1987.

He walked to the mantle and picked-up a framed easel-backed photo of General Palmer pinning the Legion of Merit medal on his blouse, the second highest award a reservist can earn in peacetime. He stared at it, reminiscing, then placed it back, ever so lightly, distressed in his grief. He stared into his J&B, swishing the ice cubes.

Beth, he thought, how is she holding up? I should have thought about her sooner. He dialed Andrew's number. Beth's sister answered the phone. Beth was asleep and under sedation. She'd give Beth the message, but to call back later.

He set his drink aside. No sense getting bombed. He phoned his office and spoke to Judy, his secretary. "I'm leaving my apartment right now. I'll be there in ten minutes. Any calls?"

"The phone hasn't stopped ringing. Kathy wants to see you as soon as you get in. She's enroute to the office right now."

"That's why I came back early. I let Bob finish the new business presentation. Has he called in yet?"

"Yes, Bob said the marketing director lost interest right after you left. He's driving back to Jersey. Going to take the afternoon off and play golf. He said every time he tees up, he's going to visualize your face on the ball. Then pow-w-w! He's really upset."

"I'll calm him down tomorrow. I had to leave. Thought he'd understand. Any calls from the army?"

"Seven from the 38th. Everyone's calling in." She ran down her list. Lieutenant Colonel Wally Livingston, Maccabee's deputy G-5 had called twice. So had Lieutenant Colonel Pete Williams, his replacement as CIMIC Team Chief for the engineer command. His three section chiefs had called, Major Klaus Ludwig, Major Gerhardt Brockmann and Major Kurt Goetz. Even his first shirt, Master Sergeant, retired, Freddy Ventura.

Maccabee walked into his agency to find a mass of pink telephone messages covering his desk. He shuffled through them hurriedly, separating the army calls from his business calls. Judy, a tall, redheaded secretary with a nose for detail and a penchant for mini skirts, walked inside. "Kathy just arrived. Shall I hold all of your business calls or may I interrupt you?"

Maccabee slumped in his chair, leaning on his armrests. "Send Kathy in and hold all my calls. I'm still out of town." He busied himself with the papers on his desk, skimming through the morning mail.

Minutes later, Major Kathy Morgan, a dynamic 31-year old career reservist, a petite brunette with a bobbed haircut, brown doleful eyes and a take-charge attitude, walked inside. She wore crisp BDU's, spit-shined black combat boots and cut a trim figure. "About time you got back," she said, tossing her army cap and late edition of the *Post* onto the long conference table. She slipped into the nearest chair by his desk. Maccabee looked into her sad, grief-stricken eyes that fought back tears welling below the surface. He didn't know what to say. He stared at her, his silence saying everything.

He finally asked, "What's the latest information? We can't sit here doing nothing. We have to make sense out of this craziness."

Morgan moved to the edge of her chair, her posture erect. "I've been on the phone with the NYPD. I spoke with three of my sergeants to see what they can learn." Maccabee knew that Morgan served as the full time AGR admin supervisor for the 245th Military Intelligence Battalion, CI counter-intelligence, which was composed of New York cops and drug enforcement agents. "I have two different teams of detectives working on the case." She explained the jurisdictional problem confronting them. "Cops from midtown can't tread on another precinct's turf. Andrew's body was found downtown. The 9th Precinct has the action."

The intercom buzzed, interrupting them. Maccabee jerked his head toward the small voicebox on his desk. Judy's alto voice filled the room. "Gretchen Lundstrom is on the phone. This is her third call."

"Who?" He frowned. "I thought I asked you not to interrupt ..." He turned toward Morgan, a perplexed look on his face.

"You better take this call," Judy pleaded. "She's very persistent."

"Who did you say it was?"

"Gretchen Lundstrom, the columnist."

"From the *Times*?" Morgan asked, interrupting. She stood and moved closer to the desk. "The one who smeared Andrew's reputation?"

"I don't want to talk to her," Maccabee declared. "I'm out!"

"I'll talk to her," Morgan snapped. She reached across Maccabee's desk and picked-up the receiver.

Maccabee held his hands up in distress. He would let them tangle, wanting no part of it.

"Hello, this is Kathy Morgan, Mr. Maccabee's executive assistant. Mr. Maccabee just returned from out-of-town. He's in an important business meeting and cannot be disturbed. Can I help you Ms. Lundstrom?"

Maccabee listened, watching Kathy's glaring eyes. He could only hear her side of the conversation. He could not understand her drift. "Yes, I see," Morgan said, pausing. "Yes, I understand." She paused longer, nodding with each comment. "You're right, I agree completely."

What's going on? Maccabee wondered. Why is Kathy baiting her?

"Yes, I understand the urgency. If you can hold the line for a few minutes, I'll try to get his attention and schedule a meeting for you." Morgan pushed the "hold" button down with a flourish. She perched on the edge of Maccabee's desk, leaning towards him. She spoke slowly, reproaching him in a derisive tone. "You never told me that

17

you knew Gretchen Lundstrom, that you met her at the German Embassy party last November."

"Yeah, I know her," Maccabee admitted, sheepishly. His face reddened.

"How quick one forgets," Morgan quipped, winking. She spoke sarcastically, buddy to buddy. "It seems that you made quite a lasting impression. The grand lady is quite impressed with your charm. And your knowledge. She wants to verify some facts about the follow-up army story she's writing and thinks that the good Colonel Maccabee is the only one who can give her the straight facts."

Maccabee squirmed in his chair, embarrassed. Morgan was making more out of the acquaintance than she should. Her needling bothered him. "Andrew and I stopped by to pay our respects to Herr Doctor, Major General Klaus Nordenfeldt of the German Territorial Forces, who was visiting here. It was a courtesy visit," he stressed, "that's all. I met Gretchen Lundstrom. She's a real pro, has a lot of class. We talked for about fifteen minutes."

"Yes-s-s," Morgan said, flashing an 'I know-it-all-look.' "Go on."

"Well-l-l, Mac. e confessed, "She turned me on. You know how it is. I made a fast pitch, asked her for a date and got nowhere."

"Did she shatter your male ego?" she taunted.

Maccabee frowned. "Hell, no. I struck-out. She didn't buy my song and dance. I was too low on the totem pole to interest her. I needed ambassador rank or at least a couple of stars on my shoulder."

"Better talk to her. Let's find out what she's after. She certainly sounds interested in you now. Okay?"

Maccabee nodded. Morgan released the "hold" button. "Ms. Lundstrom, I got through to him. Mr. Maccabee has an extremely busy schedule today. I can squeeze you in for a fifteen minute interview if you hurry over." She smiled, getting the answer she expected. "Good, I'm glad I could help." She hung up. She slipped into the chair and faced Maccabee. "Do you want me to sit in on your interview?"

He shook his head. "You really don't like her, do you?"

An angry look flashed across Morgan's face. "Not after the damage she did to General Palmer's reputation." She thought for a moment. "Be careful Colonel Maccabee," she warned. "She's not all sugar and honey. Beneath that sweet disposition is one tough lady. Sure you don't want me to sit in?"

"No, I can handle her," Maccabee answered with self-assurance.

"Watch yourself. I know her type. When she's after the big story, she'll come at you like ah, ... a rhino in heat!"

Thirty minutes later, Maccabee sat face to face with Gretchen Lundstrom. He smiled, trying to penetrate the icy reserve that she had erected around herself like an invisible barrier. Dressed smartly in a green blazer, white turtle neck sweater and navy blue skirt, Gretchen looked more poised and enticing than Maccabee remembered.

"You're a hard man to reach," Gretchen said, trying to gain his confidence. "Thanks for the interview. As I recall, you were a close friend of General Andrew Palmer. I'm sitting on a new military story that needs to be verified."

"It's about time," Maccabee replied, wondering where she obtained her facts for the "double suicide" story. "Why come to me? Why don't you go through army public affairs channels. All you have to do is call the 77th ARCOM and they'll answer your questions."

"Don't patronize me," she said, coldly. She crossed her legs, tugging at the hem of her skirt, which rose about four inches above her knees, revealing the smooth underflesh of her well-shaped thighs. Maccabee tried not to notice, but his eyes kept drifting downward. She leaned back in her chair, confident her hem-line was just right, confident she was gaining control. "The army is stone- walling every reporter who contacts them. I want to be fair to General Palmer. I want the whole story. He impressed me last Fall. You did too, David."

She sounded sincere. She paused for effect, her lilting German accent adding crispness to each word. Her sparking blue eyes reached out appealingly. "I'm sorry we couldn't get together socially, but I've been working at such a hectic pace. No time for myself. Then just when things slowed down ..."

Maccabee became impatient. "What information do you need?"

"Need?" she mimicked. She brushed her shoulder length, tawny blond hair back with her hand and glared at him, provocatively. "What are you guys trying to do? Start World War III?"

Maccabee stood. "What are you talking about?"

"Don't play head games with me David. You know exactly what I'm talking about. You were a general staff officer in the 38th Civil Affairs Command for five years. I have photographs in my possession of a personal letter from your not-too-loyal general telling the 42nd Division about military occupation plans after you guys attack Russia and the Warsaw Pact countries."

Maccabee's eyes narrowed, his temper mounting. "That's ridiculous!" He felt his voice rise. "You know better than that. And watch what you say about Andrew Palmer. I don't believe a word of it."

Lundstrom didn't back off. She remained aloof, her poise intact. She framed her next question like a sharp barb. "What is your response to the statement that the 38th is planning to conduct a military government after NATO forces attack and occupy Eastern Europe?"

"It's not true! All of NATO's plans are defensive. To defend Western Europe against a combined Soviet attack. I've never seen any plans for taking the battle east."

Lundstrom had a smug look on her face. "I suppose you've never heard about *AirLand Battle 2000,* and U.S. plans to interdict and destroy Soviet reinforcing units deep in their rear zone in Eastern Europe?"

"Of course I'm familiar with the new AirLand doctrine, but you don't have your facts straight. The deep penetration into the enemy rear will be conducted by air and missile attack, not mechanized infantry or armor. And only *after* the Soviet bloc attacks NATO, never before. It's all academic now that the Cold War is over."

Lundstrom drummed her fingers on her knee. The interview wasn't going well. She decided to provoke Maccabee into saying what she hoped to quote in her story. "The public has a right to know!" she exclaimed, her voice rising emotionally. "I can't let you trigger happy cowboys shoot-up our West German allies." She hesitated, then went on. "They're my people," she said proudly. "My people!"

"What trigger happy cowboys are you so scared of?" He thought he saw

19

Gretchen's icy resolve begin to melt. Her blue Nordic eyes reached out, challenging him. Yet, she seemed unassailable. Unreachable. He wanted to knock down the fences. To get to know her better.

"I'm scared of your MPs, that's who. They've been ordered to shoot first and ask questions later during your next NATO war game."

"You must be kidding. It's completely contrary to the new CIMIC doctrine that prohibits any show of force with our allies. It's an automatic court martial for any offender."

"I'm not kidding." She looked at him, disillusioned. "I don't believe you. You're trying to hide the facts from me."

"No, I'm not. I'm telling you the truth," he insisted. "I'm only retired three months. Uncle Sam doesn't change doctrine that fast."

Gretchen recoiled into her icy shell. Any further discussion was futile. She had stayed beyond her allotted time. She stood. "If you won't cooperate, I'll have to go with the facts I have," she said, stubbornly. She turned to leave. "Wait until you see my column tomorrow."

"If somebody has leaked secret information to you, let me show it to the ARCOM for verification."

"Too late," she retorted, dryly. "I have a deadline to make."

"Have it your way, Gretchen." He walked with her to the agency's lobby. "Let's stay in touch." She smiled, turned and walked out of the glass doors.

Where is all this leading, Maccabee wondered?

Before the next hour passed, he received a sensitive telephone call from the Pentagon, asking him to meet with Major General Bob Kelley, Chief of the Army Reserve. General Kelley had been commander of the 77th ARCOM and Maccabee's boss for four years before getting his current position. He was flying into La Guardia airport on the first shuttle tomorrow morning.

The next morning's newspapers were grim. Gretchen Lundstrom did not understate what was coming. The *Times* had devoted two-thirds of the front page to her story. The headline read:

"MILITARY SECRETS REVEALED BY GAY GENERAL TO TERRORIST LOVER!"

Large double column photos of two personal letters from General Palmer were displayed. A bold caption under the first letter read:

"U.S. HAS SECRET PLANS TO START WORLD WAR III."

The letter had a 38th Civil Affairs Command letterhead. It was addressed to the commanding general of the 42nd National Guard Division in New York, informing him that the 38th Civil Affairs Command will retain jurisdiction over all territories east of the Elbe River. All territory seized in the Democratic Republic of Germany, Czechoslovakia, Poland, Hungary and Rumania will be vested under the military government authority of the U.S. Army with the 38th CA fulfilling its role as executive agent. The letter was signed "Andy."

The caption under the second photo, read:

"FILL 'ER UP OR DIE! U.S. MP TROOPS TO SHOOT WEST GERMAN ALLIES IF THEY DON'T PUMP GAS!"

Maccabee couldn't believe his eyes. The second letter on 38th CA letterhead was addressed to the commander of the 428th Army Reserve Military Police Battalion, ordering him to instruct his troops that there may be a gas shortage in Germany during the training exercise. If price scalping occurs or fuel is denied, MPs will requisition the gas by gun point, if necessary. This letter was also signed "Andy."

The final photo featured a cover sheet marked **TOP SECRET** that partially concealed a military map of the Federal Republic of Germany.

Below it, the caption read:

"SECRET CIMIC NETWORK."

Showing some discretion, the editorial board explained that a photo of the complete map had been verified by the Pentagon, but could not be released because of national security. The text described the series of map overlays, which showed the dispositions and coordinates of U.S. Army combat and logistic forces, the location of German Territorial Forces, and the location of the CIMIC teams of the 38th Civil Affairs Command that were linked-up in a secret CIMIC Network.

Gretchen Lundstrom had scooped every major newspaper in the country. No reporter had seen the military letters and secret documents before they were taken by the police. Everyone slanted their stories on the sordid details about the gay general and the double suicide.

The television crews behaved like hound dogs, smelling the scent of a spectacular story. They swarmed onto the small Army Reserve post at Fort Totten in Bayside, looking for interviews. There was a small skeleton staff of full-timers on hand at 77th ARCOM headquarters. They weren't prepared for the avalanche that hit them. "The proper authorities are conducting a complete investigation. We cannot comment until we have more information," was all they said.

Over at the 38th Army Reserve Center, the senior full-time officer was away on leave. The junior captain and two NCOs had no media experience. The unit's public affairs officer, a reservist, was in Seattle attending a sales meeting for his company. The captain asked the ARCOM for support, but the only reply he received was: "Refer all inquiries to us." They tried to cope with investigative reporters, who were hell-bent on digging out more scandalous dirt.

Around the world, there were serious repercussions. In Washington D.C. at the White House, the Chief of Staff telephoned the Secretary of Defense: "The president wants every general grade officer given a lie detector test for homosexuality and a medical test for AIDS in the next 48 hours. Regulars, reserves and guard. No exceptions! He will not tolerate any more breaches of security. A queer general, that's just what we need in an election year."

At the Pentagon in the office of the deputy chief of staff of operations, the DCSOPS said: "A closet queen for a general! Can't trust the reserves. Task a study immediately to determine how many troops, battalions and dollars are needed to take over the Army Reserve mission with regulars."

At U.S. Army Europe headquarters in Heidelburg, Germany, the commanding general was furious: "It took us years to gain the respect of our German and NATO allies. Can you imagine what they must think of us now?"

At U.S. Army Support Command headquarters in Kaiserslautern, Germany, they said: "We'll have to get along without the reserves. Keep them at arms length and do not show them any classified documents for any reason."

At Deputy Chief of Staff of Host Nation Activities in Heidelburg, they said: "We've never seen an organization chart of the CIMIC Network. Who authorized the 38th to prepare it and why haven't we been briefed?"

At German Southern Command in Stuttgart, Germany, they said: "It is *verboten* to seize German property! The occupation is *kaput*! No more military government. CIMIC will prevail in all of Europe. West and East."

At NATO headquarters in Brussels, Belgium, the Dutch and Belgian allies said: "The Americans have lost face. We must have mutual respect and honor. CIMIC operations may be damaged beyond repair."

Back in Washington D.C. at the Army Reserve Logistic Command for Northern Germany and Benelux countries, they said: "How can we work with the Germans again? We're guilty by association. They have no use for traitors."

In New York City at the Department of Army, Public Affairs Office, there was a lone dissenter, who said: "I knew General Palmer at the Army War College. He was no fruitcake. It must be a setup."

And down south in Vicksburg, Mississippi, the home of the 47th Engineer Command, Army Reserve, they agreed: "Can't trust those damn Yankees. A faggot for a general. Our CIMIC guys must be hidin' their heads in shame."

At 10:05 a.m. on Thursday, Dave Maccabee and Major Kathy Morgan met Major General Bob Kelley at a secret closed door meeting at the Department of Army Public Affairs Office on East 57th Street. The general, a granite block of a man who looked like a linebacker on an NFL football team, sat behind a large mahogany desk, shuffling through the morning's news clippings that had been compiled for him. "We're in deep shit," he confided, gravely. "DOD has hit the panic button. The credibility of the Army Reserve is at stake."

The Chief of the Army Reserve looked intently at the two people sitting in front of him. They were one helluva PAO team, super-achievers, who complemented each other perfectly. He could always depend upon them, no matter how difficult the project or sensitive the situation.

Maccabee relaxed in a stuffed chair, laid back, but very alert. Morgan came dressed in BDUs. She sat erect on the edge of a chair, notepad in hand.

"I don't believe the newspaper stories about General Palmer," the general stated flatly. "I've known him for too many years. He was an outstanding officer. I don't believe he turned gay and committed suicide. It's all too pat."

"Yes, sir," Maccabee agreed. "No way. Not Andrew."

"We're calling every contact we have to get to the bottom of this. We have reservists working for the NYPD, FBI, DEA, Justice, DA, IRS, DIA, CIA, every spook organization you can name." The general leaned forward, confiding. "Dave, there's something not kosher about this whole mess."

Maccabee nodded. He knew the general's last remark was meant to trigger him emotionally. He kept a straight face, hoping his Jewish smarts, which he received from his Dad, and the Irish luck, which he got from his Mom and Grandpa O'Neil, might come into play. He needed all of the help he could get.

Morgan anticipated a request. "General, sir. You know the 245th CI is 85 percent NYPD. I have two teams of detectives digging for information, who report directly to me. I'm just heartbroken. I can't believe any of this nonsense about General Palmer. It couldn't happen the way they said."

The general spoke candidly. "I've asked the CID to investigate, but they don't know their way around the city. We need to get the coroner's office off its ass. I just saw a copy of the partial autopsy report, and it's a lot of crap. Talk about incompetence. I've called the mayor's office and demanded a high priority, complete microscopic autopsy and chemical analysis. Not the fast study that the medical examiner gave us." He talked directly to Maccabee. "Dave, we need to clear Andrews's name. I need your help."

Maccabee edged forward. "You've got it. What do you want me to do?"

"I want to bring you on temporary active duty, two weeks, a month, as long as it takes. You have my direct order to pull out all the stops. Leave your Madison Avenue diplomacy at home. I don't care how many toes you step on. Speed is critical. I've ordered a 24-hour telephone watch at my office in the Pentagon if you need command support to overcome any hurdles. Major Morgan will be your backup in New York. You guys are my best creative weapon. My best trouble shooters. If you live up to your past record, you should be able to come up with the answers and solve this mess for me."

Maccabee took a deep breath. Andrew Palmer had been a good friend. The man's reputation was at stake. CIMIC was in trouble, its credibility in dire need of damage repair. He had put in too much time in the reserves to let it fall apart now. "Sir, I have two suggestions. I don't think I should come on active duty. I can be more effective if I work outside the system. I won't be restricted by Army regs and can cut through red tape that gets in my way."

"If I bring you back on orders, you'll get paid for your time."

"I don't need the extra money. Everything is going smoothly at my agency. I guess it can remain small a little longer."

"Okay, if you're certain you want to do it this way. What else?"

"I want Freddy Ventura called up and put on indefinite orders. He'll need the money. I want him answering only to Kathy and me, nobody else."

Kathy spoke up. "Are you sure we need him? He's so damn irresponsible. You never know where Mr. Macho is half the time. I heard he got fired as a bouncer at some classy eastside disco."

Maccabee smiled. "You heard right. Freddy got bounced. He tried to break up a brawl and ended-up taking on both sides, including the boss's son. He now has a sales job, selling siding to homeowners. I can't picture him as a blue suede shoe salesman." He laughed, then grew serious. "We've had our problems with Freddy in the 38th, but he's the best first sergeant I know. We served together in 'Nam. He's the kind of guy you want to have around in a fire fight. He saved my ass more than once. That's why he retired when I did. Said it wouldn't be fun anymore. We're going to need his streetwise savvy, his Puerto Rican charm and maybe even his muscle."

Morgan didn't agree. "Okay, but you better keep a tight rein on him. Freddy will have every Hispanic and Afro-American reservist volunteering to help us. That is, if you can find Freddy when we need him."

General Kelley enjoyed seeing the sparks fly. "I'll have his orders cut in an hour." He paused. "Just a little command guidance. The token investigation down in the village was sloppy. Better get down there and get a good look before all of the evidence disappears. Until the NYPD reclassifies the suicides as a homicide, you can get in."

"Anything else?" Maccabee asked, wondering where to start.

"You know the 38th from the inside out. I'd like you to nose around on Saturday when they drill. I'll call the deputy commander and advise him that you're my point man and to give you carta blanche. Any questions?"

"No, sir." Maccabee stood and saluted. He shook hands with his former boss. He had never let him down. He hoped he wouldn't do it now.

Morgan also snapped to attention and saluted. She was glad to work with Colonel Maccabee again. "We do make a good team," she admitted silently, "just as long as the colonel knows who's really the boss." She spoke with a note of confidence. "We'll give it our very best, sir."

An angry scowl flashed across the general's face. "You're going to need more than that. Those classified documents didn't have legs. Someone lifted them. I want to know who. And I want to know fast!"

3

At 10:22 that night, Maccabee and Morgan followed Freddy Ventura into René Lemoine's East Village flat. Freddy, dressed in a scarlet red sports jacket, yellow turtleneck sweater and blue suede shoes fast talked his way in. He flashed his CI counter-intelligence ID card to the weary-eyed building super, who had immigrated from Mexico four years ago.

Speaking in a hurried Spanish, Freddy explained that the two plains clothes officers with him, despite their jeans and western boots, were CI agents and worked closely with the NYPD. He handed the see-nothing, know-nothing super a twenty dollar bill and gained immediate entry.

"I couldda slipped dah door's lock wid my credit card," Freddy said, as they walked inside. "Dah super says he didn't see or hear nothing' strange Tuesday night. Deese guys see everything."

"I know," Maccabee replied. "In this city, if you mind your own business, you live longer. Do you think he might remember for another twenty?"

"Nah, he told me all he knew. Nada! Didn't see a damn thing. Dat's why I told him to go back to bed." Freddy turned on an overhead light in the living room, getting his bearings. He gasped and complained: "Christ, whatta stink!"

The apartment had been left the way the police had found it. The bodies of the two suicide victims had been taken to the city morgue, where they awaited a second autopsy. The general's clothes, suicide note, Polaroid camera, gay photos, blood stained sheets, attaché case and military documents had all been taken to the 9th Precinct station, cataloged and put into a file. Everything else remained a shambles.

Maccabee walked into the bedroom with Morgan a few steps behind him. "What a mess!" he exclaimed. "Be careful, we don't want to destroy any evidence that might still be lying around. If the police ever reclassify the suicides as a homicide, they'll be back in strength, swarming all over this place with microscopic vision."

"It'll be too late," Morgan retorted. "Most of the evidence has been disturbed. They'll have no one to blame but themselves. They should have done it right the first time." She kicked aside a pile of gay erotic magazines lying on the floor by the bed. "I've asked Vito Milano, one of my sergeants at the 9th Precinct to send me a duplicate set of the police photos and schematic of the shooting, so we can get a good look at what happened."

"When will they be available?"

"Twenty-four hours for lab time, no quicker."

"Even for a high priority case like this?"

Morgan knew that her hard-charging boss's one great weakness was impatience. He never took "no" for an answer. "The NYPD doesn't work that fast. It takes time."

Maccabee didn't agree. He had to establish a sense of urgency to their efforts.

25

They had to find some hard evidence, a clue, something tangible that could point them in the right direction. "Every investigation is a process of elimination," he said. "We know we're looking for evidence, but we're not sure what we're looking for. When we see it, I hope we'll recognize it."

He looked for signs of a struggle. Any sign. An overturned chair, broken lamp, curtains pulled down. He saw no indication of a fight. He grimaced at the blood stains on the mattress, pillows and headboard. It seemed strange. He turned to Morgan and asked: "How did Andrew get here? Was he coerced or unconscious? How come nobody saw him enter the building?"

Morgan sat on the edge of the bed's mattress, trying to reconstruct the shootings. "We need to establish priorities," she said. "Fact one: General Palmer was murdered by party or parties unknown to him. Fact two: General Palmer was not a homosexual. Fact three: René Lemoine was a homosexual and may have shot the general ..."

"Go on," Maccabee prodded, "where are you heading?"

"If we agree that someone lured General Palmer into a trap, we need to concentrate on Lemoine and learn all we can about him. There's a missing link." She paused, her right eyebrow arching. "I think there was a third man."

"Why a man?"

An indignant look flooded across Morgan's face. "You guys might get your jollies off watching two lesbians perform sex, but we women find watching two homosexual men perform sex outright disgusting. There has to be a third man."

Maccabee chuckled. He admired Morgan's candor. He also respected her uncanny ability to focus tightly on a subject. She was one helluva sharp soldier, female type. Smart, tough, good marksman, good field soldier. Dressed in tight jeans and a sloppy pullover, she looked attractive. Despite the friendship that existed between them, their relationship was platonic. "It seems logical," he agreed. "We know what Andrew was all about. Let's concentrate on Lemoine."

Freddy worked his way past them into the corner of the bedroom by the night table. A burly 245 pounds, Freddy looked shorter than his six foot two height, because of the beer belly that bulged over his belt. His weight never slowed him down, not on the ballfield or the battlefield. For a 37-year old vet, he could still run fast when he had to. His straight black oily hair, dark brown eyes and swarthy complexion made people wonder about his Puerto Rican and Indian blood.

Freddy poked his foot into the stacks of gay magazines. "Look at all dis shit! Yah need a shovel to scrape it up."

"Forget about that filth." Morgan picked a greasy CCNY sweatshirt off the floor and shook it out. She held it away from her body with two fingers, trying to avoid its putrid odor. "Start digging through these clothes," she said to Freddy. "Look in the shirt pockets and trousers. There has to be some scrap of evidence we can find." Freddy reached to pick up a red plaid shirt. "And put on those latex surgical gloves I gave you," she ordered, sharply. "We can't leave any fresh fingerprints behind."

Freddy pursed his lips, annoyed. He didn't like taking orders from a female, any female, even if she was right. "No-o-o problem," he said. He slipped on the gloves and began to search through the mounds of dirty clothes.

Maccabee and Morgan put on their latex gloves, too. They dug through the debris for twenty minutes, emptying pockets, sifting through the layers of clothing. They found coins, sunglasses, keys and meaningless notes. Nothing important. They looked under the bed and found more grimy layers of erotic magazines. Freddy was right. He needed a shovel, not a sieve.

A small portable radio sat perched on the edge of the dresser, balanced precariously. Maccabee studied it, wondering if the police had dusted it for fingerprints. He opened the top drawer of the dresser and saw a pocket datebook. "I think I've found something." He skimmed through the pages, checking several months. He saw the name "Harold" scrawled on holiday week-ends. He double checked the name against the telephone directory in the back.

"What did you find?" Morgan looked at the datebook in Maccabee's hands.

"Names, addresses, telephone numbers," he answered. He turned to Freddy. "How long will it take you to copy this book?"

"Yer building is open 24-hours, ain't it? Can I use yer office?"

"Sure. You can get this duplicated and be back here in an hour."

"No-o-o problem!" Freddy assured.

Maccabee handed the datebook to Morgan as he continued to look through the top drawer. He found a Citibank checkbook, monthly bank statements and a bundle of envelopes with paid bills. He thumbed through the American Express monthly statements. "Better copy these too."

Morgan looked at the American Express statements. She focused on the January hotel bill. "Colonel Maccabee, we may have stumbled onto something. If we follow the money, maybe ..."

On Saturday morning at the 38th CA Command, Maccabee struggled not to lose his temper. He sat on the edge of a gray steel desk inside the G-2 military intelligence office. He watched Lieutenant Colonel Joseph Cherniak, the unit's G-2, a short, stocky 44 year-old reservist in BDUs, defend himself. He had been fielding a torrent of questions shot at him by the two uniformed CID investigators sent by the Pentagon. "I'm telling you the original is still here!" he said. He held the TOP SECRET document in his hand, slapping it on his desk. He shoved it roughly across the desktop at the two CID agents.

"Then how did the *Times* get their hands on a copy of the CIMIC Network?" the CID colonel demanded. "I want a list of names of everyone who worked on this classified paper. Every soldier who came in contact with it. Action officers, NCOs, typists, everyone."

"We need to know how your command's review procedures work," the CID major added, "from concept to revision to final production."

"How many people were involved in this project?" the CID colonel asked.

Maccabee sympathized with Joe Cherniak's plight. He was a good G-2. His eighteen year career in military intelligence was now at risk. Cherniak was responsible for the security of all classified documents in the command and any violations that occurred. His neck was stretched way out on this one. Maccabee decided to intercede.

"The whole G-5 CIMIC section helped write it," Maccabee said. "It was my baby from the start, linking up each of the CIMIC teams into an effective intelligence network. Everyone on the general's staff signed off on it." He paused, then spoke in somber tones. "General Palmer planned to present the CIMIC Network at OPERATION FALCON FLASH, where the U.S. and NATO general staffs would see it for the first time."

The CID colonel had been briefed that Maccabee was General Kelley's point man and not to antagonize him. He looked at Maccabee with caution, not caring for his casual safari sportsman look. "Were there any copies made of the original?" he asked.

"Hell, yes!" Maccabee answered, "but they were draft copies. We kept them under close hold." He knew the G-5 section didn't handle classified material in strict accordance with army regs. They handled the material loosely, taking it home or to their civilian jobs to type it on their personal computers. If they didn't, the work never got done. He wondered if the security breach occurred this way. He kept the question to himself.

Cherniak opened up the G-2 logbook to show the entries. "Only one final document was produced. There are no copies," he stressed. "All draft material was kept in another file."

Maccabee spoke directly to Cherniak. "Did you double check to see if the *Times'* copy is an exact match or did they pick up a draft copy?"

"It's a perfect match," the CID colonel said. "We're double checking every possibility before we go into the field." He sifted through the command's security clearance file. He fixed his eyes on Cherniak. "You say everyone in the G-5 section was cleared for TOP SECRET?"

It's time to leave, Maccabee thought. They're going to continue probing, then probe some more. He glanced at the grim faces of Captain Emil Dressler, the assistant G-2 and two female Afro-American NCOs, who were taking notes. They were dedicated professionals, who took their G-2 jobs seriously. Sergeant Laura Washington, a 36-year old matronly full time admin supervisor in BDUs, had served with Maccabee in the field. She caught his eye and walked with him to the door. She whispered, "Better check out their wives, too."

They stood outside the door of the G-2 section. "Is there anything else you want to tell me?" he asked, discreetly.

"No," she confided, adjusting her octagon-shaped fashion bifocals. "Just a thought, nothing more."

Maccabee nodded. He spoke with a note of concern in his voice. "Call me at my office the instant anything turns up. Anything unusual or irregular. Anything." He forced a thin smile. "Okay?"

"Yes sir-r," she said and walked back inside. Maccabee strode down the corridor toward the staircase that led upstairs to the G-5 section.

"Guten morgan, Herr Oberste!" Captain Rudolph Krueger, 32, tall, intent and bespectacled, sprang to his feet from behind his desk. He stood at stiff attention and clicked his heels in an exaggerated Prussian style as Maccabee walked inside the G-5 office. "We've been waiting for you, sir." Five officers and two NCOs of the G-5 CIMIC section stood behind their gray steel desks at rigid attention, their chins jutting out, their faces masking the apprehension that Maccabee knew they must be feeling.

"As you were," Maccabee said, shutting the door. He turned to the operations NCO, sergeant first class Wilfred Douglas. "Willie, I don't want any interruptions." The tall, 34-year old, Afro-American NCO, a former minor league baseball player and now IRS agent from New Rochelle, nodded. He pulled a black window shade down that said: "DO NOT DISTURB! MEETING IN PROGRESS."

Maccabee walked to the rear of the room and sat on the edge of a gray steel desk that dominated the six smaller desks of his hand-picked team of CIMIC ARTEPers. These men and women were the best field soldiers, the elite of the unit. They served as command briefers on mobile training teams, teaching the latest CIMIC procedures to the subordinate CA battalions. The ARTEP (Army Test and Evaluation) teams tested each battalion in the field, using simulated CIMIC situations that they would encounter in Europe.

The officers were infantry veterans, spoke fluent German and were proficient in CIMIC host nation procedures. During the ARTEPs, they played the role of U.S. commanders, German military officers, civilian bureaucrats and refugees. They also supervised aggressor teams that would attack the battalion defenses, using guerrilla live-play tactics and psychological operations.

"What's new on General Palmer?" Lieutenant Colonel Wallace Livingston asked in a worrisome tone. A blond curly-haired six footer who exercised daily, Livingston had been promoted from deputy to G-5 of the command. He was a bright, affable 44-year old sales manager from New York City, who always had a friendly word to say. He was married to a Chinese stewardess from Hong Kong, his second wife. Originally from the border area near El Paso, Texas, he and Liu Ann had organized a successful sales trading company, which imported men's and women's sportswear from communist China.

Before Maccabee could answer, Major Klaus Ludwig, 41, a tall, dark haired, brooding, second-generation German-American engineer from Smithtown, Long Island, interrupted. "I've never seen the morale of this unit so bad. If you saw the troops at formation this morning, man, their heads were hangin' low. If that's not bad enough, my ten-year old kid got into a fight at school. Some kid asked him if his army father was a faggot." Ludwig, a branch chief for the mobile training teams, had brought a German bride home from his active duty tour. He and Vera had three children.

"It's different with girls," said Major Gerhardt Brockmann, the ARTEP chief. "I have two daughters, ages fifteen and twelve. They came home in tears." Brockmann, 41, a stocky, balding, first generation German-American from Dusseldorf had immigrated to the U.S. when he was fifteen. He had gained his U.S. citizenship by serving with the First Cav' in Vietnam. He owned a small tool and die company in Elizabeth, New Jersey. His wife Ursula, a second generation German, worked as a passenger agent for Lufthansa Airlines at Rockefeller Center in New York City.

Maccabee understood everyone's embarrassment. The 38th was a typical army reserve "salt and pepper" unit. Four out of five members were married, three out of four had children. About eighty-five percent of the officers were white, the rest Afro-American or Hispanic. The opposite ratio existed among enlisted personnel. Maccabee smiled at Sergeant Anita Mendoza, who sat quietly at her desk, her eyes downcast. Anita, a 28-year old waitress in civilian life, had risen to admin supervisor in the reserves. Getting married last November, her pregnancy showed. Maccabee forced sentiment aside, opting for a hard-nosed approach. "The Pentagon has demanded a complete autopsy, not the half-assed job you read about in the papers."

"How long does it take?" Major Kurt Goetz asked, impatiently. A 40-year old sandy-haired second generation Swiss, who looked like a Hollywood matinee idol, Goetz was a computer specialist for an international telemarketer. He was in-charge of telecommunications for the 38th. "If the newspapers keep blasting us, I'm going to get out of the reserves. People are making nasty cracks behind my back." Goetz had served with Brockmann in the First Cav' in Vietnam. He had married a Bavarian ski instructor during his active duty tour in Germany. His wife, Erika, owned a small travel agency called Deutsch-Swiss SkiVentures.

"Let's stop feeling sorry for ourselves," Maccabee replied. "The CID is coming here to check you guys out after they meet with the deputy commander."

Livingston scratched his head, perplexed. "We can't figure out how the *Times* got its hands on our CIMIC Network. There must be a logical answer."

"Someone stole the original and copied it," Krueger suggested. A young aggressive management consultant, a second generation Austrian, Krueger had married into a wealthy Boston-Irish family. His wife Bonnie watched over their two toddlers at home. "The big question is ... who?"

"Everyone is suspect," Maccabee declared. "Is anyone in this unit hard up for cash? Has anyone been flashing a lot of money or sporting around in an expensive new car?"

"Better get rid of your Mercedes 300 SE," Krueger blurted-out. He pointed his index finger at Brockmann, teasing him. "That limo of yours cost big bucks. I'm still driving around in a beat-up Ford wagon."

Brockmann pushed the chair back from his desk with two stiff arms, indignant. "Serves you right. You need to have your own business to afford a high performance car like mine. My Mercedes will outlast your Ford twice as long." He turned to Goetz, who was laughing at him. "What about your BMW?" Before Goetz could answer, Brockmann turned back to Maccabee with a grin on his face. "Hell, we're all entrepreneurs. We know each other pretty good. Nobody I know is in trouble, nobody's over his head in debt. What I do know is ... nobody in this room stole it."

Maccabee pursued another direction. "Could somebody have taken the original document out of this office during coffee or lunch break or when you were preoccupied with another task?"

"We run a tight ship!" Ludwig protested, loudly. "No soldier can take any classified material out without our seeing it. Right Willie?"

The operations sergeant disagreed. He tried to be tactful, not to offend his superior officer. "Somebody could've taken it. Don't know who? Don't know why? But don't think we should cross the possibility out."

"Look guys," Maccabee warned. "This section has never distinguished itself in handling classified documents properly." He stood, addressing each person. "Time for a surprise showdown inspection." He walked down the center aisle that separated the rows of desks. "I want each of you to open your attaché case and put everything in it onto your desk. I want to see how many SECRET documents you're carrying."

He could see the troubled faces of the officers around him. He walked from desk to desk, frowning at what he saw. They were all guilty of mishandling classified material, carrying extracts of SECRET papers that they had condensed into a new command briefing for each of the unit's CIMIC teams.

"This is hard intelligence," he reminded them. "I used to do the same thing. I'm just as guilty as you guys. Except, I'm not involved anymore." He stood in the center aisle with everyone's eyes on him. "You need to clean up your act."

He strode to the file cabinet and yanked open the top drawer. "Willie, better check all of your section's files to make sure nothing is here that shouldn't be here."

He tried to shield his troops from anticipated harm. "You better purge your personal files. And do it quickly before the CID gets up here." Within ten minutes, Sergeant Mendoza hustled downstairs, carrying two loose files of classified papers that were headed for the shredding machine.

Maccabee sat down in his old chair at his old desk. He relaxed, glad to be back with his men. He glanced at the CIMIC briefing and thumbed through each of the slides. He nodded approval and set them aside. He looked across the room.

Goetz had started typing a message on the keyboard of a portable black terminal that looked like a laptop computer. "Want to see a demo on our new telescrambler?" he asked, keying in a tutorial.

"Is that the new XL-5?" Maccabee asked, walking over to Goetz and looking over his shoulder.

"Sure is." He patted the terminal lightly, like a proud father. "This little PC has a modem that lets us conduct classified conversations over unprotected telephone lines and radio links. The system is user-friendly and functions as a scrambler. We can encrypt and transmit secret information. Comes with a printer that lets us decrypt and receive up to 2,000 characters of text."

Livingston ambled by and stopped. "Just think of it, Dave. Our CIMIC teams can now get on a public telephone anywhere in Germany and talk to one another without worrying about the Russians listening in. We were always stymied by Germany's dumb telephone system, by Hitler's revenge. Now we can finally communicate with one another."

"I know," Maccabee replied, stepping back, speaking to the entire group. "It took a long time to develop this new technology. Your CIMIC teams down at the German local VKKs can feed CIMIC intelligence up the chain to the entire CIMIC network. The intel is more timely and accurate. The kind of hard intel you need to facilitate strong logistical support, not the standard enemy order of battle crap you get at a typical G-2 briefing."

Goetz spoke out. "Every CIMIC team has been assigned an XL-5 for FALCON FLASH. We pick-up our equipment and taped codes when we get to Germany. The codes are updated every two days, so they can't be compromised."

Maccabee eyed the men around him, coldly. He spoke in slow, deliberate terms. "You guys better guard this little jewel with your lives." He turned abruptly without waiting for acknowledgment and walked toward the door.

Livingston signaled him with an outstretched hand. "Do you have a minute?" he half-whispered. He put his arm around Maccabee's shoulder, ushering him out of the G-5 office into the corridor. They found an empty classroom down the hall, walked inside, and shut the door.

"I feel like I have a German cabal in my section," Livingston confided. "I'm the only WASP in the G-5 section. They talk like German natives, everything so fast." He threw up his hands in dismay. "I don't know what they're saying." He paused. "Dave, I know you think there's been a breach in security. Do you think there's a mole in my section?"

"Telephone call for Colonel Maccabee!"

Maccabee hurried downstairs to the commander's office, passing by a line of reservists at the supply cage. They milled about lethargically, checking out their gas masks and MOPP gear, the protective clothing that they needed to wear in a chemical warfare environment. They paid scant attention to their needs, talking quietly in groups of threes and fours. Not good, Maccabee thought, as he walked into the general's office. He spotted Colonel Herbert Zimmermann, the 52-year old acting commander, who was rummaging through the files of material at the staff conference table. Maccabee stared at General Palmer's broad mahogany desk, highly polished and unused in silent testimony.

"You have a call from Major Morgan," Zimmermann said, running his hand through his thinning red hair. "Please use the general's phone on the side table. Want me to leave?"

"No," Maccabee replied. Herb Zimmermann, like Andrew Palmer, had been a classmate at the U.S. Army War College. Maccabee was glad that he didn't have Herb's job right now. "Maccabee here," he answered.

"Colonel Maccabee, this is Major Morgan reporting in. I've just received some news from the 9th Precinct. They've changed their preliminary report from 'obvious suicide' to 'suspicious self-inflicted wounds.' They're still not calling it a homicide, but they've sealed off Lemoine's apartment and are conducting a full scale investigation. Our famous mayor has finally put the heat on."

"It's about time! What about the police photos, when do we see them?"

"Monday, at the earliest."

"It doesn't take that long to develop film. Why so long?"

"Because some stupid idiot forgot to put a 'rush job' on the film when he sent it to the color lab in New Jersey. They're closed this weekend and the police commissioner won't authorize overtime pay to open the lab."

"How's the autopsy progressing? When do we see a complete coroner's report?"

"You can't rush these people. They've been burnt once. They're proceeding with extreme caution. Best guess is Tuesday of next week."

Maccabee felt disgusted. Of all the damned things. A man's reputation has been destroyed by the media. The bureaucracy is still in slow motion. How do we get them up to speed? He shook his head. "Any messages?"

Morgan's voice mellowed, suggestively. "Yes, you've been invited to attend a Saint Patrick Day's Party next Thursday at the Bavarian Inn."

"Who invited me?"

He heard Morgan's deep chuckle on the other end of the line. "I thought you'd never ask. Gretchen Lundstrom."

"Gretchen," he repeated. "Hasn't she done enough damage? What does she want

32

now?" He hesitated. "I'll think about it. Any other messages?"

"No sir, that's all."

"Thanks. Keep in touch." They hung up.

Maccabee pulled up a chair at the conference table and faced Zimmermann. "How are you holding up, Herb?"

"As good as can be expected," the acting commander replied. "The media is driving us crazy. The center was like a zoo this morning. We had to battle our way past the television camera crews to get inside. That's why we have MPs posted outside the fences. Christ, they ambushed some of our young soldiers and asked some of the damnedest insulting questions. We almost had a couple of fist fights."

"Bill Ritter is a good PAO. Is he handling the press?"

"Yes and no. We're trying to divert them over to the 77th ARCOM. We can't get our work done. Interviews by appointment only." He looked at his watch. "Gretchen Lundstrom, the *Times* columnist, is due here any minute."

"Uh, oh!" Maccabee exclaimed. "I better get going. I've met the lady and don't want to speak to her right now." He glanced at the general's empty chair and shook his head sadly. "I have a few more things to do." He took several steps into the main corridor. There she was, striding rapidly toward him, escorted by Major Bill Ritter.

There was no way he could dodge her. Gretchen Lundstrom appeared confident, her blue eyes sparkling, her blond hair bouncing loosely over her shoulders. She wore a heavy royal blue greatcoat that fell to her ankles. It was unbuttoned at the waist, its wool folds flapping with each stride. The clicketty, click, click of her four-inch spike heels on the black tile floor echoed the length of the corridor.

Gretchen's eyes widened in startled surprise. "David, what are you doing here? I thought you had retired."

Maccabee smiled politely as she walked up to him. "Same thing as you. Trying to learn the truth."

"I'm working on a new slant." She moved closer, her four-inch heels elevating her to Maccabee's six-foot eye level. "Did you get my phone message, my invitation for Saint Patrick's Day?"

"Yeah, I received it." He stepped back two paces.

"Well-l-l, is it a date?" she asked, brazenly. Her face glowed with warmth and excitement.

Maccabee felt cornered. Yet, there was something about this bright, aggressive woman that excited him. He didn't answer.

"I'm not the enemy, David. I'm on your side." She inched closer. "Come on, David, let's bury the hatchet and be friends. We'll have fun on Saint Patrick's Day."

Fun ... at a time like this? Maccabee shook his head no, then thought better of it. What the hell, I may learn something. Who knows what information she has. He nodded yes and grinned.

"Good," Gretchen replied, beaming slyly. She turned and swished her great-coat, swinging her hips gracefully as she walked inside the general's office.

Maccabee stood aside, watching her pass. The warning buzzer in the G-3 operations office blared-out, its loud raspy sound reverberating off the walls, alerting everyone to attend a mandatory meeting.

The corridors and staircases came alive as reservists stopped what they were doing and headed toward the large classroom on the second floor. The high decibel level of animated conversation that usually erupts during training breaks was absent. The officers, NCOs and enlisted personnel filed quietly into wooden desktop chairs, seeking out friends whom they wanted to be near. Inwardly, they shared a sense of anger, betrayed by the man whom they had learned to trust. The general's misconduct brought personal disgrace to everyone in the unit. General Palmer was their general. He was the man. His betrayal was more than they could bear.

Seeing the anguish on so many faces, Maccabee wondered how the public was reacting. "Probably, just as badly," he murmured. He heard a familiar voice and looked up.

"Hey, boss!" Master Sergeant Freddy Ventura shouted, charging down the hall towards him. Freddy wore BDUs like the rest of the troops. "Gotta minute?"

Maccabee wondered why Freddy wasn't tracking down the American Express leads he had given him. "Sure, what's up? What brings you here?"

"Dey asked me to give dah next briefing. I wanted to see how my people are doin'. I recruited most of dem when I wuz in dah unit." He motioned Maccabee aside. "Wanna talk to yah, too."

"Major Morgan called," Maccabee said. "It looks like the heat is on."

"Yeah, I know. I was down at dah coroner's office dis morning. Do yah know what dat asshole did?"

"Who? The coroner?"

"No, dah medical examiner. Some goddamned Chinaman, who doesn't know his ass from shinola. Dat silly bastard never ran any chemical tests during dah first autopsy. Only took a blood sample. Says he worked a double shift and wanted to get home to his sick wife. Never spoke to dah cops at dah scene. He requested dah lab tests on a low priority."

"Kathy tells me we won't get the lab report until Tuesday."

"I'll get it sooner. My cousin Jose works at dah coroner's office. He says dey've come up wid something hush hush. As soon as he finds out what, he'll call Major Morgan at yer agency."

Two Puerto Rican typists interrupted them. "Hey, Fernando, como esta?" They were joined by three others. Maccabee felt that he should have learned Spanish instead of German, so he could understand what his troops were talking about. He watched Sergeant First Class Willie Douglas usher the chattering group into the classroom.

Douglas blocked Maccabee's path. He spoke quietly. "Sir, several NCOs want to meet with you privately. Can we come up to your office on Monday?"

"Of course." Maccabee had earned the trust of his Afro-American troops long ago, looking out for their welfare, motivating them to achieve higher levels of responsibility. Douglas had won "The Outstanding NCO of the Year" award for three straight years. "If it's urgent, we can find a vacant office and ..."

"No, sir. It can wait until Monday."

"You know the acting commander's door is always open, Willie. Colonel Zimmermann has more problems than he can handle, but I'm sure he'd see you."

"It's you we need to see. Doreen, Rosa and Tyrone asked me to arrange it."

Maccabee understood. The three sergeants were part of his ARTEP team. If they were involved, the meeting had to be important. "Sure thing.. Call my secretary at my

34

office and schedule it around ten."

Maccabee followed Douglas into the classroom. He mounted a speaker's platform and walked to the podium. He faced the troops and established instant eye contact. He spoke candidly in deep, trenchant terms. "We're all in a state of shock over General Palmer's death. We're doing our best to find out what really happened. General Palmer was not gay. I know it. You know it. He was a straight arrow. A good man. Somebody set him up. Somebody murdered him. I can't prove it yet, but I will. Somehow, we'll clear his name. So keep your cool." He turned the meeting over to Freddy, not wanting to answer any questions. He walked briskly to the back of the classroom and watched.

"How many people from Bed-Sty?" Freddy asked, his voice booming the length of the classroom.

Several NCOs and enlisted people raised their hands.

"How many from 125th Street?"

Six hands were raised.

"How many from Spanish Harlem?"

Another twelve hands went up.

"How many from dah South Bronx?"

More hands went up, practically all the NCOs and enlisted troops.

Master Sergeant Freddy Ventura strode back and forth, challenging his listeners, waving his arms dramatically. He commanded everyone's attention.

"Yer dah best damn street fighters in dah world! Hey man, what you learnt as kids growing up in dah ghetto is something dey don't teach yah in books. Yah gotta use yer common sense when it comes to anti-terrorism." He strode to the edge of the briefing platform. "What about youze officers? How many of yah live in dah city?"

Many hands shot up, about half the officers.

"How many live or work in White Plains, Yonkers and Yorktown?"

More hands went up, about a third.

Freddy pointed to some officers who had not reacted. "And where do youze guys work? In Hempstead? In Queens? Whadda about youze guys from Jersey?" He slapped his hand on his thigh, sarcastically. "Youze guys got all dah instincts to stay outta trouble. If you're walking down dah street and see something comin' down, yah get outta harm's way. If yah see a rumble starting or some punks crowding a street corner, yer smart enough to cross dah street or go dah other way. Dat's what dey teach yah in anti-terrorism survival. Use yer noodle, yer common sense."

Maccabee had heard Freddy's rear area protection briefing before. Ever since the recent terrorist threats, reservists were briefed on anti-terrorist techniques. Protective measures and travel precautions were drilled into the troops before they went overseas.

"Yah need to keep a low profile in Germany. Don't go out alone. Always travel with a buddy. Don't flash big wads of deutschmarks. Wear civvies when yah go into town. Avoid routine schedules. Watch what yah say in public places."

Freddy paused to stress the next point. "Remember, big brother Ivan is listening." He shouted: "Ivan is everywhere!"

He took a deep breath, letting the point register. He could feel everyone's eyes boring into him, including Maccabee's. He continued, talking in harsh, strident tones. "Ivan is gonna attack dah rear areas where he can cause dah greatest damage. No

35

location is safe."

He used an overhead viewer and projected the first slide. "In dah first level, dey come with enemy agents and terrorists to conduct sabotage and public disorder."

He changed acetates. "In level two, dey use Spetsnaz to raid and ambush allied forces. And to assassinate military commanders and political leaders.

"Dah Spetsnaz are bad guys. Ivan's elite. Dey are skilled in parachuting, scuba diving, silent killing, demolitions and clandestine operations. Dey operate in small teams like our rangers and green berets. Dey speak our language and wear our uniforms ... American, German, Dutch, Belgique and Brit. Dey will infiltrate by air, sea and land, maybe weeks before dah war starts.

"Dah Spetsnaz will link-up with deir agents and attack our nuclear and chemical sites. Dey will attack our command and control centers. Television and radio stations. Airfields and ports. Critical road and rail terminals. Radar and air defense sites. Telecommunications and public utilities. Remember dah blackout we had in New York? Dah Spetsnaz can bring NATO's defense to a standstill.

"Deese Spetsnaz think deir superhuman, invincible, dat nothing can stop 'em. Deir mission is everything. Dey strike fast and disappear. Dey have no fear. Victory is more important den life itself. Dey are so bad dat if one of deir comrades is wounded, dey kill him demselves. If deir commander refuses to shoot dah wounded, his deputy shoots him and dah wounded. When dey capture prisoners, men, women and children, dey torture 'em till dey talk, den kill 'em, too. Dey can only be stopped wid a bullet."

"How many Soviet agents are there in West Germany?" an NCO asked.

"How many?" Freddy repeated. He walked to the blackboard behind him, picked up a piece of chalk and scrawled in big numbers: 20,000. "Twenty thousand agents in place ... right now. And wid 80,000 ethnic Germans immigrating back to dah fatherland from Russia last year, maybe twice dat amount. Who knows, maybe more."

"How many agents does Ivan have in the United States?" another person asked.

"Don't be a wise ass!"

4

Colonel Yakov Petrovich, the Soviet Spetsnaz, dodged an incoming yellow cab. He darted across the road in front of the Pan Am terminal at the John F. Kennedy International Airport and walked to the short term parking lot. He climbed inside a leased two-tone brown Cherokee station wagon and followed a Marriott catering truck to the 150th Street exit. He drove past several rows of cargo warehouses and maintenance hangars.

The Sunday weather was cold and damp with a light annoying drizzle that kept people indoors. The husky Spetsnaz wore a blue windbreaker, sport shirt and slacks, which didn't call attention to him. He had spent the past two hours doing a fast reconnaissance of the JFK international passenger terminal and cargo areas to evaluate airport security. Just as he had thought, the airlines had concentrated security at pinpoint defense, guarding against potential terrorist attacks at passenger embarking points, watching for suspicious looking people who might try to smuggle a weapon or bomb aboard an airliner.

He checked the airport map on his clipboard. He noted the nine entry screening points in the aeronautic area, where all airport personnel present their ID cards before driving onto the ramp. A security guard searched an outgoing panel truck, looking for contraband drugs or stolen cargo taken from incoming aircraft.

He drove the Cherokee around the cargo area perimeter. Big gaps appeared in the barbed wire fences, which people had used to get in and out of the airport without being seen.

It looked too simple. He could avoid the screening points and penetrate the airport's inner defense system by scaling one of these gaps or by cutting through the barbed wire fence. Better yet, he could come in from the water's edge at Jamaica Bay, which was unguarded. "It is like sitting duck!"

He smirked. "Don't need Stinger ground-to-air missile. I sneak in, blow-up airliner with rocket launcher while aircraft is sitting on runway, and make good escape." He turned his station wagon onto Rockaway Boulevard, knowing a ground attack would not have the same high emotional impact as blowing-up the jetliner in the air over Brooklyn.

The Spetsnaz pulled the Cherokee off the road onto a sandy shoulder to get out of the traffic, wondering if the traffic was this heavy every weekend. He looked intently at the KGB strip map on his clip board. His finger traced the outline of the JFK airport, its four runways, Jamaica Bay and the surrounding Brooklyn areas.

He studied the eight alternate Stinger missile sites and the KGB recommended ambush site where the PLO terrorists would be located. The GRU agent did not trust the judgment of the KGB. "This is a military mission," he murmured. "I will decide where kill will take place, no one else!"

He had utter contempt for the Arab terrorists. This is suicide mission for them. "If they want to be martyrs like Afghan Mujahideen, I will help them. Curse their blackhearted souls!"

Petrovich steered the Cherokee back onto the highway. He parked at the Bay Harbor Mall, which was a smaller shopping center than the mile long Green Acres Mall in Valley Stream, where his safe house was located. He wandered into a men's specialty store, browsing. As he fingered a pair of Calvin Klein blue jeans, a friendly sales clerk asked: "Can I help you?"

"No, only looking," he replied in his best English. He moved about the store, admiring the variety of men's fashions on the counters and racks. Although he could speak and understand English relatively well, he felt inhibited by his Russian accent. The less he talked, the better. It was safer.

He walked into a large supermarket. "So much food on the shelves. Such great variety." He moved along the aisles, looking at different labels. He ambled back to the checkout area, surprised to see people moving though so quickly. "Not like Moscow with its scarcity of goods, where housewives queued up for hours only to go home empty handed."

The men and women shopped and socialized, speaking freely among themselves, not caring who overheard them. He tried to characterize the people who pushed shopping carts into the parking lot, loading many bags of food into their cars. The people didn't look rich, but they had spent great amounts of money at the cash register. And the parking lot, there were so many cars. Everyone seemed to have their own automobile ... workers, housewives, students, old and young. How could every adult in a family afford to buy a car?

"Was Soviet propaganda about decadent America a big lie?"

"The mission," he reminded himself. "Concentrate on mission. No more distractions." The Spetsnaz climbed back into his Cherokee and drove toward the Rockaways. He spotted a two-tone green Ford following him onto Burnside Boulevard as he passed the huge fuel storage tanks at Inwood. The KGB were following him, but he didn't care. They always watched, ready to devour anyone in their path. They did not frighten him. He would lose them easily at the proper time. Yet, he worried about his personal problem, a problem so sensitive that he could only solve it under the utmost secrecy.

Petrovich turned the Cherokee onto Davis Street, bypassing a construction crew ripping up a side street. He zigzagged in and out of the dead end streets near the Inwood golf course and marina, rejecting the area as an ambush site because of its poor cover and concealment.

The potential for discovery prior to attack was too great. He didn't trust the skill level of the PLO gunners. If he had a regular Spetsnaz hit team, they could shoot on the move and kill with their first shot. With the Arabs, there was no way to predict how they would react under the pressures of the actual attack.

He drove into Far Rockaway and Beach Channel Drive, overlooking Jamaica Bay and JFK airport in the distance. The once popular summer bungalow colony of the 1930's had disintegrated into a seedy, rundown beach-front that was now inhabited by lower class blacks and Puerto Ricans. He rejected an abandoned weather-beaten shack along the marshy inlet that faced JFK runways 40 Left and 40 Right. The area looked too lawless. They ran the risk of being attacked themselves by marauding gangs of toughs.

"We need to be mobile," he thought, disliking a static offense, which ran contrary to Spetsnaz tactics. He drove the station wagon over the Cross Bay Parkway Memorial Bridge, eyeing the JFK bay runways from the bridge's highest elevation. He drove onto a divided six lane roadway, trying to dodge the pot holes. Gray, dingy clapboard shacks and clam bars flanked the road on both sides. A NYPD white and blue police car cruised by, its two blue uniformed officers talking to each other. They ignored him.

The road narrowed. He passed through sparsely wooded tidal flats and sand dunes in the Gateway Wildlife Sanctuary with signs stating; "No parking at any time." The Spetsnaz looked for a good spot to pull over, but couldn't find one. "Good visibility to airport, good field of fire," he commented, "poor concealment and cover. Easy to get in, hard to get out."

He found a small parking area near the second bridge that crossed over to Hamilton Beach on the Brooklyn side. Visibility was excellent. JFK runway 13 Right was directly across the bay about one mile away. A Pan Am jetliner flew overhead, its engines roaring. Several cars were parked in the area, their occupants reading newspapers and watching a small fishing boat head out to sea.

"Getting better," he mused.

He drove across the bridge to Hamilton Beach, pulling the Cherokee off the road. Three young men and one woman were guzzling beer by a green Dodge van, and fishing off a low pier for sea bass and flounder. A TWA jetliner flew overhead, trying to suppress its noise to acceptable levels. It skirted the single family bungalow homes in Hamilton Beach and the high rise condos that dotted the receding salt marshes along the Belt Parkway. "Good visibility," the Spetsnaz determined, "but concealment and cover are poor."

He drove across the parkway onto 165th Avenue, skirting the windswept marshes to his left. He parked the Cherokee, climbed over a three-foot railing, and walked inland, cutting across the scrubby, decaying cord grass that led to the sand dunes at the water's edge. "Good visibility," he said. "Planes fly overhead. Good cover. Disguise PLO like fishermen. Good escape route. Drive onto Brooklyn city streets for fast getaway." He mulled over the negatives. They still risked discovery by other fishermen along the sand dunes, people walking dogs, teenagers on motor bikes or even drug addicts smoking crack or popping Quaalude.

Petrovich steered the Cherokee back onto Bay Boulevard, turning onto Shore Parkway, heading east. The marshlands and Jamaica Bay whipped by. Then a city housing development. A modern high rise condo complex. Infernal bumper to bumper traffic. Wild drivers darted in and out of lanes ahead of him. He felt trapped, fearful of a multiple car accident or police roadblock. It could lock him in time and neutralize his mission. Must plan for this contingency, and allow sufficient time for travel.

He parked at the Jamaica Bay Riding Academy on the bay side of the Belt Parkway, a location that Kolchak had recommended as the best ambush site.

The Spetsnaz looked up as another Pan Am jetliner flew directly overhead at an altitude of less than 2,000 feet. The windswept area looked isolated, consisting of sand dunes and marshes, where the PLO gunners could be hidden in clumps of tall reeds. He circled the location on his map and moved on.

He drove onto Marine Parkway, passed Floyd Bennett Field and crossed Rockaway inlet to Fort Tilden. Putting the Cherokee into four-wheel drive, he rode into an unguarded, restricted area of the deactivated army installation that once housed Nike missile batteries. Bouncing along an abandoned road, he passed a series of hidden sod covered artillery bunkers that faced the Atlantic Ocean. A jetliner circled in the distance. "Bad site. Target is too far away."

Doubling back onto Marine Parkway, Petrovich drove onto Floyd Bennett Field, another good ambush site that overlooked Jamaica Bay. He drove past the Armed Forces Reserve Center, noting that the parking lot was full. Many parked cars had bumper stickers, identifying the 162nd Engineer Brigade, U.S. Army Reserve. "Stupid KGB! They should have known the center's weekend training dates." He drove down an empty runway past a hangar, where three NYPD helicopters were parked. He frowned. A small Coast Guard cutter was tied up to a pier.

"Getting risky," he thought. He turned onto another abandoned runway, about one mile long, and drove to its farthest northeast point, unobserved. He parked at the edge of the runway and walked about fifty yards through saber tooth reeds and dense knee-high cord grass to the water's edge. He looked across the bay. JFK lay within reach, about five miles away.

An Alitalia jetliner flew overhead, cutting across the basin that separated the Jamaica Bay Riding Academy from Floyd Bennett Field. While both sites offered good concealment and cover, the Riding Academy offered the lowest risk of discovery.

Yet, the Spetsnaz knew one thing was wrong. Drastically wrong! When Kolchak selected the ambush site, he had forgotten one critical factor. The weather! The wind blew from the north. The planes landed on JFK runway 13 Right. They were landing where they were supposed to be taking off!

Petrovich slapped the palm of his hand against his knee, his face contorted in anger. "Idiots!" he exclaimed. "Planes use different runway for takeoff. Planes fly in opposite direction away from ambush site." He pulled a pair of binoculars out of a shoulder case, and watched a jetliner takeoff in the distance. It climbed rapidly beyond Stinger missile range.

He knew his earlier instincts had been correct. Kolchak had analyzed the situation when the wind was blowing from the other direction. Since the PLO gunners had only one Stinger missile, there wouldn't be time to move the gunners from one site to another by car if the wind changed. "We must get closer. We must be mobile to maneuver."

The cunning Spetsnaz formulated another plan in his mind.

"KGB be damned!"

"It's not official yet," Major Morgan said, "but every piece of evidence leads me to believe it's murder!" She faced Maccabee across a long conference table, holding a silver pocket pointer in her hands like a college professor. "There can't be any other explanation. The NYPD has reached the same conclusion."

Maccabee smiled at the way Morgan had turned his private office at the agency into a military intelligence command post. Nine large 18-inch by 24-inch layout pages were mounted on the wall, summarizing the situation. Each page listed a category and the essential elements of information. Morgan had used red magic markers to label each page with a bold title.

She was dressed in a dignified gray pinstripe suit with a simple white silk blouse, giving her an aura of efficiency. "Here are the unbiased facts that I obtained from Vito at the 9th Precinct." She pointed to the first chart titled: "Physical Evidence." She spoke rapidly in a low key, businesslike manner. "The cause of death for each decedent: gun shot wound to the head. Ballistic tests verify that both bullets were shot from the same .38 caliber revolver. The angle and distance of the shots were measured. Powder burns, smudge patterns and residual effects were analyzed. General Palmer was shot at point blank range. Muzzle to flesh."

"Which means ...?" Maccabee asked.

"The sound of the shot was probably muffled and not heard."

He nodded.

"The bullet that killed Lemoine was shot from a distance of sixteen inches. He couldn't turn the revolver on himself from that close a distance and still fire. The angle was impossible." She drew a diagram on the layout pad and handed it to Maccabee. "The killer wanted the police to think that Lemoine shot the general first, then himself."

Maccabee fidgeted in his chair, restlessly. He propped a knee up against the rounded edge of the conference table. He was dressed casually in his safari jacket, red goucho shirt, jeans and boots. "Did the killer use a silencer? Did anyone hear the shot?" He swiveled around in his chair toward Freddy, who was sitting next to him. "We need to scour that building until we find someone who heard the shots."

"I've done it boss, so have dah cops," Freddy insisted, grumbling to himself. He tugged on the open zipper of his faded brown leather bomber jacket, which he wore over a gray sweat shirt and Levi's. "Nada!" He ground a Camel into an ashtray and lit another. He had spent Sunday knocking on every apartment door in the building, but to no avail. "I've put dah word out on dah street. Something's gotta turn up."

Morgan continued briefing, as Maccabee swiveled back towards her. "It's possible that Lemoine was killed first, at least that's what the police think. There was more destruction to Lemoine's skull than the general's. Because of the distance and angle of the shot, skull fragments were blown back across the general's face and onto the headboard behind him. If it had been a suicide, we can assume Lemoine would have staged a prettier death scene. Both bodies would have been found in a neat peaceful repose, not the grotesque positions that they were found in."

"Are the police photos back yet?" Maccabee asked. He wanted to look at the details in each photo, hoping to find something that had been overlooked.

"Yes, sir, they're in. Vito sent the color negs back to the lab for dupes. Rush job, this time. We'll get a set of prints later today."

"Have they fixed the time of shooting?"

"They can only estimate an approximate time of death. The police didn't arrive on the scene until 2 o'clock on Wednesday morning. It takes eight to twelve hours before rigor mortis sets in. There was no sign of it. They still haven't found a witness who heard the shots. Their best guess is anywhere between 11:00 p.m. and 1:30 a.m."

"That's a two and a half hour time spread!" Maccabee exclaimed in disgust. "I thought the state of the art was better than that." He grabbed Freddy roughly by the sleeve. "We must get a better fix on the time or we'll never find the killer."

"I know, I know." Freddy pulled his arm loose and stood. He took a deep drag on his cigarette and stomped out of the room. He made his way down the corridor past the art studio. Bob Martin, the senior art director and partner, was arguing with a copywriter over a TV storyboard. "Nuthin' comes easy," Freddy muttered, walking into the small kitchen in the rear of the agency. The red light of the coffeemaker was "on." He poured three mugs of fresh coffee, carried them back to Maccabee's office, and handed them out.

Morgan had moved to the next chart, titled: "Fingerprints." She revealed new information. "The revolver had Lemoine's prints on it, but it was found lying in his opened hand. Vito tells me that in most suicides, the victim will continue to grasp the trigger tightly with his index finger after he's dead. This helps verify who did the shooting at the time of death."

"I've never seen that on TV."

"It's a closely guarded secret among police officers. Once a person is dead, it's impossible for someone to place a gun in his hand and have him grip it tightly. It always falls loose."

"So Lemoine didn't fire the shots."

"The killer did the shooting, then faked the double suicide, not knowing that the gun would fall loose."

"Looks like your third man theory holds up."

"The killer must have wiped his fingerprints clean or he was wearing gloves." She pointed to a second item, titled: 'Polaroid Photos.' It is so bizarre! The police identified Lemoine's fingerprints on all of the photos."

Maccabee interrupted. "Were those Polaroids shot in Lemoine's apartment or someplace else?"

"They were all shot in his apartment. The lab magnified the photos and the police checked them against their own photos, comparing the details of the molding on the bed's headboard. Everything checked out." She leaned against the wall, contemplating. "Lemoine must have posed for the photos and handled them later, never guessing he was going to be killed."

Freddy pushed his coffee mug aside. "Man, dis smells like a blackmail scam dat turned sour. We know dah general left his garage around ten. It takes about thirty minutes to drive downtown. Maybe another hour fer dah sex scene and photos."

Maccabee listened intently. "That would fix the shooting time around 11:30, wouldn't it?"

"Yeah," Freddy answered. "Anywheres between 11:30 and midnight."

"Makes sense," Maccabee agreed, looking at Morgan's next chart. "What about the handwriting analysis. What results are in?"

Her professional air of detachment dissipated. Morgan became animated. Excited. "The letters are all forgeries," she proclaimed, wetting her lips. "The evidence was there before our eyes, so obvious, we didn't see it."

A confused look cut across Maccabee's rugged face. "Obvious?"

"Absolutely. Both letters were typed on a 38th CA letterhead. Right?"

"Right."

"Both letters were signed 'Andy.' Right?"

"Right."

"But the general never used that name. He only used his proper name, 'Andrew.' He never had a nickname. His wife Beth never called him 'Andy.' The people at U.S. Chemical never called him 'Andy.' He just wasn't an 'Andy!'" She stood tall, all five feet, four inches, rocking on her toes, proud of her revelation.

"You're right," Maccabee exclaimed, slamming his open palm onto the table. "I called him 'Andrew' ... along with everyone else. The two letters had to be fake. Someone overdid it, trying to sound personal."

"Yeah," Freddy chimed in, "but how did dah killer get dah letterheads? He had to get dem from somebody in dah unit."

"There's something more insidious going on," Maccabee suggested. "Somebody is trying to discredit CIMIC, deliberately trying to mislead the press. Even Gretchen Lundstrom had her facts all twisted."

Morgan moved closer to the conference table, articulating what they all feared. "Whoever stole the letterheads had to be knowledgeable about CIMIC. Someone assigned to one of the CIMIC teams, someone we trusted."

Maccabee gritted his teeth. "I'm more concerned about the CIMIC Network. Those documents were TOP SECRET!" He glanced at the next chart, titled: "Medical Evidence," which was incomplete. He hoped the second autopsy would shed some new insights. He checked his watch. 9:42. Twenty minutes before Willie Douglas and his NCO committee were due to arrive at the agency. He faced the others and said in a somber voice, "Someone in the unit is either on the take or is being blackmailed."

"Or ... there is a mole in the unit." Morgan's face flushed as she became angry, then furious. "To think that someone we trust could be an accessory." She snapped her pointer closed, clenching it in her fist, twisting it as a violent impulse surged through her.

"Accessory?" Maccabee repeated, sitting down with his long legs sprawled out in front of him. "How do we know he isn't the killer?"

"Oh, my gosh. I assumed he was an accessory. I assumed ..."

"Never assume," Maccabee instructed, curtly. "If there's a mole, we need to dig him out. Colonel Livingston asked me about a mole at Saturday's drill."

At that moment, dressed in an expensive Brooks Brother's double breasted gray suit, Wally Livingston walked into the room, unannounced. "Did I hear my name mentioned?"

Maccabee rose and shook hands with his former deputy, who was his usual cheerful self. "Take a look at what Kathy put together. It gives you an insider's view of the latest intelligence. I hope the police are as methodical." He walked him from chart to chart, recapping each one's significance. They stopped at a final chart, titled: "Mole?"

Livingston paled, the color draining from his face. "I hope we don't have a Judas in our midst," he said, skeptically. "Thank goodness our overseas tour is only a training exercise."

"Like some coffee?" Freddy asked, gulping what was left in his mug. "I need a refill. Anybody else?" He started for the door.

"I could use a jolt." Livingston said, forcing a grin. "Hope it doesn't keep me awake all night. Liu Ann says I've been tossing and turning in my sleep for a week. I guess I'm worried."

"We all are," Maccabee retorted. He motioned Livingston to sit down. He pulled up a chair alongside him. "How is Liu Ann?"

"She's fine. She turned out to be my right arm. Works long, hard hours, but it pays. She flew with me to Shanghai last year on two different buying trips. Business is picking up. She said to say hello."

"I'm glad I don't have your expenses," Maccabee chuckled.

"You know how it is. We get to travel to some exciting vacation spots and write them off as a business expense. Liu Ann and I plan to fly to Stockholm and Helsinki on a buying trip after I return from Germany."

His secretary Judy tiptoed into the room and poked a stack of pink telephone messages into Maccabee's hands. "Do you still want me to hold your calls?"

Maccabee flipped through the messages. He handed the top one back to her, sliding the other pinks slips onto his desk. Turning aside, he said in a low voice. "Ask Bob to call Ben and tell him we'll have the comps for his brochure ready by next week." He thought for a moment. "Hold all my calls." His eyes followed her out of the office. He turned back to Livingston, tuning into his conversation with Morgan.

"It's amazing how little we know about each other in the reserves," Livingston confided. "We live in three private worlds. We see each other at weekend drills, Tuesday nights, overseas tours. We get to meet the wives and girl friends at social events. But we never see the other two worlds ... if somebody is having problems on the job or domestic problems at home."

"Humph," Maccabee grunted. "The army can't intrude into your private life like it does with the regulars. You're reservists. Your personal lives are private."

Livingston grew serious, diverting attention. "That's what troubles me. I only know the people in my section superficially. My German cabal ... anyone could be a sleeper agent. How can we possibly find out?"

Maccabee glanced at Morgan, wondering if the answer could be found outside the army intelligence community. He reached for his phone and buzzed Judy. "Please get Tim O'Brien on the phone, down at the CIA." Realizing that Morgan didn't know who O'Brien was, he explained. "Tim is a captain in the 38th and commands the headquarters company. He's one of my best ARTEPers, number one man with the aggressor force." They talked about the SBIs, the special background investigation, which everyone needed for TOP SECRET security clearance.

The intercom buzzed and the phone lit up on line two. Maccabee grabbed the receiver. "Tim, I need your help. We think there may be a mole in the unit. The FBI is checking into every unit member's bank records to see if there has been any unusual flow of cash or any serious financial problems. They're also checking individual profiles."

"What can I do to help?"

"I need the agency to pull a background check on the families of all of the officers in the 38th and their wives, going back two generations. You have a copy of the mobilization alert roster. Key it into your computer and see what turns up."

"What are you looking for in particular?"

"Any relatives still living in West Germany or eastern Europe that could have someone on a string. Better check with German counterintel to see if any names show up on their list of suspected Soviet agents."

"What about sympathizers and fellow travelers?"

"Them, too."

"I suppose you want it like yesterday? It's going to take time."

"I know. Do what you can."

Outside in the hallway, Freddy sauntered down the narrow corridor between offices, balancing two fresh mugs of coffee. He spotted Sergeant First Class Willie Douglas, Sergeant First Class Doreen Franklin, Sergeant First Class Rosa Sanchez and Sergeant Tyrone Dixon walk out of the reception area. They were all dressed neatly in business suits. "Hey, amigos!" Freddy shouted good naturedly. "How yah doing?"

"Fine and dandy," Doreen Franklin replied, warmly. In civilian life, the tall ebony-faced 36-year old professional worked as a media sales supervisor for NBC Television, calling on the most prestigious advertising agencies on Madison Avenue. "How are you doing? Heard you're back on active duty. Who you with?"

"Back with Colonel Mac again." Freddy didn't know whether to applaud or complain. "And dat lady major. Man, she's hot stuff! She can outwork any two people I know in half dah time. She's like a bulldog terrier. Once she gets her teeth into something, she never let's go." He paused, then stuck his chest out, proudly. "I report directly to her." He paused again, confiding in a low whisper. "I got her number ... maybe she can wrap Colonel Mac 'round her little finger, but I can see right through her. Gotta admit, she can anticipate what dah old man is thinking before he even thinks it."

Tyrone Dixon, 28, a paramedic and ambulance driver at Mt. Sinai Hospital, egged him on. "If she do all dat, what's dah colonel do?"

"He manages her, dat's what he do. He tells her what to do. She tells me what to do. I'm dah troops. Just me. Dey expect me to be a miracle man. Do yah know what dey want me to do?"

They shook their heads in unison, playing along with their former first sergeant.

"Dey want me to do what dah whole damn police force is trying to do. I've gotta go bangin' on doors to find out who heard two pistol shots in dah middle of dah night."

"Fernando, you're in rare form today," chuckled Rosa Sanchez, 31, an articulate legal secretary for a prominent law firm. "We're here to talk with Colonel Mac." They walked into Maccabee's office with Freddy following in their footsteps, still grumbling.

Maccabee shook hands with each of the NCOs, engaging in small talk. Seeing the serious expressions on their faces, he tried to put them at ease.

"Heard the IRS promoted you, Willie," he said, smiling. "Congratulations."

"Yes, sir. I'm movin' up in the world. Gonna be workin' out of the White Plains' office. Supervise my own section. No more commuter trains from New Rochelle to the city. Now I can have dinner with my wife and two little girls, who get to know their daddy." He smiled, pleased with himself.

"What can I do for you?"

"We just came to rap, sir, like the old days."

A dynamic, personable speaker, Doreen Franklin acted as spokesperson for the NCOs. "Colonel Mac, we can't show our faces in our neighborhoods, since the killings. Everything is coming down. It's affecting our family lives. Both my teenage sons had fights at school, sticking up for their mama's reputation. Our young reservists don't know how to cope with this kind of heat."

"Yeah," Tyrone Dixon added in a sarcastic tone. "All we hear is how whitey is sellin' us out. What do we tell dah brothers when dey ask us who dah honkies are goin' down on next?"

"Down!" Maccabee repeated, angrily. "Nobody is going down on anybody. The only person who went down was the general. And he went down for the count! He was murdered. The police report should be released later today."

"I don't mean to offend yah, colonel," Dixon apologized, "but dat's dah street talk. Willie, heah, tell me to say it like it is."

"You pay no never mind to that kind of talk!" Doreen Franklin scolded. "Our military careers are on the line. I'm proud to be in the reserves. I've attended every army school and leadership course I could take. To learn and better myself. I've worked hard to earn these stripes. I plan to be the first black female master sergeant in this command."

"I'm serious about my career, too," Willie Douglas said. "As a black NCO, I work twice as hard so I can outperform the rest. The experience I've had in the reserves helped me get my promotion at the IRS. We can't let our careers in the reserves go down the sewer."

"You've always played it straight with us, Colonel Mac," Franklin continued. "You never patronized us. You were always ready to listen to our problems and help us. Sometimes you worked us too hard, but you brought out the best in us, gave us something to reach up for."

A big grin beamed across Douglas' face. "Yeah, remember when you dropped the bomb on us at your last ARTEP, killin' off all the officers and lettin' us NCOs run the exercise. Scared the daylights out of us, but after we got over the shock, we handled it pretty good. Gave us confidence."

Morgan sat at the far end of the conference table, reflecting. Colonel Mac didn't have to prove a thing. He'd done it all in 'Nam. Freddy made sure the NCOs knew it. He was a combat commander who led by example. When the troops followed him into the field, they knew they had every chance to accomplish their mission and come back alive. He had that magic touch. He gave them a sense of purpose, motivating them to respond in a way that exceeded his own expectations. They were linked together in a strong bond of mutual trust.

"We're worried about going overseas next month and serving with the Germans." Rosa Sanchez expressed her fears in a dignified manner. "It's fine to warn us to keep a low profile in Germany, but we can't blend in like everyone else. The color of our skin stands out like a neon sign. We know the Germans call us 'schvatzes' behind our backs. That's like being called a 'nigger.' I cringe every time I hear it."

"The Germans are racists," Douglas said flat out. "It's still there, hidden just below the surface, smoldering in their Nazi past ..."

The intercom buzzed. Maccabee picked up the phone and recognized the voice of Major General Kelley, calling from the Pentagon.

"I just received the results from the coroner's office," the general said. "All of the pathological tests are in. Dave ... Andrew Palmer was raped!"

"Raped?" Maccabee uttered in disbelief.

"The son of a bitch raped him. There was sperm in Andrew's rectum and torn tissues." The general paused, then continued. "Lemoine tested negative for AIDS.

The medical examiner found a microscopic penetration in Andrew's neck, where he was injected with thorazine to knock him out. The doc thinks the killer injected the AIDS virus into him later. Then killed him."

Maccabee stared ahead, speechless.

"Dave, I want this guy. I want him bad!"

The phone call ended in silence.

Maccabee shuddered, growing angrier. "We must flush this killer out," he mumbled. He started to turn back to the NCOs. He saw Morgan standing in the outer office. She placed the phone receiver slowly back onto its hook.

She stood in the doorway, forcing back her tears. "That was Sergeant Milano down at the 9th Precinct." She fought to control her emotions "Do you know how Andrew was killed?"

"Yes, General Kelley just told me."

"Vito says it's now official. It's a homicide."

Maccabee glanced at the people in his office. They were his people, his troops. "Damn it all!" he swore. "Who in hell is attacking us? Why have they targeted the 38th? What are they going to do next?"

5

The KGB colonel walked down the three steps below street level and through the heavy glass doors of the Front Page Restaurant, one of the popular watering holes for the New York press corps.

Carrying his overcoat over his arm, Kolchak elbowed his way past the bustling crowd at the bar, three deep with reporters and freelance writers who were taking advantage of the half-price drinks during Happy Hour. The tall immaculately dressed Slav, wearing a dark business suit, spotted Gretchen Lundstrom at a corner table. He sidled past several tables and sat down. She was drinking her second manhattan cocktail.

"Sorry I'm late," he said, apologetically, "but I got here as fast as I could after getting your phone call." He draped his overcoat over the back of the chair next to him.

A Hispanic waiter came by with pad in hand. Kolchak looked up, but didn't speak. He lit a Carlton and took a deep drag, blowing the smoke in the waiter's direction. "Double Stoli on rocks and another drink for the Lady," he ordered, smiling at Gretchen, approvingly.

She wore a black sheath dress that flowed subtly, revealing well-shaped contours that were molded through rigorous hours of aerobic exercise. Gretchen's blue Nordic eyes flashed angrily. "It's a cover up!" she exclaimed. "Dmitri, it's so transparent, you'd think the police would know better than try to deceive me with their cockamamie story."

Gretchen had just come from a late afternoon press conference, where the police commissioner had announced that General Palmer's case had been reclassified from a suicide to murder. "There is nothing the police can say that will change my mind. If I hadn't seen General Palmer and René Lemoine together in bed, maybe I could have been fooled. But I saw their bodies with my own eyes. Now they want us to believe the letters were forgeries. How gullible do they think I am?"

The waiter arrived with tray and drinks in hand. He placed the vodka in front of Kolchak, who lifted it up to toast. "To truth!" Kolchak pledged, sipping his drink. He watched Gretchen down her second manhattan, push it aside, and pick up her third cocktail. "Is it possible letters were forgeries?" he asked discreetly.

"It's irrelevant at this point," Gretchen answered, acidly. "I can't stand by and let the Pentagon get away with their 'Go East' strategy. It can lead Germany into war with the Soviet Union."

The KGB controller sat impassively, masking his emotions, wondering how his seemingly perfect crime was beginning to unravel. He showed no signs of remorse, confident that he had covered his tracks. The police would not link the two murders to him. As he listened to Gretchen describe what she was going to write in tomorrow's column, he knew it was time to precondition the media, to set the second stage of his disinformation campaign in motion.

"I think you should be concerned about CIMIC," he suggested. "I read U.S. Army Civil Affairs Field Manual, which organizes military government into twenty functions. No matter how they finesse it, I do not see difference between civil affairs, CIMIC and Soviet political commissars who are assigned to military units." He looked at her blandly. "Do you know why commissars are assigned to military units?"

"Yes, I think I do," she answered, "but tell me anyhow."

"They protect the Party from subversion. Internal and external. To keep generals from gaining too much power. To prevent them from attacking the West and starting World War III."

Gretchen's eyes widened. "I never drew the same parallel between CIMIC and your commissars." She recalled the briefing at the 38th, how CIMIC operators acted as liaison between the U.S. Army and German Territorial Forces and their civilian bureaus. "Are you saying that CIMIC operators spy on our German allies?"

The KGB agent nodded with a smug look. She was responding to his manipulation as he had hoped. He could not have said it better himself. "They have opportunity to establish big intelligence network, separate from regular army intelligence channels. Can you imagine harm they could do if placed in wrong hands?" Kolchak gulped down his drink and flagged the waiter, ordering another round. "I have copy of new Civil Affairs Field Manual. CIMIC doctrine has been sanitized to hide its true mission. You must read between the lines, especially when manual describes civil operations. It is military occupation government, no matter what you call it."

Gretchen toyed with the swizzle stick in her manhattan. She felt intuitively she was on the brink of another big story. "This is all part of the AirLand Battle 2000 concept," she speculated. "I had no idea the U.S. Army had established a secret political cadre of spies." She paused in alarm, downing her manhattan. "Congress will never allow it. The public must be warned."

"Pentagon," Kolchak chided sarcastically, "in its infinite wisdom gave CIMIC responsibility in Europe to reserves, taking it away from full time professionals. Can you imagine how weekend warriors can mishandle assignment of such great magnitude?"

"A spy network hidden in the reserves!" she exclaimed, bitterly. "So that's what CIMIC is all about. I'm going to blow the whistle on ..."

The KGB controller had already phoned several media influentials who were close associates to the press secretaries to leading contenders in both the democratic party in the presidential primaries. In the spirit of *glasnost* and disarmament, Kolchak had planted new seeds of doubt, plotting to discredit the Army Reserve. "Why is Congress allowing reserves and national guard to train overseas? Can they not be trained more cheaply in United States to reduce national budget deficit?"

The contenders had been seeking an emotional issue with broad national appeal that could help them overtake the leading candidates. After huddling with their campaign managers and press secretaries, they agreed to place the issue on their national agenda and to broadcast it on network television.

Kolchak decided to stoke the furnace even further with Gretchen. He added fuel to the raging fire. He inquired innocently: "Do you think Army Reserve is a viable force ... or could billions of dollars be saved and spent better on domestic programs to help the homeless?"

"There has to be a connection," Maccabee said to the husky state trooper, who steered the patrol car up to the entrance of the Harvest Mountain Resort in Mount Pocono. Maccabee looked blandly at the faded pink facade of the shabby, second class hotel that catered to the gay crowd from New York and Philadelphia. "Lemoine trusted the killer," he said. "We know he spent several weekends here. I need to backtrack until I find the linkage."

The trooper parked the patrol car under the canopy. They walked briskly up the steps into the main lobby, ignoring its conspicuous art deco veneer. They didn't attract any attention, since the lobby was practically empty. Two gay men in their twenties, wearing flashy tie-dye T-shirts, sat on a seedy purple divan, talking. They cast raised eyebrows as the state trooper passed by and went on talking. Maccabee stopped at the registration desk and asked to see the manager. Within minutes, they were ushered into his office, which was cluttered with stacks of financial ledgers and paperwork.

"What can I do for you?" a gray-haired effeminate manager asked. He motioned them to be seated.

Maccabee flashed his army CI identification card and came right to the point. "We're conducting an investigation into the death of one of your guests, who stayed here several weekends." Maccabee glanced at his notepad. He jotted the dates down on a blank page, ripped it out and flipped it across the desk to the manager. "Your guest's name was René Lemoine. You may have read about his death in the New York newspapers."

"I saw it on TV," the manager replied in an agitated voice. He fixed a wary eye on the state trooper, who sat stiffly across from him. "Dreadful, the way everyone slanders our gay community. Look at my empty lobby. It's hurting my business."

"That's not all that was hurt!" Maccabee snapped out harshly. "My general was murdered. The trail leads here."

"We had nothing to do with it!" the manager protested vehemently. His hoarse voice jumped several octaves. He could not tear his eyes off the state trooper. He fidgeted with his hands, trying to control his nervousness.

The state trooper sat erect, dressed in a crisp gray uniform. He sat on the edge of his chair, doing what Pennsylvania state headquarters had directed him to do. Show the uniform, give moral support, and let Colonel Maccabee run with the ball.

Instant credibility can do wonders, Maccabee reflected. His phone call to General Kelley in Washington D.C. resulted in a quick call to state police headquarters in Harrisburg, then to the Swiftwater Barracks in Monroe County. They were brothers-in-arms, serving the same cause.

Maccabee pulled out a copy of Lemoine's American Express receipts for February. He read it, then shoved it across the desk in an intimidating way. "Lemoine's American Express receipts show that he paid for a room on three different weekends." He pointed his finger to the February 14th receipt, tapping it repeatedly. "Four hundred and eighty bucks is a lot of money for one person to spend on Saint Valentines Day. Looks like he paid for two people. I want the name, address and description of his companion, the guy who registered with him."

"I'll cooperate," the manager replied timidly. "Tell me what you need."

"His companion, was he the same guy each weekend? Or were they different men?"

"I don't want any trouble with the law," the manager implored, afraid that any reluctance on his part would result in endless health and fire inspections, violations and fines. The Pocono Tourist Bureau wanted to close down his gay hotel. If he didn't cooperate, he knew it could be his finish.

About forty minutes later, Maccabee and the state trooper walked out of the hotel, armed with the name and address of their quarry. Lemoine had one lover. His name was Harold Graham, a display director in Manhattan. The hotel's head bartender gave a detailed description.

"He shouldn't be hard to find," Maccabee said. He thanked the trooper for his help, and drove back to the Swiftwater Barracks on Route 611, where he had left his Chevy Blazer.

He climbed in behind the steering wheel, lamenting again over the loss of his friend. He wished he could head north to the sanctuary of his vacation home in Lake Wallenpaupack, about thirty-five minutes away, where he could be at peace with himself. The drive back to the Big Apple would take over two hours.

He checked his watch. 1:43 p.m. Plenty of time to beat the afternoon rush hour traffic at the Lincoln Tunnel. Inhaling deeply, he tried to snuff out the anger clawing at his innards. He brooded some more, dreading the ordeal ahead. He rammed the accelerator to the floorboard, and roared out onto the divided highway, pointing the Blazer east toward New York City ... and General Palmer's funeral the next day.

"Fifty-y-y thousa-an' dollars reward!" the army loudspeaker blared, "for any information leading to the arrest and conviction of the murderer of General Andrew Palmer."

Freddy Ventura sat in the front seat of the army jeep, wearing wrinkled BDUs. He handed the mike to Sergeant First Class Rosa Sanchez, who sat cramped in the back seat next to Sergeant First Class Doreen Franklin. Up front behind the steering wheel, Sergeant First Class Willie Douglas turned the jeep south on Second Avenue. They cruised downtown from 14th Street towards 4th Street, weaving in and out of the tenement studded side streets of the East Village.

They skirted the crime infested housing development on Avenue D, eyeballing the drifters hanging around. Douglas stopped and double parked on every block. They talked to neighborhood people passing by on their way home from work. The PSYOP team had been broadcasting since 6:30 p.m. nonstop. The loudspeaker, mounted on the jeep's front bumper, could project sound over three hundred yards under noisy battlefield conditions. Freddy had tuned its amplifier to full volume.

They double parked on the northeast corner of Avenue B and East 11th Street, four buildings away from where the murders had taken place. All the NCOs wore BDUs, having changed their clothes at the USAR Center in the Bronx. They had come straight from their civilian jobs. It was non-pay, something they had volunteered to do.

A $50,000.00 reward had been subsidized jointly by the Reserve Officers Association and the Civil Affairs Association. The reward was splashed across the evening newspapers in banner headlines, generating a new sense of urgency.

Rosa Sanchez pressed the button on the mike and started broadcasting a live script announcement. "Anyone who has the smallest bit of information can help us. General Palmer was our commanding officer. He was a fine officer and gave his life for our country. We must find out who assassinated him. Please help us." Rosa broadcast her message in English, then switched to Spanish, saying it a little different each time. They broadcast continuously, switching announcers, looking for a lead.

An NYPD police car followed closely behind, shadowing the PSYOP team to provide protection. The reservists were prohibited from carrying loaded weapons, even in their own self-defense, since the crime was a civil matter. The police were still in a state of shock over the senseless murder of a rookie cop in Queens. They looked at General Palmer as one of their own. They were not going to allow New York City to become a free-fire combat zone.

A round-the-clock police sweep kept the night courts busy. Every crack dealer, drug user, pimp, prostitute, mugger, thief, hustler and vagrant was pulled off the streets for questioning. A special task force of detectives, backed up by over 150 uniformed police officers, fanned out to search for suspects. They went door to door, interviewing every possible lead. They called in every informer, spoke to the kids on the streets, but didn't come up with any solid clues.

Freddy checked his watch. 11:20 p.m. Complaints about the loudspeaker's noise were lighting up the police's switchboard.

"Hey, brothers and sisters," Doreen Franklin cried out, enunciating each word in a deep thespian voice that cracked with emotion. "It was about this time last Tuesday when some hitman killed General Palmer. We're not going to let this scumbag get away with murder. What brother or sister reservist is gonna get killed next? Please ... if you have any information, please tell us."

Rosa, whose well-groomed black hair and chiseled fine features always looked neat and composed, showed signs of fatigue. She had worked hard during the day, typing a thirty page legal brief at her law firm. She had another grueling day planned for tomorrow. "I'm gonna call it a night," she said quietly to Freddy. "There's always mañana. If you drop me off at 14th Street, I'll catch a cab uptown."

Freddy nodded, signaling Douglas to head back uptown. "One more cruise around dah circuit, Willie. Something's gotta break."

"Yeah," Rosa chuckled, melodically. "I just don't want it to be me. You know how serious I am about the Army Reserve, but these tired bones have to go to work tomorrow morning. I've got to get my husband off to work, then get my kid sister Angelina off to high school."

"How old is Angelina?" Freddy asked, trying to recall when he saw her last. "Bet she's got all dah dudes standing in line."

"Don't you get any ideas, Fernando. Angelina is going to Princeton next Fall. She has a straight A average and doesn't need any distractions."

"You sound like her mama, not her big sister."

"I've raised her since she was six, after mama died. She's a good kid ... smart, ambitious, going to be an army reserve officer, too."

"Puttin' her in fer an ROTC scholarship?"

"No, I've got bigger plans for her. I'll pay her way, so she only has to serve six months on active duty before joining a reserve unit. I want her to be an officer and experience the better things in life. More than I had."

"I bet Colonel Mac can get her an ROTC scholarship. Save you about sixty grand," Freddy insisted stubbornly. "Maybe more."

She laughed, not wanting to offend his good intentions.

"I mean it. Dere ain't nothin' Colonel Mac can't do." As Douglas drove the jeep uptown, Freddy bragged some more, trying to impress Rosa. "Right now Colonel Mac's hot on dah trail. He knows who leaked the CIMIC Network to dah newspapers, knows ..."

Rosa sighed, her voice barely audible. "Freddy, you don't know what you're talking about. Stop puttin' me on." She became morose, clutched her arms tightly around herself and stared ahead silently.

Douglas drove the jeep up to the curb at Union Square. He stopped at a taxi stand. Rosa climbed out and waved good-night. "See you guys tomorrow, same time, same place." She climbed into a yellow cab and slumped wearily against the back seat. "Saint Regis Gardens," she said, "the new high rise condo on 97th Street off Third Avenue."

Freddy massaged the back of his neck, rubbing vitality into it. He grabbed the mike from Doreen and broadcast another appeal in Spanish. He checked his watch again as Douglas cruised back to 11th Street, parking by a fire hydrant in front of the murder building. 11:46. Almost time to quit. "Mucho diñero" Freddy cried out. "If anyone seen anything of interest last Tuesday night ..."

A two-tone maroon gypsy cab, a 1977 Mercury, pulled up across the street and double parked. A stout nurse in her late thirties, wearing a coat over her white uniform, dashed up the stairs into the brownstone. She unlocked the front door and hurried inside. Freddy slid out of the jeep and ran over to the cab before it could pull away. "Hey, amigo," he said in Spanish, keeping it light. "Isn't dis neighborhood off yer regular beat?"

The chubby Puerto Rican cabby looked at the husky soldier coming towards him. "Yeah, she's a regular," he answered. "Works at dah Children's Hospital in Harlem. I drive her home every night after she gets offa duty."

"Kinda expensive fer a nurse, ain't it?"

"Barter, mah man," he said cheerfully. "She looks in on my 82-year old grandma up on 138th Street twice a week. I charge her a buck a trip, same price as a subway fare. Door-to-door service. No muggers to worry 'bout."

"Do yah drop her off dis time every night?"

"Just 'bout. She gets offa work at eleven. Depends upon dah traffic."

Freddy leaned his forearm against the cab's open window. "Amigo, yah just might become a rich man. Tell me what yah remember about last Tuesday night, around dis time?"

The cabby ran his hands through his stringy black hair, perplexed. "Hey, man, I've been tearin' mah mind apart. I heard about dat big reward. Man, I could buy a new cab wid dat money."

"Did yah see anybody on dah strect? Were dere any strange cars? Come on, amigo. Think!"

"Don't jive me, man! I'm thinkin'. I can only rememba one thing and it's not

53

worth talkin' 'bout."

Freddy motioned with his fingers, gimme, gimme, doing a charade. "Tell me, man. Tell me."

"Dere was dis van, a black van parked by dat fire hydrant where yer jeep is parked. I think it wuz a Chevy, couple year old. Dat's all I rememba." He squeezed his lower lip in anguish, not recalling anything else.

Freddy persisted. He shot out questions in rapid-fire. "Were dere any signs or emblems on dah body? Any distinguishin' marks on it? Did yah see dah license plate? Wuz it New York or outta state?"

The cabby protested. "No signs, nuthin'! Man, I don't wanna play head games wid yah. Dere wuz mud splattered on dah license plate. Come to think of it, I did see a crease on dah left rear fenda."

Freddy pulled a small black notepad from his pocket, and jotted down the information. He'd call Major Morgan in the morning and have her run it through the police computer. Maybe it wasn't a wasted night, after all. "Dah elusive black van," he murmured. "At least it's a start."

The Spetsnaz made his move on Wednesday. He eluded the KGB agents who were following him through the mid-day crowds in the Green Acres Mall. He carried a pair of slacks into the men's dressing room at Alexander's and dropped them onto a bench. He sneaked out, sidling past a sales clerk and an elderly man who was trying on a sports jacket in front of a full length mirror.

Petrovich hurried into an employee's rest area and scurried past the stockroom in back. Dressed like the other stock clerks in a green cotton polo shirt and brown corduroy pants, he rushed out the rear exit, unnoticed. He sprinted behind a row of cars in the employee's rear parking lot, looking carefully over his shoulder. The KGB agents had not followed him.

Minutes later, he steered his Cherokee into the heavy commercial traffic, following a large 18-wheel Shoprite tractor trailer going north on Hook Creek Road. He doubled back three times between Springfield Gardens and Valley Stream, using the side streets among the single family shingled houses as look-out points, watching constantly for pursuers.

After two hours of steady vigilance, Petrovich was convinced he was not being followed. He checked a road map, balanced precariously on his knees, following the traffic east onto Hempstead Turnpike.

So much at risk, but the Spetsnaz enjoyed the sightseeing tour. The strip of storefronts and single-story office buildings, reminiscent of the 1950s, looked alike. One town blended into the next. Wendy's, Taco Bell, Burger King, banks, delis, video stores. So different from the modern buildings he had expected.

A small road sign "Franklin Square" came into view. Petrovich drove past the Platt Deutsch Restaurant, a famous landmark and German brauhaus, having read about the Nazi Bund meetings held there by torch light before World War II. He wondered how the townspeople had reacted to the Nazi threat.

Having checked the Nassau County Directory at Green Acres for correct numbers, Petrovich spotted the street he was looking for. He turned left onto Goldenrod

Boulevard, stopping at an old two-story red brick, slate roof house that had been built in the 1930s. The house number, 207 agreed with his notes. This was it. He slid out of the Cherokee, walked to the front door, and rang the bell.

He noticed a small yellow mezuzah fixed to the door frame above him. He waited nervously, scanning the neighborhood for any sign of danger. Nobody was in sight.

A studious dark haired man in his late forties with horn rimmed glasses, white shirt sleeves rolled up, and a black yarmulke skullcap on the back of his head opened the door. He gazed intently at the robust middle-aged man standing in the doorway, his stiff erect posture and ruddy complexion foretelling years of rugged outdoor living. "Yes, can I help you?"

The Spetsnaz felt uncomfortable and spoke in short abrupt phrases. "I am Russian Jew. Galiciana from Ukraine. I look for Jewish family, who live in Franklin Square. Their name is Helner, my cousins. I do not see name in telephone directory. I am here on short visit. Must find them before I go."

"Come in," the rabbi said warmly, escorting him inside. "I am Rabbi Cohen. Welcome to my house, welcome to America." The rabbi led the Spetsnaz through the living room into a large den at the rear of the house. "You say Helner Is your name?"

"Yes," Petrovich lied, "that is my name. I call synagogue and woman secretary tell me to come here. That you keep old records at home."

The rabbi motioned him to be seated in an old leather armchair in front of a worn mahogany desk cluttered with books and reading files. Wall-to-wall shelves of dust covered books encompassed the room, emitting an aura of history.

"I have lived in Franklin Square for over twenty years. The name does not ring a bell." The rabbi opened the top drawer of a vertical file cabinet and pulled out a metal case containing index cards. "I keep records of all the Jewish families that belong to our synagogue. All bar-mitzvahs, bas-mitzvahs, weddings and funerals." A smiling housewife poked her head into the room. "Can my wife get you some coffee?"

"Thank you, no," Petrovich stammered. He smiled politely.

"I do not see the name here," the rabbi said, thumbing through the cards, "but that doesn't mean the Helners never lived here. They could have belonged to a reform temple in Elmont or one in Hempstead." The rabbi rummaged through the file cabinet and pulled out a large dusty gray ledger. He opened it and scanned the "H's." "When did the family come to America?"

"My mother, a Jew, fought with Ukranian partisans. She died fighting Nazis. I was infant. Her family died in holocaust. Grandfather had sister who went to America at turn of century. Her name was Helner."

"I see," Rabbi Cohen replied. "We are a small congregation. The family could have moved away. Children go off to school, serve in the army, take jobs in other states, get married and have kids of their own. Their kids are just as mobile as their parents. Statistics show that the average family moves once every five years. Only God keeps track."

"How far back do your records go?"

"Our synagogue was built in 1934." The rabbi pushed his ledger aside, contemplating. "If we were computerized, I could cross-check the name against different categories. Someday, God willing ..." He pulled out another dusty ledger, marked "Funerals" and thumbed through the 1940's. "Ahaa!" he exclaimed. "Here it is." He read from the ledger. "Clara Helner, beloved wife of Jacob Maccabee, died August 24, 1943."

He pushed the ledger aside, his eyes fixing intently on Petrovich. "The Maccabees, I know that name. Abe Maccabee, one of our prominent people, a World War II hero. He married a wonderful Irish lady, raised two fine children and is now retired. Lives somewhere in Florida. His son David served as an officer with the green berets in Vietnam, won the silver star for bravery. I married their daughter Jacqueline to Lee Ackerman, an accountant, around 1973. I attended their oldest son's bar mitzvah last year."

Petrovich moved to the edge of his chair, exhilarated. Ever since learning that his mother was Jewish two years ago, he had experienced a tremendous compulsion to learn more, to search for his roots. While he respected his father, the Cossack general, he never forgave him for hiding the truth about his mother's identity. He knew his father had tried to protect him.

If the KGB discovered he was a Jew, he would be finished as a Spetsnaz. The GRU had an anti-Semitic policy of racial purity that prohibited anyone from serving who had Jewish blood going back four generations. The secret of his birth was buried with the death of his father. He had been raised as a model Soviet officer. He would not allow his secret to affect the success of his mission. "Their address? Can you tell me where they live?"

The rabbi nodded, pleased that he could be helpful. "Jackie lives in Great Neck, not far from here." He wrote her name, address and telephone number down on a sheet of paper. "She can tell you how to find David."

Maccabbee stood at stiff attention in his army dress blue uniform, replete with miniature medals, at the National Cemetery in Farmingdale. He stared resiliently at the American flag draped over General Palmer's casket. He snapped a sharp salute, his fingers barely touching the gold braided visor of his cap. The eight man honor guard fired three volleys into the damp, drizzling afternoon air. As an honorary pallbearer, Maccabee stood to the right of Colonel Zimmermann and Major Morgan.

They faced three generals who stood on the opposite side of the casket, Major General Kelley, who had flown in from Washington, the ARCOM commanding general and his deputy commander. All wore dress blues for the solemn occasion. The bereaved family sat on wooden folding chairs next to the grave site. Beth Palmer had requested that the funeral be limited to the immediate family and small circle of friends. The media had not been invited.

Head up, chin out, stomach pulled in, Maccabee adjusted his sunglasses, fighting back the hot tears that were burning his eyes. He looked squarely ahead. The bugler sounded Taps. Maccabee saluted again, holding it solemnly as he listened to the last mournful bugle call, the final reveille for his friend.

Thoughts of Andrew flashed through his subconscious like bolts of white lightning. Andrew charging out of a chopper with an M-16 rifle at-ready in the Vietnam highlands, Andrew drinking beer with him on R&R in Honolulu, Andrew and Beth dashing out of the West Point chapel as newlyweds under a canopy of raised swords, Andrew as his teammate at computer war games at the Army War College, Andrew standing in front of the troops at formation, Andrew making a difficult backhand shot at tennis. Andrew serious, Andrew carefree, Andrew ...

The chaplain folded the American flag carefully, end over end in accordance with army regulations. He handed it to Beth, who clutched it tightly against her breast, drawing an inner strength from it, showing a brave face, one that Andrew would have been proud of.

The casket was lowered slowly into the grave. Beth stood, assisted by her sister, and threw three handfuls of dirt into the grave. She sobbed quietly. The sound of the dirt and stones plopping onto the casket echoed through Maccabee's very being.

The ceremony ended. The army honor guard marched off sharply in two files behind the colors to the muffled roll of a drumbeat.

The officers and friends gathered around Beth and Andrew's mother and father, paying their final respects. Maccabee stopped and looked at her, bleary eyed. Not finding any words that were suitable, he grasped her thin hands in his. She squeezed his hands, quivering. Tears flowed down her cheeks. They stood there, holding hands tightly, their silence saying everything.

Maccabee walked away, then turned, and stared at the earth mound and gaping hole in the ground. He raised his hand and snapped a final salute, more determined than ever. "I'll find him, Andrew," he vowed. "So help me God, I'll get him."

Later that afternoon, around 4:30, Maccabee and Morgan entered Umberto's Fashion Salon, a chic woman's boutique that catered to the carriage trade on East 57th Street. Maccabee had asked Morgan to change into her green Class A uniform, complete with medals and campaign ribbons, to establish credibility. They found Harold Graham in the display director's office, buried in the lower reaches of the five story building.

The young foppish display manager looked up from the color swatch charts he was studying.

"Harold Graham?" Morgan made it sound more like a statement than a question.

"Yes, I'm Harold," he said, puzzled. "What do you want?"

Maccabee picked some color photos of window displays off the chairs in front of the desk, and tossed them onto a table near a half-dressed mannequin. He sat down and motioned Morgan to do the same.

She spoke first. "We're from CI and we'd like to ask a few questions." She flashed her CI ID card, putting it back in her shoulder purse quickly.

"What about?" Harold asked, anxiously. He pushed away from his desk. His delicate features, high pitched nasal voice, manicured fingernails and fastidious mannerisms disclosed his gay lifestyle.

"How well did you know René Lemoine?" Morgan asked.

"Oh, my God!" Harold shrieked. He clasped both of his hands across his breast, defensively, clutching his lavender silk shirt like a woman. "How did you find out?"

Maccabee wanted to steamroll right over him. He glanced at Morgan. His green eyes, still bloodshot from the funeral, registered an "I told you so" look, which was the reason he had wanted her along. He checked the zipper on the fly of his pants, unconsciously, to be sure it was fastened. "Through good police work," Maccabee growled. "We know you spent three weekends with René Lemoine at the Harvest Mountain Resort in the Poconos."

Harold's eyes widened in fright. His face paled to a colorless white. "I didn't do anything!" he shouted. "I had nothing to do with René's death."

Morgan interrupted, speaking in a motherly, reassuring tone. "Tell us what we need to know, and you'll never see us again. We're Army Intelligence, not New York police. If the cops get involved, the press will climb all over you. They'll sensationalize your relationship with René, and hound you right out of town."

He leaned against the top of his desk, breathing heavily. He sat down again. "I can't handle this!" he sobbed, uncontrollably. "I've worked too hard to get this job to lose it now."

Maccabee persisted. The sound of dirt plopping on Andrew's casket lingered in his head. "How long have you known René?" he asked, impatiently.

"We met last Fall at one of the gay bars in the Village."

"Did you live together?"

"Lord knows, I wanted René to move in with me. I begged him to stop tomcatting around with every dick that crossed his path. If he had only listened, he'd be alive today."

"Why didn't he move in with you?"

"He didn't want to be tied down with one person. I kept telling him to settle down with one lover or he was going to get AIDS. I'm simply petrified about getting it. I had three close friends die of AIDS. Once you get the disease, you're a goner in six months. It's a nightmare, even condoms don't guarantee protection. I warned René to be careful ..."

"Was he seeing anybody else regularly? Did he discuss other lovers?"

Harold stood, abruptly. "Of course, he did. We confided in each other. There was one person who seemed to dominate him, a Russian journalist he knew in Montreal."

Maccabee edged forward, intently. "Do you know the Russian's name or where he works or lives?"

Harold slid back into his chair, whimpering. "I don't know," he said. He hid his face in his hands, crying real tears. "He tried to be discreet. Now he's dead."

Maccabee bolted from his chair. "Stop acting like a baby," he shouted, moving towards him in a threatening gesture.

"I'm trying," Harold sobbed, regaining his composure. He looked up with pleading eyes. "I'm sorry."

Maccabee's anger abated. He sat down.

Everyone was quiet.

Maccabee broke the silence. "What else did René tell you about the Russian? There must be something ..."

Harold heaved a sigh of dismay. "He was so damn secretive, always trying to make me jealous."

Morgan stood and walked around the desk. She put her hand tenderly on Harold's shoulder, consoling him. "Did René leave any letters or diaries with you?"

"No," he answered, looking up appealingly. "Do you think I haven't searched my apartment for a clue? He left nothing behind. Nothing."

Maccabee squashed an impulse to grab Harold by the shirt and shake him. He shifted uneasily in his chair. "What do you know about René's terrorist activities?"

"Terrorist?" Harold repeated, shaking his head in disbelief. "René was a bitch. He had hot pants and liked a good screw. He was no terrorist!"

6

Thursday was Saint Patrick's Day. Maccabee left his agency a little before noon. He brushed past the hordes of people crowding the crosswalks during their lunch break. He trotted down the empty stairs of the 28th Street entrance of the Lexington Avenue subway. He dropped a token into the turnstile and walked onto the subway's dimly lit uptown platform. There were eight riders waiting for the next train, ignoring each other.

He had just left Morgan, who had given him an update on the latest intelligence. She had transmitted Harold Graham's information about the Russian journalist to the FBI, who agreed to do a computer search. She had also turned Freddy loose on the favorite bars and restaurants that the press frequented to see what he could learn. She had nothing else to report.

Maccabee walked to the edge of the dingy platform. He waited impatiently for the train to arrive. He peered down the subway's long, dusty tunnel tracks ... once, twice ... three times ... then saw the headlights of the local rushing towards him. He sensed the physical presence of someone getting close to him, pressing against him.

The subway roared into the station, only four car lengths away.

He looked over his shoulder. Suddenly, two huge black hairy paws grabbed at his safari jacket, pushing him into the train's path. A gravel voice rasped out: "Die, mutha fuckha!"

Maccabee reacted instinctively, pivoting on the ball of his left foot, spinning away from his assailant. His momentum carried him toward the onrushing subway. Its brakes screeched as the engineer tried to bring it to an emergency stop.

Maccabee's body uncoiled over the outside edge of the platform.

Inches separated him from instant death.

He reached back desperately for a finger grip on the outer edge of a bulkhead stanchion. Grabbing hold of it with the fat of his hand, he pulled in one hard fluid motion. He whipped his body around the stanchion, spinning back across the edge of the platform. The subway car hurtled past him, nicking the flap of his safari jacket as it ground to a stop.

Maccabee regained his balance, dropping into a judo crouch instinctively. He eyed his attacker, who gaped at him, a startled look spreading across his face. The man was big, a Jamaican with an Afro haircut, mustache and goatee, about six feet five and 250 pounds of solid muscle; the kind of gangland enforcer who is hard to hurt in a fight. He snapped open a vicious six inch switchblade knife, and lunged at Maccabee's midsection, swiping back and forth.

Maccabee jumped back, his hands and arms came up defensively. He backed away from the menacing blade. Where the hell are the transit cops? He stole a quick glance out of the side of his eyes. Never around when you need them. The big Jamaican swiped at him again.

Maccabee was ready. He caught the Jamaican's knife hand in a firm grip with his left hand, twisted it, and stepped inside his reach quickly, crouching low. He grabbed a fistful of the Jamaican's shirt with his right hand and swung his hip into him. Spinning, he flipped the man over his shoulder.

They sprawled onto the gritty concrete floor, oblivious to the people around them.

The Jamaican's knife fell to the pavement. Maccabee kicked it away. He scrambled on all fours, rising to face his attacker.

The Jamaican jumped to his feet, snarling like a pit dog. He sneered at Maccabee, looked into his blazing eyes, hesitated, then turned tail. He broke through the ring of onlookers and dashed for the exit. He leaped over the turnstile, knocking down a messenger, who had walked into the subway. The contents of his bag scattered across the floor. He ran up the staircase, two steps at a time. Two stout Polish cleaning ladies on their way home from work came down the stairs.

He grabbed them bodily by their overcoats, and threw them into Maccabee's path.

Maccabee tumbled backwards, entangled with the two hysterical women. They plummeted to the station floor below.

Maccabee pulled himself loose, and charged up the stairs. He rushed onto the street, yelling "Stop that man!" His words were lost in the clamor of the crowds, congesting at the corner crosswalk.

The traffic light turned green. A stream of taxis, cars and trucks surged up Park Avenue. Maccabee spotted the big Jamaican on the other side of Park Avenue, a half a block ahead. He watched his Afro head bob up and down in the pedestrian traffic, running away towards the Prince George, a crime-ridden hotel that housed the homeless. If he gets there, he'll be safe from any white man, including the police.

Maccabee started to jaywalk across Park Avenue. "Gimme a break!" he shouted, as a yellow cab almost clipped him. He tried again, but jumped back to avoid getting hit. The cabs were tailgating each other, blocking his path. The traffic light finally changed. His assailant had disappeared down the block and out of sight.

His anger grew. "This wasn't a mugging," he said to himself. "Some bastard just tried to kill me. A hitman, a hired killer! And he damn near pulled it off."

Maccabee calmed down. He glanced quickly at himself to assess any damage. The only telltale sign to indicate he had been in a fight was a skinned knee, where he had fallen down. He rubbed the bruised spot. "At least, I'm not hurt."

He rushed back into the subway. A female stationmaster was aiding the two injured cleaning ladies, who sat upright on the floor, examining their cuts and lacerations. "I've called for the transit cops and an ambulance," she said, as he looked down at them.

"Good," Maccabee said. His adrenaline was still pumping. He rushed out onto the subway platform and spotted the switchblade knife lying against the wall. He grasped the handle of the switchblade knife by its edge, and wrapped his handkerchief around it carefully. He snapped the blade shut. "I hope the fingerprints can be traced, but it will have to wait until later." He tucked it into the pocket of his safari jacket, and dashed into a waiting subway car as its doors were closing.

He got off at Grand Central Station and made his way up to the main concourse to the telephone booths. He phoned Morgan at his agency and told her what had happened. "Somebody is out to kill me, to put a stop to our investigation. We must be getting close."

Morgan's voice sounded worried. "Do you think it's the Russian journalist that Harold told us about?"

"I doubt it. They do their own killing. They don't take chances with contract hit men. It's too risky and can blow up in their faces."

"Then who could it be?" she asked.

"Don't know. Anything's possible." He paused, watching a tourist pick-up the phone in the next booth. "Better get me a gun permit for a Colt .45 and check out a personal weapon for me. It's a great equalizer. Better get one for yourself, too. We may need them the next time around."

"Are you coming back to the office?"

"No, I have a date with Gretchen Lundstrom, remember." He frowned. "See you after work at P.J.'s."

He walked onto the main concourse. A group of happy-go-lucky teenagers, dressed in shamrock green, were singing "When Irish Eyes Are Smiling." He hummed along, following them up through the Roosevelt Hotel and out onto 47th Street. The boisterous crowds headed cross-town toward Fifth Avenue and the Saint Patrick's Day Parade.

He chuckled, mimicking an Irish accent. "Begorra, the luck of the Irish is still with me!" The thought of cashing it in on Saint Patrick's Day disturbed him.

He took a deep breath, trying to loosen up. "I should have kicked the Jamaican in the head while I had him down. The next time the bastard won't get up."

The Saint Patrick's Day parade stepped off on schedule. Bands played. Flags waved. Drum majorettes strutted. And pep squads twirled their batons. The Police Emerald Society marched by, their bagpipes playing the shrill notes of "Scotland the Brave." Maccabee applauded, along with the thousands of spectators who lined Fifth Avenue, cheering them on.

He wanted to stay longer and watch the marching bands, but he had to move on. He darted down a side street and caught the Lexington Avenue subway at 51st Street. He glanced guardedly to his left and right, shrugged, then walked down the stairs. He stopped at the newsstand and bought a late morning edition of the *Times*. The news about 3,200 American troops flying to Honduras as a show of force to stop the Sandanistas from attacking the Contras had forced Gretchen Lundstrom's expose onto page twelve. It read:

"Pentagon's Secret Spy Network"

"How screwed-up can the woman be?" He grinned. "The way the world is heating up, Gretchen's story will get lost in the shuffle."

He rode the local to the 86th Street stop, where he got off. He threw the newspaper into a trash bin. He hadn't been to Yorkville in years. All the Hispanic and black faces he saw on 86th Street reminded him more of Fordham Avenue in the Bronx than the famous German quarter that it once was. "I'm not sure why I'm here. Why am I having lunch with Gretchen ... especially on Saint Patrick's Day."

He walked down three steps into the Bavarian Inn. He stopped to let his eyes adjust to the dim light. Yorkville's famous landmark looked like he remembered it ... a rustic German hunting lodge, replete with stuffed stag heads on the wall and Teutonic shields bearing different coats of arms.

Maccabee walked past the long polished mahogany bar. A German barmaid poured several steins of tap beer, her colorful Bavarian costume adorned with green shamrocks. He sidled past several German-American men drinking at the bar, who wore Kelly green ties and boutonnieres, celebrating like they were sons of Erin. "Everybody is Irish on Saint Patty's Day!" Maccabee chuckled.

He spotted Gretchen at a round table in the corner, talking animatedly with four businessmen. She looked up, her electric blue eyes flashing a big hello. He was taken aback. She seemed more striking, more radiant than before. His eyes widened. She wore a white tailored blouse, which plunged seductively. She sat with her legs crossed, her skirt exposing smooth well-toned legs, enough to whet his appetite. She rose to greet him.

He smiled cheerfully. They met halfway, clasping each other's hands like old friends.

"David, I'm so glad you could come," she said, warmly. She took his hand in hers affectionately and led him to a private alcove, which had been carved out of a massive wine cask. "My private sanctuary," she said, as she handed him a green Saint Patrick's Day boutonniere. "For you," she smiled. "Happy Saint Patty's Day."

Maccabee sat down. He gazed at the boutonniere for a moment, then pinned it on his safari jacket. "Happy Saint Patty's Day to you." He looked for the Bavarian waitress so he could order a drink, but she was busy serving another table. "I almost didn't make it," he said in a low voice.

"You're here, that's what counts," she said with an air of confidence.

Maccabee grinned, keeping the secret of the subway attack to himself.

She pointed to a silver ice bucket propped up on a stand next to their table, chilling a bottle of Rhineland vintage wine. "I ordered this especially for us," she said, smiling. "As a peace offering."

Maccabee didn't reply. He forced a thin smile as he pulled the bottle out of the crushed ice and looked at its label. Wiltigen from the vineyards of the Moselle Valley. The Bavarian waitress hurried to the table with a corkscrew in hand. She poured a small amount of the white wine into a silver goblet for Maccabee. He played the game. He sniffed the wine's flowery bouquet, tasted its light flavor and nodded. The waitress smiled graciously and filled both wine goblets. She poked the chilled bottle back into the ice bucket and left.

Dave held his wine goblet up to toast. "To all the news that's fit to print." He spoke with a hint of sarcasm, knowing he was treading on the famous motto of the *Times*', a guiding principle she had forsaken. He followed quickly with a second toast, his voice challenging and firm. "To objectivity and accuracy and fairness."

"I wouldn't want it any other way," Gretchen teased, tipping her glass against his. She sipped her wine.

"I'm serious," Dave replied. He knew he was a good P.R. man. He wondered how he could neutralize her biased reporting. If I can get her to make a retraction and admit that General Palmer had been murdered, it would be a start.

She sighed. "I am serious, too." She hesitated, then spoke gently. "That's why I invited you here."

They sipped the wine slowly. They looked into each other's searching eyes, waiting for the other to make the next move.

Dave spoke first, setting his wine goblet aside. "I thought you invited me to a party?" He looked casually around the room, waving his open palm in an empty gesture. "I don't see one. Where is it?"

She smiled coyly, her lips moist and inviting. "Right here," she replied. She took both his hands in hers and clasped them intimately. "Just the two of us. No distractions, no interruptions."

What is she up to? Dave wondered. He felt intimidated and withdrew his hands awkwardly.

She smiled again with disarming frankness. "We need to overcome this adversary relationship, this feeling of guarded hostility that exists between us. Let's tear the walls down and start over." Her laugh sounded hollow. "Let's make my private sanctuary our DMZ, a demilitarized zone, where we can work together as professionals ... and friends."

"Sanctuary?" Dave repeated silently to himself. I can think of better sanctuaries, like my chalet in the Poconos, my weekend retreat. He felt a sexual desire surge though his body. She's really coming on to me. I can't believe it. She always seemed so snobbish, so high above it all, so unattainable. But now ... He chuckled aloud. This is one luscious lady. Just maybe ...

He gulped the rest of the wine in his goblet.

"I'm an investigative reporter," she continued. "My job is to smell out a story and chase relentlessly. To uncover any wrong-doings, to reveal corruption and betrayal of public trust. All I can do is play my hunches, follow my gut reactions, and dig for hidden facts ... then dig some more. To talk to as many sources as possible. To get the facts. To prove out my story. Then to put everything into perspective, to tell the why of the story, how it occurred and what it means."

She eyed him carefully, disguising her in-depth interview, so she could use everything he said *for-the-record*. She had memorized a series of questions that she wanted him to answer.

"Even if it means destroying a man's reputation?" he asked, brusquely.

She controlled the excitement rising within her. She felt like a kid at a fishing hole, seeing a granddaddy trout pop out of the water, then disappear. She baited her hook and threw out her line. "Yes," she replied, "if it's deserving. If somebody invites grief upon himself, it's his problem, not mine. I report the facts, that's all."

"If he's not alive to defend himself?" He scowled at her, a feeling of animosity returning.

She shrugged, nonchalantly. She cautioned herself to let the fishing line out slowly. Wait until he nibbles the bait. "The facts speak for themselves. If they're incriminating, so be it."

The Bavarian waitress interrupted, handing each of them a large menu. "Do you want to order now or shall I come back?" She refilled their wine goblets.

"Later," Dave said, setting the menu aside as she departed. He looked at Gretchen sharply. "How did you get your hands on the classified information? The CIMIC Network was TOP SECRET!"

She played out the fishing line a little more. Her eyes expressed an intense delight. "I had a tip from a confidential source. I arrived at the murder scene ahead of the police. My photographer took the photos."

Dave felt threatened. "Why don't you reveal the name of your source? Whoever leaked the information to you."

"I can't."

"Why?"

"I have to guard my confidential sources. Once I break that trust, I have no way of getting the inside information that you guys won't divulge."

"If it's someone in the 38th, that's treason. Whoever did it has not only betrayed his country, but has been an accessory to General Palmer's murder."

"My source isn't someone in the 38th," she stated, flatly. He's nibbling, she realized. He's nibbling. Stay in control.

"Then who in hell is it?"

She shook her head, stubbornly. Tighten the tension on the line, carefully, ever so carefully. She hesitated, then asked in a skeptical tone, "Do you really think you can hoodwink me into believing that General Palmer was murdered?"

Maccabee's eyes flashed angrily. "Why are you so damn negative? Why can't you believe the evidence that's been corroborated by both the coroner and the police commissioner? How high up do you need to go?"

Gretchen refused to be placated. She became indignant. "Because I was there, right after the double suicide. It was one of the most repulsive sights I've ever seen, one that I'm not going to forget for a long time. I don't believe the commissioner's report. I can smell a cover-up. I've run into smoke screens from public officials before."

"Cover-up!" Dave exploded. "There's no cover-up involved."

He's hooked! Gretchen's warm smile vanished. She listened.

"I've spent part of my Army Reserve career in public affairs. We adhere to a policy of proactive journalism. Full disclosure to the press ... even when it hurts. We know what reporters want. Give it to them accurately and completely. All we ask in return is honest and balanced news coverage. And that the press respect classified information when it affects national security, and not disseminate it."

Gretchen's eyes flicked in a ray of amusement. Let him run with the line, the Pentagon party line. Let him twist and turn. Then reel him in.

Dave tried to read her aloof reactions, but couldn't. He decided to try one more time to set her straight. "Have you considered that the whole murder scene was staged for your benefit?"

She pulled a notepad out of her pocketbook and jotted down some notes.

"Whoa!" Dave said, holding up his right hand in warning. "I thought this was a friendly lunch, not a formal interview."

She smiled, demurely. "I'm just a working girl, remember?"

"Then, whatever I say is off-the-record, not for attribution."

"I didn't know you had anything to hide," she said. Damn it, she thought, I'm going to nail you yet. You know more than you're telling me.

"I don't have anything to hide."

"Then why off-the-record?"

He shrugged. He didn't have time to play games. "Okay, forget it. Let the questions roll."

"Why was it staged for my benefit?" she asked, sounding like the persistent, suspicious reporter that she was.

"To manipulate you into a false perception."

"False perception," she uttered with disdain. "I'm nobody's puppet. I know what I saw!"

"It was carefully staged like a one act play. Every prop carefully designed." He swallowed hard, waving the Bavarian waitress away as she approached the intimate alcove. "Those so-called TOP SECRET documents were forgeries, and we can prove it. Even Lemoine's farewell letter was a distortion of the truth to mislead the press."

"You make it sound like a sinister conspiracy," she said, staring him down. She framed her next question to achieve a specific slant for her story. "If there's a conspiracy afoot, you tell me what the Pentagon is trying to hide?" I've got you hooked, she thought. Pull him in. Now!

Dave's face grew serious. "If there's a conspiracy," he barked, "it's the other guys, not us." He ran his fingers through his blond hair in frustration. Talking to Gretchen was like crawling through a minefield where your next move can lead to disaster. "Why are you deliberately trying to discredit the Army Reserve? Do you know how much damage you've done to CIMIC? To NATO? To West Germany?"

"I am German," she snapped, proudly. "I believe in a strong NATO, in a strong Germany. Someday, Germany will be united again. I can't let you cowboys destroy Germany from within. Can't let you turn it into a battlefield to test your new tactics and equipment. Your secret CIMIC Network can't be allowed to spy on my countrymen."

"But it doesn't," Dave protested. "You don't understand how CIMIC works, and you've misinterpreted the AirLand Battle 2000 concept."

Damn! she thought. He's wiggled off the hook ... at least for now. What is it going to take to drag the facts out of him, to get him to open up? She knew she had to penetrate that hunk of masculinity, the tough shell that protects him. "David, I don't want a confrontation," she said, calmly. "I'm willing to listen."

"I don't want to argue either." He stared at her, wondering if they could ever bridge the gap, where they could work together on the same side. He shook his head, not convinced. For the time being, he had to get her off the army's back. And maybe onto her own. He knew she was getting under his skin, arousing him sexually. The wanting, the not wanting.

If it wasn't for the damn conspiracy, he'd have time to do something about it. He inhaled, deeply.

Gretchen forced back a disappointing look of resignation. She wanted to shake him, to wrap her arms around him until she squeezed him into submission.

Her eyes suddenly brightened. She recalled another question that needed to be answered. Her voice became warm and inviting. "David, how do the CIMIC teams that serve with the local German VKKs transmit secret intelligence up to higher CIMIC headquarters?"

Maccabee looked at her with disbelief. She was baiting him again. He leaned forward and spoke bluntly, "Lady, I think you're out of control!"

The Spetsnaz drove past the English Tudor house three times, slowing down to be sure the address was correct. He sped up again.

Each home on Garden Lane looked like an elegant mansion with a distinct identity of its own. The Ackerman house was set back about one hundred yards from the road. It was surrounded by majestic oak trees, blue spruces and small shrubs nestled under the eaves of the slate roof. Petrovich admired the two-story garage, which had an offshoot that connected it to a horseshoe driveway.

Homes like this, he thought, could only be owned by the capitalist rich. They reminded him of the huge estates that once were the personal domain of Russian nobility, now used as private dachas by the Soviet Politburo and army generals. Someday, I live in one ...

He drove up the circular driveway, admiring the manicured lawn. He walked to the front door and rang the bell. The sound of chimes echoed inside.

Fully expecting to see a servant, he was taken aback when Jackie Ackerman opened the door, sizing him up. She was a tall, lithe woman in her early thirties, dressed in designer jeans and a loose knit sweater. Black horn rimmed glasses were perched atop her head. She was a college professor and had been grading student papers, one still clutched in her hand. She held the door slightly ajar, smiling inquisitively. She hoped the man wasn't selling books or vacuum cleaners.

"Yes-s-s."

"You are Jacqueline Helner?" Petrovich asked abruptly in a raspy tone that sounded more like a statement than a question.

"No, my name is Ackerman," she replied, looking at the husky man that stood awkwardly in front of her, blocking out the afternoon sunlight that was streaming in through the trees. She stepped back instinctively.

"Ackerman?" he repeated in a puzzled voice. "Your father is Abraham Maccabee?"

"Yes, my maiden name is Maccabee." She wondered if this was a new sales technique. "My name before I got married. My name is Jacqueline Maccabee Ackerman." She noticed his heavy European accent, but couldn't place the country of origin. "What do you want?" she asked politely.

"Your grandmother was Clara Helner," he recited, waiting for a response.

"That's correct," Jackie answered. "Grandma Helner was Daddy's mother."

The Spetsnaz became embarrassed. He flushed slightly, feeling like a schoolboy. "My name is Yakov Helner Petrovich," he said, enunciating each syllable deliberately. He hoped he was pronouncing the words correctly. His accent continued to worry him. It could reveal his true identity to the police. "I was born in Galicia. In Ukrania. I am Jew." He became resolute, regaining his composure. "My maternal grandfather and your paternal grandmother were brother and sister. You are cousins in America." He pursed his lips and continued. "I am here on short business trip." He stepped back and turned to leave. "I am sorry I trouble you. Should not have come."

"Oh, my goodness!" Jackie opened the door wider and stepped outside. She smiled graciously. "Come in, welcome ...A Helner! I don't believe it." She took both of Yakov's hands firmly in hers and shook them in greeting. "A long lost cousin. Oh, wait till I tell Dave."

The beeper on Maccabee's belt began to buz-z-z. He and Gretchen Lundstrom were still at the Bavarian Inn, finishing a heavy German lunch and fencing with each other, neither one gaining an advantage. They were sipping cups of Irish coffee, topped with whipped cream and green creme de menthe to commemorate Saint Patrick's Day, when the beeper went off. "Can't win," Maccabee apologized, wishing Morgan had interrupted him sooner. "I need to find a phone. My office is calling."

Gretchen started to rise. "You won't be able to hear on the bar phone," she said. "I know the manager." She pointed toward an office in the rear. "Tell him that you're my guest, and you need to make a call."

"I can find my way," Maccabee said, excusing himself. He saw Gretchen signal the Bavarian waitress for the check. "She's paying," he mused, finding it awkward to let a woman pay for his meal. He rapped on the manager's door and walked into the empty office.

Minutes later, he called Morgan who picked up the phone on the first ring. "You have a call from General Kelley," she said. "You're to phone the Pentagon immediately." She gave him the OCAR's special phone number and hung-up.

Maccabee dialed. He heard the scrambler kick in. There was no mistake in the urgency in General Kelley's voice as he came on the line.

"Dave, The FBI intercepted a terrorist drop box in Central Park earlier today. They arrested a PLO courier who was traveling under a forged Iraqi passport. They're interrogating him, but he's clamed up. The FBI decoded the message he was carrying, and it's worrying the hell out of us."

Maccabee held his breath, waiting for the worst.

"It was a warning message," the general continued. "It said to prepare Stinger missile attack in New York. That's all it said."

"Stinger?" Maccabee repeated. "In New York?"

"That's right. A Stinger missile attack. That's how I heard about it. The FBI called the Pentagon to learn if any of our Stinger missiles are missing. We gave them a clean bill of health. There are no reported thefts. We've issued a high priority alert to all active army, reserve, guard and marine units to keep a close watch on their weapons and armories."

"What kind of attack?" Maccabee asked. "Does the FBI have any idea about where or when? Or what terrorist groups may be involved?"

"I wish I knew. The FBI is pumping the courier, trying their damnedest to turn him into a double agent. But these characters are zealots. They don't care if they live or die. That's what makes our civilized society so vulnerable. We're like clay pigeons, waiting for some crazy to take a pot shot at us. With modern technology, more lives are at risk than ever before."

Maccabee's mind raced ahead. "Do you think it could be a deception plot to attract the FBI's attention to a missile attack, while the terrorists plant a bomb aboard the aircraft or try to highjack it?"

"Anything's possible."

"Terrorists have been threatening for years to bring death to the streets of New York. Do you think they're finally going to do it ... or is this just another incident in their war of nerves?"

"We don't know. The FBI is locking-in on all major events that our political

68

leaders are attending in New York. I don't know what's happening over at the UN, but they're checking that out, too."

"Christ! You've got three international airports to worry about."

"Better coordinate with Colonel Ed Contino of the 38th over at JFK. Ed is in charge of airport security and might have some ideas. He'll need to keep a close watch on all domestic and international flights, incoming and outgoing. Better start developing an assumption list of worst case scenarios with appropriate time frames. If the terrorists follow their previous procedures, there'll be an execution order."

"What about the NYPD's special task force on terrorism?" Maccabee looked startled as Gretchen opened the door and ambled into the office.

Her right eyebrow arched as she overheard the words "task force on terrorism." She stood alongside Maccabee, looking puzzled.

Maccabee cradled the phone, turning toward Gretchen. "Just another minute," he snapped. He spoke into the mouthpiece. "Can't speak freely."

"I'll make it short. The NYPD's been alerted and briefed."

"How much time do you think we have between what you have and what may be coming down?" Dave spoke in guarded terms. The last thing he needed right now was another Gretchen Lundstrom blockbuster in the *Times*.

"A week, maybe two," the general estimated. "Could be longer. There's never a set pattern between a warning order and an execution order."

"Do you think there might be a connection with General Palmer's murder?"

"Dave, your guess is as good as mine." He hung up.

Gretchen studied the consternation on Maccabee's face, which he tried to mask. Something was up, she could smell it. "What's happening?" she implored. "What task force on terrorism?"

Maccabee shook his head, ruefully. "Just trying to put the pieces together. Lemoine was a communist courier. He may have been involved with terrorist groups in Quebec." He couldn't disclose the truth, but didn't want to lie to her either.

They faced each other, not saying a word.

Gretchen didn't believe him. She could see the subterfuge hidden in his eyes. He was deceiving her again.

Maccabee reached out to shake her hand. "Thanks for lunch," he said, smiling. "I admire your style. You sure know how to conduct one helluva interview. I wouldn't have missed it for anything, but I really must go."

She grasped his hand fondly in hers. "I do want to see you again," she said in a honey-tone voice. Her eyes twinkled. She leaned forward and kissed him sweetly on the lips, not a lingering kiss, but one that would bring him back for more.

Maccabee's pulse quickened. He started to respond, then checked himself. He had never met anyone like this before. She was in a league all of her own. He had to know her better. Maybe if I meet her on my turf and have the home field advantage, I can handle her. "I'd like to see you too, if you promise to help us."

Gretchen smiled, radiantly. She was going to get her story after all.

"I own a chalet in the Poconos. There's too much happening right now, but I can get away next weekend. We can go skiing. How about it?"

"Sounds great!" Gretchen's face glowed with triumph. That's it, buster. I've got you hooked!

In Great Neck, Jackie sat on the edge of the couch, pointing at a snapshot in her family photo album. The Spetsnaz gazed at it intently. "That's a picture of Grandma Clara," she said, "with Daddy before he was shipped overseas in World War II."

"Your father was infantry officer?" Petrovich asked.

"No, he was a tank commander. He served with General Patton and fought in France and Germany. He met Mom in a British convalescent center, while recovering from wounds he received in the Battle of the Bulge. Mom was Irish, a nurse. Daddy stayed in the army. He didn't come home until after the Berlin airlift ended. It was too late. Grandma died a few months before.

Petrovich turned each page of the album slowly, studying each photo. "It is hard," he confided, "to relate to family I have never known. Helner was mother's name. She was killed in Ukrania fighting Nazis in 1943. I was baby. I do not remember her. Father had no photographs, only memories. Grandfather Helner and whole family were killed at Auschwitz. Don't know how many?"

The holocaust was something Jackie had read about and seen on television. It took on a new reality. "I didn't realize ..." she stammered. "We must be second cousins. I didn't know that we had Russian blood. Grandma Helner came from Galicia in Poland."

Mother was Jew from Polish Galicia, from small village near Krakow. When Nazi storm troopers came, she escaped to Ukrania and joined partisans fighting in Pripet Marshes."

"Is that where she met your father?"

The Spetsnaz looked up. A glint of pride reflected in his eyes. "Father was captain of heroic Soviet troops. When Germans attacked Russia, they bypassed remnant army units in Ukrania in Nazi drive to Kiev. Father built fortress in Pripet Marshes. They raided at night, what you call guerrilla warfare. They attacked transportation and disrupted communication centers, disappearing into civilian population in countryside. Soviets began airlift of supplies and reinforcements to partisans. They gained strength and attacked German rear forces in East Ukrania, where they fought major battle in Carpathian Mountains."

"Did your mother fight alongside your father during this time?"

"No. She stayed hidden in small village where I was born, trying to survive Nazi terror. Soviet army was defeated in Carpathians. Father was wounded in rear guard action helping Soviet commander escape by airplane. Father led troops in breakout from German encirclement, working his way back to Pripet Marshes. Months later, when he recovered from wounds, he learned that Nazis captured mother and tortured her. She died never revealing location of hidden village. I survived with other children deep in marshes. When heroic Soviet forces sweep through Ukrania into Poland, father was promoted to major. He led Soviet armor battalion, crushing German army and destroying Berlin. He returned as Soviet hero and colonel, later became Soviet general. In 1945, he find me and take me to Moscow, where I attended school and became Soviet citizen."

Jackie reached out and held Yakov's hand gently in hers. "We're together now, my cousin," she said, reassuringly. "Here, let me show you some pictures of my husband and sons." She picked up another photo album and leafed through it, emphasizing specific events in her life.

After awhile, Petrovich asked: "Your father, where is he now?"

"Daddy retired as a major general. He and Mom live in Punta Gorda Isles, Florida. My brother Dave and I were army brats, three years in this place, three years in that, all over the world. Dave speaks fluent German."

Petrovich checked his watch, knowing the KGB would worry about his absence. Their anxiety amused him. "Your brother Dave, is he army officer?"

"Not anymore. Dave served in Vietnam with the Green Berets. He had two tours and saw too much combat. He was awarded the silver star for heroism and two purple hearts for wounds he received. He doesn't talk much about it."

"Where did he serve next?"

"He didn't." Jackie curled her legs up under her. "He came home disillusioned. The anti-war demonstrations didn't help. Deep inside his tough exterior is a sweet, sensitive individual. I should know. I grew up with him, played with him, loved him. He was my hero, my big brother. In my eyes, he can do no wrong. After he quit the army, he traveled around the country for about a year, trying to find himself. He finally settled down into a civilian job as a copywriter in New York. But the army was in his blood. A year later, he joined the Army Reserve, drilling weekends, summers and training overseas in Germany. He must have done a good job, because they kept promoting him. He recently retired as a full colonel."

Jackie jumped to her feet, impulsively. She walked briskly to an end table and picked up a princess phone. "Dave has his own advertising agency now. I must introduce you to him. We must get together."

She dialed Dave's private line and caught him just as he returned to his office. "You'll never believe what I'm going to tell you, but one of our long lost cousins from Galicia just turned up. You must meet him."

Maccabee wanted to get back to work, to get an update briefing from Morgan. The last thing he wanted was a family interruption. "We have cousins all over the U.S.," he said, flatly. "What makes this one special?"

"He's a Helner ... from the old country. That makes him special."

"I'm sorry, sis. If you've read the papers, we're trying to find out who killed General Palmer. I'm up to my eyeballs. I can't do it."

Jackie tapped her foot angrily on the floor. Her tone of voice began to rise, as she reprimanded her brother. "I don't ask many favors Dave, but this is one time I want you to think of your family first. Cousin Yakov is here on a cultural sabbatical, learning how our American system works. He's only here for three weeks. I want you to make time to see him, even if it's for a short visit. You pick the spot in Manhattan, and we'll meet you there. David ... I won't take no for an answer!"

7

For Freddy Ventura, Saint Patrick's Day wasn't over. Although it was 12:20 a.m. and theoretically the next day, Freddy was still partying. He walked into the Front Page restaurant and scanned the bar for anyone he knew. He had been barhopping all day and evening, making the rounds of the New York media's favorite watering holes. He brushed past several tipsy Irish revelers, who should have called it a night hours ago. He felt light headed himself.

He found a bar stool next to the service bar, and ordered a Bud, his fourteenth, if he hadn't lost count. He recognized a cute blond secretary, cooing an Irish lullaby into her boss' ear, snuggling up to him.

New York is fun city, Freddy thought. He glanced at another woman in her early twenties, a brunette with a frizzed-out hairdo, who smiled at him from four barstools away. She gave him the familiar "come hither" look.

"Buenos notches, amigo." A short stocky Hispanic waiter called-out, slapping Freddy on the back. "Long time, no see. How've you been?"

"Arturo!" Freddy shouted in delight, turning toward him. "It's great to see somebody from dah old neighborhood. Still live in dah Bronx?"

"Yeah, same apartment. I still live there with my mama and my two sisters. The old man took off years ago. Haven't heard from him since."

"How long yah been workin' heah?"

"About two years. It's a job. Tips are good. Make about twenty-two thou off the books. Not bad."

"Bet yer regular customers take pretty good care of yah."

Arturo punched at Freddy's arm, playfully. "You know how it is. We take good care of our regulars, give them a few freebies and they reciprocate."

Freddy pulled out a newspaper clipping from his jacket pocket. He unfolded it and held it up to the light for Arturo to see. "Recognize dis lady columnist? Her name is Gretchen Lundstrom. Works for dah *Times*."

The waiter recognized her instantly. "She's one of my regulars. Holds court twice a week. A real classy dame. "Bet she's a good lay."

"When did yah see her last?"

"Several nights ago. Monday, I think. She was here with some foreign correspondent who likes to play the role. Real intellectual. Fancy manners. You know the kind."

"Did yah hear what dey wuz talkin' about?"

Arturo grinned, sheepishly. "You know I'm not one to eavesdrop."

Freddy reared back on his stool, laughing. He reached into his pocket, pulled out a ten dollar bill, palmed it and shook hands with Arturo. Poooof, it was gone. He grinned, took a long gulp of beer. "Whadda yah remember?"

"The guy was talking about some secret spy network in the Army Reserves. He fed the lady a lotta crap ... like stopping the reserves from training overseas. He was bad news, man. Made me want to puke. A lot of my friends are in the reserves. Man, their families count on their reserve pay to survive."

"I know." Freddy agreed. "We need all dah bread we can get just to stay alive." Freddy knew he was getting closer to his quarry. "Tell me more about dis guy."

"He's been here before. I think I heard someone say he's a mucky-muck editor for some international magazine. I think he's Russian."

"When do yah get offa work?"

"Around two o'clock. After the bar closes, and we clean up. Why?"

"I gotta cousin who barkeeps at dah Press Lounge over on 48th Street. Dey've got photos of every editor and reporter framed on dah walls." Freddy reached into his wallet again. "Here's another ten fer goin' over wid me later. You'll get another twenty spot if yah recognize his face."

Freddy and Arturo slipped into the Press Lounge at 2:34 a.m., just as Estaban, the head bartender, doused the main lights. Three cocktail waitresses in scanty outfits sat at the bar, sipping Lite beers as they counted their evening tips. Saint Patrick's Day, like all holidays, paid off well. Their tips were five times more than a normal Thursday night's work.

Being the Latin lover that he was, Freddy latched onto Kerri Anne, a blond college sophomore, who worked part-time as a photographer on holidays. "Hey Estaban," Freddy called out to his bald-headed cousin, who was loading the dishwasher with dirty glasses. "Three kamikazes and make 'em strong."

It's great to get freebies, Freddy thought. "Down the hatch" he cried to Kerri Anne, who snuggled up to him affectionately. "Hey, Estaban, set 'em up again." They downed three powerful kamikazes in a row before he decided to look at the framed black and white photographs that hung on the wall.

Like many of New York's sophisticated luncheon and night spots that cater to the media trade, the walls were adorned with photographs of celebrity customers dating back to the 1950s. There were signed photos of Hollywood stars like Frank Sinatra, Sammy Davis, Jr., Dean Martin, Jerry Lewis, Lucille Ball, Bob Hope, Red Skelton, Danny Kaye, Dinah Shaw and a host of others.

Across the room were photos of media celebs like Ed Sullivan, Walter Cronkite, Edward R. Murrow, Chet Huntley, David Brinkley, Scotty Retson, Meg Greenfield, Dan Rather, Tom Brockaw, Peter Jennings, Barbara Walters; even a smiling Jimmy Breslin downing a Budweiser beer at the bar.

There was something about Kerri Anne that turned Freddy on. She was tall and thin, about five foot seven with long blond cascading curls, not particularly attractive, but spicy. Her white satin blouse was unbuttoned midway to show a hint of cleavage, not that she had much to show. Black mesh hose accentuated a great looking set of legs that drove Freddy wild. She was streamlined like a thoroughbred, born and bred for a fast track.

"C'mon, baby," Freddy pleaded, "where do yah find dah new photos? Show me some dat yah took recently."

"They're in the overflow room," she said, pointing toward the archway that led to another dining area. Sipping a fourth kamikaze and swaying to its effect, she leaned against Freddy, enjoying the warmth of his beefy arms. "There they are," she said, pointing. "The ones I took last year."

Arturo walked behind them, still nursing his third kamikaze. He looked at one photo after another. "Nada!" More photos. "Nada."

"Come on, man," Freddy implored. "Yah gotta recognize him. If he's a big shot, he's gotta be heah."

The trio moved closer to the wall, moving chairs aside. Arturo pointed to two TV celebs that he recognized, then spotted his quarry. Two familiar faces smiled into the camera. He studied the photograph closely. "That's him!" he cried. "That's the guy." He was tall, thin, blond and Russian.

Freddy recognized the man's glamorous dining partner. He winced at Maccabee's nemesis. Gretchen Lundstrom. The photograph was signed: "Best regards, Dmitri Kolchak."

"Are yah absolutely sure it's dah same guy?" Freddy asked, excitedly.

"Si! He's the one who was badmouthin' the reserves. I seen him before with other reporters."

Freddy started to pull the framed photograph off the wall. He struggled with its hook, weaving back and forth, intoxicated.

"You can't do that," Kerri Anne warned. "It belongs to the restaurant. I have negatives in my studio in Yonkers. I can make you a duplicate print, if you need one." She wrote the name and the date of the photo on a cocktail napkin and slipped it into her skirt pocket.

"Yer're a sweetheart," Freddy said. "I need that photo bad. He turned toward Arturo, as he reached into his wallet. "Heah's dah twenty I promised yah, amigo. Yah earned it." He threw his arm around Arturo's shoulder and hugged Kerri Anne closer to him, sashaying back to the bar. "One more kamikaze for dah road!" he called out to Estaban.

Freddy thought about calling Major Morgan and relaying the info to her. No, he thought, I aggravate her enough without rousing her outta bed. Who knows, Major Discreet might be ballin' it up wid somebody. He let it drop, figuring that time can take care of itself.

As they sidled up to the bar, Kerri Anne knew exactly what she wanted. She had made enough money in tips to carry her through the month. This Latin lover excited her. "My car is parked on 51st Street," she whispered softly into his ear. "How 'bout keepin' me company for the weekend, but no photos till Sunday."

Freddy ran his hand up the inside of her thigh. He felt her body quiver. He chuckled. "No-o-o problem!"

Uptown on East 87th Street, another man had a serious problem, one that tests a man's masculinity. Dmitri Kolchak rolled over in bed onto his side, frustrated and angry at himself. He heard Gretchen Lundstrom in the shower, singing in German softly to herself.

"The slut," he murmured through gritted teeth. He should have known better than try to seduce her. She had looked so lovely, lying nude in bed in the subdued lighting, reaching up for him, pulling him down towards her, smooth silken legs spread apart, waiting for him to enter. Yet, he couldn't get it up, even with her coaxing and fondling. It had been hopeless! Now, he only had one thought ... to get her to leave. He wanted to be alone.

Gretchen watched the soap suds ripple down her soft pink nipples, which still budded with sexual excitement. She stood on her tiptoes, hands high above her head, feeling the sharp stinging spray calm her emotions. She stretched her stomach and leg muscles taut, not surprised about Dmitri's behavior. She had learned years ago how to manipulate men, how to gain control and dominate them. You can't be sure of a man, she thought, until you've been to bed with him. That's where it all hangs out, she laughed. And so it did with Dmitri. She had wondered for months if he was a homosexual. Now she knew for sure.

She stepped out of the shower stall, grabbed a large Turkish bath towel and dried rapidly. She smiled, satisfied that her seduction of Dmitri had succeeded. She had learned from a pro. Her ex-husband had been a professional athlete, a domineering German stud with an enormous appetite for sex. She had been frightened at the start of their marriage. As she became more experienced, she became eager to respond, to satisfy his desires. Then to satisfy her own. To gain control over her own body, then his. The mind came next. The house, check book and career. Conflict led to divorce.

Gretchen freed herself from all restraint, engaging in sex promiscuously much like a man. She sought out new partners freely to gain advantage as she pursued her career and for the physical pleasure of the experience. Yet, she hoped someday to find a man that she could truly love, a man that could meet her on equal terms, a man she could respect.

Dressing quickly, Gretchen walked back into the bedroom. Kolchak had put on a silk Burgundy bathrobe and sipped a glass of vodka. He lit a Carlton, puffing in quick nervous spasms.

"Don't be upset," she said, trying to bolster his ego. "We had a big dinner and too much to drink." She smiled. "It could happen to anyone, Dmitri." She stood in front of the his dresser and combed her silky blond hair.

"This has never happened before," Kolchak apologized. "I'm sorry that I disappointed you. A woman as beautiful as you should have young lovers, not an old journalist like me. I should never mix business with pleasure."

Gretchen smiled coyly, looking straight into his eyes. "You've helped me a great deal in scooping the competition. Keep feeding the hot stuff to me. We must keep these Washington bureaucrats under control. Every time I think of that secret CIMIC spy network they set up in Germany, the madder I get."

She studied the Russian journalist, feeling secure in her dominance over him, while he phoned for a yellow cab.. My fame as a columnist will grow, she thought. As West Germany continues to achieve its economic miracle, my newspaper column will shape American public opinion and help the Fatherland regain its position as a superpower. Yet, she worried about the questions Maccabee had raised. Could he be right? Had she been deliberately misled? Were the communists back to their old tricks? She had to know. The Fatherland depended upon it.

She knew she needed to dig for hard intelligence. Irrefutable facts that would

75

withstand command inquiry. A wary look of suspicion glinted from her penetrating eyes. "Dmitri, where do you get your leads?" she probed.

"Through informants that I have cultivated for years," he answered, smugly. "I can't reveal their names. I think you understand why."

"Let me reframe my question," she said more abrasively. "There has to be an eyewitness to the deaths of Palmer and Lemoine, whether it was a suicide or murder. Somebody tipped you off. I beat the police to the scene by a full half hour. I want to interview your eyewitness. I swear I'll protect the identity of your informer."

"I'm sorry," Kolchak muttered, sourly. He shook his head, waving his hand limply. "I cannot share confidentiality of my sources with you or with anyone else. It is forbidden." Kolchak refused to talk anymore about it. He conversed in polite small talk during the next twenty minutes.

The doorman buzzed the intercom at 3:18. Kolchak walked Gretchen to the elevator and watched its doors close. He stood transfixed, then did an about face and walked back inside his apartment. The KGB controller paced back and forth, thinking about his problems. His *kombinatsia* was unraveling. How much had the police learned about the double murder? Did he leave any incriminating evidence behind? Why was Gretchen of all people questioning him?

His thoughts turned to the Spetsnaz. He could not be trusted. Will the Stinger attack succeed? It had to. Kolchak's career depended upon it.

He poured another vodka, sipping it slowly. He sat on the couch, hating the GRU agent. He was arrogant and impossible to deal with. He knew the Spetsnaz had disappeared, eluding his KGB agents who were skilled operatives. Where did Petrovich go? Who did he see? Was the Spetsnaz planning to betray their cause? Was he planning to defect?

Despite the early morning hour, he felt too keyed up to sleep. He picked a copy of *American Defense Magazine* off an end table, hoping to read himself to sleep. He flipped through the front pages, stopping at a story on new product development in telecommunications. His eyes fixed on the new XL-5 telescrambler that the editor said would revolutionize secret military communications in Europe. One sidebar caught his interest. The 38th Civil Affairs Command and CIMIC Network were planning to use it. He read the article again. He sensed a new target of opportunity.

By 5:05 a.m., a new scheme had fermented in his mind. Dressing quickly in a sweat suit, he jogged several blocks along Manhattan's deserted streets. His mind came to a decision. Here was a unique opportunity to prove his worth to KGB Central. KGB rules would be broken, but there wasn't enough time to seek prior approval from Moscow. He'd demonstrate his initiative and catch NATO napping a second time. It is part of my *kombinatsia*. He began to fantasize how he would be honored, his promotion to KGB general, the medals. He stepped into a telephone booth and dialed a phone number that he had memorized.

A sleepy, sultry female voice answered. "Who's calling?"

"Do you recognize my voice?" Kolchak demanded in an intimidating tone. He could picture her jerking into an upright sitting position in bed.

"Yes," she said, no longer half asleep. "I need to hear more words."

The challenge, he mused. "The sounds of silence are forever more." He paused. "Enough secrecy," he barked, abusively. "I have new mission for you."

"You promised that you wouldn't bother us again after we cooperated the last time." There was a note of frantic pleading in her voice, then stifled talk with somebody in the background.

"Listen carefully, if you value your safety. This mission will be your last. Then you go back to being typical American citizens."

"I'm listening," she said, shushing someone next to her.

"Tell our mutual friend that I want to borrow an XL-5 telescrambler for a few hours so we can inspect it and photograph it."

"My God!" she cried in dismay. "Wasn't stealing the secret CIMIC Network enough? We're not espionage agents! Why don't you leave us alone and ..."

Another voice broke into the line, a male voice, deep and combative. "We're out of this! We want no more of your goddamn spying. If I knew that General Palmer was going to be murdered, I would have blown the whistle on you, you commie son-of-a-bitch, whoever you are."

"Be silent!" Kolchak shouted, menacingly. "You will listen carefully or I will tell authorities and your wife will be deported. You know what that means. As for you my friend, you will spend rest of your life behind bars in federal prison. You will never get to spend hundred thousand dollars we deposited in your secret Swiss bank account. You are in too deep to back out now, whether you like it or not."

There was silence on the other end of the line

"You will borrow XL-5 telescrambler on Monday," Kolchak commanded. "One hour, that is all we need. Get pencil and paper."

"Damn it, man! You're going to blow our cover. It's not worth it. The feds are closing in. Have a heart for Christ's sake. It's a lot safer if I show it to you in Europe. We're going over in three weeks. I can meet you in Heidelburg or Frankfurt, wherever you want."

Kolchak knew that the agent's usefulness was coming to an end. He was expendable. "I want it now," he growled, unrelenting. "On Monday afternoon." He gave him an address in Yonkers and hung up.

He inhaled the moist early morning air. He felt like his body was drained, physically and emotionally. He jogged back to his apartment and walked inside as the alarm clock buzzed. 6:00 a.m. He poured a triple vodka, filling the rock's glass to its rim. He took a long deep gulp, then another, enjoying its jolting sensation. Feeling the vodka going to his head, he picked-up the telephone book and dialed a number. On the fourth ring, a sleepy effeminate male voice came on the line. "Who's calling at this time of night?"

"Clifford, it's me, Dmitri. How'd you like to make fast hundred dollars for thirty minutes of pleasure?"

Friday and Saturday were insufferable days for Maccabee. He suffered from a splitting headache caused by a hangover. He felt frustrated, not knowing who killed Andrew Palmer, not knowing who had tried to kill him.

He holed up in his office at the agency. On Friday, Master Sergeant Vito Milano, a NYPD detective, swung by with a gun permit. He handed an army Colt .45 caliber automatic to him. Maccabee signed a hand receipt and felt the weapon for balance, bouncing it in his hand. He didn't like the .45. It was too big and jerked when firing.

When given the choice between an NYPD .38 revolver or the army Colt.45, he opted for the more familiar.

Maccabee placed the .45 on his desk. Even with the safety latch "on," it looked imposing and out of place in an advertising agency. Since he refused to wear a shoulder holster, Maccabee wedged the .45 under his belt in the snug of his back. He wished his life hadn't become so complicated.

Even his partner, Bob Martin, who normally was a good natured art director, found time to complain. "I thought you were all through with this shit!" he exclaimed. "Are you still running an ad agency? Or have you gone back into the army? We have serious problems that only you can resolve. Jerry the frozen food man wants to know when you're going to write a new thirty second TV commercial. I told him to repeat the one on the air, that repetition counts, but you know how demanding he is. And Donald is finally coming through with a 64 page annual report. Count them. 64 pages. And he wants it done ... like yesterday. You're supposed to write it."

Maccabee had learned how to live through this type of panic with his partner. He sat at the conference table and listened, taking notes patiently. He let Martin go through his lengthy tirade and exhaust himself.

"*Time Magazine* is driving us crazy," Martin grumbled. "Our favorite client is paying ninety days slow and they're going to cut him off. You have to tell our bookkeeper to mail a partial payment. Something."

Maccabee cut in. "Easy does it. You know we don't pay one client's bills with another client's money. That's the quickest way to go bankrupt. We're in the advertising business, not the banking business."

"We're going to lose the account! They'll go to another agency, who'll help finance them. Damn it! We need larger accounts. Quality accounts, so we can win some creative awards ... and grow! You need to clear up this army mess and get some new business."

"Lighten up, we've weathered the storm before. We'll do it again. I'll call the clients." Maccabee delegated the workload, assigning the creative tasks to freelance copywriters whom he used as backup. "We'll get a biggie yet," he promised. He spent the rest of the day and the following morning on agency business.

Late Saturday afternoon, Major Morgan barged into his office. She had been drilling with her army reserve unit in the Bronx and had left early. She transcribed the messages off the agency's answering machine and was in a tiff. "Have you heard from Freddy?" she asked, anxiously. "I knew we couldn't depend upon him. Where is he? He was supposed to recon the bars and restaurants and report back to me daily. I haven't heard from him in three days."

"You can't keep Freddy on a tight rein. You need to give him some slack. He must be onto something or you would have heard from him sooner."

Morgan paced back and forth, finally sitting down at the conference table, shaking her head in disapproval. Dressed in BDUs, she was all infantry. In her book, Freddy was going to toe the line ... or else! "Probably met some blond floozy, and he's shacked up someplace."

"He'll turn up. He always does."

She walked out of Maccabee's office and returned with an armful of file folders. She slid them onto the conference table and sorted through the one marked "INTEL

FILE." Pulling a large layout pad out from behind the door, she tacked four blank pages onto the corkboard wall. She drew a large circle on each page with a black magic marker. "There seems to be four concentric circles revolving around a central axis, but the pieces don't fit together logically. First, we have the double murder of General Palmer and this Lemoine character."

She wrote the words in the first circle: **DOUBLE MURDER**

"We know the approximate time of the murder, but no eyewitness. If we could get closer to this mysterious Russian journalist, maybe ..."

She paced again, her hands in constant motion, gesturing. "Second, there's the false evidence that was left behind to smear General Palmer's name and reputation."

She wrote in the second circle: **DECEPTION**

"Plus the damage it's done to CIMIC," Maccabee added. He brushed the wavy hair back off his forehead. He sat back in his swivel chair and propped his feet up on his desk, searching for an answer. "The media has blasted the hell out of the Army Reserve. No amount of retraction will undo the havoc they've wrought." He paused. "Gretchen Lundstrom broke the first story. How did she scoop everyone else? What is she up to now?"

Morgan interrupted. "That leads me to the third concentric circle. How did the killer get the authentic letterheads and secret CIMIC Network? There has to be a mole in deep cover in the 38th CA, but we're no closer to finding him now than when we started." She inked the word into the third circle: **MOLE**

"We keep running into blind alleys."

"Any progress on the CIA background check?"

"Not yet. We've cranked the FBI in too, checking bank accounts."

Maccabee started to speak, then stopped himself.

She approached the fourth circle and inked in a big question mark. "I think the fourth circle is floating in its own orbit. The FBI intercept of a Soviet dropbox warned of a Stinger missile attack in New York."

"It could be a deception, a diversion or the real thing."

Morgan penned in five possible threats beneath the fourth circle:
- **STINGER MISSILE**
- **HIDDEN BOMB**
- **SKYJACK**
- **KIDNAPPING**
- **ASSASSINATION**

"Did you check with the U.N. to determine what heads of state may be coming to New York?"

"There's a flood of dignitaries coming and going, while the U.N. is in session. That's not our only vulnerability. We have national leaders flying into JFK, La Guardia and Newark airports from every gateway city in the U.S. and abroad. How do you protect against that kind of a threat?"

"Did you check with Ed Contino at JFK security?"

"Yes sir. It's just one more threat for him to deal with." She had a sudden thought and inked in two more threats:

DRUG SMUGGLING & GANG WAR

Maccabee's eyes hardened. "Have we contacted the DEA?"

"I have four drug enforcement agents in my CI unit. Nothing on that front so far." She pointed to the question mark. "Getting back to Contino, the Stinger threat is a new one for him. He said he'd add it to his list."

"How would he defend against a Stinger attack?"

"He said it's indefensible. Put a trained gunner on top of a Brooklyn tenement overlooking the flight paths." Her face paled as she pointed her finger at an imaginary target and pulled the trigger. "Kaaabooommmm! You just lost 350 people in the worst airplane disaster the U.S. has ever had!"

Sunday. More of the same. Maccabee awoke to the phone's incessant ringing. 10:12 a.m. Gretchen invited him to join her for a classic Sunday champagne brunch at Oscar's, a favorite Manhattan pub. "I don't think I can handle champagne or a bloody Mary at this hour," he responded, tactfully. His instincts advised him to keep her at arm's length. Yet, deep down, he knew something was pulling them together. "I have some work that I must do." He gave into a quick impulse. "Tell you what. Give me a rain check for today, and we'll get together during the week."

"If you could see me pouting," Gretchen said, "you'd know how disappointed I feel. I hoped we could see each other today."

Maccabee laughed. "Next weekend in the Poconos for sure."

After showering and doing his daily dozen, he dressed and ate a light breakfast. He walked into the living room and attacked Morgan's intelligence file, which he had brought home with him. He spread the file sheets out on the coffee table and poked at the elusive facts. There was no sign of a struggle. Lemoine must have trusted the killer, never suspecting that he was being set up for a cold-blooded murder. Why did the killer choose to inject the AIDS virus into Andrew Palmer? What purpose did it serve? If it was a setup, where did the killer get the AIDS virus? What role did the Russian journalist play in all of this? Who was he?

Maccabee shut his eyes and let his mind wander. He tried to focus on the problem the same way that he created new advertising campaigns. He concentrated, then let his subconscious take over. His thoughts became fluid, seeking new directions. He recalled a magazine article about chemical warfare. In it, Soviet military advisors had supplied chemical weapons to the Iraqis, who used the poison gas effectively against Iranian front line troops. The Soviets had also used poison gas in Afghanistan, Angola and Ethiopia. Why not supply biological weapons, too? He sat upright, staring ahead. "The bastards used the AIDS virus," he stammered aloud. "The Russian journalist must be KGB! That bastard is mission control."

He rose and walked to the window that looked out onto Third Avenue. He gazed across the rooftops. "Is the Cold War really over? Moscow's policy of *glasnost* is an unmitigated ruse to disarm us. The KGB agent is directing the Stinger missile right into our orbit. He must be stopped!"

Maccabee phoned the Pentagon and was patched straight through to Major General Kelley in his apartment at Fort Meyers. He briefed the OCAR on Morgan's intelligence analysis, describing his latest suspicions.

"I have bad news, too," the general finally said. "The FBI called me an hour ago. They've been interrogating the PLO courier since they caught him at the Soviet drop box. They haven't learned a thing." There was a pause on the line. "Ready for this?"

"Go ahead," Maccabee replied, wondering what else could go wrong.

"He killed himself. The terrorist swallowed a cyanide capsule. He had it squirreled away in the heel of his shoe. He's dead!"

"I didn't know they used cyanide anymore."

"Neither did I."

At a desolate ballfield in Far Rockaway, two blocks from Atlantic Beach, the Spetsnaz met Kolchak to discuss his operations plan. The two men, dressed in casual sports clothes, strolled around the park, chatting. Passerbys would have been shocked if they knew what was being said.

"Warning order has been received," Kolchak said, curtly. "Execution order will come 72 hours before the attack. I have new identification card for you." He handed him a Lufthansa Airlines ID card. A stamp sized photo of Petrovich was mounted in the upper left hand corner under a JFK security seal. The name Horst Gunther, Transportation Supervisor, was typed in the center.

"This ID will get you through airport security for final reconnaissance." He handed Petrovich a forged passport and a Lufthansa Airlines ticket to Frankfurt. It was dated April 9, the target date for the Stinger missile attack.

"You will be at ambush site at Jamaica Bay Riding Academy with PLO gunners as I instructed," Kolchak said, brusquely. "You have spent much time on reconnaissance. Are you satisfied with plan and escape route?"

The Spetsnaz listened impassively to the KGB controller, letting him drone on. As they walked behind the deteriorated backstop, Petrovich grabbed Kolchak by the lapel of his tweed sports jacket. He twisted it in his fist and propelled him up against a wire mesh fence, crunching him against it. "Imbecile!" he snarled, gruffly. "Your plan is no good. You must consider wind and weather factors. If wind blows from wrong direction, aircraft takes off in opposite direction and gunners cannot hit target. Mission will fail!"

He loosened his grip on the KGB agent, propping him up. Petrovich glared at Kolchak, his face only inches away. "This is GRU military operation, not KGB. I am in command. I have new plan. You will follow my orders. Understand?"

The KGB controller tried to regain his composure. He stood erect, straightening the folds of his jacket. He stepped away from the Spetsnaz. The man's cold green eyes and steel gray face terrorized him. He froze, his mind became blank. He didn't want to relinquish his authority, but ...

"Attack team must be mobile if wind shifts," Petrovich declared. "We cannot risk traffic problem or police roadblock." He visualized his new plan of attack. "I need boat with small cabin. Motorboat that fits in with other weekend boats. Smaller than one used to pick me up. I will swim from Hamilton Beach marshes to airport beach and infiltrate inner perimeter. I will spot target for PLO gunners. Boat must maneuver across bay to put gunners in shooting range of correct runway. I will identify target and coordinate by radio. Is that clear?"

Kolchak gasped when he realized his mistake. He assumed that jetliners takeoff and land on the same runways. The GRU was correct. He felt relieved the Spetsnaz had taken charge of the attack plan. Once it was completed, I will regain control. I will settle scores. The Spetsnaz will not escape my vengeance. I will liquidate him. No one will be wiser. "Let's not be angry with one another."

They walked back to the sidewalk and strolled casually toward their parked cars. "Let's not forget purpose of our mission," Kolchak confided. "The real plum is West Germany. Once we get Americans out of NATO, a neutral Germany will be united ... under Soviet hegemony and control. The American public is ripe for new treaty on disarmament and troop withdrawal. Once that happens, all of Europe will be ours."

The Spetsnaz had no tolerance for geopolitics or propaganda. He was a soldier, a GRU officer. If old GRU marshal is successful in overthrowing Gorbachev, he hoped he would eliminate KGB. They were evil men and needed to be destroyed. He looked at Kolchak, who had quickened his pace. "Comrade Kolchak," he said coldly. "I know two KGB agents have been following me. It must stop immediately!"

"I have no knowledge of anyone following you," he lied, blandly. "Are you sure it is not FBI? There has been activity at your safehouse. Some neighbor may have complained. You must be careful."

Yes, Petrovich acknowledged to himself. I must be careful. He knew he was at risk. He felt comfortable in the United States. At ease and relaxed for the first time since he could remember. It was his first taste of being his own man, of doing what he wanted to do, when he wanted to do it, without any authority dictating what he should think, say and do. If this is what Americans called freedom, it felt good. He knew he wanted to see his American cousin again, his new adopted family.

He grasped the KGB controller roughly by the crook of the arm, pulling him within earshot. "I will do final reconnaissance. I need secret phone number to communicate with you."

Kolchak nodded, trying to pry his arm loose.

The Spetsnaz pulled him closer. He whispered in a raspy voice. "Moscow ordered KGB not to follow me." He patted the P-38 automatic that fit snugly in a shoulder holster under his left armpit. "If I am followed again, there will be three dead KGB agents ... including you!"

8

Dawn patrol on Monday.

Maccabee walked to his office at daybreak, while the streets were relatively empty. His green vigilant eyes scanned in all directions, street level, upper stories, rooftops. He felt like he was on point again, his life on the line just as it had been in 'Nam, setting himself up as a target, hoping he'd see Charlie and get the first shot off. He walked rapidly, taking large strides. His right hand clasped the cold steel butt of the .45 automatic that weighted down his safari jacket pocket. At this early hour, New York was its typical self ... a city of indifference.

Nobody paid any attention to Maccabee as he crossed Park Avenue and walked into his office building. The lobby was empty. Even the elevator starter had not arrived. He rode the elevator up to his agency, relieved that nobody followed him.

At 7:39 a.m., Major Morgan burst through the portals of the reception area with a cheerful hello. She buried herself in paperwork, making early morning phone calls to contacts at the NYPD and FBI. At precisely 1000 hours, she walked into Maccabee's office to give her intel briefing. Before she started her NYPD report, Freddy Ventura charged into the office, excited and out of breath.

Wearing a flamboyant Miami Beach shirt with pink flamingos and bright yellow sun flowers, he pulled out a chair and straddled it. "I've gotta fix on dah Russian journalist!" He slid an eight by ten inch glossy photo across the conference table. "His name is Dmitri Kolchak. Dis photo wuz taken three months ago ... wid you know who at dah Press Lounge."

Maccabee peered at the photo, looked up at Morgan with a startled expression, then back again at the photo. "I'll be damned!" He handed the photo to Morgan who studied it intently.

"You did good, Freddy!" Maccabee said. "How do you know this is the guy we're looking for?"

Freddy scampered around the table and huddled over the photo. He pointed at Kolchak. "Dis friend from my old neighborhood in dah Bronx is a waiter at dah Front Page Restaurant. I showed him a pix of Gretchen Lundstrom on Saint Patty's Day. He remembered seein' her wid dis guy, who wuz bad-mouthin' dah Army Reserves."

"That doesn't make him a killer," Morgan retorted. "How do you know he's a Russian journalist?" She thought for a moment. "Where'd you get this photograph?"

Freddy grimaced. He clutched both of his hands dramatically against his barrel chest in protest, acting as if he'd been physically hurt. "Look at dat Slavic face," he chided. "It's a Rusky if I've ever seen one. Besides, Arturo says he heard him tellin' dah empress 'bout a secret spy network in dah Army Reserves. He's been seen wid other reporters. He's gotta be the mystery man. Now ... we've got dah face and dah name. All we've gotta do is run dah bum down."

"The photo?" Morgan asked, indignantly, pushing Freddy to the edge of the limb, before she cut it off. "Where'd you get it?"

A smirk crossed Freddy's beaming face. "Yah see, I know dis tall blond chick who's a photographer at dah Press Lounge. Arturo saw dah photo on dah wall framed for everyone to see. He made a positive ID. Said he'd be a witness if yah need him. Kerri Anne made three prints fer me at her private studio in Yonkers on Sunday."

Morgan's face flushed four shades of magenta. "You've been sitting on this since Thursday night and didn't call me?"

Freddy became livid, almost belligerent. "Lady ..." He swallowed his anger. "Major sir, mam! I wuz barhoppin' for yer on Thursday, all afternoon and night. I didn't run down dah photo till Friday, around three o'clock in dah mornin'. Then I hadda sashay dis dolly all the way up to her home in Yonkers, entertain her, make love to her ... so she'd be kind enough to dig through her darkroom files and find dah picture yer lookin' at. Christ, I hadda pay Arturo forty bucks outta my own money, and I musta blown another sixty bucks barhoppin'. And yah want to know why I didn't call yah. It wuz late and I wuz in dah sack ... workin'!"

"Easy now," Maccabee said in a calm influencing voice, trying to avoid a head-on collision. "I always said you had your own way of doing things, Freddy." He laughed lightly. "I do appreciate your dedication to duty."

"She wore me out!" Freddy complained. He laughed at himself and straddled the chair again. "Whadda great way to go."

Morgan didn't see any humor in Freddy's male chauvinism. She nodded with an icy stare. He did accomplish the mission... not according to the book, but at least by his own standards. She felt they were finally closing in on the conspiracy that surrounded the murder of General Palmer. She looked at Maccabee. Her question echoed his thoughts. "Is Gretchen Lundstrom part of the plot or is she being duped?"

"I wish I knew," Maccabee answered, grim faced. "She's been coming on strong, ever since Andrew's murder, pumping me for information. Her tip came from an informer. It could be Kolchak, maybe another KGB agent. Perhaps, someone else. I need to find out how deeply she's involved. If she'd reveal the name of her informant."

Morgan asked, "How do we find the Russian journalist?"

Freddy popped to his feet, becoming serious. "I checked dah phone book and couldn't find nothin'. So I called information. Dah number is unlisted."

"I'll call the NYPD," Morgan said, rising and reaching for the phone on Maccabee's desk. "They'll get the number and address for us."

"Don't bother," Freddy exclaimed. "I've got it. Yah see, I've gotta cousin Imelda. She's a supervisor for New York Tel. I called her and told her it wuz a matter of national security. She cut through all dah red tape." He read from a small memo pad. "The Rusky lives at 186 East 87th Street."

Maccabee cut in. "I suppose you've already searched his apartment?"

"Nah, not yet. I wanted to check in wid youze guys first." He grinned, cheering everyone up. "Dah day is still young. I'm on mah way."

"Better watch yourself," Maccabee warned. "We don't want Kolchak to know he's under surveillance." He paused. "Are you packing a piece?"

Freddy winked. "Yeah, boss. You know me." He pulled out a snub-nosed .38 police revolver from a hip holster, brandished it about, then slipped it home. "Me and mah baby, till death do us part."

Maccabee was determined to confront Gretchen with what he knew. He studied the two-shot photograph of Kolchak and Lundstrom and slammed it down violently. He sat at his desk, brooding. "Is she a collaborator?" he asked, not knowing what to make of Gretchen's involvement. He knew he had become infatuated with her, but that's as far as it goes. If she's part of a communist conspiracy, she'll have to suffer the consequences. He picked up his phone and called the *Times*.

Gretchen's secretary came on the line. Gretchen was downtown, covering a press conference at the World Trade Center. He left a callback message. "I must see her today. Tell her I have new information on the General Palmer murder, that it's urgent." He hung up.

He could tell intuitively there was something more insidious going on, more than murder, more than Soviet propaganda. The Stinger warning left little margin for error. He thought awhile, then energized his private network. "All conditions go!" he shouted, trying to rejuvenate himself. He picked up the phone and dialed John Howard, a second generation reservist at the FBI's central office in lower Manhattan. "John, this is Colonel Maccabee from the 38th CA. General Kelley, Chief of the Army Reserve, has authorized direct contact between my office and yours regarding the General Palmer murder."

"Yes, sir. We're briefed and on top of it," the young lieutenant answered. "The chief's not here, but if I can help, say the word."

"I need to expedite a computer search and cut through any red tape that gets in the way."

"Can do, sir. What do you need? I'm ready to copy."

"We have a hot lead on a Russian journalist, who we believe is linked to General Palmer's murder. His name is Dmitri Kolchak. I need a fast rundown on him. We believe he may be an editor for a foreign magazine. Where does he work? How long has he been in the U.S.? Does he have diplomatic immunity? Is he a KGB agent? How important is he? His home address is 186 East 87th Street in Manhattan. Please keep this on close hold. The Pentagon wants me on point. You're to be our back up."

As he hung up, an incoming call came through from a breathless Gretchen Lundstrom. "David, I've been running all over this city, it's been a whirlwind morning," she said, still gasping. "I've been to three press conferences and it's not even noon. I have two more to cover uptown. My secretary said you called, it was urgent. What new information do you have?"

"Can you meet me for drinks later this afternoon?" he asked.

"Well, ah, yes," she replied. "I come up for air around four. I'm not my own boss, David. If another story breaks, we'll have to reschedule." Her tone seemed snippy. "Why can't you tell me the news over the phone? You said it was urgent."

"It is," he snapped, disliking the arrogant German tone that he heard coming across the line. "It will keep until I see you."

"Why can't you tell me?" she coaxed. "Why don't you give me ..."

Maccabee cut her short. He couldn't tell whether her anxiety was contrived or real. He ignored the why, why, whys. "Let's meet at the Hyatt Regency. You'll find me at the upper lobby bar. At four. Okay?"

"You've scored a ten on my curiosity scale," she replied, annoyed that she couldn't pry the news out of him. She wondered if she was losing her touch. "I'll see you at four. Bye, bye."

Maccabee's jawline tensed as he hung up. He puttered about for fifteen minutes, studying Morgan's intel collection plan. She had drawn a bold red line that connected the boxes from René Lemoine in the East Village to the Harvest Mountain Resort in the Poconos to Harold Graham at Umberto's on East 57th Street to Dmitri Kolchak at the Front Page and Press Lounge restaurants, to a media box and a big question mark next to Gretchen's name.

Where will it end? The conspiracy was slowly crystallizing, but how do we stop its execution? Who is out there ... besides Kolchak?

"You have two visitors," Morgan said, striding into his office. Vito Milano, NYPD, followed close on her heels, carrying a large black suitcase. A police artist named Jimmy followed with a layout pad in hand.

Milano, a short, dark haired, muscular man in his early thirties with a bulging waistline that kept him on a constant army weight control program, flipped the suitcase onto the conference table. He pulled out six loose-leaf photo albums and opened the nearest one. "Colonel Maccabee, I'd like you to look at some mug shots that we brought with us to see if you can identify the hitman that tried to waste you."

Maccabee sat at the head of the conference table. Milano shoved the first album in front of him as Morgan hovered over his shoulder. Maccabee began thumbing through the pages. Some of the hardcase faces staring back looked like they belonged on death row. Others could have fit easily into the ranks of his enlisted troops. Faces, faces, and more faces. He shook his head, and continued flipping through the pages. He set the first album aside, then the second, third, fourth, fifth and finally sixth.

He looked up at Milano with a blank expression. "Not here. It's a face I won't forget. I had a close look at him, too."

"I'm not surprised," Milano said, stacking the albums back into the suitcase. "I had a tip from one of my snitches. Claims the hitman was an out-of-towner, an import from Miami. We're checking it out."

"From Miami?" Maccabee asked, turning to Morgan. "How does that tie in with what we know?"

She shrugged. "Don't know."

Maccabee spent the next two hours with Jimmy, the police artist, trying to sketch the likeness of the Jamaican hitman. "Rounder face, bigger eyes. No, his chin didn't look like that." On and on it went, sketch and revise, recalling details, trying to articulate what was in the mind's eye. Finally, they had it.

"I'll fax it to Miami," Milano said, "and see what they know."

Freddy found an empty seat on the Lexington Avenue local and rode it to 86th Street. He climbed the stairs to the street level and felt the cold air sting his face. He jostled his way past oncoming people until he found the white brick apartment building at 186 East 87th Street. He spoke to a portly doorman, who told him the super's name was Hernandez, who lived on the second floor. Freddy chuckled, wondering if every super in Manhattan was Hispanic.

He rang the super's bell, spoke in a hurried Spanish and made instant friends with the Puerto Rican, especially when he handed him a twenty dollar bill. Flashing his CI identity card and explaining that it was a matter of national security, Freddy learned more about Dmitri Kolchak. The man was a Russian journalist, an editor for an international magazine. The super didn't know its name. The man had renewed his three-year lease about six months ago. He kept regular hours, going to work at 8:30 every morning, not coming home until six. His evenings were irregular, usually going out. He was a quiet tenant who didn't complain much or cause any problems.

Hernandez didn't like him. "He's a racist like the rest. Calls us spics and niggers behind our backs."

Freddy slipped him another twenty for a quick look-see and the promise that nothing would be touched. Gaining access, he stepped into the vestibule with the super lingering outside. Freddy wandered through the apartment, jotting down whatever he thought was important in his black notepad. He saw a pile of magazines stacked on an end table, the six most recent issues of *New World*.

Freddy picked up a copy and flipped the pages to the index page. Dmitri Kolchak's name was listed as editor-in-chief. He scribbled his name and title into his notepad along with the name of the magazine and its business address. He skimmed through the rest of the magazine, noting the titles of the stories. "Whatta bunch of crap and lies," he mumbled. "Glad I don't have to read it."

He surveyed the IBM computer and wondered what intelligence might be stored on its hard drive. He looked closely at the nameplate and user's manual, jotting down whatever specs he could find. The microcomputer was an IBM Personal System/2 Model 80 with a 314 megabyte fixed disk drive. There was a tiny keyhole in back that locked the system. He checked the Sony TV set and VCR, looking for recorded tapes. Then he saw a shredding machine with an empty basket alongside.

After looking around for about ten minutes, Freddy saw the super growing impatient. He swore him to secrecy and left, promising him another twenty dollars for a follow up visit. Freddy had a gut feeling. If they could read what was inside the computer, they could break the case wide open. He now had Kolchak's working hours. He planned to return to Kolchak's apartment the next day. This time with a search warrant ... and Maccabee's secret weapon.

Around 1:30 that afternoon, Kolchak walked into the rear of a neighborhood photo studio, located in a small strip shopping center in Riverdale. Vladimir, the KGB chauffeur, remained outside tending the parked black van.

The KGB controller adjusted his eyes to the dim light, recognizing the matronly photographer, who was on his payroll. Two people hovered over a camera table stand, studying the secret XL-5 telescrambler. He nodded a smirking approval to the army reservist, who glared back at him.

Kolchak watched the photographer unscrew the bottom plate of the XL-5 to see the supersonic circuit boards that needed to be photographed and X-rayed.

The photographer looked up, shaking her head. "No good," she groaned. She pointed to the glob of black silicone tar that covered the circuitry. "The X-rays can't penetrate that seal."

"You must!" Kolchak barked. "I didn't go to all this trouble to steal this equipment for you to say it can't be done. You will do it." In the poor light, his ash white face turned to fury. "I order it!"

"This silicone glue is a protective cover," she tried to explain. "The manufacturer designed it to protect the computer's brain."

The KGB controller became obsessed. "You heard me," he screamed belligerently. "You X-ray it. Then photograph it. Now."

"It won't take," she argued. "The X-rays can't discriminate between one component and another with all this gook on top. If I try to melt it down, it will kill the brain."

The reservist broke in, nervously. "Don't do that!" he warned. "The equipment must be returned today in good operating condition."

"The chips are coded," she continued. "If you want to knock off this piece of equipment, you need to decode it electronically."

Kolchak stared at her, bewildered. "How do I do that?"

"Like any other decoding device. Think of this machine as a burglary safe with a combination lock. You need an electronic scanner to break into the code, to find out what the combinations are, to unlock its central brain." She touched the XL-5 lightly. "You need to monitor the machine when it transmits the coded messages."

"Coded messages," Kolchak grunted. He faced the reservist, his eyes stabbing out. He spoke in a demeaning voice. "Did you bring codes?"

"No, I only brought the tutorial," the reservist cleared his throat. "It instructs a new operator how to use the machine. The codes are separate."

"Where are codes?" Kolchak demanded in a scathing tone.

"In Europe. Each CIMIC team gets their code tape upon arrival at their assigned unit. Not until then."

"Why didn't you tell me you didn't have codes?" Kolchak finally saw the flaw in his hasty grandstand scheme. He should not have tried to improvise. If he had contacted KGB Central, they would have cautioned him about the secret codes.

"I tried to tell you, but you wouldn't listen."

Kolchak sneered and looked away disgusted.

The reservist clenched his fist. "You didn't need to jeopardize my cover. Today's a waste of time. I'll hand the codes over to the KGB when I get to Europe."

Kolchak scarcely listened. An animal instinct warned him to return the XL-5 and to cover his tracks quickly, before it was too late.

Maccabee leaned back on the bar stool at the Hyatt Regency, nursing a J&B on the rocks. His glanced at his watch. 4:15. Still no Gretchen Lundstrom. He wondered what could be holding her up.

His eyes wandered the length of the curved bar. Every seat was taken by commuters stopping by to have a quick drink before dashing home. Yuppies began to arrive in twos and threes, sidling up to the bar to order while they waited for their drinking companions to arrive.

Maccabee rehearsed in his mind what he planned to say. He'd confront Gretchen with the two-shot photo of Kolchak and her, which he'd brought along in a manila envelope. "I won't reveal too much at first. Let's hear what she has to say. Then I'll tighten the noose, first René Lemoine, then Harold Graham. I'll give her as much rope as possible."

His beeper buzzed. "Where's the nearest pay phone?" he asked the bartender, who was bent over mixing three fuzzy navels. The bartender pointed across the lobby. "I'll be back," Maccabee said, sliding off the stool.

He brushed past several yuppies waiting to be seated. He spoke to the hostess, reminding her to hold a table for two by the atrium window overlooking 42nd Street.

Waiting impatiently for an open phone, he watched over his shoulder for Gretchen to make her grand entrance. Five salesmen monopolized the phone booths, using them like private sales offices, calling in long lists of purchase orders. Finally one opened up. Maccabee glanced across the lobby again. Still no Gretchen. He dialed his office on his private line.

"Maccabee and Martin," Morgan said in a friendly voice.

"Anytime you want a job as a receptionist," he said, "you're hired."

"Don't push your luck," she laughed.

"You buzzed. What's up?"

"Your girlfriend called at 4:18 and ..."

Maccabee interrupted. "She's not my girlfriend."

"Have it your way. Miz-z Lundstrom called to say she was running for the Eastern shuttle to D.C. Has to attend a press conference at the Pentagon."

"Anything to do with us?"

"I don't think so. The Air Force is launching a new spy satellite."

"Damn it, I wanted to talk to her. How long will she be gone?"

"She said she'd be back tomorrow. She sent her apologies. Said she tried to page you at the hotel, but couldn't get through."

Maccabee hesitated. What the hell, their confrontation could wait. "Any other calls?" he asked.

"Yes, sir. Sergeant Laura Washington from the 38th G-2 office called twice. She sounded worried, but said she'd only talk to you."

Maccabee checked his watch. 4:40. Ten minutes after quitting time. He shrugged. "It's too late to call her. It'll have to wait till tomorrow. Anything else?"

"No, only a few business calls. Bob Martin took care of them. That's a wrap," she joked, trying to sound like a TV producer. "I'll see you early tomorrow."

Maccabee handed the receiver to an impatient caller. "It's all yours." He started across the lobby towards the bar, guessing that his unfinished J&B had been scoffed up by the bartender. He'd have to order another. He felt safe in the crowded bar, which was becoming more boisterous by the minute. He chuckled to himself. "I haven't been stood up in a long, long time."

Around 9:30 that night, the Spetsnaz met Kolchak in a secluded parking lot behind a large furniture store on Sunset Highway's miracle mile. He sat inside the black van on a upholstered seat facing the KGB controller, who had requested the emergency meeting. Was this just another ruse to spy on him? Petrovich wondered.

The eerie light cast weird shadows across Kolchak's face, his pale blue eyes darting back and forth, averting the Spetsnaz' glowering stare. He spoke in hushed, conspirator tones. "Your attack plan is good," he whispered, trying to ingratiate himself. "I agree that GRU must control military part of mission."

The Spetsnaz nodded. "You have secret phone number?"

Kolchak handed him a yellow slip of paper with a number scrawled on it. "You memorize number," he said, timidly, "then destroy paper."

Petrovich slipped the paper into the top pocket of his polo shirt without looking at it, his eyes boring holes into the KGB controller. "You find boat as I ordered?"

Kolchak belched. He lit a cigarette, puffing heavily. "I am working on it," he said with a wry face. "I will show boat to you by end of week." He rubbed his cheek, searching to regain the initiative. "For your approval, of course," he added in a patronizing tone.

Petrovich stared ahead. "The mission proceeds on schedule?"

"We have had a problem," Kolchak stammered, "a serious problem that does not concern you." He glanced at Vladimir for support, who sat behind the steering wheel, listening to what they were saying.

Petrovich's eyes narrowed. "What kind of problem?" he inquired in a mocking voice. He had no time for KGB intrigue. Kolchak would not have mentioned a problem, if it was not serious.

Kolchak waved an open hand toward his KGB lieutenant. "Vladimir took care of problem earlier tonight. A snoop had to be liquidated. You will read about shooting in tomorrow's newspapers." Kolchak shrugged, fatalistically. "Three bodies more or less, they are inconsequential. I lead police into blind corner, trapping them with obvious clues. My deception never fails. Authorities will not connect killings to us."

The Spetsnaz frowned. His mission was compartmentalized. Why was KGB telling him more than he should know? "So ..."

"Have you been told identity of your target?" Kolchak asked, smugly. "Did GRU name specific army reserve unit your Stinger will destroy?"

The Spetsnaz remained implacable. "No. There is no need to know. My orders are to shoot down designated jetliner with important enemy troops aboard. I am obedient officer. Orders are orders. I do not question them."

The KGB controller squirmed uncomfortably in the back of the van. He ground out the butt of his cigarette on the carpet floor and lit another. He felt a psychological need to impress the Spetsnaz with his importance. "I know name of target," he bragged, not pausing. "It is 38th Civil Affairs Command. CIMIC operators have become too strong in Germany. Your Stinger attack will eliminate this threat."

The Spetsnaz stared ahead, steadfast. He did not let Kolchak's condescending attitude fool him. Let him curry favor.

"There will be more than one attack at the airport," Kolchak revealed. "There will be diversionary attack to draw attention away from you."

Petrovich's eyes widened in surprise. "Why have I not been informed?"

"For your own protection," Kolchak smirked. "Each secret cell works independently, unknown to each other. If failure or compromise occurs with one cell, second team will continue attack. Mission will succeed."

"Diversionary attack at JFK," Petrovich repeated, undaunted. "I must know details. It may affect my plan of attack."

The KGB controller leaned forward. "Diversionary attack is KGB operation, not GRU," he stressed. "You have nothing to worry about. It is under my control. There will be disruption of communications at airport. There will be excitement and panic. You will ignore it all."

"What if army commander changes plans and unit does not board plane?"

"They will board plane as scheduled."

"How can you be positive what commander will do?"

The KGB controller puffed up to his full height, sitting erect. "Their commander is dead," Kolchak confessed, excitedly. "I shot him. I killed brigadier general with one bullet in head. There was second person who out- lived his usefulness. I killed him, too. I made it look like double suicide. Mysterious deaths were reported in newspapers and on television. Police are still confused. They will conduct endless investigation. Murders will remain unsolved. Have you seen news reports?"

The Spetsnaz nodded. He had seen a newscast on television at his safehouse, but had not imagined that KGB was involved in killings. He should have guessed. He looked at the venomous eyes of the KGB controller. He was more lethal than he had suspected. "I saw the news report," he said, flatly.

Kolchak boasted. "I have KGB agents hidden away in deep cover all over America. Me, the debonair editor who everybody respects and trusts. I monitor every agent closely. I will kill anybody who gets out of control. Anybody who threatens my operation. Anybody who gets in my way. Anybody."

Petrovich glared at him with deep distrust and foreboding.

Kolchak continued to brag. "I have built a secret network of media influentials, who do my bidding on command. Their news stories wreck havoc in American press. My *kombinatsia* will succeed."

Petrovich listened intently.

Kolchak hesitated, then spit out his deathly challenge. "I've done my part. Now you do yours!"

9

A little after 9:30 on Tuesday morning, Maccabee barged past Freddy and Hernandez the super, as they opened the door to Kolchak's apartment. He marched inside, followed by his four cohorts in civvies.

"We have a search warrant," he said to Hernandez, jabbing his thumb in John Howard's direction.

"Take a good look," the young FBI agent said politely. "It's official. It's dated today." He poked the paper in front of Hernandez, who read it slowly. He withdrew it, folded it neatly and slipped it into the breast pocket of his gray pinstripe suit. John Howard represented a new breed of army reservist. Fresh out of Fordham Law and the FBI Academy, the sun drenched blond, blue eyed six footer was a bonafide electronics technician. He played his role according to the book.

Howard spoke in short, clipped sentences, making it absolutely clear to Hernandez that Kolchak was not to be told about their entry and search. "If you want to keep your green card, you'll keep your mouth shut."

"You know what needs to be done," Maccabee said to Morgan, who had a Nikon 35mm camera strapped around her neck. "You know your priorities."

Morgan moved about the apartment clicking one shot after another, her strobe flashing at twenty second intervals. She was determined not to depend upon another photographer as she had done at Lemoine's apartment.

Maccabee's secret weapon slipped into the apartment, unobtrusively. She beat a straight line to Kolchak's computer center. Her name was Sergeant Spriggy Covalho, a second generation army reservist.

She was petite, about five feet tall, with a straight up and down figure. As a young girl, she had tagged along with her father, who had been a sergeant major in the ARCOM. A no-nonsense teenager, Spriggy gained a fast reputation with an "I can fix it, I can make it work" attitude. With an IQ of 157, she was a senior at Columbia University, majoring in mathematics with an internship at IBM's computer center. She'd been recruited by "Uncle" Dave Maccabee, her father's former commander. The ARCOM considered Spriggy to be their best computer trouble-shooter. She was only 19-years old.

Spriggy sat in the center of the horseshoe, dressed in a gaudy colored Mickey Mouse T-shirt and jeans, her everyday clothes. She scanned the IBM PS/2 keyboard and screen. She fingered the red on/off switch lightly, but did not engage it. She prepared to power up the computer. "Do you have the pass key, LT?" she asked John Howard, who hovered over her shoulder.

"The master's right here," he said, flashing a tiny silver pass key. He reached around behind the PC and inserted the key. It snapped into place. Freddy's recon had paid off. He turned the key. Within seconds, he unlocked the entire system.

Spriggy flipped the PC's red switch to ON.

She moved her chair back and studied the microprocessor, checking the user's technical manual for the fast hard disk software she had brought with her. "Don't want to see ERROR flash onto the screen."

Spriggy inserted a 3.5-inch DOS floppy disk into the drive and booted up the system. The date and time frame prompt flashed on. Her fingers raced across the keyboard. She pressed ENTER. The prompt PASSWORD? flashed onto the monitor's screen, the secret code word known only by Kolchak.

"They haven't made the security system that I can't bypass." She moved closer to the compact IBM steaming tape drive on the computer table that she connected to the microprocessor. Reaching into a shoulder bag, she produced a special 1/4 inch tape cartridge. She inserted the high performance PC Tools Deluxe program into the tape drive, and keyed-in the command: PCBACKUP.

The IBM backup system whirred into instant action.

"We're in," she said in a low key voice, "and copying." Her program bypassed the computer's password and copied a mirror image of the contents of the computer's hard disk files.

She used one high speed cartridge, copying 55 megabytes of information, which computed to about 14,000 pages of secret text. Within seven minutes flat, Spriggy had copied every secret letter, every press release, every memo, including dates and time frames of preparation and transmission that Kolchak had written and neglected to purge from his system.

She also located a string of hidden files, bypassed the code words, and copied them, too. The computer display flashed a final message: BACKUP COMPLETE. PRESS ANY KEY TO END.

Without showing any emotion, Spriggy shut down the system. "I've dumped all the files." She extracted her DOS operational disk and relocked the system. Everything looked as secure as she had found it.

"Let's head for Big Blue," she said to Howard, who continued to watch her silently. "I'll restore the contents of the cartridge onto my hard drive at the office and pull a hard copy. Whatever info I get will be a duplicate of the original data."

"You're a magician," Howard said, impressed. "If we find any incriminating evidence, I can get a court order to bug this apartment."

He pointed out the window to an apartment building located across the street. "We've established an FBI stakeout," he said, "24-hour surveillance. As soon as the judge signs off on a legal wiretap, I'll bug Kolchak's modem and telephone. We can intercept and trace all of his communications."

Howard pulled out a notepad and drew a floor plan of the apartment, indicating high traffic locations, where he would also hide miniature listening devices. "We'll be able to monitor everything that Kolchak says inside the apartment." He snapped a thumbs up signal when he was done.

Maccabee and Freddy made a complete sweep of the apartment. They had carried portable high speed duplicating equipment with them for both audio and video, the latest high tech equipment the FBI could loan them. Freddy connected the cables of their VCR duplicator to Kolchak's VCR. He powered up the unit.

Maccabee worked quickly. He inserted each of seven 120-minute VCR cassettes that Kolchak had recorded off the air on his television set. He wrote down the date and time of each recording listed on the back of each cassette's jacket.

As he completed dubbing the twelve hours of real time, Freddy called out. "Hey, boss, over heah. Looks like dah Rusky taped all his phone calls." He pointed to a portable Panasonic tape deck that was connected to Kolchak's private phone. A small plastic storage file of four audio tapes lay open on the table.

"Let's copy them," Maccabee said, advancing to the table. He used the high speed duplicator, quickly dubbing each of the four tapes. He then extracted the recording tape from the tape player, marking the counter number. He dubbed this tape, too. He reinserted it back into the tape player, rewinding it to the same counter number.

"What's this?" Maccabee asked, as he noticed a small transcriber hooked into the tape deck. He unrolled a spool of two-inch paper that automatically recorded the date, time and length of each phone call. He scanned the list of transactions. "Morgan, can you shoot this printout for me?" he asked.

She rushed to his side and looked. "If you unwind it, I'll start shooting." They worked in unison, Maccabee stretching the tape, Morgan focusing and going click, click. Five minutes later, Maccabee replaced the tape as he had found it.

Morgan used high speed Ilford XP1 black and white film so she could get it processed quickly on color processing equipment. She'd have black and white prints back within two hours. She shot everything that caught her eye, shooting three rolls of twenty exposure film. "It's better to have the shot in the can," she quipped to Maccabee, "than wish I had shot it ... later."

At 10:09 a.m., Maccabee and his four cohorts left Kolchak's apartment. They walked briskly out of the building toward his Blazer parked down the street. He wasn't sure whether any of the information they had found would hold up in court. He didn't care. He was more interested in screening the material, hoping they could finally nail Andrew's killer.

Freddy was in high spirits. He turned to the others, as they loaded the equipment onto the rear deck of the Blazer. "Dah bastard must've thought he wuz immune to search," he chuckled. "We've gotcha, yah son-of-a-bitch. We've gotcha cold!"

Maccabee steered his Blazer into the heavy stream of traffic on Lexington Avenue. He drove like a New York cabby, tailgating and jumping lanes, dodging the mass of taxis, cars, vans and trucks that wormed their way downtown. He didn't know what bothered him most ... the yellow cabs jockeying for position that slowed him down or the incessant buzzing of his incessant beeper.

"If you pull over to a corner phone stand," Morgan suggested, " I can hop out and call your office."

"No place to park," Maccabee replied, as he zipped into the middle lane. "Can't be that important. It'll have to wait."

He fought his way though the downtown traffic, almost hitting a yellow checkered cab that stopped suddenly to discharge a passenger. The crowds were congesting at the crosswalks, slowing down the traffic even more.

The broad intersection of 57th Street loomed ahead. He dropped Spriggy Covalho and John Howard off at the southwest corner so he could make the light. He watched her grab her computer bag and start cross-town toward IBM's branch office on Madison Avenue.

Maccabee sped back into the steady traffic, passing the entrance to Grand Central Station. His beeper buzzed again. "Why doesn't she let up?"

He hit a streak of green lights, drove cross-town onto Park Avenue South and pulled up at the freight entrance of his office building.

Freddy ran inside the building and came back minutes later with a porter, who unloaded the video duplicating equipment onto a dolly and pulled it inside to the freight elevators.

As Maccabee watched Morgan pull her camera bag out of the Blazer, he turned to see Vito Milano, the muscular Italian detective striding towards him from an unmarked police car parked across the street.

"It's about time you got back," Milano said. "I've been trying to reach you. Your secretary tried to call you on your beeper. I almost gave up."

Maccabee looked puzzled.

"Sergeant Milano, what are you doing here?" Morgan piped up. She stepped off the curb and rushed to the driver's side. She looked at Milano, then at Maccabee, who leaned out the Blazer's window.

"Bad news," Milano replied, sadly. He draped his arm over the side view mirror. "There's been a shoot out in the West Bronx at the 46th precinct."

Morgan interrupted. "Isn't that off your beat?"

Milano nodded. "Sergeant Nick Davila called me. He's in the 245th CI with me. He's a detective on the 46th squad."

"I know him well." Morgan snapped. "He's a good man."

"What happened?" Maccabee asked impatiently.

"One of your people got hit," Milano answered. "A soldier in the 38th CA."

"Who?" Maccabee asked, looking worried.

"Sergeant Laura Washington."

"Washington," he echoed. "Laura? How seriously is she injured?"

Milano shook his head. "She's dead. May have been killed last night."

Morgan's shocked eyes fastened on Maccabee. "She was trying to reach you yesterday afternoon," she said in a barely audible voice. "She sounded upset, but would only talk to you."

Maccabee's ruddy features turned pallid gray. He gripped the steering wheel with both hands, stiffly. "If I hadn't been chasing after Gretchen, maybe I could have saved her life," he murmured. "Why did she call?" His energy seemed to drain from his body. He felt defeated.

"Laura wuz a good G-2," Freddy groaned. "How'd she get it?"

Milano looked grim. "I'm on my way up to the Bronx. Thought you might want to come along. I'll fill you in as we drive up."

The Tremont section of the West Bronx was reminiscent of how the bombed out cities of Germany looked after World War II. Maccabee shuddered as Milano weaved his way through the maze of rubble strewn streets and deserted brick buildings that had been firebombed, gutted and ripped apart. They passed one block after another, some buildings totally demolished, others partially standing with gaping holes for windows that looked out in grim testimony.

"They average nine murders a month in this precinct," Milano said. "It's so damn crime-ridden with drugs, it's amazing there aren't more killings. Every block has seen at least one homicide."

"Dis wuz a nice neighborhood when I wuz a kid," Freddy said.

The unmarked police car rolled down the battered and broken streets, unmolested. Maccabee's steel gaze swept across a gang of black teenage punks who loitered on a street corner shooting craps. Their sullen looks of hostility glared back.

The car turned onto a dead-end street. Ahead, a swarm of blue and white NYPD cars with flashing red lights were parked at various angles along the curb, blocking off the neighborhood.

Unmarked cars, vans and emergency trucks filled the block. Uniformed officers and cops in plain clothes stood by, talking in groups of twos and threes. There were no ambulances in sight.

Milano nudged his unmarked car into an opening. They dashed out of the car and rushed toward a devastated building that once housed thirty families.   Detective Nick Davila, a dapper Hispanic officer, about five foot eight with a mop of curly black hair, intense black eyes and macho mustache, greeted them at the ravaged entrance. "Not a pretty sight," he said, as he led them into the building, stepping over debris that cluttered the hallway.

They entered the shambles of an apartment in the rear. "Drug dealers use this building as a crack house. We've closed them down two dozen times and they reopen around the corner, never missing a customer."

Maccabee stepped into the room. It looked more like a flophouse than an abandoned apartment. He noted five stained mattresses lying on the floor, an overturned table, two busted chairs and a carton overflowing with garbage in the corner. "Where was she killed?" he asked.

"Over here." The dapper detective pointed to an outline of a figure that had been chalked in white on the floor before the body was removed to the morgue. "We found four bodies. Sergeant Washington and three drug dealers."

He pointed to the overlapping chalk lines near the wall and checked his notepad. "Names were Carlos Montoya, Leo Alvarez and Chico Morales. They're convicted drug traffickers. Did time at Riker's Island with long rap sheets. Did crack, low level, not big drug dealers. All four must have been sniffing coke when they got hit. The shit was all over them. In their nostrils, in their mouths, in their eyes."

Maccabee looked at the bloodstained floor, where Washington had been gunned down. The stained wall behind it had been scraped for evidence. "When did it happen?" he asked.

"Sometime last night," Davila replied. "We'll get a better read out later today. With all the crack they sell here, it's hard to sort out the visitors from the pushers who live here."

Freddy muscled in. "Laura wuz straight. She didn't do no drugs, no sir. She didn't smoke, drink or do any of dat stuff."

"Yeah, then how come she had fresh track marks on her arm?" Davila asked. "She was still in uniform when we found her, wearing BDUs. Must have come straight from the reserve center."

"How far away are we from the center?" Maccabee asked.

Milano answered. "About ten, twelve blocks."

Maccabee turned to Freddy. "Where does she live?" He wondered what route she took and if she had told any other reservist where she was going.

Freddy looked confused. "I'm not sure," he answered. "Somewheres in dah south Bronx. Takes dah subway home every night."

"We're checking it out," Davila assured. "I've got a team over at the center right now questioning the fulltimers."

Maccabee swallowed hard. "Who found her body?"

"Some neighborhood kid," Davila replied. "He heard a dog howling and came looking. Found all four bodies blown apart in that corner. Whoever did them in used a submachine gun, riddled the hell out of them."

"Any clues who did it?"

"Not yet. We're talking to all our informants, going over the names of suspects." He paused, curling his mustache thoughtfully. "Looks like a drug vendetta. We don't know if it's a Jamaican posse, Hispanic gang or Mafioso. One thing we're sure about, it's drug related. The shooters didn't take anyone's wallet, jewelry or watch. This rub out was a warning to somebody."

"Didn't anyone hear or see the killers?"

The detective snorted. "Not in this neighborhood. We have shootings, stabbings, people thrown off roof tops, people's heads bashed in with baseball bats, people suffocated. Witnesses are too terrified or too apathetic to talk. Nobody sees a damn thing."

"Anything else I should know?"

"Yeah, are you ready for this. It's a zi-i-n-ger!"

Maccabee's green eyes widened.

"She was carrying a CIMIC Troop Overseas Deployment List in her purse, classified TOP SECRET." He paused. "How does that grab you?"

Maccabee was speechless. He knew Laura was a competent intel sergeant, who took pride in her work. She knew better than to walk around with a TOP SECRET document on her person after working hours. The string of coincidences began to weigh him down. First Andrew, now Laura.

"What if this shoot out isn't drug related?" he asked, sensing a connection. Andrew Palmer's and René Lemoine's double murder had been staged to look like an apparent suicide. This gang vendetta looked too pat.

The detective forced a wry smile. "We have a good homicide solve rate in this precinct, best in the city. It'll take time, but we'll find the killers."

Maccabee felt stymied. What did Laura know that killed her? Who was the mastermind behind all this?

The news hit the afternoon newspapers and evening television and radio newscasts like a shock wave. **Bronx Massacre!**"

Sergeant Washington's name was featured with three dead drug dealers.

Major General Kelley at the Pentagon prevailed upon the media to withhold disclosure of the TOP SECRET document. Maccabee could picture Gretchen Lundstrom winging homeward to drop the death knell on the reserve's latest lapse in security and all of its ramifications.

He sat stonefaced in the commander's office at the 38th's reserve center in the Bronx. The normal Tuesday night admin activities had ground to a standstill. Reservists poured in early, wondering what was happening.

Maccabee saw Colonel Zimmermann, the acting commander, was at wit's end. He had taken charge of the unit, acting like a bull in a china shop. "I have a unit to run," he argued without showing any sign of sympathy. "Washington's murder is a police matter. We can't waste our time trying to learn why she had the classified document on her. The NYPD gets paid for that. Let them earn their salary."

The freckled face marketing executive ran his fingers nervously through his thinning sandy hair, ignoring the two fulltimers who sat quietly at the conference table, listening. "Christ! I only have two weeks to get our CIMIC teams off to FALCON FLASH."

"You'll have to bear with me," Maccabee urged. "If I can't use this office, I'll ..." He started to rise.

"No, go ahead with your questioning," Zimmermann snapped. "I don't want to miss anything important."

Maccabee nodded a go-ahead to the fulltimers to retell their story.

"Laura walked out of here at 4:30 along with the rest of us," Captain Jeff Keller said. The tall, skinny, intense admin officer adjusted his specs. "She said she was going home. The last time I saw her, she was walking up Hall of Fame Drive toward University Avenue."

"Anybody with her?"

Sergeant Lydia Castro, an olive skinned admin specialist with long black hair tied into a bun, spoke up. She sat erect with her hands folded in her lap, trying to control her emotions. "I wuz wid her," she said, softly. "I hadda go shoppin' on Fordham Road. I left Laura at University Place. That wuz dah last time I saw her." She started to cry. "She wuz headin' down 183rd Street toward dah el. She takes dah subway home every night."

"Where does she live? What stop does she get off at?"

"She rides number four local to 149th Street. Takes about fifteen minutes. She lives on Grand Concourse in dah Mott Haven section."

Maccabee grimaced. He wondered if she ever reached the subway. Her body had been found in the Tremont section, a long distance away.

"What direction were you going, Jeff?"

"The usual," he said, flippantly. "The Deegan to the G.W. Bridge, across the Hudson, off at Fort Lee and home to eat with the missus."

"Who else was in the building yesterday afternoon?"

The high strung captain held Monday's sign-in sheet in his hand. "We had a string of people doing mandays, getting ready for their overseas training." He handed Maccabee the list.

He studied the names briefly. He looked up and dismissed Keller and Castro. "Send in Colonel Cherniak and Captain Dressler from G-2." He looked at the sign-in log. Every section was represented, G-1, G-2, G-3, G-4, and G-5.

The door opened. Lieutenant Colonel Livingston stuck his head inside. "If it's okay, I'd like to join you." The amicable sales executive walked inside and dropped onto a padded leather couch. Minutes later, Cherniak and Dressler arrived. They sat at the conference table, facing Maccabee.

Cherniak handed the G-2 intelligence log book to Maccabee with a grave look on his face. "The CIMIC troop list for the Transportation Command is the only one missing. All other troop lists are accounted for in the G-3 file. The TRANSCOM list was logged in two months ago. Nobody logged it out."

Maccabee stared ahead, considering all the possibilities. "Who was in the G-2 cage yesterday?"

"I was, for one," Livingston interjected in his usual good natured way. "I had to update the CIMIC SOP for the Engineer Command. Logged it out in the morning, logged it back in around four."

Maccabee addressed his friend. "Did you see Laura leave the center?"

Livingston shook his head. "I worked right through lunch, so I pulled out a few minutes early. Didn't see her leave."

Maccabee read the daily log. "Everyone checked out his documents and returned them properly. Nobody in G-3 had their hands on the troop list." He paused, dismayed. "What possessed Laura to take it?"

"Maybe she was supporting an expensive drug habit," Livingston volunteered. "Crack's not cheap. It's happened before."

The two G-2 officers shook their heads in disbelief.

"What if ..." Maccabee suggested, "what if it was a plant? That somebody stole it from your safe and planted it on Laura's body?"

Zimmermann spoke up. "How many thefts can we have in this unit? We're still trying to find out who stole the CIMIC network document?"

"Then how did it disappear?" Livingston asked, innocently.

Cherniak answered. "I can only think of one thing. You know how it is around quitting time. Everybody brings in their classified files at the same time, logging them all in at once. Sergeant Washington probably had the safe's file drawer open. Somebody could have walked in and lifted the troop list during the confusion."

Maccabee turned to Livingston. "Wally, did you see any outsiders in the G-2 cage that shouldn't have been there?"

"No," Livingston said. "Just my guys from G-5, Brockmann and Goetz. And Kerner and Ozir from G-3. Nobody else."

Captain Dressler cut in. "Sergeant Washington was a sharp soldier. She would have seen something strange going on. Nobody can just walk in and take a secret document without her knowing it."

"That's the trouble," Maccabee said. "Laura knew something. She called my office twice yesterday afternoon. She had something important to tell me."

Everyone remained silent, waiting.

"I was out," Maccabee lamented, feeling his insides gnawing away, painfully. "Whatever she wanted to tell me, that's what caused her death."

The next two days for Maccabee were sheer pandemonium. Gretchen's column in the *Times* blasted the security breakdown at the reserve center, just as he had expected. He read her headline.

"G-2 SGT FOUND DEAD WITH TOP SECRET DOCUMENT."

Then the subhead.

"Can NCOs Be Trusted?"

Why couldn't she tone down her copy? Now she was stabbing at the very heart of the reserves. The NCOs run the army. He threw the paper down in disgust.

He pressed his intercom and asked his secretary, Judy, to call Gretchen. Moments later, he learned Gretchen had left town to cover a major news story. She'd be back on Friday. He left a call back message.

On the brighter side, Spriggy had duped Kolchak's computer data bank successfully. Maccabee and Morgan poured over twenty eight volumes of computer printouts, consisting of about five hundred pages each. They tried diligently to make sense out of the reams of information.

After the first few hours of analysis, he directed Spriggy to dupe her hard disk copy, which he Federal Xed to the Pentagon for content analysis. Telephone calls ranged back and forth, assigning topic guidelines, descriptive phrases and time frames that would be factored into meaningful categories. He ordered all modem traffic to be reported on both a qualitative and quantitative basis. All transmissions were to be cross-checked by name, address, telephone number and subject matter; then cross-checked again with the audio and video tapes that he also forwarded.

After sixteen hours of constant phone calls, he dispatched Morgan to the Pentagon so she could key in her intel collection plan and make snap judgments on the scene. She flew to Washington, D.C. on Thursday's noon shuttle.

Having worked around the clock, Maccabee sat alone in his office, surrounded by twenty-eight volumes of computer printouts. He pushed them aside. Despite his ability to speed read, he felt like he was on a treadmill.

His mind jumped from one killing to the next, from Andrew to Laura, and back again. There were still no hard clues on Laura's murder. He blamed himself for both their deaths. If he had only been there when they needed him.

He slipped into a state of self-pity. It felt like one of his darkest moments in 'Nam, when everything seemed like it was lost. When all he wanted to do was to crawl into a hole and pull the dirt over him, hoping the danger would go away.

But it didn't. It never does. He knew he had to confront the crisis head on. To end the guilt trip. He blinked his eyes, forcing himself out of the lethargy. Somehow he'd pull it out, just like he did in 'Nam.

He tried to focus on Laura.

His secretary rapped on the door. "I think you need to speak to a couple of friends." She stepped aside as Sergeants First Class Willie Douglas and Doreen Franklin walked into his office. Dressed immaculately in business suits, both NCOs had a look of despair pasted across their faces.

Maccabee rose to greet them.

"We can only stay a minute, Colonel Mac," Doreen said, anxiously. "We're flabbergasted about what the papers say about Laura."

"It couldn't happen that way!" Willie exclaimed, excitedly.

"It's preposterous!" Doreen declared. "Laura led a good life. No way did she freak out. She wasn't into drugs or booze." Doreen began to choke with emotion. "We went to high school together. She was so square and righteous, that girl, that she scared off every man that crossed her path." She sobbed, blurting out, "Somebody framed her! Just like the general."

Maccabee waved them into chairs by the conference table. He pointed to the stacks of computer printouts spread across the table. "We're getting close to General Palmer's killer. Major Morgan flew to the Pentagon to analyze this material on high speed computers. The FBI's involved. We're hoping for an early breakthrough."

Willie looked livid. He mustered control of his temper. Maccabee had never seen him so angry. "The hitman?" he asked. "Is it the same guy?"

"Possibly," Maccabee replied. "There's too much of a coincidence. Both murders were staged to deceive us." He stopped short. He couldn't say anything else.

"How we goin' to find Laura's killer?" Willie asked.

Maccabee thought for a minute, then paced in a small circle. He began to feel better, like his old self. "If Laura was set up, someone had to finger her, point her out to the killer. I don't know how she ended up in the Tremont section, but I bet she was mugged and dragged into a vehicle."

"Lydia tells me she was walking down 183rd Street," Doreen said. "If the police can't do their jobs, we'll do it for them."

"I like to run a loudspeaker patrol like we did in the Village," Willie requested.

"Good idea," Maccabee replied. "Get over to the PSYOP battalion and check out two jeeps and loudspeakers. You have my authorization. Start combing the area where Laura was seen last."

He looked at the two senior NCOs, who climbed to their feet slowly. The color that had drained from their ebony faces began to return. Maccabee walked them to the door. "Somebody out there saw Laura kidnapped. You know how stiff-lipped the locals are with the police."

He paused as an idea gripped him. He reached into his wallet and pulled out three twenties. "A lot of kids play on the streets before supper time. Use this money and buy a couple cases of Hershey candy bars. Start handing them out. Maybe some ten-year old saw what happened."

On Friday morning, Maccabee received a flash report from Morgan. "We lucked out on the first run," she disclosed, excitedly. "Kolchak knew General Palmer was going to be murdered before it occurred. The IBM disks prove it. He sent out the news story to a network of media sympathizers across the country. The original message was recorded on March 8, 1988 at 5:06 p.m. in the computer's directory, six hours before the murder took place. The message was transmitted by modem at four the next morning."

"The bastard knew about it!" Maccabee fumed, gnashing his teeth. "Was there any other incriminating evidence?"

101

"We're still checking it out. Looks like Kolchak has been waging a Soviet disinformation campaign with the liberal press for years."

"Did he set Andrew up? Did you find a smoking gun?"

"Kolchak was involved, but we don't know who pulled the trigger."

"Anything else?"

"Kolchak outfoxed himself when he recorded his phone calls. There were transcriptions of two calls made to Gretchen Lundstrom, one where he didn't speak, one where he did. He made his second call at 12:32 a.m., about thirty minutes after General Palmer was killed."

Maccabee held his breath, expecting the worst.

"Kolchak told her about the murder and its location. Looks like your girlfriend was not an accomplice, but was duped into complicity."

Maccabee protested. "She's not my girlfriend." He let his breath out slowly, knowing that he had confirmed his weekend date with Gretchen.

"They had a rendezvous at Kolchak's apartment. After reading the transcripts, I'm not sure who seduced whom."

Maccabee winced. "Did Kolchak have anything to do with Laura's murder?"

"Don't know. We plan to cross-check the tapes on Sergeant Washington over the weekend. We're also checking on the Stinger missile threat. I'll have an intel summary on Monday."

Freddy barged into his office, looking bleary eyed and raunchy from his all night vigil in search of a lead to Laura's killer. "Dat neighborhood is somethin' else," he complained. "I covered an eight block radius from University Place to Jerome Avenue. Didn't come up wid one lead."

"Are the people talking?"

"Yeah, dey're Kinda closed-mouthed, but dey talk to me."

Maccabee briefed Freddy quickly on what he had learned from Morgan. "We still don't know if Kolchak is a KGB assassin or a Soviet propagandist. The M.O.s for Andrew's murder and Laura's are similar. Kolchak's propaganda campaign is based on deception. Right?"

The burly Latino straddled a chair. "Right."

"Let's assume Laura found something hot, maybe even discovered who the mole is. Somehow the mole found out and panicked. Maybe Kolchak moved fast to eliminate her, to stage the drug murder scene to protect his conspiracy."

Freddy stood. He paced back and forth, listening intensely.

"The killer had to be the mole, a hired hitman or KGB assassin, maybe Kolchak. Whoever did it had to follow Laura until she was out of Sergeant Castro's sight."

"Somebody hadda finger her," Freddy said.

Maccabee nodded. "Yeah, there were lots of photos around on Andrew, but none on Laura. Only the mole knew what she looked like. My guess is the mole followed her by car, not on foot."

"It ain't safe fer an anglo to walk deese streets alone, day or night."

Maccabee thought back to his days at the reserve center. "Everybody zips out of the parking lot, making a beeline straight for the Deegan Expressway and the Cross Bronx Expressway."

"Dat's right. Everybody goes in dah same direction."

"Whoever went in the opposite direction either fingered or killed her."

Later that day, Maccabee and Freddy sat at the conference table, planning how to determine who went in the opposite direction. If Morgan could photograph selected cars at Tuesday night's admin drill, maybe they could get the word out on the street. Unless someone came up with a new lead, there was little they could do until then.

"It's time to call it a day." Maccabee nudged his sidekick, becoming personal. "Going to see, ah ... what's her name? The photographer?"

"Yah better believe it. Her name's Kerri Anne. She's somethin' fine!"

"Falling in love again?"

"Yah know me, boss. Never can tell."

"Get going," Maccabee laughed. "See you Monday." He waved good-bye, picked up his Blazer and drove cross-town to a parking lot on the westside.

He walked through the heavy glass doors of the *Times* Building and rode the elevator up to the editorial offices and asked for Gretchen.

After ten minutes of waiting, she burst though a door, carrying a small overnight suitcase. She had an eager look of anticipation on her face. "Hi! I'm ready. Sorry to keep you waiting, but I had to change clothes."

She looked more like a college coed than a high paid newspaper columnist. She wore a bulky knit beige sweater that clung suggestively to her supple body. Low slung hip-hugger pants left little to his imagination. She carried a brown leather, flight jacket over her shoulder.

Maccabee stared at her and smiled.

She reached up without hesitating and kissed Maccabee tenderly on his lips. A short "hello" kiss that turned his adrenaline onto fast forward. "Let's go," she said, grabbing his arm in hers, snugly. "I didn't think this weekend would ever come."

10

The drive to Maccabee's retreat in the Poconos went quickly, once they passed the Lincoln Tunnel and commuter traffic. They acted spontaneously like two young people discovering each other for the first time. They talked and listened, then talked some more. Small talk, nothing important. For the first time in weeks, Dave felt himself letting go, letting her magnetism engulf him. He cruised along Interstate 84 with one eye peeled on the road, the other on Gretchen.

An early Spring snow had swept down unexpectedly from Canada, white-washing the gray forest one last time before warm weather arrived. Gretchen felt bubbly, uninhibited. There was something so masculine about Dave, something so appealing. He was finally unwinding, becoming his real self, just like she knew he would. Charming, carefree, a gentle boyish aggressiveness overtook him. Gretchen knew she was beginning to penetrate his defenses. She had to know everything.

It was almost 7:45 when they turned off the highway at the Hamlin exit. Dave shifted the Blazer into 4-wheel drive, as he turned onto a snow-covered country road that sloped down to Wallenpaupack Creek. Everything looked so fresh and clean and crisp. "There it is," he said, pointing to the white stucco gate that his headlights illuminated. The sign read: "Forest Haven. Private Property." He turned and drove up a sharp curving hill for three-quarters of a mile. He plowed through a small snow drift into a driveway and parked in front of a rustic chalet. Snow and ice still clung to the tall evergreens and oak trees that towered majestically sixty feet high above them, guarding the smaller elm and maple trees. Snow was pancaked on their branches. Frozen icicles pointed down, creating a frozen canopy of serenity.

"I love the snow," Dave said. "It's like God decided to paint the earth white, cleansing it of all its filth and anguish and violence." He grinned, afraid that she might laugh at him. "I feel closer to God here. It's my private sanctuary. The silence, the solitude, even the loneliness are good. It gives you time to hibernate, to recharge your batteries, to gain an inner strength, to take a fresh look at life."

"It's lovely," Gretchen said, as she uncurled her long lithe legs and slid gracefully out of the Blazer. She grasped her overnight suitcase and followed Dave onto the deck. They stamped loose snow off their shoes and walked inside. Dave switched on the lights and turned the thermostat up to eighty degrees to warm up the house.

"It's just the way I knew it would be." Gretchen walked into the living room, which had been built around a fieldstone fireplace that rose to the ceiling. Her eyes followed the cathedral ceiling to the exposed oak rafters that led to the banistered loft and master bedroom upstairs. She noticed a large ski rack protruding from a wall, holding Rossignol downhill and cross country skis. A 12-gauge Remington shotgun hung from a gun rack over the mantle. Three fishing rods and a fishing net were locked in a rack on the far wall. "Needs a woman's touch," she thought.

"I'm starved," Dave said, "Let's go out to dinner. I know a perfect place. I'll start a fire now, and the house'll be nice and warm when we return." He walked Gretchen into the den, which served as a guest room. "Why don't you drop your things here. We can wash up and go as we are."

Gretchen faced him and said, "I'd like to change, if you don't mind. I want this first night to be something special." She started to unpack her suitcase.

Dave went back into the living room, and dumped a bag of instant charcoal briquettes onto the fireplace grate and lit them. Within minutes, the charcoal glowed red. He shoveled peat coal onto the hot coal bed, watching the blue flames spread.

Around nine that evening, they drove to the Chateau, a popular nightclub overlooking Lake Wallenpaupack. While checking Gretchen's long royal blue greatcoat, Dave stared longingly at her figure, saying, "Well now!"

She wore a Grecian gown of alluring beige chiffon with silk cord criss-crossed delicately over her voluptuous bosom. The soft gathers of fabric fell suggestively to her four-inch spike-heel sandals, creating an illusion of high undaunted spirits. The subtle slant of her blue Nordic eyes was bewitching. The vibrant glow of high cheek bones added to her classic beauty.

They ordered scotch sours, gazing at each other through the flickering candlelight. "Enjoying yourself?" Dave asked as he set the menu aside.

"It's delightful." She placed two fingers against her cheek and stared romantically at him. He looked dashing and debonair, now that he had agreed to wear his white dinner jacket, stud shirt and bow tie. They sipped their frosted cocktails slowly, toasting each other.

Dave watched two couples on the dance floor. He rose and put out his hand for Gretchen. "Like to dance?"

"Love to." She felt the wild, irrational part of herself taking hold.

They slid onto the dance floor, moving gracefully to the rhythmic beat of a rumba, swaying to its lilting melody. Gretchen glided across the dance floor like she was floating on a thin wisp of air. Dave had a strong lead, holding her firmly in his arms. She followed his every step, her movements very sexual.

Dave felt everyone's eyes upon them. The two couples moved off the dance floor, watching them. He tried to be nonchalant. Yet, he knew he was performing.

She laughed. "Dave, you do a wonderful rumba. I didn't know the Green Berets were this versatile." They glided smoothly from one dance pattern to another as if they'd been dance partners for years. He pulled her closer, swaying to the coaxing rhythms. He felt captivated by the subtle fragrance of her Shalimar perfume. He sensed her willing response. He brushed a light kiss across her cheek when they slid together. The band played another rumba, "Love Me Lazy, Love Me Good." He watched her swirl to its tantalizing beat. Her well-rounded hips rolled melodically under the flowing chiffon. She clung to him buoyantly as the music ended.

Dave led her back to the table, whispering into her ear. "Dancing is the only custom where you can take a woman in your arms in public and nobody will complain. And you looked great!"

"It was fun! Let's dance again, Dave. I want to dance, dance, dance." They had two more cocktails, then ordered prime ribs for dinner. The evening raced by. On the dance floor again, Gretchen shut her eyes, enraptured. They danced to a medley of love songs from the fifties. Dave hummed along, singing what lyrics he knew. She snuggled closer, still scheming, but not wanting to lose the moment.

Strolling back to the table, Gretchen feared her emotions had taken charge, catapulting her towards a new threshold. She sat down and stared into the glowing candlelight, fighting to control herself rationally. She took his hand in hers. "Dave, can I get serious for a minute?"

"Sure." He leaned forward, smiling pleasantly. "What's on your mind?"

She played with the pearl dinner ring on her finger. "I've had second thoughts about the two army murders. I think you're holding something back. The two cases are linked to each other. Why can't you level with me and tell me everything?"

Dave's smile vanished. He caught his breath. There it was, out in the open. Was all this romance just a come-on? "The two cases are tied to each other," he said, reluctantly. "I can't prove it yet, but I will."

"Why won't you trust me?" she asked, articulating each word with clipped Germanic precision. "I am only trying to get to the truth. You have an excellent reputation as a PAO and publicist. We're on the same side. We need you. I need you. Why can't you take me into your confidence?" She looked at him closely. His eyes seemed to reflect a deep sense of mistrust.

Dave leaned forward, staring at the cocktail glass in front of him. He jostled it, then set it aside. "I believe in a free press," he said. "I admire people who are willing to stand up and say this is what I think is right, this is what I think is wrong. It takes courage, conviction and honesty. With one caveat."

"Which is?"

"Responsibility."

"Are you suggesting that I'm not responsible?"

"I'm not suggesting anything. I worry when I see reporters mishandle a story and stir up a lot of trouble, because they didn't do their homework. I worry when I see reporters sensationalize a story to enhance their careers or to help their publishers sell more newspapers. You're in the news business, not the entertainment business."

Gretchen edged closer to Dave, trying to avoid an argument. "I bust my butt chasing down a story. I've antagonized people, intimidated them, grilled them ... flattered, cajoled, persuaded, even pleaded with them to get them to talk. People are scared to talk. They're afraid they might lose their jobs, their reputations, their freedom, and in some cases, even their lives."

Dave ordered another round of scotch sours. He listened intently.

"I only react to what I see. That's why I keep digging and asking why."

The waiter placed two cocktails on the table and left. Gretchen forced a thin smile. She sipped the scotch.

"What happens when the facts don't support your opinion? You can be a very stubborn woman."

She giggled. "Not always, well, ... sometimes I'm stubborn."

"We've all been victimized by a clever Soviet deception campaign, by a murderous conspiracy that you spurn and deny."

"That's not so!" A flush reddened her face. Her temper flared. "I'm a professional journalist. If I make a mistake, I'll be the first to admit it. Some people accuse me of being an ambitious, conniving and cunning woman. It's partially true, but

I don't get entree into the corridors of power by being timid or self-serving."

Dave signaled the waiter. "I don't want to argue with you. This isn't the time or place." He scanned the check, used his American Express Gold Card and signed the receipt. It had started out as a great evening, but it had turned into a shambles. They drove back to the chalet in silence.

"Come on," Dave said, as they sat before the fireplace, sipping cognac from crystal snifters. "Let's lighten up. No more business talk, okay?" They sat together on the couch facing the slow burning blue flames of the fireplace.

Gretchen's temper flared again. "I'm not a child, I'm a woman. If I want to talk business, I will!" Her fiery blue eyes challenged him, trying to disarm him and draw him into her web.

Dave slid across the couch and faced her, saying, "Then talk."

"I need to know how your CIMIC network operates, how it communicates secret information to U.S. commanders without the Germans knowing?"

He sat erect, annoyed by her question. He decided to confide in her. "If you want to talk about secret information, let's talk about your friend, Dmitri Kolchak."

She let out a low gasp. Her blue eyes widened in shock.

"He's a Soviet spy, KGB, not the simple editor you thought he was."

" I can't believe it."

"Kolchak knew about General Palmer's murder before it occurred. That's why he was able to tip you off, so you could scoop the other newspapers. He was using you as a pawn, duping you ... along with hundreds of other editors across the country. The FBI has him under close surveillance."

"How did you find out? How long have you known that Kolchak was my informant? What evidence have they found?"

"Hard incriminating evidence, the kind that stands up in court. I've seen it."

"I knew you were withholding information from me. When can I see it?"

"My deputy is down at the Pentagon processing the data over the weekend. It's classified and on close hold. There's another serious threat involved that we can't talk about. Hundreds of lives may be involved. You must respect our need for secrecy."

Gretchen eyed him bleakly, spellbound. "Was Kolchak involved in Sergeant Washington's murder?"

"We're not sure, but the FBI is checking it out." He hesitated, watching her closely. "I'm sharing highly sensitive information with you. If Kolchak gets wind of it, I'll know who told him. You better not leak it, not until we're ready."

Gretchen slid closer to Dave. She grasped his chin firmly in her hand and forced him to look into her eyes, enticing him. "I promise I won't tell a soul. But you must give me your word that I'll get a full blown briefing before you go public. One more scoop, that's all I need."

Dave's eyebrows arched slightly. He waited.

"I had misgivings after writing Sergeant Washington's story. I jumped to conclusions too fast. The evidence looked so clear at the time." She snuggled closer, pulling his arm around her shoulder. "I need you David. We can do so many things together. We can make things right."

Dave settled back, looking at her inquisitively.

"I'm dying to know one more fact?"

"What's that?"

"Silly, but my curiosity is getting the best of me. I'd like to know how your CIMIC operators will circumvent German channels of intelligence."

He jumped up. It finally came to him. Gretchen had been pursuing him since Andrew was murdered. She wasn't Kolchak's pawn. She was an unguided missile, pursuing her own trajectory. "Damn it! You've been chasing after me, so you can write your BIG STORY about the reserves. It's business and only business with you."

"It's not true!" she cried, her blue eyes becoming misty. Tears welled up and flooded down her cheeks, streaking the flawless finish of her make-up. She sobbed quietly, rejected and hurt.

"You had me going, really going. I was falling for you, hook, line and sinker!"

She stood and confronted him aggressively. Her eyes blazed with fury. "I have a complete dossier on you. I studied it. I lived with it. You're the key to these damn murders, to this whole conspiracy. I have nothing against the reserves." She began to cry. "I had this dumb photograph of you. Stupid me! You turned out to be more than I expected, more than I ever wanted."

Dave offered her his handkerchief, but she slapped his hand away. "I have no pride left," she cried. "I'm beginning to love you, David Maccabee. But you're afraid to let go. Afraid to fall in love. What will it take?" She ran to the den, crying uncontrollably. She slammed the door behind her.

Dave sat in the dark for about an hour. He sipped two fingers of cognac and brooded. "I need to talk to Gretchen, to comfort her, but we'll only argue again." He trudged up the banistered staircase to his bedroom, closing the door. He undressed and lay in bed in his skivvies, staring into space. Gretchen's presence remained with him, unnerving him. He couldn't sleep. She'd been right about one thing. He didn't want to fall in love, didn't want to be hurt. "Am I acting stupid? What if she is a newshound? What difference does it make? She's brainy and bold, so different from other women I've known.".

He wondered if Gretchen had cried herself to sleep. Was she still wearing her evening gown or had she slipped into a nightgown? "Can she be lying there, nude ... waiting for me?" He closed his eyes, trying to shut her out of his mind. Sleep was hopeless, his mind too active. He took a fast shower in the upstairs bathroom and dried haphazardly. His wavy brown hair and muscular shoulders glistened with droplets of water. He donned a pair of sweatpants and tiptoed downstairs. He heard her taking a shower in the main bathroom. "I guess she couldn't sleep either."

He walked to the portable bar and mixed two hot toddies. He rapped lightly on the bathroom door, still hearing the steady downpour in the shower.. "Room service! Are you decent?"

The shower stopped. "For you, anytime!"

Dave chuckled. "I've been behaving like a jerk." He opened the door a crack, placed the hot toddy on the floor and withdrew his hand quickly. A hot steamy cloud laced with sweet fragrant Shalimar enveloped him.

"Cheers!" he toasted, taking a deep gulp of the hot toddy. "I've been thinking, maybe we can work closer together."

"David, that's wonderful!" she squealed from inside the bathroom. Minutes later, the door opened wide. She stood quietly on the threshold, clad in a white terrycloth robe with a sash tied loosely around her. She sipped the toddy, her face aglow. She looked deliciously demure.

A gasp escaped his lips. He tried to find his voice. "How do you feel?"

"Wonderful. Every pore in my body feels like a million dollars. The shower was so invigorating." A startled look crossed her face. "David, you're still wet!" She rushed to the bathroom and hurried back with a large bath towel. "You're worse than a little boy!" She backed him up against the bar, drying his wavy brown hair vigorously.

She suddenly wrapped the towel around his neck, tugging on it playfully. She reached up on her tiptoes, clinging to the towel, and planted a warm, ardent kiss on his lips. Her nimble fingers slid onto his bare shoulders, messaging his sinewy muscles. Her long fingernails dug into his flesh. "Mm-m-m-m-m."

Dave let his hot toddy slip to the carpet. "Come on," he pleaded, rearing back, trying to fend her off. A chill raced down his spine. He seized Gretchen by her shoulders, trying to stop her impetuous teasing. The sash on her terrycloth robe began to loosen. Dave gazed down into her saucy blue eyes. Her robe fell wide open.

He stared into a gaping chasm of two firmly pointed breasts, escaping all restraint. Two luscious mountains of joy, perfectly rounded and velvety white, jutted upwards, straining to be kissed. Desire overwhelmed him.

He lifted Gretchen into his arms. She wrapped her hands around his neck.

"Oh-h-h, David." Her robe fell away, revealing her sensuous nude body.

Dave carried her upstairs to his bedroom, his heart thumping in double time. He crushed his mouth onto hers. He threw himself on top of her, embracing her. They rolled across the king size bed, her robe more off than on, his bristly chest clamped firmly against her velvety breasts.

He kissed her passionately, the white torrid heat of their bodies crying out convulsively for more. His fingers played magic tricks across thousands of silky goose bumps that quivered on her slithery body. He caressed her. Fondled her. His passion became gentle and tender. Her skin was so fair. His fingers played across the flat of her tummy, deftly working his way upward to the deep velvet smoothness of her breasts.

"Oh-h-h-h-h, I love you David," she whispered out of sheer ecstasy. She knew she was losing control, getting swept up in his strength and masculinity. She answered his every movement, countering with hot responses of her own.

He opened his lips wide and thrust them full upon one of her budding nipples, trying to swallow it whole. His tongue darted around its swelling edge, nipping its pink splendor. Then over to her other breast, kissing and nuzzling, feeling her engulf him in desire.

Gretchen jerked her feverish body in wild, frenzied movements to the circular movement of Dave's hand while it played across her pelvic bone. He drew small deft circles that made her cry-out and melt inside. She felt the heat of his strong, virile body driving into her, lustful and wanting. Every muscle, every sinew, every nerve sent electrifying shock waves shooting through her. "My *liebe*," she cried softly in German. "My love, I have finally found you." He was hers. All hers.

His finger fumbled with the draw string on his sweatpants. He ripped them off. He had an urgent need to satisfy her every hunger. He kissed her feverish lips. His tongue darted inside like a serpent, finding her warm welcome tongue striking back. The sweet taste of love ravished him. Her hot scorching body thrusted up wildly. Her breath came in short hot bursts. He felt like they were burning up. He wanted to devour her, to climb inside her skin. "I want to eat you," he whispered. "I want to eat you alive."

The hole opened wide. Petrovich whipped his brown two-toned Cherokee station wagon into the empty space at 72 miles per hour, cruising in the fast lane through the heavy Sunday traffic on Rockaway Boulevard. Tailgating a Ford sedan, the Spetsnaz steered the Cherokee back into the inside lane. He ignored the two swarthy skinned Arab terrorists sitting in the back. The muscular Spetsnaz, wearing a blue windbreaker, sports shirt and slacks, enjoyed darting in and out of traffic, slowing down only when he saw a patrol car. The freedom of being able to drive fast, drive anywhere, exhilarated him. He had become edgy and irritable. The drive made him feel cheerful. Two more weeks and the mission would be over.

He caught fast glimpses of people passing by, oblivious to the peril that threatened them. He liked what he saw in America. So many cars, so many happy faces. Everybody rushing somewhere at such frantic paces.

He began to see America in a different light. Are these people my enemy? How many people will I kill in Stinger attack? Target must be destroyed. Enemy aircraft, enemy soldiers. But innocent civilians? Hundreds will be killed in sky, maybe thousands more on the ground when jetliner crashes into city. The civilians are not faceless targets. They are people with names, families, futures. What have they done to deserve tragic death?

I spend years in fighting units living like animal, suffering hardships and hatred to become what I am, risking death itself. For what? To become mass murderer?

He tried to steel himself against showing any sign of remorse. He owed it to his son, Gregorievich, and to his comrades who had been killed by American-made Stingers in Afghanistan.

He became depressed and angry. This was not war. The Soviets were turning him into assassin. He was soldier, not assassin. That was KGB work. Why must I turn peaceful skies over JFK into battlefield? Maybe it was time to leave army, to start new life?

He liked his new family, the Helner-Maccabee-Ackermans. He looked forward to seeing Jackie again and meeting her brother David. "Do I want to return to Russia? I will not be disloyal. I will obey GRU code of silence and never reveal truth about Spetsnaz forces. I will never defect. I may leave army, but never defect."

He wheeled the Cherokee onto Old Channel Lane, a salt water channel that runs parallel to JFK before it empties into Jamaica Bay. He dismissed the strange, compelling thoughts running through his head, remembering that he was a professional soldier on important GRU mission. He would not fail.

Following the directions that Kolchak had given him, he spotted the weather-beaten, brown shingled bungalow that looked out on the marshy channel. He drove across a patchwork of sandy scrub grass and parked in the backyard. Petrovich signaled to two dark haired, medium-built Arabs and pointed at the 28-foot cabin cruiser that was tied up to a dilapidated mooring. Petrovich walked briskly to the water's edge, scowling as he looked back over his shoulder at the two Arab gunners, who trudged lethargically across the sand swept ground.

He stepped lightly over the loose boards of the gangplank that led to the boat. He stopped short, angered by the sight of Kolchak, who continued to harass him. The KGB chieftain, dressed in a blue sports blazer and black turtleneck sweater, talked to a KGB agent, Vladimir, whom he recognized. An iron wall of indifference arose within Petrovich. He climbed aboard the boat.

Kolchak greeted him with a smirk on his face. "The boat meets with your approval?" He tried to mask his loathing for the GRU colonel, which increased with each encounter. "Vladimir drove boat from Freeport yesterday."

Petrovich looked impassively at the KGB controller. His icy gaze swept the length of the boat. The cabin cruiser was white with navy blue racing stripes. It looked like a typical weekend boat with a small sleeper compartment , accept this one will hide the two PLO gunners and Stinger missile until the time came for the attack. The canvas tarpaulin that covered the navy blue vinyl seats could be stowed in back, providing sufficient space at the stern for the gunners to aim and shoot.

"Boat is good," the Spetsnaz acknowledged. He turned to Kolchak and spoke disdainfully. "Why are you here?" Petrovich scanned the nearby houses and sand dunes. "You risk whole operation! Police may follow you. You must stay undercover, no matter what."

The cunning journalist laughed, disarmingly. "You are in America, my comrade. There are no secret police looking over our shoulders. Nothing to worry about." He hesitated, not wanting to offend his adversary. "I wanted to see for myself that boat meets with your expectations." He paused. "No more surprises, I assure you."

Kolchak shifted his weight, nervously, as the brutish Spetsnaz stared him down. He retreated several steps, then whined. "I am no neophyte in art of terrorism. I will be careful. Next time we meet will be to celebrate your mission's success."

Petrovich nodded his approval. A jumbo jetliner thundered overhead on its final leg before landing. He had reconned JFK six times, and the wind conditions kept shifting, sometimes twice on the same day. There was no way to predict which way the planes would takeoff. He ushered the PLO gunners below, showing them where they would hide on the day of the attack. Walking to the boat's stern, he demonstrated their aiming positions, and where they'd stand when firing the missile.

His decision to be mobile was correct. The Sunday traffic on the Beltway was just as heavy as weekday traffic. To be landlocked in traffic jam could abort the mission. He sent the gunners back to the Cherokee to keep them out of sight. He saw two five-gallon fuel tanks lying on their side near the gangplank. He checked the boat's fuel gauge. It read full.

He sat on the boat's gunwale, talking gruffly to Kolchak as a senior officer speaks to an inferior. He visualized the military tactics. "I infiltrate JFK's defense. I use Lufthansa air cargo truck to identify and track target."

He checked a small codebook for the radio frequencies that they would use, jotted them down on a sheet of paper and handed it to Kolchak. "I place beeper on target while loading at passenger terminal. I maintain radio silence until target pulls away from passenger dock. I follow beeping signal down runway. I break silence to

111

announce takeoff runway number and direction. I follow target as it taxis, break silence again, when target is in number one position for takeoff. Boat will not break radio silence for any reason!"

Kolchak looked at the wooden deck with downcast eyes. The burly Spetsnaz continued to intimidate him. He hated taking orders from him. They were of equal rank, both colonels. His high handed GRU ways would end soon. When mission was complete, Kolchak decided he would settle accounts with him, KGB-style. "I have assigned KGB agent Drachev to help Vladimir pilot boat and monitor radio transmissions. They will not break radio silence."

Kolchak tried to hide a smug look on his face, now that he had intervened. He didn't trust the PLO gunners. Despite Soviet training, they had trouble operating radio frequencies. Moscow Central will applaud the precautions he had taken. "If something goes wrong, Drachev knows how to shoot Stinger missile." He lit a cigarette, inhaling deeply. "How do we verify your radio signal from boat?"

"Your response will be big explosion in sky!"

On Sunday morning, Dave jogged up the stairs to the chalet, taking two stairs at a time. He carried a jug of apple cider that he had bought in town. Sliding the heavy glass doors aside, he walked into the living room. The sweet smell of sauerbraten drifted from the kitchen. "Gretchen?"

"Hi! I'm in the kitchen cooking."

Walking past her to the refrigerator, Dave pulled out a tray of ice cubes and poured two tall classes of apple cider. He turned and leaned against the wall, holding the two drinks. Gretchen wore a white cotton bikini midriff blouse and hip hugger pants. She had her back to him, stirring the gravy. She waved a wooden spoon.

"Greatest thirst quencher in the world," Dave said, as he sipped the cider slowly. He stared at the faint outline of Gretchen's panties when she bent over the stove. It aroused him. He placed the two drinks onto the kitchen backboard and sneaked up behind her. He placed his strong arms around her slender waist, where the white satin skin showed. He squeezed her, lifting her inches off the floor.

"Dave!" she yelled. Her toes retouched the floor. She turned her head and caught a kiss under the ear, enjoying it as he hugged her affectionately.

"You smell delicious."

"Sweet cabbage, silly."

"I know what I smell. This ole schnozola never lies. You smell great!" He nuzzled against the nape of her neck, nipping at her ear.

"Davey!" she shuddered. "Now stop that. Can't you see I'm cooking?"

"Uh, huh." Dave slid his arms loosely around her waist again. This time she crossed her arms over his, overlapping their hands, drawing him closer, pressing tightly against his loins. She suddenly spun around in his arms, stretched up on her tiptoes and kissed him soundly on the lips. "There! That should keep you until after dinner." She turned back to the stove.

Dave picked up his glass of cider. One more moment, and I'd have carried her bodily up to the bedroom. Dinner be damned. He gulped down the cider.

"Wait for me!" Gretchen rushed to his side. She snatched up her glass and clinked it against Dave's. "What do we drink to?"

"To us." He lifted her chin with his forefinger and kissed her gently.

"The dinner!" she shrieked, forcing herself away. She rushed to the stove and stirred the gravy, trying to keep it from sticking to the bottom of the pan. "I worked so hard on it yesterday, I can't let it burn."

He followed her to the stove and inhaled. Shalimar's flowery fragrance mingled with the savory flavor of sauerbraten. "Smells wonderful." He placed his arms around her again, while she wrestled with the pan. Dave ran his fingers across the flat of her tummy, then slowly up the inside of her midriff blouse. He felt the cool ripples of tiny goose bumps. He cupped his hands over her warm budding nipples. He pulled her closer, running his tongue along the hollow of her neck. "Oh, Davey," she purr-red. "Please, I can't stand it much longer. The dinner. ..."

"It'll keep." He flicked the switch to "off" and lifted the pan away from the burner. He kissed her again. He reached down for her legs. She sprang into his arms, responding to the fire within her. She kissed him passionately, as he carried her into a burning world of bliss.

She felt the coolness of the bed sheets beneath her. She heard her breath come in short quick gasps, matched by his heavy panting. She felt Dave unbutton her blouse and slip it off, its coolness replaced by his hot pressing lips. His tongue played fantasies on her budding nipples. His hands whipped off her pants and panties in one swooping stroke. She pulled him tighter, feeling his bristly chest pressed against her tender breasts. They kissed ardently, their tongues darting in and out, challenging each other. She felt the strength of his hard torrid heat begin to enter. Slowly. Freely. Then, Oh-h-h-h ... so deeply. She rose to meet him. Faster. Harder. Harder! They plummeted toward a cliff. Faster. Don't stop. Not yet, keep going ...

They plunged off.

They lay in each other's arms, their passion spent.

They kissed each other tenderly, their breathing slowing down, their eyes saying everything. Dave rolled onto his side and gazed at her glistening body. He ran his finger lazily along her thigh, tickling her.

She grabbed his hand and pulled him towards her. "Have I told you lately that I love you?"

"No, tell me."

"I love you." She kissed him sweetly. "I want to say it over and over." She wrapped her arms around his neck, her nude body slipping under his. "I love you so very much."

"I love you too," Dave whispered. He had never shared his emotions this openly before. He found it unnerving.

"Hold me, Davey. Hold me tight. Don't ever let me go."

They lay there quietly. "Davey, the dinner!"

Dave placed his forefinger over her lips and kissed her. "I turned the stove off. I always like a late dinner."

She nestled closer to him, smiling. They lay that way for about a half hour, submerging themselves in each other. Dave inched closer, feeling the warmth of her body. A marvelous sensation overtook him. His fingers played across her warm thigh, lingering just below her pelvic bone, poking gently for a spot that made her squirm. He

113

drew her closer, running his fingers over the rich fullness of her breasts, messaging the growing firmness of her pink nipples.

"Oh, Davey-y-y," she responded, "don't you ever get enough?"

"Do you want me to?"

"I love you." Gretchen pulled Dave's head onto her breast. They felt themselves hurtling towards each other in a hypnotic trance. His lips found hers, the sweet intoxication drowning him. Their naked bodies mingled ... pressing, wanting, trying to climb into each other's skin ... they clutched wildly, rising higher and higher ... a warm, icy smoothness surged to the surface, coming, bursting, shooting for the stars and outer space.

They soared beyond the farthest galaxy. Then ... they were spent. They drifted calmly into a peaceful slumber.

They awoke to the incessant ringing of the telephone. Draping his blanket around himself Indian-style, Dave answered curtly: "Maccabee. Go."

"Colonel Maccabee, Major Morgan here, calling from the Pentagon."

"What's up, Kathy?"

"You sound half asleep. It's only eight o'clock. Did I wake you?"

"Yeah, but I'm alert now. How are you guys doing?"

"We've nailed our suspect. Kolchak was up to his neck in the conspiracy to kill General Palmer. We can't pin the murder on him yet, but the conspiracy evidence is conclusive. The FBI has a court order to tap his telephone line. They put a five man surveillance team on his tail, starting tonight."

"Why don't they arrest him and interrogate him?"

"He'd clam up if they do. They need to follow him and see if he leads them to the mole. The risks are too great. We still don't know if the threat of the Stinger attack is true. We need more hard intelligence."

"What about Laura's death? Was there any linkage?"

"We drew a zero, but that doesn't mean he wasn't involved. He may have handled her murder differently. The FBI is looking for angles."

"When are you returning to New York?"

"I'll catch the first shuttle tomorrow. I'll brief you at 1000 hours."

"Good work, Kathy. See you tomorrow." He hung up.

Gretchen had dressed and stood within hearing distance. She had a troubled look on her face. "Arrest who?"

"Kolchak," Dave answered. "The FBI confirmed that he's the chief conspirator in General Palmer's murder, just as we suspected. They're giving him some slack, hoping he'll lead us to the killers."

Dave looked at himself and chuckled. "I better get rid of this blanket and get dressed while you make dinner. I need to return to New York tonight."

As he slipped into his clothes, Gretchen said. "I want an exclusive! I want to interview Kolchak immediately after the FBI arrests him."

"Sure," Dave replied, wondering whether Gretchen was still chasing after the Pulitzer Prize. "Someone has to keep you honest."

114

11

"The FBI wants us out of the action," Major Morgan said to Maccabee and Freddy, as she paced in front of her intel board like a lioness protecting her lair.

Having landed at La Guardia earlier in the morning, she had caught a cab directly to the agency, arriving in the conference room minutes before her scheduled 10 o'clock briefing.

Still dressed in her army class A uniform, Morgan was highly adept as a command briefer. She spoke in strong assertive tones. "The FBI has put a full team onto Kolchak in New York. He's a KGB colonel. Worked in London, Hong Kong, Damascus, Baghdad and Berlin under different alias. The guys over at Langley say he's never been involved with anything big, an unimportant functionary who moves from assignment to assignment. That's why nobody paid any attention to him here. The NSC has invited themselves into the operation. They want to know why the KGB is running a covert operation and trying to subvert General Secretary Gorbachev's peaceful overtures to the U.S."

"What is the NSC doing about it?" Maccabee asked.

Morgan shook her head, exasperated. "Everything is TOP SECRET. I asked and they said I didn't have a need-to-know."

Maccabee gritted his teeth. "Let's review what we have."

Morgan was all business. "Kolchak wrote a detailed news release about General Palmer's murder four and a half hours before the murder happened. Eleven full hours before it was transmitted by modem to his secret media network."

"Did Kolchak commit the rape and murder?"

"He's my number one candidate," she snapped. "The telephone tapes prove he's a homosexual. Did he pull the trigger?" She shrugged. "I don't know. His videotape shows he tried to establish an alibi. He taped NBC for three hours from 9:30 p.m. to 12:30 on March 9th, so he could say later that he was home watching TV. His big mistake. He forgot to wipe the programs off the videotape. His prints were all over the cartridge, so we know he used it."

"What else?"

"Kolchak wrote a series of pitch letters and press releases that he sent to the journalists in his network. The FBI analysts are tracking the releases and correlating them to actual news stories that appeared on TV and in newspapers and magazines."

"Did you come up with anything on Laura?"

"No, there were no telephone calls or computer messages."

Freddy interrupted. "It don't make no sense! Why would dah bastard wanna kill Laura? She wuz good people."

Maccabee swiveled in his chair toward Freddy. "She tried to phone me twice on the day she was killed. She must have heard or seen something that caused someone to react quickly. If Kolchak was involved, he may have used his office phone or a pay phone on the street."

Morgan asked Maccabee, "Do you remember anything that she might have said to you previously?"

Maccabee rubbed his neck, trying to remember. "I don't recall ..."

Freddy broke in, disrupting Maccabee's train of thought. "What about dah Queen Bee? Man, she showed up at dah murder scene first. We need to interrogate her. Dose photos she took, dat's tamperin' wid evidence, wid national security. She's guilty as hell! Den dat story she wrote about Laura, man, dat wuz dah last straw."

Morgan didn't have any respect for Lundstrom, either. She had created enough grief for General Palmer, Sergeant Washington, the Army Reserve ... and now she was toying with Maccabee's emotions. "The FBI doesn't want to arrest her yet. They said she'd be released within an hour of her arrest. First Amendment rights."

She paused and asked Maccabee in a discreet tone, "Did you know Gretchen Lundstrom is a German alien? She's been working in the U.S. for over fifteen years, and has never applied for U.S. citizenship? That she returns to Germany for one month every year to retain her German citizenship?"

Maccabee flushing slightly. "I didn't know."

"The FBI's afraid to arrest her. She'd get wise and tip off Kolchak. The FBI has staked out her apartment and tapped her phone."

Maccabee felt his face growing redder. "I spent the weekend with her. She's a lot nicer than you think, a different person when you get to know her. She knows she's been duped by Kolchak. She overreacted and made mistakes. She'll make amends when we discover who the killer is. Don't worry , I have her under control."

"Better watch what you say on the telephone to her," Morgan reminded. "The FBI is listening. Don't say I didn't warn you."

"Then we're out of it?" Maccabee asked, perplexed.

"No!" Morgan answered, emphatically. "General Kelley wants us to stay with it. Jurisdictional disputes be damned!" She smiled, apologetically. "His words, not mine." She continued, speaking rapidly. "General Kelley wants us to find the killer. He wants the mole uncovered in the 38th CA. The Army Reserve and CIMIC have lost face in NATO. The threat of a Stinger missile attack could be a diversion for a bomb attack or be the real thing. He's worried. I'm worried."

Maccabee knew they were getting closer. Yet, everything was so damn complicated. The rape, the murder, the series of screw-ups, the Soviet propaganda, the threat of a Stinger attack, a dead Soviet courier, the second murder, more propaganda. Even his affair with Gretchen. Where is it leading to? It worried him more than he wanted to admit.

Around 8:45 Tuesday night, Freddy was on the prowl again. He stalked East 87th Street from Third Avenue to Madison, his burly shape hunched over, hands buried deep in his pockets. His dark brown eyes scanned everywhere. He felt the eyes of the FBI watching him from their stakeout across the street. He knew he'd catch hell the next day when his name popped up on their report. "Screw 'em!" he grumbled. "Gotta find someone who saw somethin'."

He felt like his ass was dragging, prowling the Bronx in the daytime, Manhattan in the evening. If one murder wasn't bad enough, he was torn between two. The sidewalk was empty, accept for garbage pails and plastic garbage bags stacked up at the curb for pickup. On his second tour around the block, he kicked a garbage pail lid that had fallen to the sidewalk. It clanged, scraping across the cement pavement, shattering the neighborhood silence. Curtains parted in three tenement windows above him. Curious eyes peered down, then disappeared behind drawn curtains.

Freddy hoped the NCOs were having better luck in the Bronx, looking for a lead to Laura's killer. Willie Douglas ran a three-man PSYOP loudspeaker patrol, Doreen Franklin another.

As he stooping to pick up the garbage pail lid, Freddy looked up into the glaring eyes of Ramon Garcia, a Puerto Rican doorman, who was trying to control three cocker spaniels on a triple leash that were yelping and trying to break loose. "Watcha doin', man?" he asked, belligerently. "That's my lid."

"Killin' time, amigo. Just lookin'" Freddy said, bending over to pet a black cocker spaniel. "Yah walk deese dogs every night?"

"Yeah." Garcia curbed the dogs, watching them squat and crap into the gutter. He carried a doggie-doo shovel and broom in his hand and swept up behind them. "I'm out heah every night."

"What time?"

"Dis time, man. After dah tenants get home, eat and feed deir dogs."

"Dis time every night?"

"Yeah, same time, every night. You a cop or P.I.?"

Freddy reached into his billfold and flashed his CI card. He produced a small photo of Kolchak and held it up to the street light. "Know dis guy?" Garcia studied it for a brief moment. "Yeah, he's dah Rusky dat lives down dah street. Not a bad guy for a commie. Keeps to himself, don't say much to nobody. Don't own no dog."

"Does he have a car at one of dah parking garages?"

"Nah, never saw one. He rides a cab or bus to work."

Freddy put his arm around the doorman, speaking confidentially. "Ever see him ride in a black van?"

Garcia looked puzzled. The spaniels yanked on the leash, pulling him towards Third Avenue. "Nah, er-ah ... wait." He stopped short, remembering. "Yeah, I saw a chauffeur pick him up in a black Chevy van several times. One of dose vans from dah Rusky mission. Had diplomatic plates."

"How can yah be so sure?"

"I got kinda close a coupla times. Read dah license plate real good. Red, white and blue. Said DIPLOMAT, big and clear. Some smudged numbers."

Freddy wanted to hug the doorman. "Yah didn't happen to see dis guy on dah night of March 8th?"

Garcia reined the dogs in, shortening the leash to control their pulling. "Yah must be kidding. How am I supposed to remember one night from dah next? What day is today?"

Freddy laughed, loudly. "Hey, amigo, I have dah same problem, not keepin' track too good. March 8th wuz a Tuesday night, three weeks ago."

"Three weeks ago," he repeated, his voice rising. "Yeah, I remember. I saw dah Rusky get into dah van three weeks ago, Tuesday night."

"How can yah be sure it wuz March 8th?"

"How can I forget. Tuesday night, dat's my wife's bingo night, every Tuesday

117

night. Dat's dah night Mrs. Gumble's labrador got into a fight wid a German shepherd. Almost got his ear bit off. Tuesday night, positively."

"Did yah see dah license plate? Wuz it dah same one?"

"Nah, didn't get dat close, but it wuz dah same van. Hadda scratch on dah right front fender. Same van, no mistake about it."

Freddy handed a ten dollar bill to Garcia. His persistency had paid off. First a crease on the left rear fender, now one on the right front fender. Maybe dah suckers used dah van in dah Bronx, too. He'd have to check it out. He chuckled to himself. "Dah elusive black Chevy van wuz elusive no more."

Wednesday was a bad day for Maccabee. It started off on a bad note and never seemed to improve. Maccabee's first phone call came from General Kelley at the Pentagon, offering no advice, but keeping the pressure up. His second call came from Colonel Zimmermann, the acting commander of the 38th. He briefed Maccabee on the ODT overseas deployment list. "I'm flying to Heidelburg with the advance party next Wednesday. The CIMIC teams depart Saturday afternoon. We received our travel tickets from Fort Hamilton. We're flying Pan Am from JFK, not MAC out of Philly. The troops should be happy, no long bus drive to the terminal."

"Have you come up with any new insights into Laura's murder?" Maccabee asked. "She was too good of an NCO to violate security procedures. I can't believe she walked out of the center with a TOP SECRET document without logging it out. She didn't have any reason to be carrying the troop list."

"You're sure it's not wishful thinking on your part?" Zimmermann asked with a note of skepticism. "You've always protected your people. That's your weakness. You're too damn loyal. You defend them first, even when you know they've done something wrong, then straighten them out later. You need to face the facts. We know there's a mole in the unit. Somebody stole the CIMIC network. Sergeant Washington turns up dead with another classified document. Has it occurred to you that she might have been on her way to meet whoever is paying her off, that she planned to get the TRANSCOM troop list back in the safe before anyone missed it? That Sergeant Washington is the mole!"

Maccabee's face grew livid. "I hear what you're saying, but I don't believe it." He thought for a moment, then continued. "Six officers were in the building, one fulltimer and five on mandays. Livingston, Brockmann, Goetz, Kerner and Ozir. I'd trust my life with any one of them. What were they working on? Any connection with General Palmer's murder?"

"Colonel Cherniak and Captain Dressler are working with the CID? Christ Dave, we're only one week away from ODT and the unit isn't ready. We need to put these murders behind us and get moving. I'm neglecting my job. My wife Helga is pissed off at me. I had to cancel a freebie weekend that my wife's brother set up for us at the Dortsmund Hotel in the Catskills. It was supposed to be a going-away gift from Werner, who manages the hotel. Helga's going without me. And I'm stuck in the Bronx drowning in paperwork."

"Hang on," Maccabee urged. "Maybe you can still get away. Please keep me posted on any progress."

"Yeah, and a happy holiday weekend to you." He hung-up.

Maccabee had forgotten that Easter was coming up. Madison Avenue and Park Avenue shut down at one o'clock on Good Friday, giving their employees a long weekend. This year Easter and Passover came on the same weekend. Maccabee thought about his Dad and Mom, who were vacationing in Puerto Vallarta, Mexico. He had great respect for his Dad as a field commander. They had a special relationship, and he missed talking to him, especially with all of the problems breaking around him. He looked at a stack of pink telephone messages that had been building up over the past few days, all unanswered.

His secretary Judy rang him on the intercom. "Call from your sister, are you in? She called twice yesterday."

"Sure," Maccabee said. "Put her on."

Jackie's voice had a stern, hard edge to it. "David you promised to have lunch with me this week, and I haven't been able to reach you."

"Welcome to the club."

"You promised to meet with cousin Yakov. He's only here for two more weeks. And only God knows when we'll see him again."

"Jackie, I'm up to my ass in crocodiles. I can't get away right now."

"You promised to have lunch with us. David, this is important!"

"Can't do it, sis." Major Morgan walked into his office, waving another pink telephone slip in the air.

"Then if you won't have lunch with us, will you come Friday night? I'm planning to have a small seder, since Mom and Dad are in Mexico and Lee's parents are vacationing in Boca Raton. Yakov said he'd come."

"Okay, okay, I'll be there."

"Your word?"

"You've got it." He hung-up.

Major Morgan flashed a bright good morning smile, blocking Freddy's path, who tried to enter the room. "Fourth call from Gretchen Lundstrom," she taunted. "On line three." Pivoting, she stiff-armed Freddy and pushed him back into the outer office. "Not your turn yet, take a number."

Maccabee snapped the phone's third button down and heard Gretchen's voice. "Dave, is that you? I've been trying to reach you since yesterday."

"I've been up to my ears in ..." His mind began to work double time.

"I miss-s-s you," Gretchen said. "I'm having another one of my whirlwind weeks. I'm flying to Albany tonight, then Hilton Head tomorrow. I thought you might want to meet me there so we could spend the weekend together."

"Can't do it," Maccabee answered. "My sister's been bugging me to have dinner with a long lost cousin. I have to attend a seder at her house Friday night." He started to invite her, then realized he couldn't. If he showed up with a date for Passover, Jackie would think he was getting serious. She'd been pressuring him to get married for years. He had enough problems without adding to them. "How about spending Sunday with me in the city?"

There was a brief silence on the other end. "I'll try." Another pause. "Are there any new developments about you know who?" Before he could answer, she said, quickly. "Don't forget, you promised me an exclusive."

"When I have something new to report to the press, you'll be the first to hear." He hoped she'd stop her constant calling.

"I love you," she whispered, waiting for a reply.

Maccabee found the words difficult to say. "Yeah, me, too."

And so the morning went, one telephone call after another. Wally Livingston, Pete Williams, Klaus Ludwig, Gerhardt Brockmann, Rudy Krueger, Joe Cherniak from the 38th. Even the NCOs called in -- Willie Douglas and Doreen Franklin. Everyone in his section checked in, wanting reassurance from Big Daddy, everyone except Kurt Goetz, who was doing a 72-hour turnaround flight to attend a global telemarketing conference in Geneva.

Despite the interruptions, Freddy briefed Maccabee and Morgan. Upon hearing his report, Maccabee called the FBI, wanting to use their resources to find the Soviet black van and impound it, to turn the FBI lab technicians loose. The elusive black Chevy van linked it all together. Every instinct convinced him that Kolchak had committed the murder.

Despite Freddy's breakthrough, his fax machine printed out a "cease and desist" from the FBI, until he received further instructions.

Within thirty minutes, John Howard, the young blond FBI agent from the 77th ARCOM, appeared. "Our hands are tied. We can't touch the van. It has diplomatic plates. Diplomatic immunity protects it from seizure. According to the law, any attempt to enter the vehicle is like an attack on the territory of the Soviet Union. Even if there's incriminating evidence in the van, we can't use it."

"Bullshit!" the husky Puerto Rican shouted. "Yah can take yer diplomatic immunity and shove it!" He cast a deadpan expression and turned to Maccabee. "I'll meander over tonight and look fer a van wid a couple of crease marks."

Maccabee shook his head, visibly angry. He knew they'd have to back off. "I'm sorry Freddy, but if you're caught, it could cause an international incident."

Thursday wasn't any better than Wednesday. On his way into the office at 7:30 a.m., Maccabee picked-up a copy of the *Post*. He stared at a mug shot on the front page. The sneering face of a big Jamaican with an Afro haircut, mustache and goatee stared back at him.

The *Post's* headline stated:

"HITMAN GETS HIT!"

The copy was short. "Police find body of Felix Ambray, gangland enforcer of Queens cocaine posse, dead in trunk of abandoned car in Staten Island. Ambray had been shot twice in the back of his head, execution style. Ambray was on the FBI's 'Most Wanted List' for more than a dozen unsolved murders. No clues to the gangland murder were reported."

Maccabee sighed, He patted the .45 automatic that was nestled under his belt in the small of his back. He felt relieved, knowing he'd never see that cruel, haunting face again.

He found detective Vito Milano with a copy of the *Post* doubled up under his arm waiting for him at the agency. "I see you read the paper," the muscular Italian said. "A patrol car found his body early this morning. Didn't take long for the papers to report it. I almost called you, but figured I'd wait until you came to work."

Maccabee unlocked the door of the agency and ushered Milano inside. He turned on the lights and flipped the thermostat up to seventy-two degrees. They walked into his office and faced each other across the conference table. Milano unfolded the newspaper and slid it across the table's surface. "Is this the guy?"

Maccabee picked up the newspaper, then laid it down. "That's him. That's the bastard who tried to push me off the subway platform. Looks like he got what he had coming." He sat down, relaxing.

Milano pulled up a chair and straddled it. "Ambray should have been wasted a long time ago. He was a hitman for a Jamaican drug posse that took its orders from some big shot drug lord in Colombia. He also worked freelance. Spent time in the pen twice, three years for assault and battery, five years for intent to kill with a deadly weapon. He moved around quite a bit, Miami, Newark, Detroit, now New York."

Edging closer to the table, Maccabee asked, intently, "Do you think he was part of the hit team that killed Sergeant Washington in the Bronx last week?"

"I don't think so. Ambray liked to act alone."

"What about all these informers I've seen on TV, hasn't anyone come forward to identify the hit team? Are there any eyewitnesses yet?"

"We've talked to every snitch on the street. We're still sorting through the crap they're giving us. Not one, mind you, not one person described your big Jamaican hitman." He smacked his lips, lingering on his next point. "Does the name Hector Sanchez mean anything to you?"

Maccabee reflected for a moment. "No, never heard of him. Who is he?"

"If I believe an anonymous phone call, he's the man who hired the Jamaican to kill you."

"Why me?"

"Colonel, you know we're a small family in the reserves. Freddy Ventura and I go back a long way. Freddy tells me there may be a mole in the 38th, someone who stole the CIMIC Network that I read about in the papers. Maybe the same someone who stole the troop list and fingered Sergeant Washington. Somehow, you scared hell out of this guy Sanchez, because he's the one who paid the Jamaican."

"How can you be sure?"

"I'm not. That's what bothers me. My info came from an anonymous phone call, a woman's voice. Sing song, Jamaican. May have been Ambray's girlfriend."

"What did she tell you about Sanchez?"

"He paid Ambray five thousand bucks for the hit."

Maccabee frowned, whistling softly. "I didn't know I came so cheap." He inhaled slowly. "Any connection with the Colombian drug cartel?"

Milano nodded. "We cross-checked his prints with DEA and hit a windfall. They've been watching him for awhile. He's a commie, a dedicated Marxist courier. He was born in Buenos Aires. He left Argentina in 1973, one step ahead of the generals. His Marxist father and mother were captured, tortured and executed. Sanchez escaped to Havana, then Mexico City before coming to the United States. He's been laundering Colombian drug money for Castro."

121

"That's how he knew the Jamaican?"

"Probably."

The name didn't register. "I don't understand. How does he fit in?"

Milano leaned forward, intently. "Whoever stole the CIMIC Network and the TRANSCOM troop list had to be an insider at the 38th, right?"

"Right."

"Well, that insider was his accomplice. His wife. Sanchez is married to a Puerto Rican sergeant in your unit. Her name is Rosa Sanchez."

"Holy shit," Maccabee murmured, "not Rosa. She's an outstanding NCO. Everyone respects her. And you got all this on a tip, unsolicited?" He ran his fingers through his wavy brown hair, bewildered. "Where is this guy, Hector Sanchez? We need to get our hands on him quickly and interrogate him."

"We have an all points search going on right now for both Hector and Rosa. I hope we find them before they end up like your buddy from Jamaica."

Late Thursday afternoon, Freddy rode in an army jeep with Willie Douglas, scouting the crowded Hispanic tenements on Aqueduct Avenue in the West Bronx. Both men wore BDUs. It was about 4:45 p.m., and the neighborhood kids were home from school, playing rambunctiously.

Willie steered the jeep onto Grand Avenue, dodging a group of teenage boys, who were playing stickball in the middle of the street. A group of twelve-year old girls were jumping Double Dutch rope on the sidewalk. Three women sat on a stoop, speaking Spanish, watching pre-schoolers chase each other in a game of tag.

"Let's stop heah," Freddy suggested, leaning out the front seat. He turned on the amplifier and keyed the mike to the loudspeaker. Willie double parked the jeep near a fire hydrant. "Hey kids," Freddy shouted in Spanish. "We got FREE Hershey bars to give away. C'mon over!"

The two friendly soldiers were overrun with boisterous kids of every age, who crawled over the jeep with their hands outstretched. Freddy could barely hear his voice above the clamor, as kids came back for seconds, yelling "Gimme, gimme!"

A precocious eight-year old in pigtails climbed onto Freddy's lap and planted a big kiss on his cheek. "My name is Alicia," she said. "I'd like an extra candy bar, so I can have the energy to study real hard tonight."

"What grade are yah in?" Freddy asked, playing along with her.

"Third grade," little Alicia replied proudly, showing off to six other third-graders who pressed against the jeep.

"Tell yah what," Freddy said, "I'll give yah a second candy bar and maybe one to yer girlfriends, if yah answer a question right."

Alicia beamed at her girlfriends and shouted. "Did you hear that, we get a second Hershey bar if I guess the right answer."

Freddy showed a photo of Sergeant Washington at an NCO picnic at West Point, serving hamburgers to children not much older than Alicia. "Have yah ever seen dis woman before? She passed heah last week on Monday afternoon at dis time on her way to dah subway. She wuz wearin' a uniform like mine."

"Let me see," little Alicia said. She studied the photo carefully, then turned to her favorite girlfriend and said, "I want to be a sergeant in the army when I grow up. Don't you?"

"Who said she wuz a sergeant?" Freddy asked, becoming excited.

"She told me!" Alicia said, indignantly. She placed both little fists on her hips like she had seen adults do on television to make her point.

"Do yah know her or are yah just saying so to get an extra Hershey bar?"

Little Alicia jumped off Freddy's lap and started to walk away. "You can keep your Hershey bar!" she taunted, angrily. "I know an army sergeant when I see one. She always said hello to me." She climbed back onto the edge of the jeep. "I haven't seen her since those nasty men took her away."

The two soldiers glanced at each other in eager anticipation. "Can yah tell me what dey looked like?"

"They were big men with yellow hair. They wore black coats and large sunglasses like the bad guys wear on TV."

"Only two men?" Freddy asked, holding up two fingers.

"That's all I saw. Two men grabbing her and another driving the van."

"A van," Freddy repeated, elated. "What color van wuz it?"

Alicia climbed back onto Freddy's lap. She took the photo out of his hand and looked at it. "She was a nice lady. I hope they didn't hurt her."

"What color wuz dah van?" Freddy asked, impatiently.

She hesitated, then recalled. "Black! It was a black van."

"Where did it happen?" Freddy asked. "Where did dey grab her?"

Alicia pointed toward Grand Avenue. "Down the block, right after she said hello to me. The van was parked down the street."

Willie listened attentively. He recorded the conversation on a tiny Sony voice-activated dictaphone hidden in his shirt pocket. He wanted to hug the little girl, just like he hugged his own little girls when they did something good. He remained impassive, listening.

"Did yah see any strangers on dah block followin' her?" Freddy asked.

A puzzled look crept across Alicia's face. "I don't remember seeing anybody walking behind her."

Another third-grader pushed her way onto Freddy's broad lap, sharing him with her playmate. "My name is Maria. I'm Alicia's best friend." She nudged Alicia in the ribs. "Remember the big white car that kept flashing its lights, the one that ran over Isabel's new rubber ball?"

Alicia's mouth gaped open. "Now I remember," she said. "That's what a best friend is for." She smiled. "I remember a big shiny white car."

"Who wuz drivin' it? A man or woman?"

Alicia turned to Maria and shook her head. "I don't remember. Do you?"

Maria shook her head back. "No."

"Wuz dah driver wearin' an army uniform?" Freddy persisted.

The two youngsters shook their heads again.

Freddy hugged each girl with his beefy arms and gave them six boxes of Hershey's. He wrote down their names, addresses and phone numbers.

As they sped back to the reserve center to call Maccabee, Freddy said to Willie, "I knew Laura wuz straight! We've been beatin' our brains out fer over a week looking fer an eyewitness. Those commie bastards kidnapped her right under dah noses of deese kids."

"Yeah," Willie replied. "Thank God for third-graders!"

Later that evening, Kolchak booted-up his personal IBM computer at his apartment. Wearing a burgundy lounging robe with no underclothes on, the wily KGB controller pursed his lips nervously. He basked in an aura of foolhardy, self-indulgence. His fingers raced across the computer's keyboard, writing the press release that would shock the world.

Kolchak mocked the Spetsnaz' response about "big explosion in sky!" It motivated him to write his finest *kombinatsia*, his creme de la creme. A Russian proverb surged through his mind: "The devil does not come until he is called." He will be summoned with a BANG! One more week and it would be over.

He wrote the headline and subhead for the Stinger attack.

TERRORISTS SHOOT DOWN PAN AM JETLINER OVER JFK!

350 DIE IN AIR, 1,500 DIE ON GROUND AS PLANE CRASHES INTO BROOKLYN NEIGHBORHOOD!

Then, the lead. "350 passengers were killed today when a terrorist Stinger ground-to-air missile blasted a Pan Am 747 jumbo jetliner out of the sky, while it was taking-off from JFK airport in New York. In this greatest air disaster ever, 1,500 people were killed in a blazing inferno, and another 3,500 injured when the Pan Am 747 crashed into the inner city. Apartment houses and tenements burst into flames as the earsplitting roar and cartwheeling debris crushed their dwellings. The catastrophic crash cut a swath of wreckage and death across a ten mile radius like a fiery meteor falling from the sky ..."

His eyes became glazed. His imagination took hold, fantasizing about what was to come. He wrote a different slant for a second story.

"225 U.S. ARMY RESERVISTS DIE IN PAN AM JETLINER CATASTROPHE! 125 FROM TRI-STATE AREA."

He wanted to trigger an emotional response. "Families mourn the tragic loss of their loved ones -- brothers, sisters, sons and daughters, neighbors and friends who were lost on Pan Am's Flight 000. Men and women who were snuffed out in the prime of their lives, serving their country proudly as citizen soldiers. Alive one day, gone the next. Lost, irrevocably. Dead!

"Why were they flying to Europe for a NATO training exercise? The Cold War with the Soviet Union is over. In the spirit of *glasnost*, the U.S. should pull back, reduce tensions and disarm. The Russians want peace, not war. We can train our soldiers at home bases in the U.S. Remember the lessons of Viet Nam. It's time to bring our troops home.

"Let the sacrifice of these brave, patriotic American reservists not be in vain. It must never happen again. The NATO alliance is passé. It is time to stop spending billions of dollars to defend Europe, when the only thing Europeans want is a safe, nuclear free, peaceful continent. NATO is obsolete. War is obsolete. Bring our troops home NOW!"

Kolchak scanned the monitor and printed a hard copy. He read the story aloud, then edited the copy. His fingers stroked the keyboard's functional keys, cutting and pasting, omitting needless words. He read the revised copy aloud, still not satisfied.

He started another story. "An exclusive for Gretchen," he chortled, thinking this headline would be the clincher.

"CIA STINGER MISSILE SHOOTS DOWN PAN AM 747!"

He wanted his copy to be provocative. "A fatality of errors led to the tragic shoot-down of Pan Am Flight 000. According to reliable sources in the mideast, the missile used to shoot-down the Pan Am 747 with 350 people aboard, including 225 U.S. Army Reservists, was an American-made Stinger ground-to-air missile. This weapon was originally sold by the CIA to a secret organization in Pakistan for shipment to the Moslem Mujahideen guerrillas fighting the Soviets in Afghanistan. Instead, the Pakiis sold the Stinger to a Islamic fundamentalist group, who donated it to a fanatic splinter group of PLO terrorists.

"This same CIA Stinger missile was used to destroy the Pan Am jetliner in retaliation for the U.S. Navy's bombardment of Islamic martyrs in Beirut, Lebanon. When will the string of retaliatory attacks end? When will the U.S. stop interfering in the affairs of third world countries? It's time to stop subsidizing surrogate warfare."

Kolchak had another week to fine tune the copy before he transmitted it by modem to Gretchen and his network of agents. The only additional information that needed to be inserted was the correct date of the attack, the flight number and the specific number of casualties.

The KGB controller knew the success of his *kombinatsia* depended upon the Spetsnaz, how well he and the PLO gunners executed his plan. He worried about the Spetsnaz' reliability. He tried to force his personal animosity aside. A foreboding surged through his brain. He mumbled to himself, then spoke aloud. "The Spetsnaz is acting strange. Something is wrong! I must report his irregular behavior to KGB Central in Moscow."

He dressed quickly, deciding to go to the Soviet embassy, where he would transmit a secret coded message to his superiors. He pranced across the room, admiring his devious work, oblivious to the miniature listening device in the ceiling that picked-up every word he uttered.

In the apartment across the street, John Howard, dressed in a jogging suit with ear phones wrapped around his head, listened to Kolchak's words being recorded on magnetic reel-to-reel tape. He turned to his FBI partner, who listened in on another headset. "Better call the chief. This stuff is hot!"

12

Friday was the beginning of a three-day holiday weekend. Good Friday, the first night of Passover, April Fool's Day, Easter Sunday; the good times that people enjoy

Yet, a state of bedlam reined from the moment Maccabee walked into his office around eight o'clock that morning.

He strode briskly past Morgan, who was busy typing Freddy's latest breakthrough on her daily intel report. As he walked into his office, Vito Milano waylaid him in the doorway with his first calamity of the morning.

"More bad news," Vito Milano said. "Hector Sanchez is dead! Shot twice behind the ear, executed Mafia style. Two .38 slugs. His body was found in a garbage dumpster beneath the Queensboro Bridge. His wallet was in his pocket. We made a positive fix. Whoever killed him wanted us to know who he was."

Maccabee slammed his fist onto the desk. "Damn!" he swore angrily. "We needed to talk to that son-of-a-bitch. If he was the mole behind ..."

The detective droned on. "His body was dragged about eight feet before it was tossed into the dumpster. Left a messy trail of blood. He was probably executed in another location, then brought here. We're running a ballistics test to see if the same gun was used that killed your Jamaican buddy. Who knows, maybe we'll get another anonymous tip."

"What about Rosa?" Maccabee asked anxiously. He still couldn't believe she had betrayed their trust, betrayed her country.

"I didn't get to her apartment fast enough yesterday. She and her kid sister have skipped. That's a pretty swanky apartment building that she lives in. The concierge said she hurried out yesterday afternoon, carrying two overnight suitcases. Didn't say when she'd be back."

"Then she's on the run?"

"Looks like it. We're keeping her involvement under wraps until we find her. No release to the press, just minimum disclosure about Hector."

"Have you searched Rosa's apartment?"

"We have a search warrant, and we're going in soon."

"What about those kids up in the Bronx, who saw Sergeant Washington get abducted? Freddy and Willie broke that one open."

Milano grunted. "The public schools are open today to make up for snow days. Nick Diaz will check it out after the kids get home from class. We're keeping this report under close wraps, too."

Maccabee hesitated, then asked, "You can get Hector's and Rosa's social security numbers, can't you?"

"Yeah, I can get Rosa's from Captain Keller at the center. I can get Hector's, too. Why do you need them?"

126

"I like you to use your influence at Motor Vehicle and find out what make and color cars they own. There could be two cars. Better check it out with the concierge at Rosa's apartment building. He'll know what they drive. Find out what parking garage they use and double-check there, too."

Milano picked the logic up quickly. "If one is a big white car ..."

"Exactly," Maccabee replied. "It closes the loop."

"I'll stay in touch." Milano twirled and left.

Maccabee sunk into his swivel chair, propping his legs up on his desk. He stared out the window, listlessly. He grappled with thoughts that became enmeshed with other thoughts. He tried to sort them out, recalling the KISS principle. He murmured to himself, "Keep it simple, stupid."

Morgan rushed into his office, waving a typed transcript in her hands. "Before you reach for the phone again, we need to talk," she said. "I transcribed Freddy's interrogation of little Alicia and Maria. It's dynamite! The two kids identified a big white shiny car that flashed a signal to the black van. That's the closest we've come to identifying the mole in the 38th."

"I know," Maccabee replied. "I'm having Vito check out Hector's and Rosa's car. They may have owned two and ..."

Freddy stormed into the office, exuding confidence. "Whadda 'bout Rosa's car?" he asked, overhearing Maccabee's comment. "I wuz friends wid dem."

Maccabee smiled. "Remind me to give you an attaboy for yesterday. Willie, too." He looked up into Freddy's wide grinning face. He stood, and slapped him solidly on his beefy shoulder. "Good job!"

Freddy stole a look at Morgan, who smiled knowingly at him. He sucked in his beer belly, puffing up to his full six foot two inch height. "Whadda yah need to know?"

"Did Hector and Rosa own one car or two?" Maccabee asked.

"Dey each hadda car of deir own. If I think what yer thinkin', yer on dah wrong track. Rosa drove a red '88 Camaro. Hector bought a new Ford Thunderbird. It wuz black wid neat white racin' stripes."

"Are you sure?"

"Yeah, boss, I'm sure. Dey didn't own a white car."

Maccabee looked at Morgan again, stymied. "If Rosa isn't the mole, who fingered Sergeant Washington? Who followed her in a white car?"

"Maybe there's more than one mole in the 38th," Morgan speculated. "I know it sounds crazy, but what if there are two moles, both under deep cover, neither one knowing the other. If Rosa stole the CIMIC network and the TRANSCOM troop list, the second mole may have been ordered to kill Hector as a warning to Rosa."

"Why didn't he kill Rosa, too?"

"Probably wanted to, but she disappeared before he could find her." Morgan tapped her pencil nervously on the conference table. "I think I'll visit the 38th on Tuesday night. It's the unit's last admin meeting before the troops go overseas. Every officer and NCO is required to be there. I'll photograph every white car in the parking lot. Then we match cars, license plates and owners to our list of suspects ..."

"Let's hope one of them owns a big shiny white car."

To bring a semblance of order to the chaos that whirled around him, Maccabee set aside the hunt for the moles during the afternoon. He shuddered at the thought of a

Stinger attack, but set that threat aside, too. That was police work. The FBI also knew what it was doing.

He wrestled with the public relations dilemma that engulfed the Army Reserve. It was premature to go public with the latest intelligence. While it could clear up some of the mystery behind General Palmer's and Sergeant Washington's murders, it would only spook the Soviets and drive Kolchak under- ground. More time was needed to solve the conspiracy. Yet, he knew there was a dire need for damage control, not later, but now.

"I feel like my hands are shackled," he complained to Morgan, who faced him across the conference table. "We need to start rebuilding the image of the Army Reserve. What's happening in PAOland?"

"The usual," she reported. "The 77th ARCOM has the action. They're issuing daily communiqués, trying to keep the press off their backs. It's a reserve matter. The Pentagon is staying out of it. The ARCOM and the 38th are getting all the heat!"

"What about the image?"

"What image? It's so badly tarnished ..." She rolled her eyes, looking up.

Maccabee broke in. "We must do something. We need to think proactive, to plan ahead. To have a plan ready to roll out as soon as the time is right."

"Don't get your head befuddled with image, colonel," she cautioned. "We need to find the mole, and stop the bloodshed. Let's not go off on a tangent."

Maccabee didn't listen. "We can toss two balls up into the air at the same time and juggle them. We need to get organized and mobilize our PAO assets. Let's get the heavy hitters from my old News Strike Force." He scrawled three names on a sheet of paper. "These are the guys I want. Get their tails up here as fast as you can. They have contacts with media influentials all over this city."

Morgan looked at the list of names and smiled. She would have asked for the same people. Sergeant Major Robert Cord and Lieutenant Colonel Gene Daniels had retired. Sergeant Dottie Jackson had resigned to have a baby, followed by two more. They were professional P.R. practitioners and had worked for blue chip companies.

"I want them recalled to active duty, cleared for TOP SECRET on a need-to-know basis and read into the problem by early next week. We can't keep sitting here and let the image deteriorate any more. We must rebuild our credibility. Our troops are flying to Europe next week. They need to have pride in their unit. They need to hold their heads high and look everybody straight in the eye. They need to feel good about themselves again."

Maccabee stood and paced back and forth. "I want a BIG IDEA! We must give it a sense of importance. A sense of urgency." He sat down again and discussed alternative strategies. "We can leak some facts discreetly, revealing that the police are closing in on Andrew's killer ..."

"But that will scare Kolchak," she argued, trying to foresee the pitfalls. "He might hop a plane back to Moscow and then ..."

"I know," Maccabee said, thoughtfully, seeking another solution. "We could hint that the four murders are all linked together in a sinister plot, but that would have the same effect."

Morgan was not to be repulsed. "I can think of another strategy."

"What is it?"

"Do nothing," she quipped. "Let Kolchak think he's fooled us until the FBI and police unravel ..."

"Want to mail him an April Fool's Day card?"

She cast an angry look. "Don't be silly! It's the best course of action. If the media is dumb enough to tie the three murders to drugs, Kolchak will feel safe. He doesn't know the FBI has him under surveillance. He could do something stupid, and then we'll have him."

Maccabee scratched his head. "There has to be another way." He grew silent, then nodded. "I guess you're right. Okay, let's plan and wait."

His intercom buzzed. He ignored it. It buzzed again, repeatedly. Maccabee sighed, stood and stretched. He walked to his desk and pressed the button on the intercom. His secretary Judy's voice filled the room. "Gretchen Lundstrom phoning from Hilton Head, demanding to speak with you."

"Put her through," Maccabee chuckled, wondering whether Gretchen really demanded or Judy thought she was demanding. Hell, it'll be good talking to her. Morgan rose and left the room.

"Maccabee, here."

"H! love! I miss you." Her voice sounded spirited and sincere.

He laughed. "I'm beginning to miss you, too."

"Anything new on you-know-who?"

Uh, oh, his warning bell flashed on. "The police are muddling along," he answered in half-truth. He wondered if he could trust her fully. "Nothing new."

"I just had a brilliant idea."

Maccabee listened.

"Why don't you use me as bait, and lure you-know-who into a trap. Once he knows that he's compromised, we can turn him into a double agent."

As evening darkness enveloped the city and its suburbs in a cloak of security, Dave Maccabee sat at his sister's dinner table in Great Neck. They were celebrating the first night of the Jewish Passover. Lee Ackerman, acting the patriarch in a navy blue suit, sat at the head of the seder table. He wore a black yarmulke on this head and had a silk Hebrew prayer shawl wrapped around his shoulders. His two sons, Michael, fourteen, and Jeremy, twelve, sat to his right, wearing white yarmulkes and prayer shawls.

Dave sat across the table from his nephews. Seated next to him was his new cousin ... Yakov Helner Petrovich ... from Galicia and Moscow.

Dave felt awkward in his prayer shawl and white yarmulke. He grew rest- less during the formality of the long, tedious seder ceremony. He hadn't spoken Hebrew since his Bar Mitzvah, so he followed the Haggadah prayer book in English. Lee recited the passages slowly, relating to his two sons the story of the Israelite exodus from Egypt. He explained the rites and symbols, glorifying the traditions of the feast of freedom.

During the final benediction when the silver goblets were filled for the fourth time, Dave watched his Galiciana cousin with greater curiosity. His cousin seemed to share the same discomfort as the seder droned on. Yakov sat ramrod erect, reminding Dave of a military cadet sitting at attention. He fidgeted with his yarmulke on the back of his head. His watchful hooded eyes followed every movement at the table, missing nothing.

As they raised their wine goblets to make a toast, Lee's reading of the Haggadah had a biting touch: "May he who broke Pharaoh's yoke for ever shatter all fetters of oppression and hasten the day when swords shall, at last, be broken and wars ended. Soon may He cause the glad tidings of redemption to be heard in all lands, so that mankind -- freed from violence and from wrong, and united in an eternal covenant of brotherhood -- may celebrate the universal Passover in the name of our God of freedom."

"Amen," Dave said, glad that the ritual was nearing its end.

"Amen," Yakov repeated. In name of freedom, he thought, when will fighting stop? He couldn't bring his son Gregorievich back from the dead, but he could save other young lives. America must stop selling weapons to enemies of Soviet Union. His mission will shock America into submission. Then, there will be peace. On this special night, he questioned, is there another way?

They tipped their wine goblets in a final toast to God, the King of the Universe, saying, "Next year in Jerusalem." Yakov wondered if God was alive. If so, maybe he, Yakov Helner Petrovich, was God's messenger of death. He shut his eyes, momentarily, stilling the evil thoughts of impending doom.

During the dinner conversation, young Jeremy bragged about Dave's military exploits to Yakov. "Do you know that Uncle Dave was a Green Beret in 'Nam? Fought with the Montagnards in the highlands. Killed over forty VCs in one battle. His outpost was overrun, almost wiped out. Uncle Dave grabbed a machine gun and blasted his way out, and ..."

"That's enough war talk," Dave said, feeling his face reddening.

"Uncle Dave was G-5 in the 38th Civil Affairs Command," Jeremy boasted. "He developed the new CIMIC concept that the U.S. Army uses in NATO ..."

"Jeremy!" Dave cut in, reprimanding his nephew. "That's enough." He knew that his curly-headed nephew idolized him, but he felt embarrassed in front of his robust cousin. He looked at Yakov closely, sensing a kinship of arms. "Have you served in the Soviet army?"

Yakov stiffened when Jeremy mentioned the 38th Civil Affairs Command. He wondered if Dave was still in unit? Was Dave flying to Europe next week? Kolchak had identified the 38th as target. Am I on collision course with cousin Dave? I must find out. He remained impassive, masking any show of emotion.

In his search for his roots, Yakov planned to listen and learn, but to say little. His Russian accent sounded harsh, even to his own ears. The less he said, the safer his GRU identity. "Yes, like all patriotic citizens of Soviet Union, I have been soldier in heroic Soviet army."

"Infantry or armor?"

"Infantry, air assault. Mountain warfare."

"See any action in Afghanistan?"

Yakov Helner Petrovich nodded, his mind working rapidly. He stopped eating, placed his knife and fork down, and folded his hands together on the edge of the table. "I fight Moslem fanatics in mountains of Afghanistan." He looked at his two hands, clenching them as he grasped the trigger of an imaginary machine gun. "I never forget feeling of intense power, of cold steel vibrating in my hands when firing machine gun from helicopter gunship. Every muscle quivering in total unity with weapon. I still see red tracers spitting out death to target. I try to forget. Too much killing. Too much destruction. That's now behind me."

His words had a chilling edge. He felt cheated, vengeful. If Moscow had only let him raid Moslem sanctuaries in Pakistan, we could have destroyed American arsenal and liquidated rebels. My son would be alive today. We win war, not lose it. Bureaucrats were to blame.

He wanted to share his despair and war stories with cousin Dave, to tell him about the brutality and fighting he had experienced, to tell him how his son had died courageously. His cousin would understand. David was special forces, just like Yakov. Green Beret. Spetsnaz. They were the same. He and his cousin were alike in many ways. They were colonels. Elite. Someday, I find out who is better man.

For now, Yakov kept his thoughts to himself, sidestepping any more army talk. "I now teach in gymnasium. I work with Young Pioneers. Teach swimming, marksmanship, long range navigation and sports parachuting."

"Eat, eat," Jackie interjected, pushing a large serving bowl of mashed potatoes across the table. The tall, lithesome brunette arose and brought a platter of stuffed derma from the kitchen. She dished out hot servings to everyone around the table. "This is a family feast, a time to rejoice."

They ate and talked and ate some more.

"This is my first seder," Yakov said to Dave. "Your sister is good cook." He munched on a flat piece of matzo, holding it up. "To think, I never eat matzo before." He patted the white skullcap on the back of his head. "Never wear yarmulke before." He laughed. "Never celebrate being Jew before."

Dave was intrigued by his Russian cousin. "I'm surprised the communists let you come to America. Aren't they afraid you may defect?"

"I have unblemished record. I am politically reliable."

"Your father was a general in the Red Army?"

He nodded twice. "Your father, a general, too?"

A proud smile spread across Dave's face. "Dad retired as a major general. I'd like you to meet him someday. He was a helluva field commander. Fought with Patton in World War II and Abrams in 'Nam. You'll like him."

"My father was Soviet partisan hero in Great Patriotic War. He died two years ago. He is buried in Cemetery of Heroes in Moscow."

Dave wondered about his cousin's Jewish heritage. "What was your rank?"

"I was captain," he lied. "Why do you ask?"

"I didn't know the communists allowed Jews to serve as officers."

"They do not know I am Jew. I do not know myself until two years ago. My father tell me on his deathbed. He keep it secret all these years. He raise me to be model Soviet citizen." He went on to tell how his father and mother met, while fighting the Nazis in Galicia and Ukraine, how he grew up in Moscow. He stayed close to the truth about his boyhood, but guarded his military career carefully.

After awhile, Yakov's curiosity prevailed. "Have you been to Germany?"

"Yeah," Dave answered. "I spent five years on NATO exercises as a G-5, CIMIC officer. Served in Baumholder with the engineers."

131

"Are you still in Army Reserve?"

"No, I retired after twenty years. I'm in the retired reserves. I can be mobilized only in the event of a major war."

"You do not fly to Germany with reserves for any reason?" Yakov needed total reassurance that his cousin would not fly with the 38th next week.

"I'm out, a civilian. Have you been to Germany?"

Yakov harbored a deep hatred against Germany. The Nazis had murdered his Jewish mother. His country had been raped and pillaged, over twenty million people killed. "I spent time in Democratic Republic of Germany in Warsaw Pact maneuvers before Cold War ended. Nazi descendants run Germany today. They change uniforms and allegiance. Nazi swastika for Red star. They do not change their ways. They still think they are superior race. They are aggressive, dangerous people. They must be kept weak and divided. East and west."

"The West Germans are different from the ones you knew," Dave explained, trying to avoid stereotyping their national character. "The Federal Republic of Germany is a democratic parliamentary republic. The Germans that I've served with are responsible officers, who have sworn to protect their democratic constitution. The German population enjoys its freedom and high standard of living. Their democratic principles have never been stronger."

"Not true," Yakov argued. "You think Germans atone for sins of Nazi past? I have seen with my own eyes West German businessmen sell chemical warfare equipment to Iraqi generals in Baghdad. You see difference between good and bad Germans? Explain difference between Nazi fathers who used poison gas to kill six million Jews, and Nazi descendants who sell poison gas to Iraqis to kill Moslems. Explain how West German businessmen sell nuclear secrets and high technology equipment to Soviets and Third World countries. Beware, my cousin, your German allies will drag America into war of conquest. Do not trust Germans of any kind. We must keep them under jackboot!"

Dave heaved a deep sigh. "Who can we trust? We don't choose our enemies. They choose us. Who knows what friendly will turn against us, and what enemy will join our side? I share your apprehension. Every time I go to Germany, I feel a latent hostility lurking below the surface, a resurgence of German nationalism waiting to rise again." His jaw jutted out resolutely. "I fear no one. My guard is always up."

An insight flashed through Dave's mind. His cousin, there was something hard and remote in his eyes, something that he was hiding. Dave couldn't put his finger on it, but he felt it intuitively.

Later that night as Dave and Yakov said good-bye to Jackie and Lee, Dave bumped deliberately into his burly Russian cousin. He wanted to see if Yakov was as strong as he looked, to see how far he could knock him off balance. Dave was surprised. Yakov didn't budge, his center of gravity anchored to the floor. Dave bounced off Yakov like he had run into a brick wall.

"Are you all right?" Yakov asked, helping Dave regain his footing.

Dave laughed. He gripped Yakov's right hand in a firm handshake. He said to himself, "If trouble comes, I'd want cousin Yakov on my side."

At 7:00 a.m. on Easter Sunday in New Rochelle, Sergeant First Class Willie Douglas snapped photos of his two pajama clad daughters, Natalie, age six, and Nora, age eight, as they scampered into the living room, hunting for Easter eggs. Willie loved his wife Sharon and daughters. He'd miss them while he trained in Germany.

At 7:15 a.m. on Easter Sunday on the Grand Concourse in the Bronx, Sergeant Tyrone Dixon arrived at his sister Gloria's apartment, carrying a large chocolate Easter bunny that was wrapped with a big red bow for his four year old niece, who met her favorite uncle with a big hug and many kisses.

At 7:30 a.m. on Easter Sunday on Bruner Avenue in the Bronx, Sergeant First Class Doreen Franklin rolled her two teenage sons out of bed. Despite their protests, Victor, age sixteen, and Phillip, age fifteen, started dressing for their family's Easter pilgrimage to church and grandma's.

At 8:15 a.m. in Manhattan's SOHO district, Sergeant Laurie Martin crawled out from beneath her patchwork quilts onto the hardwood floor. A display manager, she had joined the reserves as a lark. Everyone said she was good at giving orders. She dressed to visit her 92-year old aunt in a nursing home.

At 8:30 a.m. in Shrub Oak in northern Westchester, Captain Tim O'Brien, company commander and CIA agent, awakened to the smell of frying bacon as his wife Susan readied their twelve-year old daughter, Colleen, and ten-year old son, Ethan, for their drive to St. Patrick's Church in Yorktown.

At 8:45 a.m. in Elizabeth, New Jersey, Major Gerhardt Brockmann awakened his wife Ursula for church. He worried about her plan to fly to Germany on her Lufthansa secretary's pass to visit him on his middle weekend. Wives never came along. Since money wasn't an obstacle, was this a smart thing to do?

At 9:00 a.m. in Medford, a suburb of Trenton, New Jersey, Captain Rudolph Krueger, studied his personal CIMIC files for the German VBK where he'd be assigned. He heard his wife Bonnie readying his two small daughters for church, knowing that he'd miss them when he went overseas.

At 9:15 a.m. in Smithtown, Long Island, Major Klaus Ludwig, ushered his German-born wife Vera and three quarreling young children into their Audi for the ride to church. Fighting, always fighting. Klaus looked forward to getting away from the squabbling kids for his two week tour of active duty.

At 9:45 a.m. in a luxury apartment on Manhattan's Sutton Place, Major Kurt Goetz glared at his slumbering, Bavarian-born wife Erika. He wished he'd never married her and stayed a grunt. Her whole life was her travel agency. She was getting in over her head. Was the big Swiss bank account worth it?

At 10:00 a.m. in another luxury apartment in mid-Manhattan, Lieutenant Colonel Wally Livingston dreaded being away from his company for two weeks. Imports had increased and the big bucks were pouring in. His Chinese wife and partner, Liu Ann, assured him that she'd manage everything, and not to worry.

At 3:00 p.m. in the South Bronx, Freddy Ventura visited his aging mother, who resided in the old neighborhood. He carried a bag full of barbecued chicken that he'd bought at the local bordega, and a bottle of Chablis white wine. He ran out of conversation after the first ten minutes, but his visit was appreciated.

At 3:28 p.m., Sergeant First Class Rosa Sanchez telephoned Freddy at his mother's apartment. "Freddy, I'm in trouble, you've got to help me."

"How'd yah know I wuz heah?"

"I've been calling all over the city. We used to date when I was single or have you forgotten?"

"It's a holiday, Rosa. Mama's two feet away. I don't want to worry her."

"Freddy, I need help. They murdered Hector! They're after me, too!" Her voice became hysterical. "The police are looking for me and Angelina. Freddy, what am I going to do?"

The big Puerto Rican felt no pity for Sanchez. Rosa had been one of his favorites, a superstar among the Hispanics in the unit. She had betrayed them all. He had no stomach for traitors. "Turn yerself in, dat's what yah should do. Tell dah cops everythin' yah know, it'll go easier on yah."

"I didn't do anything, it was Hector. I only brought home blank stationery with the 38th's letterhead and a letter to the troops from General Palmer with his signature on it. That's all. I had no idea Hector was giving it to his Marxist friends. I swear it. I had no idea he was involved in General Palmer's murder." She began to cry.

"What about dah CIMIC network. Dat wuz TOP SECRET. Why did yah steal it? You knew it wuz classified!"

"I didn't steal it!" she screamed, still sobbing. "I swear it! I never took it, only the stationery and the letter. Hector confessed that he never saw the CIMIC Network, that it must have been stolen by another agent."

"What about dah TRANSCOM troop list? I suppose yah didn't steal dat either. That yah had nothin' to do wid Laura's kidnappin' and murder?"

"I'm innocent!" she shrieked. "We had nothing to do with Laura's death."

Freddy shook his head in disbelief. "I don't believe yah."

"It's the truth. I loved Hector, you gotta understand. Please help me. I need to cop a plea. I need to protect Angelina. I was sending her to Princeton. The scandal will destroy my sister. Freddy, you've got to help."

"Let me get hold of Colonel Mac or Major Morgan and see what dey say. Probably tell yah dah same thing, to turn yerself in."

At 6:40 p.m. on Easter Sunday, Freddy Ventura escorted Rosa Sanchez into the FBI's office in lower Manhattan. Maccabee and Morgan met them at the door, along with FBI agent John Howard from the 77th ARCOM, who had been pulled off of Kolchak's stakeout for this secret meeting.

The foursome led Rosa into a large corner office in the rear of the building. Two FBI agents dressed in neat business suits stood as they entered. Detective Milano, NYPD, tugged at the window cord and dropped the venetian blinds.

Maccabee spoke in solemn tones to Rosa. "You are in deep trouble. My best advice to you is to make a complete confession, tell the FBI everything you know. It'll go a lot easier on you."

Rosa, who normally was a fastidious dresser, looked terrible. Her long black hair was disheveled. She wore no makeup. Her eyes were red-rimmed and bloodshot from crying. She looked like she had slept in the blouse and skirt she was wearing. "I'll cooperate, Colonel Mac, just like I told Freddy."

134

Vito Milano took her hand and walked her to a chair in front of a large walnut desk. He snapped a desk tape recorder to "ON." He read Rosa her Miranda rights from a small card he carried. She barely listened, a look of anxiety clouding her face.

"I want a lawyer," she said, abruptly, after Milano stopped reading.

John Howard pulled a chair up to her, hoping to get her to talk. They were almost the same age. "You're entitled to a lawyer," he said, calmly. "If you want one, Vito will see that you get one. You don't have to tell us anything, if you don't want to."

Maccabee sat on the edge of the desk, facing Rosa. "The FBI has agreed to place your sister Angelina under their witness protection program," he said. "You won't have to worry about her."

Rosa ran her fingers through her unkempt hair, distraught. "Thank you."

"I don't have time to deal with lawyers," Maccabee declared, impatiently. "Five people have been murdered, including your husband. You've turned yourself in. You'll be safe under protective custody. I need answers, Rosa. Honest answers."

"How do I know you won't break your word?" Rosa asked. "How do I know that Angelina will be safe, that I'll be safe?"

Maccabee was tight-lipped. "You have my word." He swept his hand toward the others in the room. "And that of the FBI and NYPD."

Rosa looked helplessly at Freddy, then Howard and Milano, who all nodded their assent. "If anything happens to Angelina, I'll deny everything I tell you."

"Nothing is going to happen to her," Maccabee promised. He turned to Milano and asked, "Have you picked Angelina up at the address in the Bronx?"

Milano nodded. "I pulled Nick Diaz away from his Easter Sunday dinner. He has her in custody. She's safe from any vendetta."

Maccabee tried to win her confidence. "Freddy tells me you denied stealing a copy of the CIMIC Network. Is this true? Did you or Hector take it?"

"No, I swear I never took it!" she replied.

"Did Hector visit the reserve center?" Maccabee asked. "Was he around when you had access to the classified files?"

"He never came to the center."

"Did you ever take the files home with you or to your office to type?"

"No, I never did. I only had time to do it at the center."

Maccabee remained placid, switching topics. "Does the name Dmitri Kolchak mean anything to you?"

Rosa stared, a blank expression on her face. "No, I never heard that name."

"Who did Hector report to? Who was his Marxist contact?"

"I don't know. Hector never told me. He said that I'd be insulated, that I couldn't be held as an accomplice if he was arrested."

Milano interrupted. "We searched her apartment and found a name in Hector's diary. We've brought Roberto Perez in for questioning. He's a Cuban émigré from Miami, a known Marxist. He took the fifth. We'll sweat it out of him."

Maccabee's tone hardened. "Did Hector say anything about a Stinger?"

Rosa looked puzzled. "Stinger?" she repeated, hoarsely.

"That's right," Maccabee snapped. "Stinger. What does that mean?"

Rosa shrugged. "I don't know. I think it's the name of a cocktail, brandy and creme de menthe. I had it after dinner several times."

"Come on Rosa, don't get cute with me," Maccabee said angrily. "You know what a Stinger missile is."

"That Stinger," she answered, recalling its military description. "It's an air defense, shoulder fired, ground-to-air missile. We identify it in our soldier skill qualification test."

"Did Hector ever mention it?"

"No, never. Hector was a socialist. He was afraid of guns. He preached the overthrow of government through nonviolence."

Maccabee shook his head in dismay. He stood and let FBI agent Howard proceed with the questioning. Time was running out. If Rosa was telling the truth and she and Hector didn't steal the CIMIC Network, then somebody else stole it. Damn it! We're back to where we started. Who's the mole in deep cover in the 38th? Somebody had access to the secret files, somebody Sergeant Washington suspected.

If he had only answered Laura's phone call in time. He blamed himself for her death. Time was running out. The FBI will give Rosa a lie detector test. They need to know whom Hector reported to. What if she was telling the truth ... and didn't know?

On Monday afternoon around two o'clock, in a heavily wooded section of Central Park near East 96th Street, a ten-year old black boy pocketed a five dollar bill and hurried to a tall gnarled oak tree. He placed a tiny band-aid, 1/4 by 1 1/2 inches, into a small cavity at the base of the tree trunk as he had been instructed. He looked back over his shoulder in the direction of the mysterious person who had given him the money. The person had vanished. The boy shrugged and ambled away.

Moments later, a blond pigtailed cyclist, who looked like she was 16, crashed her bicycle into the same oak tree. She reached into the hole of the tree trunk and found the band-aid. Without dislodging the tiny red ripcord, she lifted the flap of the paper wrapper, being careful not to tear it. She peeled the white plastic strip off the gauze and found a microdot that was no bigger than a pinhead. Reaching into her jacket, she pulled out a tiny cartridge, the size of a pocket calculator. She snapped the lid open, inserted the microdot and activated the high speed microfilm processor.

"Twenty seconds, do it." She extracted the original microdot, slid it back into the band-aid, sealed the outer wrapper, and tucked it into the hollow of the tree just the way she had found it. Popping a wheelie, the freckle-faced girl pedaled away. The entire action took eighty-nine seconds.

The FBI stakeout at the KGB dead letter box had paid off. The pigtailed cyclist was a special FBI agent, aged 26. She pedaled her bike rapidly to a nearby FBI mobile van, which was parked inconspicuously on Fifth Avenue.

She handed the cartridge to a bespectacled FBI agent in a gray sweatsuit. He took the high speed microfilm from her and placed it on a Kodak photo enlarger inside the van. Within minutes, he read the secret KGB message and telephoned the intercept to the FBI's command post downtown.

The terse message was a KGB execution order. "Target: Pan Am Flight 120. April 9. Attack and destroy!"

13

On Monday, Maccabee's lunch was delicious, delightful ... and all Gretchen. She had flown into La Guardia earlier that morning, invited Maccabee to her apartment around noon and flew into his arms as he walked through the door into the foyer. It was pure sex from the moment he saw her. Animal sex. Pure unadulterated lust.

Maccabee struggled to control his emotions, which pounded away with unexpected fury. He became obsessed, overwhelmed by the sensuality of her craving body clinging to his. Gretchen's blue Nordic eyes and coquettish smile flared out brazenly, enticing him, exciting him.

"I've missed you so!" Gretchen cried.

Dave gasped. She wore a powder blue negligee, its flimsy see-through veil exposing her freshly showered, marvelously scented body. He gazed into the cleavage of two voluptuously rounded pink breasts, a flat tummy and tufts of soft, blond curly hair beckoning below.

She stood on her tiptoes, yanking his safari jacket off by the sleeves. She ripped at the buttons on his shirt, clawing to get to his bare skin. She kissed him feverishly.

Dave cast aside all restraint. "I've missed you, too," he cried. He ran his hands inside her negligee, feeling the satin finish of her bare skin against his fingertips. He planted a fiery kiss on the softness of her neck, then slid down onto her pink, titillating breasts. His tongue indulged in a hundred ravishing fantasies.

Gretchen tugged violently at his belt buckle and zipper with both hands, prying them loose. She tore his pants open and plunged her hand deep into his jockey shorts. She gasped as her fingers caressed his hot throbbing shaft. "I love you, I adore you," she cried-out, wantonly. "Make love to me now!"

Dave swept Gretchen up into his arms, tripping on his trousers that had fallen to his ankles. He stepped out of his pants, naked from the waist down and carried her into the bedroom. They plunged onto the edge of Gretchen's heart-shaped bed, clutching, grabbing, embracing.

They kissed each other breathlessly, murmuring erotic words of longing. They ran their hands over each other's glowing bodies, inflaming each other. Suddenly Dave felt Gretchen slip out from under him, climb on top and straddle his loins. He laid back as she guided his joystick into her warm, juicy lovebox, rising to meet her movements.

A look of ecstasy glowed on her radiant face. She sat erect in the saddle, mounted proudly on his manhood like a jockey mounts a thoroughbred race horse. She cantered ever so slowly before the grandstand. Her palms reached down onto his hairy chest, pushing in perfect rhythm, reining him in to follow her commands. Her pointed breasts rose and fell in perfect unison with each gyration. Her blue eyes seemed to mellow on each downward thrust, a woman confidently in love.

She groaned, uttering gasps of joy. "I love you, I love you, my *liebe*!" She quickened the pace, moving into a slow gallop. She was a woman in control, dominating her man like only a German woman knows how.

She shut her eyes, blissfully. Her groans came more rapidly. "Not yet," she pleaded. "It feels so good, keep moving, oh-h-h-h-h ..." She felt like a raging inferno, hurtling toward a rapturous climax.

Suddenly, she felt herself being lifted up and away, being tossed out of the saddle. "Don't stop!" she cried out in dismay. She felt stranded, left up in the air in a vacuum, abandoned in a sea of unfulfilled emptiness.

"Dave-y-y-y!" she shrieked, as he flipped her onto her back. He climbed on top of her, re-entering her dripping sluiceway in lustful frenzy. She rose to meet him, wrapping her heels tightly into the small curvature of his back. He was in command. She didn't care. "Oh, my lov-v-v-v."

They moved quicker, faster, humping like a jackhammer.

Quicker, faster.

"My lov-v-v-v, I'm coming, I'm coming, I'm ..."

The floodgates burst open. Love poured forth.

They lay together, exhausted. Their sweating bodies glistened in the dim artificial light. They fell asleep in each others arms.

When they awoke later that afternoon and snacked in her dining room, she talked about Hilton Head and the environmental debate that was raging there. It was a good story, the kind that would get national coverage. As she told Dave about it, she knew he was only half-listening. He tried to be attentive, but his mind kept wandering.

After awhile, she brought up the subject she really wanted to talk about. Dmitri Kolchak. "I can't understand why it's taking the FBI so long to crack your super spy conspiracy," she finally said. "If Dmitri Kolchak is the master spy you think he is, I have a brilliant idea how to trap him."

Dave attempted a grin. There was no way to restrain this woman. "Okay, Gretchen, what's your brilliant idea?"

"The best way to catch a thief is with another thief. Right?"

Dave nodded.

"Why don't we lure Dmitri into a trap? He trusts me implicitly. He thinks he controls me like a puppet on a string. Except this puppet pulls her own strings."

Dave watched her with utter amazement. She could be so feminine one moment, so dynamic and aggressive the next. "Keep going," he said. "What strings are you talking about."

"Mine, silly." She smiled confidently, imitating a puppeteer pulling on strings.

She continued, "I can tell Dmitri that simple little me blundered into another closely guarded military secret at the 38th, a secret that's so hush hush, I've been sworn not to reveal it. It's bound to peak his curiosity. Since the FBI is bugging his phone lines at home and at his office, they can record any report he makes to Moscow. We'd catch him in a ironclad act of espionage, confront him with the evidence and turn him into a double agent. He's a very proud man, a classic overachiever. He can't afford to go back to Moscow in disgrace. It would be the end of him."

Dave's grin broadened into a wide smile. This is one smart lady, he thought, maybe too smart. "It could work," he said. "What closely guarded military secret do you suggest? Do you plan to invent one?"

"The military secret that you've been running a smokescreen on ... every time I bring it up. The new technology that the CIMIC operators will use in Germany to bypass the normal NATO chain of command."

A watchful, steadfast look crept into Dave's eyes. He listened.

"You don't have to tell me everything," she pleaded, "just enough to whet Dmitri's appetite. You know, a general description of the equipment, how it works, who transmits the secret data, who receives it."

She saw the look of alarm filter across his face. "Trust me on this one. Once you've turned him, you'll learn all you need to know about General Palmer's murder, about his entire KGB spy network in the U.S."

A sudden grimness overtook Dave. "I'll have to think about it," he said. "If we serve up a military secret, the Pentagon will have to okay it first." He forced a grin. "We have no intention of sharing our CIMIC plans with the Russians."

On Tuesday evening around 7:30, Maccabee pulled Lieutenant Colonel Wally Livingston out of the 38th commander's staff meeting, where final preparations were being made for the unit's overseas departure. They made their way up the back staircase to an empty classroom on the second floor. Maccabee closed the door and straddled a folding chair. He faced his friend and confidant, trying to mask the seeds of doubt running through his mind. He spoke in a solemn, deliberate tone.

"What did you do during the day Sergeant Washington was killed?" he asked. "How did you spend it? What specific tasks did you work on?"

Livingston, who was dressed in a dark pinstriped business suit, sat down. He crossed his legs casually. "Specific tasks?" he repeated in a friendly manner.

"I know we've been through this before, but tell me again. What secret material were you working with? How often did you visit the G-2 section? Who was there? Did you see anything strange? What was Laura doing?"

The affable deputy turned on his charm. Sincerity pierced the air. "I've searched my memory, over and over," he confided. "It was a quiet day, everything routine. I worked on my CIMIC briefing. I logged it out in the morning, back in at the end of the day. Goetz and Brockmann were both here on mandays, preparing briefings for their CIMIC teams."

"Did they log their material back in at the same time you did?"

Livingston thought for a moment, running his fingers through his curly blond hair. "Not exactly."

"What do you mean?"

"I didn't see too much of Brockmann. I worked upstairs all day in the G-5 section. Brockmann spent most of the time working by himself. He said he needed to be alone so he could think without any distractions. I think he used the OER room downstairs."

"Did anybody see him there?"

Livingston shrugged. "Don't know. I was busy. Brockmann is a good field grade officer. If I have to spend my time looking over his shoulder, I'll replace him."

"What about Goetz? What was he working on? Did he log out with you?"

Livingston shook his head. "He was all over the place, in and out a couple of times. Worked across the hall most of the day. Logged out ten minutes before me."

Maccabee gripped the top of his folding chair tightly, his knuckles glinting white. "Did you guys have lunch together?"

"Nope, I brown-bagged it. Ate in. I think Brockmann did, too." He smiled, winking at Maccabee. "Goetz took his usual two hour executive lunch."

"Two hours?" Maccabee edged forward intently.

"Well, not exactly. I didn't keep tabs on him. You know how he is, fast tracked, ticket punched in the right places, always playing the angles."

Maccabee smiled. He was genuinely fond of Kurt Goetz, a hard-charger like himself. Goetz and Brockmann had both distinguished themselves in combat as platoon leaders with the First Cav' in 'Nam. Yet, they were so different. Goetz was ambitious, a compulsive ladder-climber, a swinging bachelor who had finally met his match in a not-too-happy marriage. Brockmann was steadfast, a solid hitter who could be counted on to get the job done. He had married after returning from 'Nam, and was a dedicated family man.

"How's Jerry's business doing?"

"Okay," Livingston scoffed, disparagingly. "The way Brockmann tells it, he's barely keeping ahead of his creditors. The competition is starting to overwhelm him."

Maccabee rose, unlimbering his tall frame. "What about your business, Wally? How are you doing?"

"Couldn't be better. The money is rolling in, more than we ever expected." He stood, grinning smugly. "I hate the thought of being away for two whole weeks. Liu Ann is good with customers, but my key accounts only want to talk to me."

Maccabee hesitated, as he walked toward the door. He tried to focus on the reality of the situation, setting friendship aside. There had to be an answer to the shadowy maze that kept engulfing him. He stared at Wally and spoke tight-lipped. "Somebody saw something or did something that alarmed Sergeant Washington. That's why she tried to call me. Twice. She saw something that blew someone's cover, something that cost Laura her life."

Livingston inhaled, matching Maccabee stride for stride as they walked down the corridor toward the G-5 section. "As much as I hate to say it," Livingston said, almost too innocently. "It has to be either Brockmann or Goetz. One of them has to be the mole. I can't figure it out any other way."

They walked inside the G-5 section. Gerhardt Brockmann and Kurt Goetz sat at their steel gray desks with their feet propped up on their desktops. They stopped talking and swiveled to a more erect position. Both men had taken off their business suit jackets, which hung on a corner coat rack. Their long sleeve shirt cuffs were rolled up two turns, their ties loosened.

Maccabee sat on the edge of Brockmann's desk with a determined look on his face. "Jerry, we've had a breakthrough on Sergeant Washington's murder, an eye witness who can identify the car that flashed a signal to Laura's killers. I'm searching for the motive. Laura discovered something. I think there's a Russian mole under deep cover hiding inside this unit."

Brockmann jerked to his full, robust height, a startled look flooding across his face. "Come on, boss! You can't think it's me."

Livingston eyes widened in surprise. "Whose car did they identify?" he asked, breathlessly, looking back at Goetz, who seemed uneasy.

"The police are working on it," Maccabee replied, turning back toward Brockmann and glaring at him. "I want to know what you were specifically doing here on the day Laura was murdered?"

Brockmann became agitated and emotional. "Come on, boss," he rasped, excitedly. "You know what I was doing here." He hesitated, then ran his palm across his anguished face. "I was doing this, that and the next thing."

He jumped to his feet, waving his hands high in the air. "Here, I'll show you. Let me show you what I was doing." He walked to the file cabinet and pulled the top drawer open. He flipped through several file folders, then turned around red-faced. "Shit, Willie's got it in his safe."

Maccabee tried to suppress a laugh, but couldn't. Brockmann brought his nervous excitement under control. He acted like many first generation German-Americans. They were loyal Americans, two-hundred percent. Maccabee couldn't visualize him committing any act of treachery.

"Sit down," Maccabee said. "Nobody is accusing you of anything."

The big German flopped into his chair, still concerned. "I have a big problem. My wife wants to fly to Germany while we're overseas. What am I gonna do? Ursula has her heart set on it. She's a secretary at Lufthansa and gets a free pass. I've tried to talk her out of it, but she's stubborn and won't listen. I know we're not supposed to bring our wives, but ..."

"If she lives on the local economy, there shouldn't be a problem," Maccabee said, glancing at Livingston.

The amiable G-5 nodded. "Better make sure her visit doesn't interfere with your work," Livingston said. "If you're out partying every night, you won't be worth a damn."

"She wants to come on the middle weekend. She's promised to keep a low profile. It's our money, so what the hell. One problem after the other."

"That's the least of our problems," Maccabee snapped. "If you guys could only remember. Something triggered Laura to call me. Try to remember. Anything unusual?" He swung around toward Goetz and asked. "You came in unexpectedly. You weren't scheduled for a manday. How come?"

"I missed a few Tuesday nights, flying to Geneva on business," he answered. "I practiced on the XL-5 for two hours during the early morning so I'll know how to use it when I get to Europe. I worked on my CIMIC briefing during the rest of the day."

Maccabee felt a strong bond to the two infantrymen. Livingston had to be wrong in his conclusion. Somebody else in the center had to be the mole. "It's so damn complex," he muttered.

"Everything was a lot simpler in 'Nam," Goetz said, attempting a grin. "I've seen guys shot, blown apart, decapitated, garroted, stabbed, bombed, napalmed. This is nothing." He paused, trying to reassure Maccabee. "We muddled through it there. We'll muddle through it here. Somehow, we'll get through it."

"Shit!" Brockmann added. "Things were complex there, too. Christ, we didn't know who the Goddamned enemy was."

"Yeah," Goetz agreed. "I couldn't tell. I was up at Ia Drang in the central highlands." He glanced at Maccabee. "Where were you? You were up in Laos with the Montagnards playing Daniel Boone, weren't you?"

Maccabee nodded.

"Not the way I heard it," Brockmann laughed. "Sounded more like Davey Crockett at the Alamo, where you guys fought to the last man."

"You at least knew who the enemy was up there," Goetz continued without hesitation. "Man, we were down in the Drang River Valley. Christ, when we'd sweep the Goddamn villages, I didn't know who the enemy was half the time. Couldn't tell the difference between the VCs and the peasants. Hell, the enemy was anybody who pointed a gun at me or charged in my direction. You'd shoot first, ask questions later. That's the only way we survived."

"Remember our first mission with the Air Cav'?" Brockmann asked, "When we flew into the Drang Valley and landed on a VC headquarters? Man, I was scared shitless."

"Me too," Goetz recalled. "I was so damned scared, I was yelling go, go, go to my guys as we came out of that chopper at the LZ. I almost shit in my pants. I couldn't let on that I was more scared than they were. There was more damn lead flying through that killing zone, most of it inbound, coming right at us."

"Shit, I remember that day. It's a day I'll never forget," Brockmann said. "I didn't know which way to crawl. We had lead coming at us from every direction. I looked up and saw muzzle flashes coming down from the top of this tree. I never did see the sniper, only the gun flashes from his AK-47. I tried to turn, but it was too late. That's how I got hit."

Goetz tipped his head back, grinning. "At least you saw where it came from. My platoon caught it from three sides. It was like a hornet's nest. There was no way you could hide from that stuff. Never did see the enemy. Stood up once in five foot elephant grass, trying to pull my men together and that was it. Man, I was down, bleeding bad. It's amazing we ever got out of there alive."

"It was a crazy war," Brockmann insisted. "Who's the enemy? How many times did we ask that question?"

"It was a critical problem," Maccabee said. "Every time we fortified a hamlet, we never knew if the peasants supported us or if they were VC infiltrators or VC sympathizers reconning our positions."

"Recon, hell," Brockmann stated, turning to Goetz. "Remember that day our company swept the hamlets near Bong Son and that woman came running out of her hooch with a grenade tucked under her skirts, what were they called?"

"*Ao dai*," Goetz answered, "That's the name for the whole outfit. Tunic, split skirts and pantaloons."

"She tossed the grenade and wiped out my third squad. Good troopers, every one of them."

"Yeah," Goetz replied, sarcastically. "If your troops weren't so busy burning down the hooches, maybe she wouldn't have thrown a grenade at you."

"Yeah, screw you!" Brockmann swore, grinning.

"Hey number one, GI," Goetz mimicked in a high pitched Vietnamese accent. "Me not VC, me not VC!" His voice returned to normal. "Then she reaches under her *ao dai* and pulls out a grenade." He paused, his voice growing somber. "I saw it happen twice. We wasted the broad so damned fast, she looked like chopped meat."

"That's right," Brockmann agreed. "You waste 'em quick."

"Life was simpler then," Goetz grumbled, lapsing into his current miseries. "My goddamned wife. I hardly see Erika anymore. She's a pain in the ass. She won't do what I tell her to do. That damned company of hers, she spends more time traveling to Europe than here in New York. One problem after another. What a mess! I should have stayed single."

"You sound like you're headed for divorce," Brockmann said.

"Yeah," Goetz growled. "I wish it was that simple."

Livingston sat behind the large desk by the window, seemingly amused by the entire conversation. "It's not that difficult to get divorced. My first marriage was a disaster. That's when I made all my mistakes. Now that I'm married to Liu Ann, it's one happy love affair. Life couldn't be nicer."

Goetz brooded. "Okay, how do I get rid of my wife?"

Brockmann chimed in. "You heard the man. Stop bitching about her. If you can't live happily with her, then get a good divorce attorney."

"Yeah, but how is it going to look on my record?" Goetz whined. "My ticket is punched. I'm the right pedigree, I've graduated from the right schools, had the right jobs, commanded the right units, got the right medals. Shit, man, you get divorced, that don't look good. You know how General Kelley is. He's a good Irish Catholic. He doesn't believe in divorce, so I've got to put up with all my wife's shit. All her problems. There's no way out."

Young Captain Rudolph Krueger had walked into the room, laden down with several folders of the CIMIC force structure for the German Territorial Army. He dumped them onto his desk, listening.

He finally interrupted. "With all due respect, sirs," he said, intently, "we have a lot of work to do tonight before I fly out with the advance party tomorrow. Can we shelve the war stories and personal problems and get on with business?"

Maccabee's eyes fastened on his comrades. They belonged to an elite brotherhood of arms. They had shared a moment of destiny, where brave men put their lives on the line to protect one another. A short terrifying moment in time that can never be recaptured in civilian life, that can never be truly understood by someone who has not experienced combat. These were his men, his team. Yet, Maccabee knew deep in his gut that one of them was a traitor.

Outside in the fenced in parking lot, Major Morgan parked her beige VW van in a designated spot for visitors. She stepped quickly out of the van, scanning the lot. She carried a Nikon camera, which had a compact strobe flash attached on top.

Dressed in BDUs, she walked through the rows of parked vehicles, searching for white cars. It didn't take long. She spotted a new '88 El Dorado Cadillac and photographed it from the front, then the rear. She pulled out a notepad from her top pocket and jotted down its license plate number.

She spotted another white car, a sleek '87 white Ferrari sports car that was parked in the commander's reserved parking spot. She photographed it and jotted down its license number. Then she spotted two more shiny white cars, parked side by side near the back fence. One was an '87 BMW, the other an '84 Buick. She snapped photos of them, too.

That was it. Four shiny white cars. The rest were cars and trucks of various makes and shades, solids and two-tones. They didn't matter.

She walked inside the heavy green doors of the center, signed the visitor's log and walked toward the G-2 intelligence section cage. She entered, sensing a feeling of gloom that pervaded the area. Sergeant Laura Washington's name plate was missing from her empty desk.

"I have a list of four cars and their license plate numbers that I need to identify," she said to Captain Dressler, who stood at attention when she walked in. She handed him the sheet of paper.

The young G-2 captain checked the list against a master log.

Minutes later, Morgan walked out of the center with her list of confirmed suspects. She planned to process her film the first thing in the morning. Then Freddy would show the photos to the Puerto Rican third graders after school to see which car they could identify.

She climbed back into her van, shuddering at the thought of what she had to do. She culled over her list of suspects. She dreaded telling Maccabee that each suspect was an officer, a close personal friend.

Morgan forced back the tears brimming in her eyes, recalling the creed they all swore to follow. "Duty, honor, country!"

14

The next morning about eight, Maccabee stood on the steps of Pan Am's international terminal at JFK. He watched the advance party of the 38th check into the passenger departure area.

Each of the reservists wore civilian clothes and carried a civilian passport, maintaining a low military profile to avoid giving a skyjacker an obvious target. Each reservist carried two cumbersome duffel bags to the weigh in scale. One contained a steel helmet, field equipment, uniforms and supplies; the other bag contained a gas mask and bulky MOPP gear, the protective chemical warfare clothing that would be worn during the NATO exercise. They all packed their army dog tags, ID cards and orders into their duffel bags for safekeeping.

Colonel Herb Zimmermann, the 38th's acting commander, walked back to where Maccabee was standing. "Thanks for seeing us off, but it really wasn't necessary." He shook hands, turned, and pointed at the troops. "All present and accounted for, except one." He counted off their names: "Colonel Cherniak, Captain Dressler from G-2; Captain Krueger from G-5, Captain Keller and Sergeants Brown, Carter and Jones from G-1." He grimaced, when he mentioned the last name. "One NCO from G-5 is absent: Sergeant First Class Sanchez."

"The FBI is interrogating Rosa downtown," Maccabee said, quietly. "She's cooperating. There's a good chance the Pentagon will authorize her flight to Germany with the rest of the unit on Saturday. Nobody in the unit knows that she's been arrested, and we're trying to keep it that way. We have to flush out the Soviet spy, wherever he's hiding. She's our best decoy."

"How serious do you think the Stinger threat is, Dave?"

"Very serious. It could be a Stinger, it could be a bomb. We're not taking any chances. That's why Big Ed was pulled off Saturday's flight. Contino is in charge of airport security at JFK. The Pentagon wants him on the ground, to establish an emergency command post."

"If it was my decision, I'd cancel Saturday's flight, close down the airport. But I was overruled."

Maccabee put his arm over Zimmermann's shoulder, ushering the worried commander into a corner of the promenade, where they could not be overheard. "That was my first reaction, too. Cancel the flight, send our troops down to Philly and fly them out on the next MAC military airlift flight."

Zimmermann's face flushed with anger. He shuddered, wanting to pull back, fearing that the situation was out of control. "It is the only sensible thing to do. Why is the Pentagon keeping the threat a Goddamn secret? We should alert everyone that's booked on the flight. They should be given a choice, at least told their lives may be in jeopardy." Pangs of conscience tore through him. "Christ, Dave, we're playing with hundreds of people's lives. We have one hundred and twelve troops aboard that flight. They may all be killed!"

"It's not our decision. It went all the way to the top, to the FBI and to the Pentagon. Terrorists can't be allowed to close down JFK. It would be like closing down our international airline system, It's a damned if we do, damned if we don't strategy. A lot of jurisdictions are involved. All the appropriate agencies have been alerted: the FBI, Federal Aviation Agency, Pan Am, the mayor's office, the NYPD, NYFD, even the Coast Guard."

"What about the CIMIC teams from Kansas City and Saint Paul that connect with Flight 120?"

"They're being diverted, rescheduled through flights out of Washington."

Zimmermann pressed closer to Maccabee, his reddened face inches away, almost snarling. "That's *selective* alert! If the plane gets blown away, who takes the fall? How do you explain who lives, who dies?"

Maccabee took two steps backwards, giving himself some breathing space. He shook his head, resolutely. "The commander-in-chief made the decision. Keep the LOCs, the lines of communication, open. They may be interdicted in a real war situation, but some CIMIC teams will get through."

"But this is supposed to be a war game, not a real war."

Watching Pan Am's flight taxi out of the holding area, Maccabee left the observation balcony and walked back onto the sidewalk, thinking. The CIMIC advance party was on its way safely. God willing, the main group would follow on Saturday.

He walked toward the International Airlines Arrival building that housed the international flag carriers. Stopping at an outdoor pay phone, he called ahead to Ed Contino who answered the phone on its first ring. "All cool at your end?"

"It's a go! We checked the plane out from top to bottom, electronic sniffer, dogs, the works. Everything's A-OK. Come on up. Tell the guard at the desk to call me, and I'll come down and give you a personal escort."

Hanging up, Maccabee walked another block to the Port of Authority Operations Center and control tower. He looked up anxiously each time a jetliner thundered overhead on takeoff. Walking into the building, he stopped at the reception desk, where he signed the logbook, was issued a visitors ID pass, and waited while the guard called upstairs. Five minutes later, he rode the elevator up to the fifth floor under Contino's personal escort.

Big Ed was an amicable sort. He was 37, six feet five inches tall, weighed about 220 pounds, had black wavy hair and bushy eyebrows. He was a low key, non-assuming type of professional manager, a rising star in the 38th. He led Maccabee into his large corner window office that looked out onto JFK's aeronautical area and four major runways.

Maccabee glanced at the big map behind Contino's desk, which showed an outline of the restricted perimeter road network that connected the eighty two airlines, tenants, buildings and cargo area at the international airport. A map of Brooklyn, Queens and Long Island was mounted on the adjacent wall. Two security men in civilian attire worked on a series of large scale grid enlargements of the local neighborhoods that lay along JFK's flight paths.

"We're setting up a command post here in my office and one in the control tower above us. We'll have all of the key players in one room at the same time if we need a fast decision."

"What protective measures are you taking?"

"The first step was to confirm the authenticity of the threat. Now that we know it's credible, we've beefed up internal security. On Saturday, we'll conduct intensive inspections at all passenger screening points, and at the nine major screening points that lead to the aeronautical area. We can't lock the place up like a drum. There's too much happening during peak traffic hours with all the wide-body aircraft arriving and departing. Each airline is responsible for its own security. We're in contact with the FAA and Pan Am. If it's a bomb threat, we should be able to sniff it out. If it's a Stinger, well ... we've never had that kind of threat before."

"What help are you getting?"

"All we can get," Contino replied. "The minute the FBI warned that an aircraft might get blown up over New York City, we had everybody and their brother-in-laws involved. We're getting maximum support from the NYPD." He pointed to a large red-lined trace on the map surrounding the airport. "The NYPD will bottle up the area and flood the streets with blue suiters. How they guard against a terrorist attack from one of a thousand different rooftops, ... well, it defies the imagination."

Maccabee turned away from the map and watched a TWA jetliner takeoff on a nearby runway. He turned back to Contino and the map. "What about chopper support? How many choppers can the NYPD provide?"

"I'm not sure. They have three or four over at Floyd Bennett Field, observation types. The Coast Guard has two large choppers at Governor's Island. There are a lot of rooftops, sand dunes and marshes out there, a helluva lot of turf to cover."

Looking at his friend's worried face, Maccabee knew that Big Ed would probably get an ulcer before the weekend passed. The big man tried to hide his distress, but he wasn't convincing. "I hate playing defense. We must take the initiative."

Contino sat on the edge of his desk, stroking his chin. "I have one or two hole cards to play. I just don't know ..."

"We do have one advantage," Maccabee confided, "a small one, but it's still an advantage."

"Advantage? What kind of advantage?"

"We know that an unknown person or persons are out there on the perimeter, about to perpetrate a mass murder. What they don't know is that we know. For what it's worth, that's our edge."

On his way back to Manhattan, Maccabee drove past the MP sentry gate at Fort Totten, the home of the 77th U.S. Army Reserve Command. He parked his Chevy Blazer in a small parking lot behind the ARCOM headquarters building and walked briskly across the wooden bridge into the operations center.

Waving at a few familiar faces, he poked his head into Major Claude LaSalle's office, the assistant chief of staff for air support.

"Claude, have you been briefed that I'll need air support on Saturday?"

The stocky, balding pilot, dressed in an aviator's jump suit, looked up from his paperwork. "Colonel Maccabee, how are you, sir?" LaSalle rose and shook hands with his old boss. "Good to see you." He stood erect alongside his desk, a serious look on his face. "Our CG, the commanding general, got the word from General Kelley yesterday. I've got two Hueys standing by at Stewart. The flight plan is laid on for 10:00 a.m. sharp."

Maccabee looked at the flight assignment board. "Who's piloting?"

LaSalle rubbed his thinned, balding head. "Since you're involved, I've got Huey One. Chief Johnson is co-pilot. Posner and Tomkins will fly the second aircraft. We'll touchdown at Totten at 10:45 and standby. What's our next destination?"

"Floyd Bennett Field. Better call ahead and make arrangements to refuel there. Once we get airborne, we're going to need maximum loitering time."

"Anything else?"

"Yeah," Maccabee said, feeling his energy surge. "I want two M-60 machine guns bolted down in each of the choppers, plus full boxes of ammo. We'll also need eight sets of high-powered binoculars. Better requisition four M-16 rifles with scopes and plenty of ammo, too."

The pilot's eyes widened in surprise. "What kind of drill is this?"

"It's not a drill. It's the real thing."

Wheeling the Chevy Blazer into his parking garage on East 26th Street about two o'clock in the afternoon, Maccabee flipped the keys to the parking attendant. "I'll need the Blazer at seven sharp on Saturday morning. Army business." Ten minutes later, he rode the elevator up to his agency. He found Major Morgan agonizing over reams of computerized intel reports. She jotted down a summary of a recent highlight that was consistent with operational necessity. She looked up as Maccabee walked over to her desk.

She tapped her hand lightly as she spoke. "My best guess is that they've compartmentalized their spy operation. They've isolated each activity. Sergeant Sanchez confessed all that she knows, which isn't very much. Her husband evidently manipulated her. If the police could have only caught him before he was murdered." She shook her head in dismay and went on. "The FBI gave Rosa a lie detector's test. She didn't steal the CIMIC Network proposal or copy it."

"Then who did?"

"That's not all," she continued. "There's a new complication."

Maccabee was sorry he had interrupted. If he could only curtail his impatience. "Go ahead. What else is there?"

"Lieutenant John Howard called from the FBI. They've been bugging Kolchak's apartment and overheard him talking to himself and ..."

Maccabee interrupted again. "Talking to himself, they bugged him talking to himself. Christ, the next thing you know, they'll be able to bug what a person is thinking."

Morgan chuckled.. "They came pretty close. He was mumbling whatever thoughts were running through his head. Stream of consciousness. He was complaining about a Spetsnaz who is acting ..."

148

Maccabee broke in again. "Spetsnaz?"

"Yes, sir."

"Here in New York?"

"I think so."

"Holy Christ!" Maccabee stood, jamming his hands into his pockets. He walked in a small circle, his anxiety mounting.

"The FBI asked for background information on Spetsnaz forces, which I forwarded to them."

"They don't operate in the U.S.," Maccabee snapped. "I've read about unconfirmed sightings in Alaska, but they haven't been proved." He sat down again, his eyes probing intently. "Do you think there's any connection with the Stinger threat?" He knew the answer before Morgan replied.

"It's a strong possibility."

Maccabee's mind rushed ahead, saying what he and Morgan already knew. "They're GRU. Soviet army intelligence. They operate like our Rangers and Green Berets. They operate in teams of four, eight and twelve."

They stared at each other, saying nothing.

Maccabee tried to delve beneath the surface for an explanation. Suddenly, he snapped his fingers, coming to a conclusion. "The bomb threat is a deception. Those bastards are really planning to shoot down a jetliner! Somehow, they've smuggled a Stinger missile into the country. I can feel it intuitively."

He stood, his jaw jutting out stubbornly. "We must follow our instincts. If a Spetsnaz team has targeted the 38th ..."

Morgan walked out from behind her desk, clasping a notepad in her hand. "Here's what Kolchak said." She looked at her notes and read aloud. "The Spetsnaz is acting strange. Something is wrong. I must report his irregular behavior to Moscow Central."

Maccabee rubbed the scar on his chin. "Did the FBI monitor his phone or intercept any computer messages he may have sent by modem?"

"They're bugging everything. He left his apartment shortly after making the comment. The FBI followed him to the Soviet Embassy, where he must have secretly transmitted his message."

"The one saving grace I remember from 'Nam is that the other side is usually just as screwed up as ours, maybe more so." Maccabee straddled the cane back chair, swiveling it in an arc to face Morgan, who was pacing back and forth.

He became angry as another thought bubbled to the surface. "The Spetsnaz could be the hitman, the assassin who murdered General Palmer, René Lemoine, Hector Sanchez and what's-his-name, the Jamaican?" He paused, then continued. "If Kolchak is the brains, the KGB controller, then your hunch about the operation being compartmentalized is correct."

Morgan's face became livid, thinking about Andrew Palmer. She sat down again at her desk, drumming her fingers nervously. "If the 38th is targeted," she said, "the sleeper agent had inside information about the flight plans of the unit. How else could the KGB know the flight number?"

Maccabee sat across the desk from his harried associate. She looked tired, her hair stringing down over one eye, unlike her fastidious self. He moistened his lips, then asked, "Who was involved in getting the airline tickets? We don't tell the troops the specific flight number until the day of departure. That's confidential information. How many people knew?"

"There's Rudy Kane at Fort Hamilton's travel desk, he's reliable. Then, the admin section at the 38th," she said, brushing her hair back. "Captain Keller and Sergeants Brown, Carter and Jones flew out with the advance party. They can be trusted."

"Nobody is above suspicion," Maccabee cautioned. "How can you be so sure?"

"I just know. It's a feeling a woman can have."

He sat quietly staring into space, reflecting. "How can an outsider find out what flight you're on?"

"I checked with Colonel Contino a little earlier today. It's not too difficult. All you need is one airline ticket agent on your payroll. Any airline will do. They tap into each other's computer reservation system on a routine basis. They're always swapping information with one another."

Maccabee probed further, knowing that there had to be an answer. "What about travel agents, they all have computers?"

"It's not the same thing. They can only punch up reservations that they make. Nothing else. They use the SPNR system."

"What's an SPNR?"

"It stands for Secure Passenger Name Record. Every name and reservation is protected. Can you imagine what mayhem could occur if a computer freak could penetrate the system and destroy or change the reservations?"

Maccabee had his answer. He said, simply. "Then the mole had a friend at the airlines."

Freddy sat on the cement stoop of the tenement building on Grand Avenue in the West Bronx, waiting for the neighborhood kids to return home from school. He flipped through the pages of the *Daily News*, checking the ball scores and racing results. Dressed in a brown flight jacket, gray sweatshirt and jeans, he fit easily into the neighborhood.

He looked up as little Alicia Alvarez turned the corner, carrying an armful of textbooks under her arm. She headed in his direction without noticing him. The precocious third-grader seemed to be the leader of her small group of girlfriends, who flanked her on both sides. She talked animatedly to each of them, enjoying their company. Her pigtails bounced against the collar of the open blue wool coat. She suddenly spotted Freddy, who rose to his full height as she approached. Her little mouth gaped open dramatically in surprise.

"Hi!" Freddy said. "Rememba me?"

Alicia strutted up to him, acting haughty like an actress she had seen on TV. "Where's your uniform?" she asked, putting on airs for her girlfriends to see.

"I'm not on duty," Freddy answered, beaming his let's-be-friends smile. He sat down on the chilly stoop, folded the newspaper on its horizontal fold and set it aside. He reached into his jacket pocket and pulled four Kodacolor photos out of an envelope. He studied each one of them for a brief moment, ignoring the youngsters.

Alicia and her friends sidled up to him, their curiosity aroused. "Can I see?" Alicia asked, as she sat down next to Freddy.

150

He looked at her and flashed another big smile. "No-o-o problem," he answered. He handed Alicia a photo of Colonel Zimmermann's shiny white '87 Ferrari sports car. "Is dis dah car yah saw dah day Sergeant Washington wuz grabbed?" he asked.

She took the colored photo in her hands, exclaiming, "Oh, wow!"

She turned and showed it to her best friend, Maria Gonzolo, who had squirmed into a sitting position next to her. "Far out!" Maria exclaimed. She handed the photo back to Alicia. The three other little girls craned their necks so they could see, too.

Alicia handed the photo back to Freddy. "No, that's not the one."

"Yer sure it's not dah sports car?" Freddy asked, poking it in front of her.

"No, no, it's not that car," Alicia replied, strongly.

Freddy pulled the second photo out of the stack. He showed Lieutenant Colonel Livingston's shiny white '88 Cadillac El Dorado. "Is dis dah car?"

She looked at the photo, her brown almond eyes growing wide. "Out of sight!" she exclaimed, bubbling over. "That's the car. I remember it."

She showed it to Maria. "That's it!" she cried. "That's it."

Freddy dealt Alicia the third photo, Major Gerhardt Brockmann's shiny white '84 Buick. "What about dis photo, ever see dis car before?"

"Cool! Man, I want to ride in one of those," Alicia exclaimed.

"Is dat dah car?" Freddy asked.

"Nah, that's not it," Alicia answered. "'Twas the other one."

"Let me see," Maria demanded. She pulled the photo out of Alicia's hand and not to be outdone, screamed, "That's totally awesome!"

"Is dat dah car?" Freddy asked Maria, fixing an icy gaze on her.

"That's the one!" Maria shouted.

Freddy reversed the two photos, poking the second photo at Maria. "Not the Caddy, but the Buick? Right?"

"Right on," she replied.

Alicia refused to change her mind. "It's the Caddy, I know it's the Caddy."

Freddy brushed his moppish black hair back, not liking what he was hearing. "Hey wait a minute kids, I got one more to show yah." He flipped the fourth photo at them, Major Kurt Goetz' shiny white '87 BMW. "Whatta 'bout dis car? Wuz dis dah car yah saw?"

"That's intense!" Alicia said. "I think it was this one."

Maria looked over her shoulder. "No, it was that one." She pointed to the white Caddy.

"I thought yah said dah Buick," Freddy complained. "Okay, let's start all over." He held up the photo of the '87 Ferrari. "It's not dah sports car. Right?"

Both little girls shook their heads, "No."

Freddy pocketed the photo of the Ferrari. He held up the photo of the Caddy. "Is dis dah car?"

Alicia scratched her head, confused. "I'm not sure. Maybe it was the last one."

"It was the last one!" Maria shrieked. "I'm sure of it."

"I don't agree," Alicia argued in a reprimanding voice. "It was the Caddy."

"Okay," Freddy said. "Let's eliminate the Buick." He flashed the Buick photo in front of the girls one last time. "It's not dis car?"

"Oh, my God," Maria confessed. "I don't know. Maybe it was the Buick." She turned to Alicia for help. "Wasn't that the car I liked best?"

Little Alicia pursed her lips, bewildered. "I don't know. It looks different now." She fingered the photo of the Buick, then the BMW, then the Caddy. She shook her head each time. "It was a big shiny car, that's all I remember." She felt tears beginning to well up in her eyes.

Maria put her arms around her best friend, consoling her. "I'm not sure either," she whispered. "It looks different now."

Freddy flashed the photo of the Caddy again.

"I think it was this one," Alicia insisted.

"I think it was that one," Maria said, pointing to the BMW photo that Freddy held in his other hand.

Freddy shook his head in despair. "Come on, kids. Deese cars look totally different. Which one wuz it?"

"It was new, it was new," Alicia repeated. "It was shiny, it was big and shiny like Maria says."

Freddy flipped the three photos up into the air and watched them float to the sidewalk. "Youze don't know, do yah?"

He reached down, picked the photos up and fanned them like a poker hand. He looked at the Caddy and Buick and BMW. It had all seemed so simple. Everything had finally come together, waiting to be ID'd by an eyewitness. "Damn it!" he grumbled. "We got three suspects out dere, and we don't know which one fingered Laura. Who dah hell wuz it?"

He stood and looked down into the dejected eyes of the two third-graders. "Thanks, kids. Yah tried real hard." He forced a wide smile, saying, "No-o-o problem ... at least we know who to watch."

At 4:28 that afternoon, Vladimir, a tall heavy-built Soviet chauffeur, and two female secretaries from the Soviet mission, strolled nonchalantly into Central Park. He looked repeatedly over his shoulder, his eyes darting this way and that. Not seeing any danger, he walked into a wooded section, stopping at the gnarled oak tree. He squatted low and reached into the hole at the base of the tree. He pulled out the tiny band-aid and slid it into his pocket. He and his friends walked briskly out of the park. They split-up instantly. Each ran in a different direction.

Two FBI agents in business suits, using binoculars from a high vantage point about one hundred yards away, jumped to their feet and followed them. As they hurried onto Fifth Avenue, one agent followed Vladimir, who rounded the corner on 97th Street. The second agent signaled a cruising blue Ford van, which came to an abrupt halt. He pointed to the two secretaries running south on Fifth Avenue and east on 96th Street. The two agents chased after them. The van followed the first agent, who pursued the Soviet chauffeur.

Vladimir ran across Madison Avenue and turned downtown. He rushed into a glass-enclosed telephone booth on the corner of 96th Street. Working rapidly, he ripped open the band-aid and placed the microdot into a compact microfilm reader-printer, which measured about twelve inches square. The device processed the negative into a positive print instantly. He used a high power microscopic lens to read the secret message.

Seconds later, he thumbed a quarter into the pay phone and dialed quickly, ignoring the screeching noise of the Con Edison crew working with jackhammers a few feet away.

The first FBI agent spotted Vladimir talking on the telephone. He signaled his partner, whose Ford van rounded the corner. Inside the van, another agent with headphones on his head listened to the microwave interceptor, trying to hear and record the Russian's telephone conversation. The Con Edison jackhammers drowned out his words.

Vladimir looked up the street. He spotted a clean-cut, well dressed young man loitering against a telephone pole. He appeared to be entirely out of his element in this rough neighborhood. Vladimir flicked his cigarette lighter and ignited the microfilm negative and positive print. He watched them both go up in flames.

He walked back onto the street and flagged a passing yellow cab. Getting inside, he breathed a sigh of relief, pleased that the FBI had not arrested him.

Kolchak placed the receiver down on its hook, delighted that the execution order had finally come through. He walked out of his office at *New World Magazine*, crossed First Avenue and walked cross-town to Third Avenue. He browsed at several specialty shops, admiring the window displays, checked his watch repeatedly. At 4:50 p.m., he walked down the flight of stairs into the IND subway station at 53rd Street. He found an open pay phone on the lower subway platform.

At 5:00 o'clock sharp, he dialed a telephone number that he had memorized, calling a pay phone in the Green Acre Shopping Mall in Valley Stream. The E train roared into the station, muffling the relay of the execution order to the GRU agent on the other end.

Kolchak brushed past a mob of rush hour people charging toward the subway's open doors and made his way upstairs back onto the street. He glanced quickly to his left and right, saw nothing but a surging mass of people hurrying home. Despite previous espionage training that agents are most vulnerable to exposure during a covert mission, Kolchak had grown soft and careless in his plush job in Manhattan. He didn't notice the FBI agents following him, who melted into the streaming crowd.

Walking downtown, Kolchak headed for the Front Page. It was time to indulge in a Stoli or two. That night, he'd write the finishing touches to his propaganda campaign.

He sat at the crowded bar, immersed in his diabolic thoughts. "They'll never pin murders on me," he murmured. "It's old news, like it never happened." An intense evil look flared from his eyes. In 48-hours, his mission will be history. He fantasized how Moscow would applaud his *kombinatsia*, how he would be promoted to KGB general after the shoot down of Pan Am Flight 120.

Then, he thought about the Spetsnaz. He would not tolerate his deviation from Party policy. He looked forward to settling the score at the airport. He decided to catch a limousine to JFK on Saturday afternoon ... and to enjoy the fireworks.

The Spetsnaz hung up the receiver of the pay phone in front of Alexander's, angered by the final execution order.

He cut across the mall's aisle, dodging the oncoming people and made his way to the exit. His eyes darted vigilantly back and forth. He zigzagged into the parking lot, looking around. Nobody followed him. He made his way to his Cherokee and drove to the safehouse, located a few blocks away.

He stifled the desire to call his cousin Jackie, his army discipline controlling the situation. As distressful as the mission seemed, he knew he was Spetsnaz. He would do what was expected of him ... or, he could ...

He shook his head, hoping Moscow might still call off the attack. 48-hours remained before zero hour.

Petrovich walked inside the bungalow, readying himself for the ordeal ahead. He repeated the execution order to himself. "Flight 120. April 9. Attack and destroy!" He sat down on the living room sofa next to the phone and thumbed through the yellow pages until he found Pan Am. He dialed reservations and asked for the flight time of Flight 120 on April 9.

The passenger clerk spoke courteously. "The plane departs at 4:00 p.m."

The two PLO terrorists walked into the room. The leader, Abdallah Bakr, was five foot four inches tall, about 120 pounds, dark skinned with haunting black eyes that remembered the U.S. naval bombardment of Beirut. His wife and two children were never found under the rubble of their apartment building. His assistant, Mohammed Abdahlwadis, a Shiite Muslim like himself, survived the Phalangist massacre at the Shatilla refugee camp in Beirut. Smaller in stature, Mohammed carried the Stinger launcher and placed it onto the floor.

Petrovich picked up the launcher and swung it snugly onto his right shoulder, using little physical exertion. He squinted through the optical sight and aimed at an imaginary target.

The Stinger was a packaged missile system, consisting of a disposable launch tube, a high explosive hit-to-kill warhead, an infra-red navigation seeker and a dual thrust rocket motor. It measured five feet long and weighed only thirty pounds.   The Spetsnaz demonstrated the optical sighting. "Gunner will acquire target visually. Find target in optical sight. Turn on missile's infra-red guidance sensor that will lock onto aircraft's engines. Don't forget to lead aircraft before firing. Then, launch missile."

He scowled at the terrorists. "You fire-and-forget," he said, worrying that visual target acquisition could be their greatest vulnerability.

"Point and shoot!"

The two gunners listened, impassively. They resented the Russian's condescending attitude towards them. They had trained enough. They knew how to use the Stinger missile. They didn't need more practice. Their ayatollah demanded a *ghassas*, an eye for an eye. They would not fail in their martyrdom. "Allah is great!" each man repeated. "It is Allah's will that I become a martyr."

15

For Maccabee, Thursday morning was not only a total loss, it was devastating. One hammer blow came after the next. The FBI had reported to Major Morgan, identifying Boris Vladimir, the Soviet chauffeur, as a lieutenant in the KGB. They had not been able to overhear or trace his telephone call after he had picked up the execution order in Central Park.

The FBI team, which had been assigned to track Kolchak, had been equally unsuccessful. They had no idea where the Soviet hit team was hiding. There had to be a safehouse, but where?

"They've got Kolchak's apartment staked-out," Morgan said, "Something has to break soon." She kept poking at her intelligence file, rereading the raw data, trying to find something that she might have overlooked.

Maccabee stormed around the office, totally frustrated. He had argued vehemently over the telephone with General Kelley. "We need to warn the troops about the threat! They're going to be sitting ducks, up there. They must have a fighting chance for survival. They're my friends ..."

The general's decision was final. "There will be no breaches of security. The Pentagon has declared the mission will proceed as planned. All precautionary steps are being taken to protect our troops. We will do what we need to do." No further discussion was allowed.

After hanging up the telephone, Maccabee slammed his fist onto his desk, upsetting the incoming file, which scattered across the floor. He picked the papers up angrily and stuffed them back into the file.

Freddy milled about the office, moving from one chair to the other, volunteering different scenarios about the big shiny white car ... none of them practical.

"If the kids could have only remembered," Maccabee complained.

Morgan set aside her paperwork and walked into Maccabee's office, overhearing his comment. "Colonel, the girls are only eight-years old," she said in a rebuking tone. "Would you have remembered at that age?"

Maccabee shook his head. His ruddy face flushed crimson with embarrassment. "I guess it was too much to hope for."

"Everything looks big and shiny when you're a third-grader," she continued.

Freddy blurted out, "Boss, I know dah suspects are friends of yers, but so wuz General Palmer."

Maccabee cast an angry eye of warning at Freddy, who ignored the look and plunged ahead.

"Yah gotta dissect each one of dere alibis, one of dem is up to his ears in deese murders. First, General Palmer gets killed. Yah damn near get wasted. Den, he bird-dogs Laura and fingers her murder. Hector Sanchez gets a bullet in dah brain. Where's it gonna end? Dah troops leave fer Germany on Saturday. And a Spetsnaz team is waitin' to shoot 'em down with a Stinger."

Maccabee and Morgan looked at each other grim faced. Freddy was telling the painful truth.

"Christ, boss!" Freddy continued, callously. "If dis were 'Nam, we'd arrest dah three suspects and work 'em over till we got dah truth."

Maccabee shook his head at his erstwhile NCO, trying to contain his anger. "This isn't 'Nam, and we're not talking about interrogating VC prisoners. You're talking about three dedicated army officers with fine military records. Wally Livingston is an outstanding officer. Jerry Brockmann and Kurt Goetz have fine combat records. We don't have any hard evidence to lock them up. It's all circumstantial. The driver of the shiny white car that fingered Sergeant Washington could have been someone else."

Freddy became argumentative. "I say we arrest dem," he blustered, "and squeeze dem until dey tell us what we needda know. Time's runnin' out!"

Morgan sat quietly at the conference table, listening to Freddy and wondering when Maccabee would reveal what he knew. She gave him an appealing, go-ahead-and-tell him look.

Maccabee read her signal and nodded. "The FBI have put all three officers under surveillance. If one of them is guilty, we're going to give him a little more rope. Maybe, he'll lead us to the Stinger hit team before it's too late."

"If he turns up sick for the flight on Saturday morning," Morgan interjected, "we'll have our man. At that point, we turn the screws."

Freddy wasn't to be put down. "What if he doesn't know 'bout dah Stinger attack? What if he's a sacrificial lamb?"

Maccabee's ruddy features purpled. He glared at Freddy for speaking his mind. "It's possible. That's the dilemma we face."

Freddy looked hard at Maccabee, recognizing that he had pushed him to the limit. Not willing to give up, he pursued a different direction.

"Deese guys are all married to foreigners. Dere wives work wid foreign companies. Dere wives run dem like dey hadda ball and chain."

Maccabee's eyes widened. His mouth gaped open. A forgotten thought buried deep within his subconscious burst into clarity. He looked at Morgan, then back at Freddy, who droned on.

Maccabee jumped to his feet. He slammed the flat of his palm onto his desk, its hollow sound reverberating across the room. "That's it!" he recalled. "That's what Laura said to me the day the CID interviewed Colonel Cherniak and Dressler. She said to check out the wives. I've been trying to jog my memory all this time."

He punched Freddy in the fat of his biceps, driving him against the wall with a surprised look on his face. "Freddy, you're a genius," he said, grinning.

He turned to Morgan, who had risen to her feet. He snapped out a quick command. "Get Tim O'Brien up here. It's about time the CIA gets off its duff. Where in hell is the spouse report you asked for? Tell Tim I want a fast readout on the Advance Party as well as the Main Body."

Kolchak sat at his computer command post in his apartment Thursday evening,

156

waiting for his modem to activate. The staccato sound of the printer filled the air as a coded message from KGB Central rushed across the page. He tore the sheet off, opened up his secret code book and deciphered the message. His eyes gleamed with anticipation as he read it.

"Alert! (Eyes Only): New background check on Spetsnaz reveals forged birth certificate and parentage transgression. Criminal violations under investigation. Loyalty now questionable. Maintain utmost vigilance. Arrest Spetsnaz and return to Moscow via Aeroflot when mission completed."

He read the message aloud three times, not wanting to miss any nuances. He committed it to memory. It was more than he had hoped for. He inserted the message into his shredding machine and watched it disappear.

Kolchak sprawled onto the couch in the living room, propping his feet up on the coffee table. He lit a cigarette and inhaled deeply. Moscow had vindicated his suspicions about the Spetsnaz. He wondered what crimes Petrovich had committed against the Party, against the country. "He's guilty as hell," he muttered. "War hero, be damned!"

A diabolical thought crept through his mind. Since the Spetsnaz had infiltrated into the country two days before General Palmer's assassination, why not frame him for murder?

Kolchak's imagination took over. He'd frame the Spetsnaz for all eight killings ... the army general, Lemoine, the black sergeant, the three junkies, Sanchez, even the Jamaican.

"Why not?" he mumbled. "The Pentagon's Order of Battle lists the mission of Spetsnaz forces. Level Two includes assassination of political leaders and army generals, disruption of communications and transportation. It is made to order for my *kombinatsia*, for more disinformation and deception."

Wait, he thought. Why disclose his identity as Spetsnaz? He looks European. He could pass for German or Pole. Why link him to Russia? He's GRU, military intelligence. Not KGB, not espionage. CIA has no record of him.

Yes, he smirked. Why not give him new identity? He began to weave a new maze of deception, distorting the truth to suit his purposes. He knew the Spetsnaz would be carrying a forged West German passport, which was part of the KGB escape plan. After Stinger mission is completed, I will find Spetsnaz and kill him in self defense. I will identify him as international terrorist, a double agent who was employed by East German intelligence and PLO, a renegade spy that KGB was hunting. How was I to know he planned to blow up Pan Am jetliner? I am Soviet journalist. People pass confidential information to me. I cannot divulge source. I only report facts.

Nobody will believe East German and PLO authorities, when they deny knowledge of attack. The media will demand retribution, then support U.S. troop withdrawal from NATO to avoid more casualties. The Americans will be grateful for my killing the terrorist. And Moscow will be saved cost of embarrassing trial and execution of Spetsnaz.

Kolchak sat erect, jerking the cigarette out of his lips. "Why should I put myself at risk?" he reflected. "I use someone else to pull trigger."

He picked up the phone and dialed the Soviet Embassy. He arranged a midnight rendezvous with a KGB assassin, who was trained to kill silently in public places.

Dead-end. Deadlock. Dead. The impending thoughts of disaster haunted Maccabee. Friday turned into a day of anguish and depression. Still no breakthrough. Only doubt, distress and dismay.

Maccabee busied himself at his office, shuffling through intel reports that Morgan had placed on his desk. He sighed listlessly, trying to read between the lines, searching for the elusive answer buried somewhere in the mass of paperwork.

"Damn it all!" he exclaimed, despairing over the treachery. Somebody had to be on the inside. Somebody betrayed his trust. He fought with himself, thinking the unthinkable.

Words and images blurred into an impenetrable maze. His eyelids grew heavy from worry and lack of sleep. He blinked his bloodshot eyes, refocusing them. He thought about Kolchak, then Gretchen, then the mole.

Suddenly, a sharp recollection jolted his brain. "Morgan, get in here," he shouted. He rummaged through one pile of computer printouts after another, searching with furious intensity.

"What's come over you!" Morgan cried out, rushing into his office. She held a stiletto letter opener in one hand and a large unopened manila envelope in the other. "What are you doing?"

Maccabee yanked at one page after another, spewing the printouts across his desk, spilling the accordion folds onto the floor. "The time frames," he muttered. "Where are your time frames?"

"What time frames?" Morgan asked in a state of irritation. She looked over his shoulder. "What are you looking for?" She glared at Maccabee, then at the clutter of reports that she'd have to straighten out later. "If you'll only stop for a minute and tell me what you're looking for."

Maccabee stopped shuffling through the printouts and looked up. "The time frames," he repeated in an agitated tone. "Kolchak's tapes. I need to see the sequence of time for each search of his apartment."

"Why do you need it?" she asked. She took the printout from Maccabee's hands and tried to straighten the pile on his desk.

"There's a time lag that we forgot about." Maccabee looked sharply at his associate, his confidence returning. "A couple of days elapsed between the time we searched Kolchak's place and when the FBI tapped his phone. How much of a time gap was there? We missed it."

Morgan's mouth gaped open in surprise. She pushed the printouts aside, and sat facing Maccabee. She ran her fingers through the bobbed hair on her forehead. "You're right," she said, flustered. "There was a time gap." She stood. "I have the dates and time sequence in another file. It was so obvious, I missed it." She rushed out of the office. Minutes later, she returned with three manila files in her hands.

They poured over the information, checking specific times. "Here it is," she finally said, pointing to a diary of events. "Freddy reconned Kolchak's apartment on Monday, 21 March. Lieutenant Howard got a search warrant the next day, Tuesday, 22

March. That's when we searched Kolchak's apartment and Spriggy did a computer dump."

"How much time transpired after that to analyze the data? When did the FBI obtain a court order to tap Kolchak's lines?"

Morgan switched files and rummaged through her notes. "Here it is. Thursday, 24 March." She looked up, her eyes shining brightly. "There was a 36-hour time gap! Who did Kolchak talk to during that time? Could he have called the mole?"

Maccabee shook his head. "I don't know."

"What if he called the Spetsnaz?"

"The Spetsnaz? It's possible." Maccabee struggled with a nagging thought buried deep in his subconscious. He kept reaching for a vague shadowy image ... the Spetsnaz, but it kept eluding him.

Another thought broke to the surface. He jumped to his feet. "Get John Howard and Spriggy on the phone." He checked his watch. 11:40. "There's plenty of time left to run another computer dump and dupe the tape on Kolchak's answering machine before he returns home from work. Get them moving fast. I want a flash report before the end of the day."

Morgan rushed from the room toward her desk in the outer office. She passed Tim O'Brien of the CIA, who walked inside. She placed two quick calls, spoke to each party and ordered them into instant action.

She walked back to Maccabee's office and flashed a thumbs up signal.

Maccabee nodded and waved Morgan to join them at the conference table, where he and O'Brien were talking. "Tim has the CIA spouse report we've been waiting for." He pointed to the CIA executive report that was spread out in front of him. The information was terse, compiling intelligence from CIA field offices in Frankfurt, Germany with domestic FBI background reports.

O'Brien, a tall, wavy haired, blue eyed Irishman, had a friendly face that blended easily into a crowd. He spoke in a carefree manner. "I wish I had something positive for you, but none if it looks incriminating."

"Tell me what you have on the primary suspects," Maccabee said, staring at the younger officer. He crossed his legs and listened intently.

The CIA agent opened the file, *Gerhardt and Ursula Brockmann.* "Ursula is second generation German-American, born in Milwaukee, Wisconsin, 12 August 1950. Her father, Heinz Schuster, age 69, was born in Leipzig, East Germany. Served as panzer officer in Werhmacht until capture by Russians on eastern front. Prisoner in Siberia until release in '47. He immigrated to West Germany, then to Milwaukee the following year, where he settled, married and raised a family. He worked as an auto mechanic for Ford, then Volkswagen until retirement at age 65. According to his passport, he has visited Germany once a year since the mid-sixties. Ursula's paternal grandfather was also an army officer, wounded on the eastern front, settled in Dresden, East Germany. He worked as a low level communist bureaucrat in internal security until his death in '81. No record of contact between son and father or granddaughter and grandfather during this time period."

"What about Ursula's mother?" Maccabee asked.

"Nothing there." O'Brien read more of his file. "Name Hilda Knapp, age 68, born in Milwaukee. Married Heinz Schuster, November '49. Occupation, housewife.

Ursula was an only child. Maternal grandparents were both born in Chicago. Grandfather served with U.S. Navy in Pacific during World War II. Hard hat at Schlitz brewery. Now retired. One hundred percent American."

"And Ursula?"

"Graduated from University of Wisconsin, June '67, majored in political science. Was involved in peace demonstrations. Came to New York City in '68. Worked for Lufthansa German Airlines as a reservation clerk. Speaks fluent German. Married Gerhardt in June '69. Stopped working to raise two kids. Returned to Lufthansa's Rockefeller Center office in '84. Her passport indicates annual trips to Frankfurt from '68 to '72, a hiatus, then again in '84 to '87."

"Did the dates of her annual trips match that of her father's?"

O'Brien looked surprised. He checked his notes again. "It's a match during '68 and '69. The dates don't match after that."

"Did Jerry accompany her to Germany on these trips?"

O'Brien checked another report. He nodded. "Yeah, '84 to '87 check out. They flew over and back together."

Maccabee looked perplexed, not knowing what to make of the report. "Jerry doesn't have any living relatives in Germany, if I remember?"

O'Brien set the report down. "He's an orphan. His family was killed during the war. He was an army mascot, adopted by a GI, a mechanical engineer who raised him in Elizabeth, New Jersey. The whole family looks clean."

Maccabee blew his breath out forcibly. "Cross off one suspect," he said to Morgan, who sat attentively by his side.

"Suspect number two," O'Brien said in a businesslike tone. He picked up the report and began reading. *Kurt and Erika Goetz.* Kurt's a second generation Swiss and his credentials are impeccable, both military and civilian. Kurt's father was a vice president at Swiss GeoPrecision before retiring and Kurt's following in his footsteps. You're familiar with his military record."

It's his wife I want to know about. What have you learned about her?"

"Erika was born and raised in Garmisch, Bavaria, near the famous ski resort at Zugsitze Mountain. That's about sixty miles south of Munich."

Maccabee cut in. "I know where it's at. I skied there."

"That's how Kurt met her. Skiing the Zugsitze. Erika was a ski instructor. He met her on R&R while on active duty. Married her two weeks later and brought her back to the states."

"Dates?" Morgan asked, wanting to check each detail carefully.

"Born 9 January 1944, Garmisch, Bavaria. Married 12 March '71 in Baden Baden. She's president of Deutsch-Swiss Ski Ventures, incorporated in State of New York on 5 November '73, in Bavaria, Germany on 12 December '73 and Geneva, Switzerland on 20 January '74. She conducts business and maintains bank accounts in all three countries. Her passport shows numerous trips to Munich and Geneva. They never had any children."

"How successful is her business?" Maccabee asked. "Are there any signs of financial problems?"

O'Brien shrugged. "It's difficult to tell. We checked her IRS returns, business and personal. She sells over two million dollars each year in ski tours and condo rentals

160

and plows her profits back into real estate investments. We're trying to track down her Swiss holdings, but you know how tight-lipped the Geneva bankers are. So far, we haven't found any irregularities." He chuckled aloud. "Kurt married one helluva smart business lady. I wish I'd done as well."

Morgan interrupted, finding the comment chauvinistic. "What about her mother and father? Do they live in Germany or in the U.S.?"

O'Brien checked his notes again, disconcerted. "Her father, Eric Zwickau was an alpine ski champion. He was killed in Norway, November '43. Her mother and grandparents were killed in allied bombing raids in March '44, two months after she was born. She was raised by a spinster aunt, Helene Zwickau, who died of cancer in Munich in '61."

"How did she manage during the ten years before she met Kurt? She was only seventeen."

O'Brien's face grew long. "I guess she was a born skier like her father. She became a ski instructor, that's all I have."

"Scratch suspect number two," Maccabee said, trying again not to think the unthinkable. "What have you got on Wally's wife Liu Ann?" He turned to Morgan, explaining, "I knew his first wife Louise, a conservative Texan whose great grandfather was a state senator. She was so straight laced, it's a wonder their marriage lasted as long as it did."

O'Brien pulled out his third file. *"Wallace and Liu Anne Livingston."* He looked up, sensing Maccabee's eyes stabbing at him. "Liu Ann Chang. Born October '47 in Yingtak, a small village in Kwantung Province in southern China. Entered Hong Kong with older brother as illegal immigrants in '63. Employed as seamstress in Hong Kong sweatshop in Kowloon. Fought her way out as concubine to Chinese casino owner, then mistress to Brit manager of Hong Kong Chinese trading company. Attended night school, earned degree in '72 in textile management with his backing."

Morgan interrupted. "I thought she was an airline stewardess."

"She left the Brit in '76. No information on her whereabouts during the next two years. She popped-up again in '79 as an airline stewardess for a local Brit charter service, ferrying cargo and people between Hong Kong and the communist mainland. Joined Pan Am in '82, flew the Pacific rim. Met Livingston in '84 on one of his Far East buying trips. Her flight schedule coincides with his buying trips to Hong Kong, Taiwan, Shanghai, Rome and Paris. She married Livingston in '86. They started an import company, purchasing sportswear in mainland China for shipment to the U.S."

"Wally told me the bucks are rolling in," Maccabee said. "Did you check their IRS tax returns? How prosperous are they?"

O'Brien shook his head. "They've come into a pile of money. We think they're running a double set of books, one for us, one for their communist suppliers. They netted four hundred thousand dollars last year, after taxes. Claim they hit it big at a gambling casino in Macao, then reinvested their winnings in buying more goods for their company."

"Any way to check it out?"

"We're trying, but the Portuguese casino owners have clamed up."

"Do you think he's laundering money through his company?"

"It's either that or Wally's on one helluva roll!"

161

Maccabee stared at O'Brien, fearing the worst. "How could Wally get so damn involved? I've known him for years. I'd trust him with my life."

"I'd play it cagey, if I were you," O'Brien warned. "We don't have anything incriminating yet, but we're pluggin' away."

Morgan broke in, ticking off an open question on her check list. "What about Liu Ann's parents? What info do you have on them?"

O'Brien wavered. "Not much. They were wealthy landowners before the revolution. They're supposed to be rehabilitated and living somewhere in central China, but our agents haven't been able to confirm it."

"Have your agents talked to her brother?" Morgan persisted.

O'Brien winced, referring to his notes. "He's dead. Killed by Hong Kong coast patrol in May '76 while resisting arrest on a Chinese junk for gun smuggling." He stood and began to pace. "Her whole background sounds fishy."

The phone rang several times. Maccabee ignored it, engulfed in mental anguish. He stared out the window, oblivious to the bustling late afternoon crowds hurrying by on Park Avenue. Seconds later, his secretary buzzed him on the intercom. "Important call from John Howard."

Maccabee leaned awkwardly over his desk and picked up the receiver. "Maccabee here."

An urgent voice surged across the wire. "It's John Howard, sir. We couldn't get in. Kolchak took the day off. He's working in his apartment."

"Damn it!" Maccabee exclaimed. "That's the last thing we needed." He held the receiver aside and spoke directly to Morgan. "Kolchak's in his apartment. They didn't get inside."

Maccabee pursed his lips, thinking quickly. He spoke into the mouthpiece. "Where are you calling from?"

"Me and Spriggy are holed up across the street at the FBI stakeout. We're watching every move he makes."

"Good," Maccabee snapped. "I want you two to stay put where you are ... even if you have to work around-the-clock. Don't leave for any reason. It's imperative that you gain entry to Kolchak's apartment the minute he leaves. You must dupe his tapes. We need the information desperately. Call me the instant you analyze the information. If you can't reach me here, I'll be at my apartment. You have my number?"

"Yes, sir, I know the number. We'll do our best."

"We're running out of time, John. The unit flies out tomorrow. A lot of people are depending upon us."

"We're hangin' in, sir."

"Good." Maccabee hung-up. He sat on the edge of his desk, stymied.

O'Brien approached him. "I need to get back to my office. We're still trying to unravel all this stuff. If we get any new information, you'll be the first to know."

"Thanks for the briefing," Maccabee replied. "Keep the hot line open."

"I have a question."

"Shoot."

"Do you know why I've been pulled off tomorrow's overseas flight? My orders have been canceled. What's going on?"

Maccabee glanced at Morgan, surprised. "Did you know that O'Brien's orders were changed?"

Freddy walked into the office at that moment, smiling. "Anybody lookin' fer me?"

"No," Morgan snapped. "We were too busy to notice you were missing." She looked appealingly at Maccabee, saying, "I had no idea his orders were changed." She hurried to the outer office to phone the 38th to see if any other selective cancellations had been made.

"It's embarrassing," O'Brien said to Maccabee. "My wife's throwing a big dinner party tonight as a send off for my ODT tour. The entire family is coming, even Father Paul is coming to offer his blessings. How do I tell them I'm not flying to Germany?"

Maccabee felt the pressure seething inside him, ready to explode. How much of the conspiracy could he keep to himself? How much could he share? He turned to Freddy and made a snap decision. "Here's our second shooter. You ride shotgun with me tomorrow in Huey One." He pointed toward O'Brien. "Tim rides shotgun with Morgan in Huey Two."

Kolchak sweated it out in his apartment, wondering if Friday afternoon would ever end. He was too pent-up to concentrate on anything, but his *Kombinatsia*. He knew he was balanced precariously on a tightrope, treading a dangerous path. One wrong move, and everything could go astray.

He focused on the Spetsnaz. He had to set him up for the kill, one step at a time. His mission came first. Pan Am Flight 120 had to be destroyed. Then, and only then, would he terminate the Spetsnaz.

He tuned his television to CNN at five and watched the hourly news report. At six, he switched channels to NBC, first Chuck Scarborough and the local news; at seven, Tom Brokaw and the network news. Finally, at 7:30, he called Gretchen at home to set the final move of his conspiracy in motion.

She picked up the phone on the third ring. "Hello, this is Gretchen."

"Hallo, mein liebe fraulein. This is Dmitri."

"And what do I owe this call to?" she asked icily, wondering what Kolchak was up to. Gretchen still wore a green cardigan, simple white blouse and navy skirt from work, having arrived home ten minutes earlier.

"I have new story for you, another scoop." He paused briefly for effect, then asked, "You are interested?"

She forced a thin laugh. "Of course. Let me get a pencil and notepad." She returned moments later, wanting to record the gist of his story. "Go ahead," she said, flatly. "I'm ready to copy."

"A reliable source at Soviet embassy has informed me that international terrorist named Horst Gunther will fly to La Guardia Airport on Monday night. He is hired assassin. Very dangerous man. Informants say his mission is to highjack Eastern Airline shuttle and blow it up on runway at National Airport in Washington D.C."

He hesitated, waiting for the shock to sink in. He continued to establish the big lie. "Assassin is responsible for murder of General Palmer and Sergeant Washington. He must be stopped before he kills more people."

"Where did you get this information, Dmitri?" Gretchen asked, coldly.

"I told you. From unidentified reliable source. I cannot reveal his name. I am

163

sworn to secrecy. Why do you question me?"

"Why?" she repeated, baiting him. "Because you've been feeding me false information, and I've been reporting it like it's the gospel. Those days are kaput! Come clean, Dmitri, I want to know where you're getting all your information so I can verify it before I call my editors." She paused, then asked curtly, "Why don't you inform the police? Why call me?"

"I can't tell police," he rasped in a whining voice. "If word gets out I informed, I will be killed."

"Don't be dramatic," Gretchen scoffed. "Who's going to kill you?"

Kolchak thought quickly. The conversation was not going the way he had planned. "I overhear KGB talking, that's where I get information. KGB say terrorist must be stopped at all costs."

"You're afraid the KGB will kill you, if you report the terrorist threat to the police?" She reflected momentarily, then spoke caustically. Her Germanic inflection pierced Kolchak's defenses, acrimoniously. "If you don't warn the police, I will."

"No!" he cried. "KGB has set a trap at La Guardia to capture terrorist, to turn him over to proper authorities in Europe. If you tell police, they will swarm all over airport. Gunther will evade police and escape, like he has done many times in past."

"Who is this man, Horst Gunther? What do you know about him?"

"He is former Nazi Gestapo officer. He works for West German BND, special security in Bundesnachrichtendienst. He is double agent, employed by East German Stasi. Espionage. That's how KGB learn about his mission."

"You say Horst Gunther is a spy for the Federal Republic of Germany?" she mocked, arrogantly. "And Bonn doesn't know he works for the Stasi?"

"Yes," he lied, struggling with his story. "He is citizen of West Germany, carries West German passport. But he is double agent for Democratic People's Republic of Germany. He is radical who wants to stop CIMIC, who wants to stop West Germany from becoming Americanized, who wants to go back to old ways. One unified country under one supreme leader. One communist leader. That's why he killed General Palmer. Now he plans to blow-up plane in Washington." His voice became distraught. "You must help me. Swear you will not reveal to police what I have said. It is KGB matter. KGB will settle score with Gunther. I want you to win Pulitzer for scoop."

Gretchen stared at the phone in disbelief. There was no end to the man's intrigue. "Is Gunther in New York City at this moment?"

"No," he lied, vehemently. "He flies to La Guardia on Monday night from midwest, coming from Cincinnati or Kansas City."

She knew he had answered too quickly. He's lying, she reflected. How dumb does he think I am? "What time is Gunther's flight?"

Kolchak paused, wondering if he had said too much. "Monday night. During rush hour when airport is crowded. Between six and seven o'clock."

Gretchen copied his comments in shorthand. "What does he look like? How will you recognize him?" Now she had him boxed into a corner.

"Look like?" he rasped, testily. "He looks German, that's how he looks. He'll be wearing a Lufthansa workman's uniform. He's a killer. If trapped, he'll shoot on sight." He swallowed hard, then pleaded in a dry, exasperated voice. "As one professional journalist to another, swear to me you will not alert police or reveal source of story. Swear it.'"

There was a moment of silence. Gretchen shuddered. Her distrust deepened. She answered deviously with a note of rancor in her voice. "I swear it. I won't spoil your little surprise or disclose my source of information. Freedom of the press, remember?" She hung up.

Across the street at the FBI stakeout, an FBI agent in rumpled clothes with a headset over his ears sat by a tape recorder. "Did you hear that?" he asked John Howard and Spriggy Covalho who stood nearby. "This guy never stops scheming. That's the damnedest yarn I've heard. We'd better call central control. Looks like the big hit is scheduled Monday night, not tomorrow."

"I don't know," Howard replied. "This guy is slippery. He could be leading us on. Do you think he knows his line is tapped?"

"Nah-h-h," the FBI agent replied. "I've been on too many wire taps. A suspect will choke up when he tries to con you. This sounds real to me. He hasn't the faintest idea we're listening in."

Spriggy watched a second FBI agent in gray sweats scan the front apartment window through a set of high powered binoculars. "What's he doing now?" she asked.

"Nothing much. Pouring himself a vodka and watching television. It looks like it's going to be a long night."

"How're we going to get him out of there?" Spriggy asked. "There must be more information about Gunther in Kolchak's computer."

"We could start a small fire in the basement," the FBI agent suggested.

"Just what we need," Howard quipped. "A street full of wailing police sirens and flashing red lights." He laughed. "We don't have any other choice, but to wait Kolchak out. The next move's up to him."

Gretchen stared at the phone after hanging up on Kolchak. She took off her cardigan jacket and threw it across the back of her couch. She walked to the standup bar in the corner of the living room and poured herself a stiff Johnny Walker Black Label. Leaning back against the fluffy cushions on her couch, she downed the scotch slowly, angered over Kolchak's duplicity.

Gathering her thoughts, she rose and walked to the end table. She picked up the phone and touched the redial button for Dave's apartment. The phone rang three times, then clicked into his answering machine mode. She sighed impatiently, then left a message.

She tapped the redial for his agency. This time she found her quarry. Morgan came onto the line, then Maccabee.

"Dave, I have something important to discuss with you," she said, "I have new informa ..."

Maccabee cut her short. "I can't talk to you right now. All hell's breaking loose. It'll have to wait until tomorrow."

"But Dave," she argued. "It's important."

"Can't help it. I'm in a meeting. There are people in my office. Can't talk. I'll see you tomorrow night."

"It can't wait until then," she insisted. "I need to see you sooner."

"Can't do it. Need to see the troops off tomorrow. I'll call you after I leave the airport. Have to go. Bye." The phone clicked off to a buz-z-z.

She slammed down the receiver, infuriated. This was not the Dave she knew and loved. It was so unlike him to cut her off like this. What type of emergency had occurred to dominate all of his attention?

GRetchen now knew what she had to do. Grabbing her spring coat, she rushed out of her apartment building, and flagged a cab cruising down the street. Pulling her overcoat tightly around her, she jumped into the back seat.

"Where to, lady?" the cabby asked.

"To the Federal Republic of Germany's Mission to the UN," she answered. "It's located at 600 Third Avenue." She leaned back against the stark leather seat, wondering who Horst Gunther really was.

She watched the city street lights roll by, realizing that Kolchak was trying to set somebody up for liquidation. This is one time he isn't going to manipulate me, she mused. Two can play at the same game.

She thought about General Palmer's and Lemoine's murders. How it had all been staged for her benefit. Then the drug massacre in the South Bronx, when Sergeant Washington was murdered. That shoot out had been staged, too. Then the gangland murders of Sanchez and the Jamaican enforcer. All senseless, unanswered killings.

"How deeply involved is Kolchak in these murders? Is he a KGB assassin, maybe even the mastermind behind all of these killings? I won't put up his lies any longer."

The taxi pulled up to the West German mission and stopped. Gretchen paid the cabby and gave him a five dollar tip for good luck. His as well as hers. She opened the door and swung her shapely legs out the door. She stood on the empty sidewalk, then walked briskly to the entrance. Her four-inch, stiletto heels echoed in the eerie, dim lit night.

She rang the night bell and waited impatiently. "I'm going to get to the bottom of this conspiracy before the night ends. Kolchak is far more dangerous than I ever thought."

The door to the mission opened. She walked inside.

166

16

On Saturday morning, the sky was overcast. A gray ominous cloud hovered about 3,500 feet over the U.S. Army Reserve Center in the Bronx. The temperature was cool, the air crisp with a little breeze stirring. The reservists arrived in ones and twos in private cars. They climbed out of their vehicles, pulled the duffel bags out of their trunks, and stacked them on the sidewalk in front of the two chartered Greyhound buses that were parked nose to tail. Their cargo side gates were wide open.

Maccabee, dressed in his safari jacket, red shirt and beige slacks, moved among the enlisted troops, talking about their trip to Germany. For some, it was their first trip on an airplane. For others, it was another chance to take photos, buy souvenirs and earn some extra money. The senior NCOs circled around Maccabee, joining in the small talk.

Everyone wore civilian sports clothes for the long flight to Frankfurt. They were all enthusiastic, their spirits high. Some of the male soldiers introduced their wives to one another. The women were dressed in a bright array of floral colored blouses, miniskirts and jumpsuits. They looked like a cheerful Bronx neighborhood group waiting to go on a picnic. The male spouses socialized with one another in the background, their kids staying close.

"Sure wish you were comin' with us," Sergeant First Class Willie Douglas said, smiling. "Hey kids, come meet Colonel Maccabee." And so it went, one person after another.

Sergeant First Class Doreen Franklin, whose smiling ebony features always gave Maccabee a lift, waved at him as he passed. She called roll from her clipboard for the second time in the morning, trying to maintain platoon integrity: "Rodriquez, Rojas, Rosado, Rosales, Rosario, Royal, Rubino, Salazar Estella, Salazar Luis, Salazar Sandra, Sampson, Santana, Schmidt, Scott ..."

They answered "si, yeah and heah." They drifted about, practicing their Berlitz German, excited about getting out of the ghetto, even if it was only for two weeks.

Colonel Chuck Bailey, the G-1, a competent efficiency expert with a machine gun mind and propensity for achievement, acted as senior officer for the flight. He huddled with Major Jerry Brockmann, who broke away when he spotted Maccabee and walked towards him. "Didn't expect to see you here Dave. Bet you'd like to come with us."

Maccabee nodded. "Wanted to say good-bye and wish you good luck." He grasped his right hand in a firm handshake. He turned as Major Kurt Goetz dumped his two duffel bags onto the sidewalk with a thud.

"When do we start loading our bags into the busses?" Goetz asked, joining the foursome.

"Any time now," Bailey snapped. He signaled Sergeant Douglas and walked towards him. A loading party started piling the duffel bags into the charter busses.

"Anybody see Livingston?" Brockmann asked, as he stood on his tip toes, swiveling his head around to scan above the crowd.

"Nah," Goetz replied, shaking his head. "I haven't seen him. Hope he doesn't miss the flight."

Brockmann shrugged. "It's not like Wally. You know how he likes to worry. He always shows up at least fifteen minutes before a meeting starts, before we go any place." A look of concern spread across his face. He spoke to Maccabee in a hushed voice. "Do you think he's sick?"

Maccabee frowned, concealing his doubts. "I don't know." He stretched his neck out, his head high, trying to spot his friend. He didn't see him.

Goetz laughed, throwing his arm around Brockmann's shoulder. "Hey buddy, it's you and me against the world, just like in 'Nam." He chuckled, winking playfully. "I wonder what beautiful frauleins may be waiting to meet us at the gambling casinos in Baden Baden?"

"My wife's flying over," Brockmann confided. "She's keeping a close watch on me this time." He laughed good naturedly. "I'm sorry ole buddy, but you're gonna have to do a solo and get into temptation's way all by yourself."

The two officers jostled each other as soldiers often do, whiling away their time. Maccabee forced a grim smile, missing the camaraderie of ODT. He checked his wristwatch. 10:32. Two hours and forty minutes had passed since the first roll call. Livingston still hadn't showed up.

Maccabee felt his anxiety rising, fearing the worst. He didn't want to believe Wally was the mole. Yet now, every thought screamed out for retribution. Wally was a KGB spy. Wally had betrayed their trust. Wally had been involved in all of these murders. He deserved the stiffest penalty. Maybe death! He fought with himself, trying to control his vivid imagination. He didn't want to believe it. Not Wally ...

He caught Bailey's eye and took him aside. "Any word from Livingston yet?" he asked, stiff-lipped. "Has he phoned in yet? Did he call in sick?"

Bailey shook his head. "Not a word. He's the only one missing."

"Did anyone call his apartment?"

The personnel officer nodded. He pointed toward his admin NCO, Sergeant Lopez. "Carlos called thirty minutes ago. Nobody answered the phone."

Maccabee grimaced, knowing he'd have to phone the FBI as soon as the troops left for the airport. Should he wait, he wondered? If Wally and Liu Ann are on the run, we need to nail them quick. Liu Ann. He shook his head. How could Wally get so deeply involved with a Chinese concubine? Liu Ann was a curse upon his good name. Maccabee paced back and forth, his thoughts growing darker and darker.

He talked quietly with Brockmann and Goetz until 10:45, when the troops lined up to board the buses. They advanced in single file, climbing inside.

Collette Perkins, a tall, dynamic, talkative high school teacher and wife of Major Thomas Perkins, the hard-nosed 44-year old mechanical engineer from Patterson, New Jersey, tugged on Maccabee's arm. She had a worried look on her face. "Dave, you take good care of my Tommy!" Maccabee felt embarrassed for Perkins, who was within earshot. Normally, Maccabee would have told her Perkins was old enough to take care of himself. This time Maccabee kept silent.

Maccabee's eyes widened, his face spread into a grin. A shiny white Cadillac screeched to a halt. It parked diagonally in front of the lead bus. Maccabee breathed a sigh of relief.

Wally Livingston threw open the door on the passenger side and leaped out. He opened up the back door and yanked-out two duffel bags and an attaché case. He looked up at Maccabee, his face flushed with nervousness. "If anything could go wrong today, it did," he complained.

He thrust one duffel bag into Maccabee's hands and threw the other over his shoulder. He grabbed his attaché case with his other hand. "First, they had my car buried in the garage. Took over a half hour before the lone attendant drove it out. Then I had a flat tire on the FDR Drive. Ever have a flat tire in all that traffic? It's dangerous as hell. I was damn near run over a dozen times. You'd think these crazy drivers would have mercy."

Livingston swung his duffel bag into the arms of an NCO inside the lead bus, still talking to Maccabee over his shoulder. "I sure hope this isn't a bad omen for our tour of duty." He grabbed the second duffel bag from Maccabee and flipped it inside. "What a helluva way to start." He climbed onto the first step of the bus, then leaned back out. He waved good-bye to his wife, who had double parked the Cadillac down the street. She waved back.

Maccabee snapped a thumbs up signal to his former deputy, flashing a genuine grin. "Have a good trip, old friend. See you in two weeks."

The door to the charter bus closed. The driver revved up the engine, and pulled away from the curb. Maccabee walked over to Liu Ann, regretting his earlier ugly thoughts. "Heard you had trouble getting here. At least, Wally didn't miss the bus."

Liu Ann, a tall willowy woman with classic Chinese features, looked up from the open window. High cheekbones, large almond eyes and a full mouth masked a hidden arrogance that lurked beneath the surface of her flawless porcelain face. "I came within inches of being killed," she said, icily. "Wally was changing the right front tire when this maniac almost side-swiped us. I couldn't believe it. Even the police car parked behind us couldn't wave him off!"

She glared at Maccabee and spoke in a condescending tone. "Wally is no use to me now. I trust your war games are worth it." Having made her point, she closed the window and drove away.

Maccabee stood transfixed, watching the Cadillac disappear around the corner. He didn't know what to make out of her last comment.

An enormous burden had been lifted from his shoulders. "Thank goodness, Wally is not the mole," he murmured.

He walked briskly to his Chevy Blazer, still searching for an answer. "I'm back to where I started. Who in hell is the mole?" He wheeled the Blazer into traffic and onto the Cross Bronx Expressway. He sped across the Whitestone Bridge towards Fort Totten and the waiting Hueys. For the reservists, it would be a day of "hurry up and wait." For Maccabee, it was time to scramble.

Slowing down at the sentry gate, Maccabee flashed his ID card to the female MP with a pixie haircut and starched BDUs and drove onto the sleepy, isolated Army Reserve post. He drove around the parade field and rolled onto the chopper pad located at the far nook of the post. Morgan, O'Brien and Freddy, dressed in BDUs, stood about fifty yards from the waiting Hueys, whose twirling props kicked up clouds of dust.

As Maccabee climbed out of his Blazer, Freddy ran up to him, puffing, out of breath. "I checked out both machine guns, loaded dah belts. We've got M-16s, a grenade launcher and lotsa ammo." He pointed toward LaSalle, who climbed out of Huey One. "We're all set to go."

Maccabee signaled LaSalle to stay aboard. Before he could run to the chopper, O'Brien rushed up to him, grabbed him by the arm and shepherded him into the wooden operations shack, where they could hear each other speak above the clamorous din of the choppers.

"I have some news for you. Some good, some bad. Just came in from our CIA office in Bremerhaven. Want to hear it?"

Maccabee nodded. "Hell, yes. Let's hear the bad news first."

O'Brien didn't know how to say it tactfully. He blurted it out. "The chief says Gretchen Lundstrom is a spy. I'm sorry boss, but it looks like your girlfriend works for a foreign government."

Maccabee laughed. "She's been a thorn in our side, sensationalizing the news," he said defensively, "but she's no Russian spy." He put his arm around O'Brien's shoulder and started walking him toward the door. "You guys in the CIA need to coordinate better with the FBI. The bureau has evidence that proves she's innocent. She was manipulated by a KGB agent. They're watching her closely."

O'Brien stopped in his tracks. "I didn't say Russian spy." He paused. " She's BND ... German secret service."

"Come on, Tim. Gretchen's on a fast track, but not that fast."

They stood in the doorway, facing each other, grim-faced.

"How much do you know about Gretchen's background before she came to the United States?"

The question unnerved Maccabee. There had always been something about Gretchen that troubled him. Her damn German superiority. Her resourcefulness. "She told me that she grew up in war torn Germany and had a domineering mother, whom she never got along with. She worked as a domestic, first for the Brits, then here. She became a reporter in the mid-seventies."

"Did you know her father was a German U-boat officer?"

Maccabee ran his hand through his hair, recalling. "She said he was a submariner, disillusioned about the war, never the same afterwards. Was depth charged one time too many. She visits him once a year."

"Her old man was first officer on the U-boat that smuggled in a hoard of Nazi gold to Argentina before WWII ended. What she hasn't told you is that her father is a right wing extremist who lives on a fat pension from a secret Swiss bank account. We think she may be a sleeper." O'Brien chuckled, then continued quickly. "Not just with you boss, but planted here to become a media influential, to shape the news to support a strong Federal Republic of Germany, possibly the resurgence of the Fourth Reich."

Maccabee's mouth was agape. "You're serious, aren't you?"

"Absolutely. It's bad enough searching for spies who steal high tech military secrets and sell them to our enemies for cash. Now we have to ferret out NATO spies, who want to undermine our government to achieve their country's political goals.

Where will it end?"

"I can't believe it," Maccabee shouted, angrily. He slammed his fist into the wall, splintering the soft wooden paneling. "Do you have irrefutable proof?"

"Yes, we do," O'Brien answered. He stepped back, putting a safe distance between Maccabee and himself. "It could be worse. At least, we're on the same side." He scratched his curly head. "I think we are, aren't we?"

"Damn it all!" Maccabee cocked his fist to strike the wall again, then thought better of it. He rubbed the skinned knuckles on his hand, wondering which felt worse, the bruised knuckles or his bruised ego. "I feel like I've been taken! How dumb can I be? It's like falling in love with a Goddamned whore."

O'Brien tugged on his arm, pulling him through the door and outside. "C'mon, boss, it's not that bad. She's still a friendly. If you need to vex your anger, let's get airborne and find those terrorists."

The two officers hunkered down and ran toward their choppers. As Maccabee approached Huey One, he flashed a thumbs-up signal to the pilot. He climbed aboard, plopped into a jump seat and grabbed a set of headphones. Freddy climbed in behind him. Within minutes the two Hueys were airborne, enroute to Floyd Bennett Field and their search for the Stinger.

While the two Greyhound buses headed toward the Whitestone Bridge, Vladimir outfoxed the FBI for the second time in two days. A Soviet chauffeur, who closely resembled Vladimir, drove a black limousine out of the Soviet mission's garage and headed over the George Washington Bridge into New Jersey toward Newark Airport. A team of three FBI cars followed, one ahead, two behind, leapfrogging caravan style. A fourth FBI team that stayed behind spotted a female driver wheel the elusive black Chevy van into the heavy morning traffic.

Tanya Szabo, a 25-year old KGB agent, trained in high speed escape and evasion, whipped the van through the morning traffic like a veteran race track driver. She pulled a brodie on the Queensboro Bridge, jumped lanes and lost the FBI car going in the opposite direction. She raced downtown and zipped into the Midtown Tunnel. She sped across the Brooklyn Queens Expressway towards JFK with KGB Lieutenants Vladimir and Drachev sitting in the rear.

A Mongolian by birth, the short stocky, moon-faced brunette drove the van into the quiet town of Valley Stream, where the Soviet safehouse was located. Szabo turned into a narrow driveway between two cedar shake bungalows on 250th Street and parked next to the kitchen porch. Vladimir opened the van's sliding side door and jumped to the ground without being observed. He returned within minutes, cradling the Stinger missile under his arm. The two PLO terrorists followed closely behind.

Backing out of the alley, Szabo drove the van back onto Sunrise Highway. She was right on schedule. 11:15. She followed the Belt Parkway and then veered off onto Rockaway Boulevard. Twelve minutes later, she drove onto the sandy driveway of the ramshackle bungalow on Old Channel Lane and parked by the water's edge. Vladimir opened the van's sliding side door and leaped to the ground first. The others followed quickly.

They climbed aboard the 28-foot cabin cruiser. Mohammed and Abdallah carried

171

the Stinger into the forward cabin below. They removed it from its protective casing and laid it on a velvet padded berth, caressing it fanatically. "Death to the United States," they whispered. They slipped off their shoes, checked their wrist watches and waited to do their noon prayers.

Vladimir climbed up the boat's ladder onto the command bridge and sat hulking in the captain's chair behind the steering wheel. He started the engine. Drachev, fair-headed, short and muscular with a gymnast's build, cast off the bow and stern lines, jumped aboard and climbed up the ladder onto the bridge. Vladimir steered the cabin cruiser slowly into mid-channel at about five knots per hour, trying not to make a wake. The foursome were dressed in blue windbreakers, gray sweatshirts and jeans. They looked like casual weekend sailors about to go fishing. Jamaica Bay and JFK airport lay less than one mile away to starboard.

Szabo wheeled the black van toward Rockaway Boulevard and JFK. She had been trained in the KGB art of silent killing in public places. Having proved her worth in Geneva and Hong Kong, Szabo mulled over her midnight rendezvous with Colonel Kolchak. She was ready for the task ahead, to liquidate the Spetsnaz in a crowded lobby at the airport at Kolchak's command.

Yet, she had serious misgivings about her mission. She steered the van into the heavy westbound traffic on the Belt Parkway. She tried to concentrate on her driving, maneuvering the van into the inside lane.

She spotted the green signs to JFK and watched for the access road. Kolchak, she brooded, why did the Soviet under-secretary in-charge of intelligence warn her to watch the KGB master spy? If KGB Central in Moscow is worried about too many killings, why is Kolchak planning another murder in such a high visible area?

She regretted Kolchak had sworn her to silence. Torn by divided loyalties, her pulse beat faster as she drove into the short term parking lot by the International Terminal. "Is Comrade Kolchak following KGB orders or is he on a ruthless blood rampage, paying off old scores?"

The Spetsnaz drove his Cherokee into JFK's employee parking lot number seven. He rode the employee bus to the Lufthansa cargo building, where he got off. He wore a gray workmen's uniform with the Lufthansa yellow logo embroidered on back. It covered his black frogman's diving suit, which had dried out from his early morning swim in to JFK. He carried a large black tool box that contained a radio set, honing system, and a crumpled brown paper lunch bag with a loaf of French bread inside. A medium size canvas totebag hung innocently from his shoulder, containing a theatrical makeup kit, extra clothes, a secret GRU passport and GRU paraphernalia.

Petrovich walked inside the large warehouse and made his way to the employee's area. Once inside, he searched for locker number 332. He found it without any difficulty and used the key Kolchak had given him. Yanking the locker door open, he found a wallet and forged passport on the locker's top shelf. He pinned a special JFK identification card onto his uniform. It was a computer controlled, class one, red holograph ID card that gave him access to all high security areas. His new name: Horst Gunther, occupation, transportation supervisor.

He walked to the assignment board, grabbed a piece of white chalk and logged

172

himself in. He found a time card with Gunther's name on it and punched it into the time clock. 12:44.

He walked out of the warehouse and into the parking lot, carrying his tool kit and totebag. A small Lufthansa three-quarter ton cargo truck awaited him. He found the keys under the front seat, started the engine and drove onto the cargo service road toward the central terminal area.

The Spetsnaz entered the restricted high security area through the airport's back door. He stopped at Guard Post G and showed his ID. The guard looked at it carefully, noted the license plate on the rear of the truck, which had been previously logged. He waved him through.

Petrovich drove onto the ramp, dodging a yellow tow tug pulling four dollies of baggage to an awaiting British Airways jetliner. "It is not difficult to penetrate security," he murmured, "when we pay people to do our dirty work. Once on Soviet payroll, they are slaves forever."

He drove slowly at fifteen miles per hour, keeping close to the airline buildings, weaving around a red Marriott food catering lift truck servicing a TWA jetliner. A blue and white police car cruised by slowly, its patrolmen looking for something.

The Spetsnaz stared straight ahead, as he drove around the inside perimeter of the International Airlines Arrival building. He drew up near a green tailed Alitalia departure on the west wing, stopping next to a sanitation lift truck. Another blue and white police car cruised into view, circling the Pan American terminal just ahead. He wondered why security had tightened-up.

Turning, he steered the truck across the hardstand and past the taxiing area to a remote spot on runway 4 Right. A four-man construction crew was patching a crack near the edge of the runway. They didn't notice him as he jumped out of the truck.

The Spetsnaz walked to the seawall, unobserved. . He pulled the loaf of French bread out of his paper lunch bag and tore it into chunks, throwing them into the salt water. Seagulls appeared out of nowhere, dove for the morsels, then swooped away. The Spetsnaz slid down the breakwater piling to the water's edge. Spotting a blue bobber in the water that he had inserted earlier in the morning, he fished out a small watertight canvas bag. He slipped it inside the front of his work uniform and walked casually back to the truck. The construction crew continued with their repair work, ignoring him completely.

Petrovich drove back toward the Lufthansa service area, pleased that his pre-dawn swim from Hamilton Beach had succeeded. He opened the canvas bag and grasped a tiny black electronic sensor, which he planned to place on Pan Am Flight 120 before it taxied away. He drove past the TWA and British Airways terminals.

As he approached Guard Post G, he saw a tighter security net. Two guards with clipboards inspected a Federal Express van, checking the van's manifest against the packages inside. Four DHL worldwide express vans were lined up behind it. He wheeled his truck out of harms way, deciding to stay inside the security perimeter.

Petrovich drove back to the Lufthansa arrivals and departure area on the East Wing and parked the truck near a screening point. Getting out, he walked inside the terminal to find a pay phone.

He called Kolchak at home, using the unlisted number he had been given. When the KGB controller answered, he asked, "Has there been change to mission?"

173

There was a one word reply. "Nyet!"

Petrovich hung-up. He walked downstairs to the employee area and back out through the screening area. He climbed back into the Lufthansa truck and tried to relax. He watched the jetliners takeoff on runway 4 Left, noticing that the wind conditions were negligible. Unless the weather changes drastically, the KGB boat will be in perfect position to shoot down the Pan Am plane as it flies over Jamaica Bay.

The Spetsnaz listened to the FAA radio frequency in his truck, and the weather reports were favorable. As he sunk deeper into the seat, his dilemma nagged at him. No amount of killing would bring back his son or his fallen comrades. The thought of mass murder, of revenge, left a sour taste in his mouth. "Why do I invite grief on myself? Why do I let Moscow turn me into mad dog killer? Soviet government is evil. If I walk away now, I drop allegiance to Soviet government. I still be loyal to my people, to my country." He looked at his watch. 12:58. He waited.

Kolchak flung the phone down violently, upsetting the ash tray on the end table in his apartment. "The GRU cannot be trusted!" he spat out, belligerently. The call had taken all of six seconds. Kolchak wanted to know if everything was going according to plan. The blockhead did not give him sufficient time to ask.

Kolchak stomped around his living room, disturbed there was nothing more he could do. He had fine tuned his propaganda press releases, churning them into formidable backgrounders. He had set the timer of his IBM computer to transmit his propaganda by modem to catch the evening news deadlines. He grew impatient.

He worried about KGB Central's directive to arrest the Spetznaz. Why hadn't the KGB Director sent more information? Is Moscow changing signals and running for cover? Maybe I shouldn't kill him? Maybe I should do as I am ordered?

He wiped his dry lips nervously, looking for a cigarette.

No, he thought. The Spetsnaz is too dangerous to capture. If he smells a trap, I could end up the victim, not him. He lit a Carlton and dragged deeply on it. He paced back and forth, arguing with himself.

Is Moscow setting me up? His survival instincts were creating havoc with his stomach. A deep belch echoed from its lower extremities. He rushed to the medicine cabinet in the bathroom, and popped two Alka Seltzer tablets into a glass of water. He downed it in three gulps, trying to settle his queasy digestive system.

He couldn't stand it any longer. At 1:25, he called a taxi for his rendezvous with Tanya Szabo at the Pan Am Clipper Club at JFK. As he draped his overcoat over his shoulders and reached for the doorknob, the phone rang again.

He hoped the Spetsnaz was calling again. Rushing back into the room, he picked the phone up on the fourth ring. "This is Dmitri Kolchak."

An impatient Gretchen Lundstrom cut in. "Dmitri, I want better answers than the ones you've been feeding me." Her voice was harsh and antagonistic. "I checked out your story about the highjacker, Horst Gunther, your so-called West German intelligence officer, who's supposed to be a Stasi double agent. It's a lot of crap, like everything else you've been feeding me."

The Soviet controller stiffened, his breath coming in short gasps.

"You forget that I have friends at the West German Mission to the UN," she chided, sarcastically. "You should not underestimate me."

Kolchak held his breath, clenching the phone tightly, his knuckles turning white.

"The Federal Republic of Germany's intelligence service denies that any espionage agent by the name of Horst Gunther ever existed."

"They don't trust you with secrets," he insisted. "You're a journalist. That's why I give skyjack story to you as big exclusive."

The doorman's intercom buzzed. "Yer taxi is waiting at dah curb."

"Dmitri, we need to have an understanding ..."

Kolchak cut her off, abruptly. "I can't talk any more. You must wait. I have taxi waiting downstairs. I must go to airport immediately!"

"But Dmitri ..."

He slammed the phone down violently and rushed for the elevator.

Gretchen stared at her phone. Nobody does that to me and gets away with it! She redialed his number, angrily, and heard the phone ring five times. Then his answering machine clicked on.

She hung up. What was so damn important at the airport that he can't talk to me? We've played cat and mouse far too long. Something big must be coming to a climax. I can feel it.

She had dressed to go shopping at Saks Fifth Avenue. She wore a tailored Ann Klein black wool jumpsuit that was tapered to reveal her long, lean look. She paced to and fro across the living room carpet in stocking feet. She sprawled out on the couch, then stood again. If Gunther was supposed to highjack a plane at La Guardia on Monday evening, why was Dmitri rushing to the airport now?

She sat down, tapped the auto redial on her phone for Dave's apartment. She slipped on a pair of four-inch spike-heeled I. Miller black pumps, cradling the receiver between her shoulder and ear. The phone rang three times, then a recording came on. "Damn! Where is he? Just when I need him the most."

She left a message on Maccabee's answering machine and hung up. Thrusting both hands into her jumpsuit's deep pockets, she walked to the picture window. She stared at the gray New York skyline, disconcerted. She tried to think logically. Dave had been too busy to talk to me last night. He hasn't called back. He knows I love him. Why won't he open up and let me help?

She struggled with her emotions, bringing them under control. She grew angrier, thinking about Dmitri. How he lied. How he tried to manipulate me. His last words echoed in her mind. "I must go to airport immediately." What's so damn important about the airport? It's only Saturday, two days before Herr Gunther comes to town. Two days before ...

Suddenly, a clairvoyant perception struck her. "He's highjacking the plane today!" she bellowed. "Dave said he had to see the troops off at the airport." This sudden awareness shocked her into action. Pulling out her telephone directory from a cluttered drawer on an end table, she skimmed rapidly through the pages until she found the phone number for the 38th Civil Affairs Command. Her fingers tapped out the numbers quickly.

After four rings, a reservist from another unit, who was passing by the 38th's empty admin office, picked up the phone. "Nobody heah from the 38th," he said. "They gone to Germany for two weeks."

"Can you tell me the airline and flight number?" she asked, anxiously.

"I dunno," he answered, blandly. "Most flights leave around five or six o'clock. I heard some guy mention Pan Am."

"Do you know what airport they're flying out of?"

"Yeah, lady. JFK."

"Thank you." She hung up, then hit the auto redial to her city editor at the *Times*. "I want a chopper standing by for me in twenty minutes at the East 23rd Street heliport. There may be a highjack brewing at JFK. Keep it under wraps until I'm positive."

She placed a second phone call to the Undersecretary for Cultural Affairs at the West German Mission to the U.N. She spoke tersely to her controller. "The KGB plans to highjack a Pan Am jetliner tonight. They're targeting the 38th CA Command!! They're trying to subvert CIMIC and our NATO alliance."

She hung up, grabbed her purse and rushed for the door. Stopping in mid-stride, she turned and darted back into the bedroom. She opened her night table drawer. A black plastic 9mm Beretta automatic was tucked under a vanity case. She inspected it, ejected the ammunition clip, then slapped it back into firing position. She slipped the lightweight automatic into her purse, and hurried out the door.

"If I know Dmitri," she murmured, "he'll be lushing it up at the Pan Am Clipper Club. It has the best unobstructed view of all the runways." Not the one on the upper concourse, she remembered, but the one on the rooftop level. I have to find Kolchak and grill him ... before it's too late.

Across the street from Kolchak's apartment at the FBI stakeout, John Howard sat in a dazed condition, his eardrums aching. He had the headset tuned to full volume, when Kolchak slammed the phone down on Gretchen. He listened to his partner play back the recording of Kolchak's first conversation, knowing that he couldn't trace a six-second call.

"Damn it! That must have been the Spetsnaz who called! Strange way to verify an execution order." Howard used the FBI frequency on his cellular phone to call the FBI Ford parked down the street. "The red vulture is about to fly. He's taking a taxi to JFK. Follow him and keep in touch. As soon as he clears midtown, me and Spriggy will go over and dupe his tape recorder and do a computer dump."

Howard played back the second recording, wondering what Colonel Mac's lady friend was up to. "What do you make of this highjack talk?"

"Beats me," his partner answered. "He called it skyjack. She calls it highjack. Sounds like someone's planning to hoist a plane in our backyard."

"Better phone our guys over at Lundstrom's apartment building," Howard suggested. "Let's find out if she's made any more calls."

He turned toward Sergeant Spriggy Covalho, who was dressed in her Mickey Mouse T-shirt and jeans. Saturday was an ARCOM drill day for her reserve unit, and the commanding general had approved her stint with the FBI as equivalent duty for pay purposes. "About ready to go?" Howard asked.

Spriggy looked up from a computer magazine she was reading. "Shouldn't take as long the second time around." She patted her totebag and the software inside. "Just tell me when."

On the second pass over the Belt Parkway in Huey One, Maccabee peered down at the congested traffic jam below. The NYPD had set up a roadblock near a housing development complex and had diverted three lanes of traffic into one. Maccabee had helped engineer the NYPD game plan to delay and disrupt all traffic leading into JFK. If the terrorists used surface transportation, this simple strategy could upset their time schedule.

Using high powered binoculars, Maccabee spotted NYPD blue suiters who were patrolling the apartment building rooftops. The NYPD had redeployed teams of uniformed and plainclothes cops from each of the city's five boroughs, placing them in a one mile semicircle around JFK. Every off-duty police officer and brown suit traffic cop had been recalled.

"There are too many rooftops to watch," Maccabee shouted to Freddy, who kneeled alongside him. They passed over the sandy marshlands along the Jamaica Riding Academy and saw NYPD dog handler teams patrolling the empty beaches.

The chopper veered inland over Brooklyn, circling the old red brick apartment buildings that dotted the landscape along Flatbush Avenue. If I could only have army reserve troops on the ground, Maccabee thought, I could dissect every city block. I need troops on those rooftops and beaches. Yet, he knew deploying the reserves was against orders. JFK had to be kept open at all costs, despite the risk to his friends in the 38th. Any leak to the press would warn the terrorists, who could strike at another time of their choosing.

Adjusting the headset atop his head, Maccabee checked the map on his clipboard. The NYPD had established a defensive perimeter around JFK. Major LaSalle, piloting Huey One, tuned into the JFK control tower, which controlled the three NYPD observation choppers and two Coast Guard choppers that were all airborne. Each helicopter had been assigned a specific geographic grid to patrol. With the heavy incoming and outgoing air traffic, each chopper had been assigned a specific altitude. The danger of a mid-air collision preyed on everyone's minds.

The two army choppers had been deployed as a roving patrol to seek any target of opportunity. Maccabee selected the flight path over Jamaica Bay and the Rockaways. He radioed Major Morgan and Captain O'Brien, who were flying in Huey Two over Long Beach and the south shore. "Anything down there unusual?"

"Nothing here, sir," Major Morgan shouted, over the roar of the helicopter's engine. She scanned the desolate sand dunes along Atlantic Beach, flying over the empty beach clubs and condos. "There goes another jetliner," she said, pointing to a TWA jetliner taking off from JFK outbound runway 4 Right. The aircraft climbed quickly and veered across the Inwood fuel tanks and Far Rockaway, heading out across the Atlantic Ocean.

An inbound Air France airbus roared overhead on its final approach. The big bird settled slowly onto inbound runway 4 Left. Maccabee gazed out the other side of the Huey. Another jetliner circled east on its approach path toward the Rockaways and

JFK. The jetliners were now landing at two minute intervals.

He checked his wristwatch. 2:59. Only two hours left before Pan Am's scheduled departure for Flight 120. "Let's double back and fly over the Inwood fuel tanks again," he said in a worried voice over the intercom.

"Rogah, Inwood tanks," LaSalle confirmed, banking the chopper across the wildlife tidal flats towards the Cross Bay Parkway, which cut across Jamaica Bay. They headed toward a boat marina. A lonely white cabin cruiser with blue racing stripes on its hull fished off an inlet near the far shore.

At 3:04, an agitated Dmitri Kolchak sat frustrated in the back seat of a yellow cab, stuck in traffic. The taxi had made good time, driving across the FDR Bridge and Grand Central Parkway until it screeched to a slowdown in the heavy backed-up traffic on the Van Wyck Expressway. "Some expressway," he murmured, watching the cab crawl bumper-to-bumper for almost fifteen minutes. The normal fifty minute trip had dragged into an hour and a half ... with no let up. He rolled down the window and tried to see what was holding up the traffic. About a quarter mile ahead, two lanes of cars were merging into his lane, getting ahead of him. "Can't we use the city streets?" he shouted to the driver.

"I'm not a magician," the cabby answered, resentfully, his head bobbing left and right, trying to see ahead. "I see flashing lights. Must be police cars. With this traffic jam, it must be a humdinger of an accident."

Kolchak wouldn't be mollified. He looked out the rear window, but didn't see two gray FBI sedans, following three car lengths behind. He became more irritable. He hated to sacrifice a deep cover mole on Flight 120, but he still held the mole's wife on a string. The man has outlived his usefulness. He knows too much. No love lost between him and wife. He sighed with utter disdain. I find her another husband.

The yellow cab crept forward two car lengths, then jerked to a stop, idling. The traffic was at a standstill. Kolchak finally lost his composure. "I must catch plane!" he screamed, vehemently. "You get me to JFK before 3:30. I must not be late!"

17

"Boarding for Pan Am Flight One Two Oh will be delayed one hour," echoed across Pan Am's public address system. The troopers of the 38th were visibly annoyed. They milled about aimlessly in groups of threes and fours at Gate 7, holding their tickets and boarding passes. Some stood, some sat. Others drifted back past the security magnetometer screening point and out onto the main concourse that led to the USO lounge for the armed forces and the duty-free shops.

Major Jerry Brockmann, Major Klaus Ludwig and Major Kurt Goetz browsed through Bloomies, Cartier and several other boutiques. They wandered down the concourse, observing the throng of passengers scurrying about. Some read books, guarding zealously their carry-on luggage, others slept sprawled across the confines of narrow uncomfortable seats, others paced back and forth restlessly.

The trio engaged in people-watching, noting the international character of the horde of people passing by, trying to guess their country of origin. Light skin, dark skin, mixed breeds, Asians and blacks. People from every social class and continent. Old, young, marrieds, singles, students, children, infants; wearing every conceivable mode of dress; carrying a colorful array of suitcases, handbags, totebags and backpacks; chattering in foreign languages they had never heard. They felt like strangers in their own land.

After awhile, they wandered back toward the military baggage check-in counter, where army reservists from another unit were huddling. They decided to get some fresh air and walked through the heavy glass doors that opened magnetically for them. They sauntered out onto the sidewalk.

Goetz lit a Marlboro as he watched incoming taxis drop off passengers and luggage at the hub of the horseshoe on the upper level, where they stood. He turned to Brockmann, confiding, "I'm not going to miss the rat race. It's good to get away from Erika and the job, even if it's only for two weeks. I should have stayed in the army. Life was a lot simpler then."

"Yeah-h," Brockmann grinned. "You were getting your damn ass shot off. You forget what it was like. I don't want to go through that hell again. Six weeks in the hospital, man that was enough. We paid our dues. I don't want any more of it."

"Why did you stay in the reserves?" Goetz asked, seriously.

Brockmann shrugged. "Same as you. I couldn't let go. Once you wear the uniform, it's glued to your back. It's part of me. The money doesn't hurt either. All of my army reserve pay goes into a college fund for my kids. If something happens to me, at least they have a jump on life." He smiled, then added, "I'm a diplomat warrior now, no more charging up hills to the sound of gunfire. I'm an *offizier* ... and a gentleman, ready for a two week gentleman's tour."

Goetz laughed, nudging him. "I still think you should come to Baden Baden with

179

me. We can hit the casino. Your wife is no different than mine. Bring Ursula along for luck. I'm sure she'd like the excitement. Maybe you'll get lucky and win."

"Are you kidding!" Brockmann laughed. "My wife will never believe me again when I tell her I work sixteen hours a day in Germany. All she has to do is see me screw around with you one night. Life will never be the same."

"Come on, Jerry," Goetz kidded. "I'm not that bad an influence."

"Who says?" Brockmann jabbed his buddy in the arm. He turned to Ludwig and started to walk back inside the terminal. "Where's Livingston? I haven't seen him since we checked-in our duffel bags."

"Where do you think?" Ludwig answered. "Wally's a frequent flyer, flies first class wherever he goes. He's at the Clipper Club Lounge on the top deck, conducting last minute business. Probably set the phone booth up like a sales office. Do you know what that crazy workaholic told me he was going to do?"

"What?" Brockmann asked, humorously.

"He told me he had to make a long distance phone call to Hong Kong, to some Chinese businessman from Shanghai. He had to fax a purchase order to him at the Marco Polo Club. I don't know about Wally. He never stops working."

"I've been there," Goetz said, trying to impress his buddies. "It's one of those ver-ry British-h-h colonial clubs, where western bankers meet with Chinese communist businessmen on neutral turf. They have some gorgeous Chinese hostesses there. High priced call girls, but ver-ry good." He winked, promiscuously, rubbing his close-cropped sandy blond hair. "Ver-ry nice!"

"Shouldn't be calling Hong Kong on personal business," Brockmann chided. "Silly bastard, doesn't he know he's on active duty now?"

"He'll miss the flight," Ludwig said. "Hope he knows what he's doing."

"If he misses the flight, he misses it," Brockmann murmured. "He should know better." He checked his watch. 3:24. "Come on," he chortled, "Let's go inside. I want to check our departure time." He and Ludwig walked back through the open doors into the terminal's departure reception area.

"I'll catch up to you guys in a minute," Goetz said. "I want to finish smoking my cigarette." He blew a thin smoke ring that dissipated into the air. His eyes followed his two buddies as they greeted an incoming busload of army reservists dressed in BDUs, who had come in through the front entrance. The reservists stacked their duffel bags at the military baggage check-in counter, awaiting a charter flight to Fort Bragg, North Carolina.

Goetz inhaled deeply, glad to be alone. He tried to relax, to control a premonition of danger that gnawed persistently in his stomach, turning it into twisted knots. He wanted to force his life with Erika out of his mind. Their marriage had failed. It was beyond redemption. He was over his head. He wished he had never met her. How to cope ...

At 3:26, a yellow cab pulled up, it's exhaust pipes spewing out a fuming cloud of blue carbon monoxide. Goetz turned away, choking slightly. He noticed the shoelace on his right shoe had become undone. As he turned and knelt down to tie it, he didn't notice the tall agitated Kolchak thrust the cab door open and dart directly into the terminal. Neither man saw the other.

180

Kolchak charged ahead, turning to the right once he walked inside. He made a straight path toward the Clipper Club, passing the Port of Authority security guards, who manned the magnetometer check-in screening point for gates three to seven. He pushed the "up" button on the elevator, impatiently.

Minutes later, he stepped inside, and rode it up one flight to the rooftop level. He stepped out into a hallway, looked out a glass door onto the rooftop parking lot, then hurried through a heavy oak paneled door into the VIP lounge. He showed his Clipper Club ID card at the reception desk.

Saying little, he strode across the thick, well-worn blue carpet, oblivious to the elegance around him. Tanya Szabo looked up from reading a magazine. She sat in an upholstered chair in an empty alcove underneath a nostalgic Pan Am advertisement, reminiscent of Pan Am's days of glory.

As Kolchak hurried towards her, he walked past Wally Livingston without seeing him. Livingston sat at a computer station, his back turned blindly to the aisle, typing a message in a sheltered alcove that was arranged as a business office for Clipper Club cardholders.

Szabo set aside a cup of coffee on the red marble coffee table as Kolchak approached. She started to rise.

Kolchak motioned her to continue drinking with a flourish of his hand. The luxury lounge was relatively empty. A bartender busied himself at the square-shaped bar in the center of the room, not noticing him.

Kolchak sat on the edge of a small cane-backed settee across from her and spoke softly in Russian. He instructed her to follow him closely when he leaves to meet the Spetsnaz after the missile attack. He reviewed her mission and nodded with satisfaction when she told him how she planned to terminate the hated GRU colonel. "I want him dead!" he said, ruthlessly.

He reached inside his suit jacket and handed her an Aeroflot ticket for a flight to Moscow later that night.

He rose without further comment and walked to the far corner of the lounge, an isolated vantage point that overlooked the two JFK bay runways and Jamaica Bay. He snapped his finger loudly and signaled the bartender who looked up from polishing a wine goblet. "Double Stoli!" he barked, "with slice of lemon."

Kolchak plumped into an overstuffed couch. He glanced at the flight information on the black and white television monitor above him. He frowned as he read the data. "Pan Am Flight 120. DELAY. Departs 1800 hours."

He checked his watch. 3:42. Picking up a copy of Fortune, he tried to read it, but couldn't concentrate. He looked out the skyview window and watched a British Airways Concorde land on the bay runway.

"Stay calm," he said to himself. "The first attack ... the diversion, should come at any time."

Kolchak knew he'd be insulated. There will be limited casualties and mayhem, nothing else. He felt no pangs of conscience.

He waited for the main event, smirking with eager anticipation. It would come soon enough. He had the best seat in the house.

At 3:42, a checkered cab pulled up to the Pan Am rear entrance of the International West Wing at the hub of the horseshoe, about ten feet from where Goetz had been standing. The two women inside did not notice the fair-haired troubled man take one last drag of his cigarette, grind it out under his heel, and walk inside toward his buddies at the military check-in counter.

They were too intent with the purpose of their trip. A young woman of college age, dressed in a black leather jacket and skin tight blue jeans, climbed out first. Samar Zahid, a short, sorrowful-eyed Syrian with black hair streaming down her back, was an exchange student at San Diego State University. She reached inside the cab and struggled with a heavy, oversized, black leather suitcase, which she dragged onto the curb. She lifted the bulky suitcase onto a two-wheel mini luggage cart and strapped it onto the aluminum frame.

She helped Utafa al-Birwa, who was dressed in a traditional black Arab headdress and chador that fell to her ankles, crawl awkwardly out of the cab. A black cloth veil, masking most of her shriveled, weather-beaten face, revealed two dark tormented eyes that had witnessed more pain than her 36-years could endure.

They spoke Arabic in a barely audible whisper. The younger woman pulled the luggage cart with one hand, while grasping the arm of the older woman with the other. She led her through the rear glass door into the terminal, unnoticed. She sat her down in an empty row of four brown seats, located against the far wall of a vacant stairwell.

The two women stared with glaring hostility at the soldiers milling about at the check-in counter. Samar Zahid took the older woman's hands in hers, clutching them tightly. "Inshallah," she whispered. "God willing."

The older distraught woman forced back tears. Utafa al-Birwa, a Shiite Moslem, had spent her entire life in the Jebaliya Refugee Camp in the Gaza strip. Her husband Ahmed had joined Fatah as a freedom fighter. He had been killed by Israeli Bedouin anti-terrorist trackers, when he tried to infiltrate from Jordan.

Two teenage sons, Hasan and Hisham, had been killed throwing petrol bombs at a passing Israeli jeep during the Intifada uprising. In retribution, her house had been bulldozed to rubble. When PLO agents recruited her for terrorist training in Iraq, she volunteered willingly to become a martyr, to fly to America, to make the Great Satan pay a debt of blood.

The older woman nodded good-bye.

Zahid rushed from the terminal and climbed into the waiting cab. "Take me to La Guardia airport," she said. "American Airlines. I have to fly to California."

Inside, Utafa al-Birwa clutched the chador cloak firmly around her body like an Indian blanket. She felt the unyielding weight of an Uzi submachine gun, harnessed under yards of stiff black cloth. She trembled as she rehearsed in her mind how she had to pull out the safety pin, before she threw the Soviet-made hand grenade, which was hitched to her waistband for quick removal.

She rose wearily to her feet, hearing ... but not understanding an announcement made in English that blared over the loudspeakers.

"This is a security check. All unattended baggage will be removed by security personnel. This is a security measure. Repeat. All unattended baggage will be removed by security personnel."

She trudged slowly toward the enemy, toward the American soldiers in civilian clothing, milling about at the passenger counter. She wanted to plant the grenade at their feet before she fired the Uzi.

Major Brockmann was joking with a blond female passenger agent at the counter, showing her a wallet-size photo of his wife Ursula in a Lufthansa uniform and their two children. Major Ludwi stood nearby, looking on.

No one saw the evil eye of vengeance plodding slowly towards them.

Maccabee adjusted the headset so he could speak into the mike freely, as Huey One swept over the sand dunes of Rockaway Peninsula and Floyd Bennet Field. He had received permission from the JFK control tower to fly at rooftop level. He looked back over his shoulder and spotted a police chopper hovering over a brick tenement building in lower Brooklyn, searching for but not finding any sign of the terrorists. Two small coast guard cutters crept close to the west shore of Jamaica Bay, searching from the water's edge.

At 3:46, the voice of Major LaSalle, the pilot, surged across the intercom. "Switch to channel two for Colonel Contino at JFK tower."

Maccabee flipped the switch. "Maccabee here, go."

The unmistakable voice of Big Ed bellowed across the static. "I've been directed to advise you that the FBI has identified the mole. Howard and Covalho broke the case wide open. They duped Kolchak's telephone tape recorder. Your hunch was right. There was a time gap. Kolchak received a critical call on Wednesday night."

"Sensational!" Maccabee could hear himself yell over the roar of the engine. He pressed the headphones tighter to his ears. "What did they learn?"

"Plenty. Enough to send two people to jail for the rest of their lives."

Maccabee pressed his lips tight, waiting to hear the inevitable.

"I have a verbatim. Want to hear it?"

"Hell, yes. Damn it, who called him? Who's the mole?"

A woman's voice broke through the static, tinged with a caustic, icy inflection. "Dmitri, you've pushed me too far. If you'd only listened to our warning, we could have provided you with the XL-5 telescrambler in Germany, where the secret code is available. But no, you had to see it here. What good did it do you? My husband pleaded with you not to blow his cover. There was no need for you to murder Sergeant Washington, no reason at all."

Kolchak's familiar voice echoed across the static. "There was big reason. Your husband phoned me at my magazine in state of panic. Sergeant Washington became suspicious. She saw your husband take telescrambler out of headquarters and bring it back after our meeting. She confronted him with her discovery, and planned to report the breach of security to his commander that night. She had to be stopped. There was no other way."

"The police will find out," she said in a frightened voice.

"No, they won't," Kolchak said. "We've covered our tracks too well. Your husband pointed her out to us. That's all he did. He was not involved in shootings. Don't worry, your cover is safe. Nobody will find out." He laughed in a mocking tone. "Sometimes, we take one risk too many."

"I hope you're satisfied," she said, angrily. "Stealing the CIMIC network was one thing, getting involved in murder is too much. You didn't have to murder the general. I'm out of it. I don't ever want to hear from you again. We're through. Finished. I quit."

"I had to shoot General Palmer. It was part of grand scheme, one far too complicated for you to comprehend."

"You heard me Dmitri," she argued. "I quit."

"My dear, Moscow does not look kindly on resignations," he answered in a patronizing voice. "I would reconsider your hasty act, if I were you. If FBI learns of your treachery, you face arrest and deportation. Years of harsh imprisonment in mother country. You never get to spend hundred thousand dollars you salt away in Geneva bank."

Big Ed Contino's voice stepped on a string of icy, feminine profanity that faded into garble. "Recognize her voice?" he asked.

"Yeah," Maccabee replied. "I never liked that witch."

"How'd you spell that?"

"With a capital `B'!" Maccabee snapped back. "I never understood what he saw in her. How could he let her manipulate him into an act of treason?"

"Don't discount her beauty. Maybe she was very good in bed."

"Not that good!" Maccabee snapped. "No woman is worth betraying your country for." Maccabee cringed, not wanting to believe what he had heard. "What happened to all his years of service, to his fine military record? How could he throw it away for greed and lust?"

Maccabee felt the pain and torment of betrayal, especially from someone he trusted. He could see her face, so prim and proper. It dissolved, supplanted by Gretchen's lovely features. He shut his eyes, trying to wipe away her image.

Big Ed's voice penetrated his thoughts. "Our friend should be boarding the jetliner any time now. There's a surprise waiting for him on the other side of the pond."

Maccabee exhaled deeply, regaining his toughness. "Surprise, what kind?"

"The FBI plans to double him, to turn him into a double agent. With or without the compliance of his sweet, adorable wife."

Maccabee's anger mounted. "Has the FBI picked her up for questioning?"

"Nope. They came up empty handed. She wasn't at her office or at her apartment. Just a matter of time. They'll find her."

"What does the FBI think? Does she know anything about the Stinger?"

"A disconnect on that one. The FBI doesn't confide in me."

"Christ! If she knows and hasn't told her husband, she could be setting him up for a kill?"

"Anything's possible. Maybe she knows, maybe she doesn't. That's why you guys better get hot."

"What about Kolchak? You heard his confession. He pulled the trigger. What else do we need? Pull him in and work him over."

"No can do, my friend. The FBI wants to give him more rope. He has a big mouth. Hopefully, he'll ID the highjacker, lead us to the Spetsnaz missile team before it's too late. Concentrate on the hunt, ole buddy. Over and out."

Maccabee grimaced, imagining the worst of things and hating himself for it. Gretchen's face flashed through his mind like a kaleidoscope of acid rain. The love, the trust, the hurt, the betrayal. How stupid can a man be? How far can a man fall? How long will it take to get over her?

"The mission," he mumbled. "Focus on it..." He leaned out the hatch. He spotted four army jeeps with tripod mounted M-60 machine guns, manned by white helmeted MPs, scouting the abandoned missile bunkers at Fort Tilden. Two more jeeps wormed their way across the windswept sand dunes facing the Atlantic Ocean, searching for the terrorists. "Where the hell are they?"

Kurt Goetz called back to his buddies at the military check-in counter. "I'm going down to the USO Lounge to get some coffee and watch TV." He waved at Jerry Brockmann, who looked up, gave him a sign of recognition and went on talking to the blond passenger clerk.

Goetz walked about twenty strides, stopped and turned. Out of his peripheral vision, he saw the lady in a black Arab headdress and flowing ankle-length cloak trudge slowly away from her suitcase, which stood upright on the luggage cart, unattended.

He had just heard the loudspeaker announcement. "All unattended baggage will be removed by security personnel."

"What's going on?" he muttered. He stared hard at the strange looking woman, who chanted something quietly to herself. She shuffled directly towards the passenger counter about thirty yards away, her right hand tugging at an object hidden under her robes. She held her left arm rigidly at her side, her elbow crooked awkwardly against what could be another hard object.

"A suitcase bomb!" Years of combat training and conditioning jolted him into action. Instinct took over. He rushed diagonally towards the woman, measuring the fifteen yards that separated them. Fifteen desperate yards that placed him between her and his buddies at the passenger counter. Without taking his eyes off her, he scanned the area for security guards. He saw a uniformed blue suiter at the screening point down the corridor start into motion, talking into his walkie-talkie and tugging at his holster. The guard was about a hundred yards away, too far to be any good.

"Watch-out Jerry!" he shouted, as he ran towards her. "Get outta there. She has a bomb in her suitcase!"

The woman turned, wide-eyed, freezing in her tracks. She saw a man with short sandy hair rushing towards her in a frenzy, shouting.

In that flash of an instant, Goetz relived a nightmarish scene from which he could never escape. It was 'Nam again. A no-name village, burnt hooches, dead VC lying in grotesque positions. A Vietnamese woman in her twenties, dressed in a straw conical hat and black pajamas, walking toward his platoon sergeant, begging for help. Without warning, she pulls a grenade out from underneath the slit of her tunic and throws it. Thirteen good men are torn apart by the shrapnel, thirteen body bags shipped back home to the U.S. Four weeks for Goetz to recover from his wounds in a field hospital, purple heart number two.

Goetz' eyes widened as the dreaded VC image dissolved into the hateful eyes of the veiled Arab terrorist. He sprinted hard, his feet pounding onto the corridor floor. He lowered his head and shoulders like a charging bull, closing the distance.

Utafa al-Birwa pulled the grenade loose from her waistband. She held it in front of her cloak, gripping it tightly. Her finger clutched the safety ring. She tugged. It came loose. Eight seconds to explode. She raised her arm back over her head, turning towards the baggage counter to lob it.

"Grenade!" Goetz shouted, as loud as he could. "Gre-na-a-a d-e!"

She saw the soldiers and civilians dive for the floor with looks of shock and bewilderment on their faces. "Not here, not in New York," she could hear them thinking.

Goetz smashed into her, driving his shoulder into her mid-section, slamming her onto the floor in a sprawling heap. The grenade squirted out of her open hand like a fumbled football, its ugly metallic sound echoing each time it bounced on the floor.

Seven seconds. Six, five, four ...

He scampered on all fours after the rolling grenade.

Three seconds, two seconds ...

He picked it up, saw the unused stairwell behind him and tossed it.

One second ...

He fell flat on his face and covered his head with his hands.

A loud explosion engulfed the vacant stairwell. Steel fragments tore into the exterior wall, staircase and locked door below, ripping them apart. The stairwell contained the explosion, as if the grenade had been dropped into an empty hole. Miraculously, nobody was hurt.

The PLO terrorist regained her feet, screaming hysterically. She had been robbed of her vengeance, cheated by the sandy-haired American. She jerked the Uzi submachine gun loose from the strap under her cloak. "Where are you?" she screamed, determined to end his interference.

Goetz regained his footing about eight yards away. He saw her wave the Uzi menacingly in his direction. He saw her index finger tighten on the trigger. In that fleeting moment, he knew his life was over.

Mustering his courage, instinctively, he charged right at her, yelling an awesome combat cry, "Rangah-h!"

He heard shouts of warning and a flurry of pistol shots coming from the distance. It was too late.

The Uzi spouted flame as he rushed into its muzzle. Hot metal tore into his chest, spinning him around. He sprawled onto the ground, clutching at his bleeding wounds. His vision blurred.

He looked up in time to see the terrorist slump to the ground under a hail of gunfire. Blue suiters and airport marshals circled around her prostrate body. Somebody kicked away the Uzi, nudging her lifeless form with his black shoes. "She's dead," he heard someone say.

He began to choke on his own saliva. Breathing became difficult. He looked up into the face of Jerry Brockmann, who kept shouting, "Medic! Someone get a medic!"

Jerry cradled Kurt's head in his arm, pleading with him. "Hang on, buddy. Help is coming. You damn fool, you didn't have to charge the Uzi. Don't die on me. You're gonna make it."

Goetz could see a blurry circle of strange faces staring down at him. His life began to slip away like a bad dream. He felt like he was drowning. He reached up with his

186

hand and grabbed Brockmann by the shirt, so he could hear. "It's better this way," he gasped. "It was Erika's fault. She made me do it. She got me in over my head. There was no turning back."

He began to cough up blood. His body convulsed one last time. He lay rigid in Brockmann's arms.

Tears streamed down Brockmann's face. He placed Kurt's head gently onto the floor, running his fingers over the dead man's eyes to close them. He looked down at Goetz with pride and respect. Kurt had sacrificed his life to save his buddies. Brockmann knew he owed his life to his comrade-in-arms, to his buddy. Ludwig, too. Probably another two dozen people, if the grenade had hit its mark.

He stood, brushing away his tears. Airport emergency personnel appeared in droves, moving him aside and clearing the area. Members of a bomb disposal unit carried the terrorist suitcase down the stairwell and outside into a bomb disposal container, in the event it contained an explosive. It didn't.

An airport marshal shepherded Brockmann and Ludwig towards the security screening point, assuring them that the next of kin would be notified and funeral arrangements coordinated properly. They were soon surrounded by troopers from the 38th, asking what happened. Brockmann shook his head sadly and let Ludwig do the talking.

An announcement blared-out across the loudspeaker system. "Pan Am Flight One Two Oh will board at Gate 7 at 1630 hours."

Brockmann started walking slowly toward the gate. Minutes later, Wally Livingston popped out of the Clipper Club elevator, rushed through security and ran up to Brockmann. "Just heard about Kurt. My God, how did it happen?"

Brockmann continued to shake his head, mumbling, "I'll tell you later on the plane." He pulled out his ticket and boarding pass, wondering what Kurt had meant. "It was Erika's fault. She made me do it. She got me in over my head. There was no turning back." Kurt knew he was dying. Why did he need to apologize?

Livingston stopped to look out the window of the terminal and watched a Marriott food service truck drive away from the Pan Am jumbo jet North Sea. A yellow tow tug pushed the aircraft away from the terminal.

Two brown security cars flanked the aircraft. The tow tug pulled the jetliner toward a hardstand two hundred yards away.

"Something irregular is going on," Livingston said to Brockmann, as they milled about awaiting the final order to board. "It looks like they're going to switch planes on us." He didn't understand the on-again, off-again scheduling, why Pan Am kept changing departure times. The delay from 1700 hours to 1800 hours appeared to be routine. Moving the boarding time back to 1630 hours meant they'd probably be leaving at the original time. It seemed confusing. Now they were switching planes.

At 4:33, another announcement came over the loudspeaker. "All passengers on Pan Am Flight One Two Oh proceed downstairs to the lower level, where you will be bussed to the aircraft."

The waiting civilian and military passengers looked at one another with confused expressions on their faces. They carried their handbags and followed the Pan Am passenger agent down the stairwell to the final security screening point. They placed their carry-on luggage onto another X-ray baggage machine and shuffled past a walk-through metal detector. Each person was frisked by a security guard with an electronic wand.

They proceeded past the final security check to a special holding area. They waited.

Another agonizing ten minutes passed. Finally, they were ushered outside into two double-size passengermate busses that drove them to the hardstand, where they were lifted by a hydraulic scissors-like elevator to the Pan Am North Sea's main hatch. They walked inside and sat down in their assigned seats.

Livingston and Brockmann sat together on the starboard side. Wally offered Jerry the aisle seat and tried to encourage him to talk. The effort was fruitless. Livingston resigned himself to a restful flight, recognizing Brockmann would eventually talk, but only at a time of his choosing. There was little he could do to hasten the event. The tragic loss of Kurt Goetz weighed heavily on everyone's mind.

At 5:34, the jetliner's intercom came on. "This is your captain speaking. We're sorry for the delay, but we're following new security measures. We should be taxiing shortly. Our new time of departure is 1745 hours."

18

The Spetsnaz was worried. He had watched airport guards throw a security blanket over the Pan Am North Sea during the past thirty minutes. He saw police cars patrol a forty yard perimeter around the Pan Am terminal. Every ground crew member, who drove or walked into the restricted area, had been challenged to show identification. Dog handlers with German shepherds sniffed the baggage dollies and service vehicles near the aircraft for explosives. Although he couldn't see it, Petrovich suspected that the dogs had inspected the inside passenger compartment, sniffing for explosives, too.

He wanted to place the beeper on the aircraft, but saw that he couldn't get close enough to do it. He sat in the cab of the cargo truck, parked by the Lufthansa departure area, brooding.

He listened to the voice transmissions on the truck's radio set, switching frequencies between the control tower and police. The control tower had changed runways around three o'clock, switching from the bay runways to the foul weather runways.

At first, he thought the switch was made because of wind conditions. Now he didn't know. The planes were taking off on runway 4 Right, flying directly over the Inwood fuel tanks and nearby inlet, where the cabin cruiser was waiting in ambush.

At 3:56, he heard a Port of Authority emergency police report: "Terrorist attack in Pan Am International Departure building, East Wing, upper level. Grenade attack. Arab terrorist with submachine gun. Two people down. Ambulances and bomb disposal unit come quick!"

He swore at his bad luck. Stealth was essential to success of mission. He recalled a Russian proverb his father had often repeated: "Even the falcon does not fly higher than the sun."

How could KGB idiots allow this to happen? To permit terrorists to commit random act of violence during crucial operation. Why choose Pan Am terminal for attack? Why not attack another airline?

Petrovich glared at the sky, his anger raging in intensity. "Is it possible?" he questioned, "Kolchak! Did he conduct diversionary attack to fool enemy or to wake him up? What game was KGB controller playing?"

At 4:16, he heard another police report: "Condition red, code three."

He watched a yellow tow tug pull the North Sea out to a hardstand, escorted by two security cars. He noted the aircraft's identification number on its tail and wrote down its number. N5273. The police had become too visible. He gave up on the beeper and decided to track the jetliner visually with his binoculars.

"They know!" Petrovich grumbled. Stupid Kolchak talked too much. No, he is incompetent, but not disloyal. He shut his eyes, trying to squelch his anguish.

He suddenly remembered the boyhood stories he had heard about the God of the

Hebrews. "My God," he whispered aloud. "Do I believe in you?"

He hesitated, shaking his head. He didn't know. Finally, his mind rendered a difficult decision, one that had been troubling him for weeks.

"I cannot be disloyal to army. God forgive me for what I do."

The Spetsnaz could feel his mission unraveling. He knew he had to get closer to the Pan Am jetliner to follow it visually. He recalled his earlier reconnaissance. He drove the cargo truck past the International Airlines Arrivals building, giving the Pan Am terminal a wide berth. He cruised down the restricted perimeter road past the police garage, where he had seen emergency vehicles lined up.

He parked the Lufthansa cargo truck alongside a prefab maintenance shed. He sauntered back to the garage, looking for the nearest ambulance, carrying his black tool kit and canvas totebag. Finding one unattended, he climbed inside, unobserved. Using his Spetsnaz training, he hot-wired the vehicle to start its engine. He found a white smock behind the driver's seat and put it on over his coveralls. He wheeled the white ambulance back onto the perimeter road and drove it to a midpoint on the paved tarmac, where departing aircraft were lined-up, awaiting takeoff instructions.

A police car rolled by. The uniformed officers inside waved at him. Petrovich forced a sly smile and waved back.

Petrovich tried to relax, but didn't dare. He recalled the success of his Spetsnaz team during a Warsaw Pact war game, when he used an ambulance to penetrate white army headquarters. With all the present confusion at JFK, he hoped his tactic would work again.

Two planemate busses were lifted up to the North Sea. More time elapsed as passengers made their way onto the plane. The scissors-lift descended. The busses pulled away. The door to the hatchway finally closed. The waiting ended. He followed the aircraft from a safe distance as it taxied slowly ahead to a standby position for take-off. He tracked number N5273 with his binoculars. It was number six in line.

The Spetsnaz pulled a micro shortwave radio out of his tool kit and tuned it to the planned cabin cruiser frequency. Forty-five minute delay may have unnerved PLO terrorists ...

He broke radio silence, using his electronic scrambler. His secret message took five seconds to transmit. "Aircraft departs runway four right. Repeat, runway four ro-me-o. Will confirm."

The Pan Am North Sea moved up to position number five.

Then four, three, two and ...

Aboard the KGB cabin cruiser, discipline had fallen apart. Vladimir crashed his fist into Abdallah's rib cage, smashing him back against the boat's bulkhead. The thin PLO terrorist clutched his stomach, gasping for air. He slipped to the wooden deck.

"You will follow orders! My orders. I am senior officer." The husky KGB lieutenant grabbed Abdallah by his shirt and threw him bodily down a small ladder into the sleeper compartment.

He turned toward the second PLO terrorist, snarling at him. "You will obey my orders!" Vladimir's dark eyes blazed. He raised his fist to strike Mohammed, who started to advance, but had second thoughts. He retreated into the safety of the compartment below, commiserating with his fellow Arab.

The second KGB lieutenant, Drachev, a wiry, muscular agent, cradled the Stinger in his arms, having snatched it from Abdallah. "We should kill these black-asses and feed them to sharks. I can shoot missile and hit target."

"No, comrade. We do not deviate from orders." Vladimir pulled a black P-38 automatic from a shoulder holster and pointed it at Abdallah, who was crawling out of the hatch on all fours. "You stay below until I tell you to come on deck."

He checked his watch anxiously, four minutes since the last time. He tried to fight the fear gnawing at him. Why doesn't aircraft takeoff on time? What caused long delay? Why doesn't Spetsnaz call? He stepped closer to Abdallah, trying to reason with him. "Time for killing is getting close."

The Arab terrorist had an anguished look on his face. He had struggled through the afternoon at a feverish pitch, awaiting the radio signal that never came. The takeoff had been scheduled for 5:00 p.m. Forty-five minutes had passed. Something was wrong, drastically wrong. The Spetsnaz had been killed or captured. The target had already taken off. He had to shoot down the next jetliner. Any jetliner ...

Abdallah tightened the red band on his head, which inscription said: "Death to America!" He crawled up the ladder, mumbling: "I must shoot missile at jetliner. It is Allah's will!"

"One more step," Vladimir warned, pointing his automatic within inches of Abdallah's forehead, "and I shoot."

The Arab stopped in his tracks. He gazed at Vladimir, then Drachev, with hatred in his eyes. If I only have pistol, I kill them both. He reached for a seven-inch curved dagger that was tucked into his boot.

"Idiot!" Drachev shouted, as he placed the Stinger back under the heavy tarpaulin. He pulled a P-38 automatic out of a shoulder holster, awaiting the fanatic's charge. "Army helicopter fly over our boat one hour ago. We must look like fishermen until attack order comes on radio. We must not panic!"

The VHF radio in the boat's cockpit began to crackle. Drachev dashed over to it, flicked up the volume control and listened intently to the message that was deciphered electronically. The Spetsnaz had not let them down.

"Aircraft departs runway four right. Repeat four ro-me-o. Will confirm."

Vladimir holstered his P-38. He motioned to the Arab terrorists to come up on deck. Drachev handed the deadly Stinger launcher and missile to Abdallah, leading him to the stern of the boat. He pointed directly across the bay at JFK runway four right, about two miles away.

"In few minutes when I give order, you ready Stinger weapon. Prepare to sight, track and engage target. Aircraft will fly directly overhead."

The Huey One almost clipped the few scrub trees that dotted the beaches along Floyd Bennett Field that overlooked Jamaica Bay. Maccabee could feel the mental stress wearing him down. He pulled Freddy, who was leaning out of the side of the chopper, back within earshot. He shouted over the roar of the rotary engine. "There's a shooter down there someplace. I can smell it! Those are my people about to takeoff. We've got to save them. Freddy, where would you hide if you were the shooter?"

"Come off it boss," Freddy pleaded, excitedly. "We've been thru dis question fifty times! I'd be down dere on dah mainland, not out in dah Rockaways where we been. I'd wanna shoot and scoot. I wouldn't wanna get my ass trapped on some peninsula where I couldn't get away."

Maccabee pressed the switch on his mike and spoke to LaSalle, the pilot. "Let's make one last sweep at rooftop level over the Hamilton Beach marshes, before we play Big Ed's hole card. I don't care how many people we scare." He checked his wristwatch. 5:44. "Patch me in to Contino."

Minutes later, Big Ed's deep voice came onto the air. "We're at a standstill. I'm holding Flight One Two Oh in position number two. We've swept the aircraft clean. It's a GO. Every precaution has been taken."

"Any sign of the terrorists?"

"Yeah, we've had an incident down here. PLO terrorist. Some broad from Gaza, wearing one of those long black Arab robes, tried to waste our troops with a grenade, then an Uzi. An air marshal shot her before she could do too much damage. Didn't want to burden you with another problem. Don't know if she was a diversionary tactic to confuse us about the would-be highjacker or if she's a harbinger of the main attack. The Stinger threat's looking worse."

"Any casualties?"

"Yeah, one KIA. A major. Looks like he cashed it in the way he wanted, fighting like a hero. It could have been worse. He saved a lot of lives."

"Who bought it?"

"Sorry, ole buddy, but we lost our `double'."

"Kurt?"

Freddy, who was listening in on his earphones, bellowed over the din of the twirling blades, "Holy shit!"

Maccabee was speechless. He looked up at his first sergeant, who hung halfway out the side hatch, with a shocked look on his face.

"Unless his old lady talks, we'll never find out what caused him to betray his country. Maybe it's better this way."

Maccabee found his voice. "Has the FBI arrested Erika yet?"

"Still no word. She may be on the run. We won't release Goetz' name to the media until we find her."

Maccabee looked out the side hatch of the chopper as the Brooklyn marshlands came into view. If there was a Spetsnaz team out there, he had to find them. "What about the police? What the hell are they doing?"

"They've flooded their patrols along the flight path. No sign of any activity. Nothing!"

There had to be a breakthrough. Something. Anything. "What about Kolchak? Has the FBI interrogated him yet?"

"Wait one. General Kelley's here with me. FBI, police commissioner, the works." Two minutes of crackling static elapsed.

Maccabee hung out the side of the Huey looking down as the chopper swept over the red brick bungalows and small manicured lawns along Hamilton Beach. His eyes began to sting from the wind and eye strain of trying to see through rooftops and impenetrable walls. He blinked, trying to focus better, then perched his tinted sunglasses on the bridge of his nose.

Big Ed's deep voice came back on the air. "Kolchak was tied-up in the traffic jam and road block on Van Wyck Expressway. He arrived at the Pan Am about 3:30. He rushed up to the Clipper Club before the terrorist incident occurred. Another ten minutes and he would have walked right into it. He's been acting jumpy, bugging the reception clerk to find out when the plane is taking-off. We've been feeding him all kinds of garbage. He doesn't know the FBI's tailing him."

Maccabee's voice was filled with foreboding. "What else can we do?"

"Pray a little. We've done all we can do at this end. I'm going to release the flight for takeoff."

Maccabee turned from his vigil and looked at Major LaSalle in the cockpit. He tapped him on the shoulder, speaking on the intercom. "Let's get on point and flush those bastards out!"

He toggled his switch back to Big Ed on the tower channel. "Okay, Ed, play your hole card."

The prolonged wait had frayed the nerves of the Spetsnaz almost beyond his endurance. He sat cramped behind the steering wheel of the ambulance, anxiety gripping him. He had escaped detection. *How much longer can I get away with it?*

Three jumbo jets that were positioned behind the North Sea moved ahead of the Pan Am jet and took off. Twelve minutes had elapsed since he had radioed the boat.

Another police car sped by, the patrolmen barely glancing at him.

He was thankful the ambulance hadn't been missed. He listened to the control tower's frequency, but didn't understand all the jargon coming across the airwaves.

Suddenly, he heard: "Flight One Two Oh is cleared for takeoff."

The control tower's next instructions devastated him.

"Divert to runway thirteen lee-mah. All aircraft are holding. Takeoff and good luck."

Petrovich watched the big Pan Am clipper turn away from the runway that the other jetliners were using. It lumbered slowly across the apron toward a new runway that ran perpendicular in the opposite direction.

The Spetsnaz grabbed an airport map and unfolded it. He saw quickly what his adversaries were doing. "They try to outfox me."

He flicked on the power of his portable VHF radio and called the KGB cabin cruiser. "Emergency alert! Aircraft on new runway, thirteen left. Repeat, new runway thir-teen lee-mah. Change location immediately!"

The two KGB agents aboard the cabin cruiser were shocked when they heard the message. "Change location immediately!" The two PLO terrorists had become impossible to deal with, especially after receiving the Spetsnaz' first radio signal.

Abdallah and Mohammed sat in the stern of the boat, their hands playing with the tarpaulin that covered the Stinger. Their cruel yellow eyes gave testament to their revolutionary zeal. They swore a silent oath each time a jetliner passed over their heads, awaiting the final signal.

Spotting the new runway location, Vladimir snapped on the boat's engine and rammed the throttle forward, surging into a high burst speed. The boat's bow arched high in the air, leaping out of the water, almost tossing the terrorists overboard. Vladimir whipped the steering wheel hard to port as the powerful twin engines churned up huge geysers of white foam.

The boat roared out of the Inwood inlet into mid-channel, dashing across Jamaica Bay. "We are too far away from new runway," Vladimir shouted. "We must get closer for shot. Maximum range to hit low flying target is four miles."

The cabin cruiser raced toward the Cross Island Bay Bridge, holding a steady course for the Rockaway Inlet, which ran between Breezy Point and Brooklyn before it emptied into the Atlantic Ocean. Vladimir steered straight for the bridge and a new KGB shooting point, six miles away.

Drachev scurried down the ladder from the command bridge toward the stern. He tried to steady his footing as the boat sliced through the choppy water. "Take tarpaulin off Stinger," he shouted to the PLO gunners. "Prepare to sight target visually!"

Maccabee hunkered over the M-60 machine gun, traversing it slowly on its tripod. The Huey One hovered momentarily over the fishing pier at Hamilton Beach Park, waiting for the North Sea to taxi across the divider aprons to runway 13 Left.

Alternative courses of enemy actions flashed through his mind. He tried to think like an enemy gunner, to get into his mind-set. Where would he hide? "We've looked at every obvious location," he murmured. "Every fixed location that ..."

Suddenly, a stroke of brilliance surged forth. "That's it!" he shouted to Freddy, looking out across the bay. "It's so damn obvious, we didn't see it."

"What's dat?" Freddy asked, hunching over him so he could hear.

Maccabee rushed to the cockpit, tapping LaSalle on the shoulder. He pointed across the bay, yelling over the chatter of the roaring engine.

"Quick. Head across the bay. Remember that white cabin cruiser we saw fishing in the inlet near the Inwood fuel tanks, the one with the blue racing stripes? It's too damn cold to be fishing today. That's why there are no other boats out."

He paused, putting the pieces of the puzzle all together.

"They're mobile, damn it. They're flanking us, and coming in from the seaward side."

The veteran pilot jammed the throttles forward. Huey One peeled off, darting across the bay.

In the distance, Maccabee saw the cabin cruiser racing toward the Cross Island Bay bridge, slicing through the choppy water at about 45 knots.

He spoke into his mike, cold and unemotionally. "JFK control tower, this is army chopper seven seven one. We have enemy boat in sight!"

The Spetsnaz drove the ambulance past the International Airlines Arrivals building toward the Pan Am terminal. His penetrating green eyes fastened on the North Sea and followed it as it turned onto runway 13 Left.

Petrovich braked his vehicle to a stop on a hardstand, overlooking the runway. He kept his engine idling. He looked guardedly to the left, to the right, over his shoulder, then ahead again, remaining vigilant. No sign of interference. No police. No security guards. No discovery. Not yet. A few minutes more ...

He concentrated totally on his mission. He was Soviet soldier. GRU. Spetsnaz. Tough. Loyal. Obedient. Follow orders. No second thoughts. No recriminations. He wiped all seeds of morality from his mind.

I will not fail. The mission. The target. His pulse pounded, his breath quickened. He knew he was on the edge. A thin sneer creased his broad face. He inhaled deeply, modulating the controlled excitement he had learned to accept before going into battle.

He actuated his VHF radio set.

The North Sea revved its jet engines and moved slowly off the blocks. The jumbo jetliner rolled down the runway, picking up speed. Accelerating. Faster and faster.

The Spetsnaz held the microphone to his lips. He spoke in a hushed, commanding voice. "Aircraft taking off on bay runway thirteen left. Repeat, bay runway thir-teen lee-mah. Out."

He drove the ambulance back toward the International Airlines Arrivals building with a watchful eye, still looking for signs of danger. He skirted the aeronautical area by the Pan Am passenger terminal. As he had guessed, the tight security ring around Pan Am had been relaxed as soon as the aircraft had taxied away.

Petrovich needed a vantage point, a safe place to witness the big explosion.

Instinct warned him to keep going, to park at another airline. He drove past Air France, Sabena, Air India, and El Al baggage areas on the West Wing. The S.A.S. loading bridge popped into view. He braked the ambulance to a stop by the Alitalia service area. He jumped out. He slipped the white smock off of his Lufthansa workman's uniform, grabbed his tool kit and totebag, and rushed inside the employee's door.

An onslaught of last minute doubts flashed through his mind. Will Arabs aim Stinger like I trained them? Will they lead target properly? Will they blow it away?

He hurried up the empty staircase toward the main concourse and the observation deck, where he planned to meet Kolchak. As he found a stairwell window, he looked out across the bay runway.

The big heavy bird lifted gracefully into the sky ...

19

Two green and olive, camouflage-striped F-4 Phantom II jets roared into view, whipping across JFK bay runway 13 Left. Their sleek wheels almost touched down on the cement pavement. They soared upwards, flames spouting from their twin jet engines.

The lead F-4 banked upwards to the right, chasing the tail of the North Sea, staying about two hundred feet behind it. The second Phantom II, only five seconds behind, climbed to the left, bracketing the wake of the jumbo jetliner. Both tactical fighter-bombers maintained the same rate of speed as the Pan Am 747. They climbed at 150 knots, gaining speed.

Up front in the lead Phantom, Major Steve Merrit, a tall, angular stringbean of a pilot with a hawk-like nose from the New Jersey Air National Guard out of McGuire Air Force Base, clicked his mike. "JFK control, this is FURY Six Oh Two, ridin' shotgun."

"FURY Six Oh Two, JFK control. Maintain fifty yard separation from aircraft. Initiate countermeasures. Report any missile sighting on radar."

"JFK control, this is FURY Six Oh Two, roger that." Flicking on his intercom, Merrit talked to his bombardier-navigator, who rode in the back seat. "Let 'er rip!"

"There she goes, hot and sizzling!" The BN squeezed the chaff release button, dispensing a cluster of three infrared flares. Traveling at the same air speed, the three IR flares ignited instantly behind the zooming jets, spitting out a white-hot core of flashing red flame. The IR flares presented a false target, drawing any heat-seeking missile into its orbit to confuse and neutralize it. The heat seeker would hone-in on the IR flare instead of the jet aircraft and self-destruct.

"Nobody's gonna let this jetliner takeoff naked and unprotected," Merrit shouted to his BN. An attorney in civilian life, Merrit had flown 163 close-air support missions in South Vietnam. He had never flown this kind of close-air support before, but the mission intrigued him. "Zap 'em again," he cried, "one every ten seconds until we get out to sea."

Merrit's wingman chased closely behind in the second Phantom II, dispensing a second cluster of IR flares in a defensive pattern to protect the jetliner as it zoomed skyward. They had used IR flares effectively against SAM heat seeking missiles when they flew air cover for bombing runs in the deadly skies of North Vietnam. Why not use them closer to home?

When the Spetsnaz spotted the two Phantom fighters roar across the runway at truck-top level from his window perch in the employee's stairwell, he dreaded what might happen next. He ran up the stairs to the corridor that led to the passenger waiting

196

area. He could hear his footsteps echoing on the hard floor as he bounded past several people milling about on the observation deck that looked out on Jamaica Bay. He shouldered his way past three middle aged couples, who glared at him, but said nothing.

Ignoring them, he pushed his way to the rail at the gigantic skyview window and looked out..

Everything was happening too fast. Everything was falling apart at the same time.

He watched the two Air Force chase-planes fly cover for the Pan Am 747. As soon as he saw the first cluster of red flares ignite, he knew Moscow had underestimated the Americans. They looked so soft and complacent, so vulnerable. It should have been an easy kill. But the Americans, they are so ... unpredictable ...

The generals should have known better. Their scheme to use America to bring down Gorbachev was stupid! Working with KGB, even worse! There should have been better way to keep strong Soviet army intact.

"Win or lose ... it will be over in few minutes," he murmured to himself. "If the PLO gunners lead aircraft properly, maybe Stinger missile will discriminate between flares and heat exhaust of aircraft, maybe ..."

He looked at the people near him. They talked quietly among themselves, shuffling their feet, bored and impatient. They looked out the skyview window, watching everything, seeing nothing. They checked their watches, waiting nervously for an anticipated arrival. Nobody seemed to pay any attention to him.

He stood at the skyview window, transfixed. He knew he had to keep moving, to act natural. His safety was now in jeopardy. He clutched his canvas totebag, knowing he had to change clothes quickly. He had to find Kolchak before the assassin betrayed him. Then he could put his escape plan into effect.   Glancing down the corridor, he spotted a sign to the men's restroom. Yet, he couldn't tear his eyes away from the window and the big bang coming in the sky.

The Huey One dipped its nose and roared across the bay on a direct collision course with the white cabin cruiser, hell-bent to intercept it as it darted out from under the Cross Island Bay Bridge. Maccabee hung out the side of the port hatch with binoculars fixed to his eyes. He strained to see what was happening on the boat. He couldn't tell. The boat's superstructure, the command bridge, obscured everything behind it.

"I'm going to make a low level head-on pass," LaSalle shouted into his intercom. "If they have a Stinger missile team aboard, they have three options. They can shoot straight up, shoot from starboard side or shoot out from the stern. The command bridge on the boat is like an obstacle. There isn't enough room up there for the gunner to shoot straight ahead." He jammed the chopper's throttle to the firewall, getting all the speed he could from his aging craft.

"We need to eyeball 'em, close up, to make sure they're bad guys, before we waste 'em," Maccabee warned, not wanting to blow an innocent bystander out of the water. That type of accident was the last thing he needed.

"They'll need to turn the boat around when they get into firing range," he shouted. "The gunner has to acquire the target visually before he initiates his optical sights. We must destroy them before they fire. Once that missile is launched, it's bye bye baby.

The Stinger will guide automatically to the target within fifteen seconds."

LaSalle dropped the chopper down to fifteen feet above the whitecaps, racing headlong toward the target. Maccabee rushed mid-ship to the starboard side and looked out. The choppy white caps rushed dangerously towards him. He felt skittish. His legs became light and watery. He ground his boots into the thin armor plating below him. He realized that he was out of his element. The water rushed closer and closer.

He shunted Freddy away from the M-60 machine gun and crouched behind it. He grasped the grip and trigger guard firmly in his hands. The cold glistening steel gave him a sense of power.

Freddy sat on the outside edge of the open hatch, his feet dangling over the chopper's side. He held a 40-MM pump-action grenade launcher tightly in his hands. He pointed it in the direction of their quarry.

"We're coming up on them, about one hundred yards away," LaSalle hollered over the intercom. He pulled the yoke hard to the left and banked the chopper at a 45-degree angle to get a better view of the boat from the cockpit. He spotted three men in the stern, two trying to aim the Stinger in the direction of the Pan Am jet that was soaring away from them on a perpendicular course. A third man tugged at the weapon, trying to dislodge it from the other two, pointing toward the oncoming chopper.

"Bandits at one o'clock!" Freddy shouted over the roar of the engine, as he saw the Stinger missile. "Deir bad guys fer sure." He swung back inside the chopper to assist Maccabee at the machine gun. He shook several belts of 7.62-mm ammunition loose, ammo that would feed into the machine gun at 200 rounds per minute. He inserted a grenade into his deadly weapon, cradling it in his beefy arms.

LaSalle banked the chopper and brought it abreast of the racing cabin cruiser. He flicked the radio transmit button on the control tower frequency. He spoke in a low, modulated voice. "JFK control, this is army chopper Seven Seven One. We have bad guys in sight. Confirm cabin cruiser with Stinger missile on stern, ready to fire."

The control tower's response was instantaneous. "We copy Seven Seven One. Engage target."

Aboard the cabin cruiser, bedlam had broken out again among the gunners. As the army helicopter bore down on them, Vladimir could see his boat was still beyond effective shooting range. "Another half mile, and we take chance!"

He jerked the steering wheel hard to port and skidded into a wide turn, trying to evade the chopper. He spun the wheel back sharply, seeing a red buoy rushing towards him along the shoreline. The boat's hull brushed past it, narrowly averting disaster.

He swerved to starboard again, cutting the wheel back and forth, barely hanging on to his captain's seat. The boat zigzagged to the west and Floyd Bennett Field in the distance. "Hold it steady," he heard himself cry. "More power. Faster!"

He looked back over his shoulder, seeing surging water from the boat's wake cascade into the boat's well each time he cut the wheel. He didn't want to swamp the boat and wash anyone overboard. He flicked on the bilge pump. A geyser of gurgling seawater gushed out.

In the boat's stern, Drachev grabbed the Stinger launcher from Mohammed hands. He smashed the metal tube against his nose, wrenching it away. The terrorist slumped to the deck and lay there, bleeding, hurt and semiconscious. Abdallah held onto the boat's rail, steadying himself as water gushed over him. He grabbed a long curved dagger from the sheath in his boot and lunged at the KGB agent.

The Russian jumped aside, backing into the ladder that led to the command bridge. He held the Stinger up defensively, away from his body. "Here," Drachev cried, pressing it forward. "Take Stinger and aim at jetliner."

He thrust the weapon into the terrorist's hands, knocking the dagger to the deck. He kicked it aside, grabbing the Arab roughly. He pointed at the three jet aircraft flying out of their firing zone. "Aim!"

The overzealous Abdallah spotted the Pan Am jetliner and two Phantom II fighters. He remembered his training. Shouldering the launcher, he placed his right eye against the optical sight and focused on the jetliner. He activated the weapon.

Drachev screamed into his ear. "Lead target!"

Abdallah couldn't remember how far to lead the target. It was flying too fast, flying out of his range. The boat pitched into another zigzag turn. Churning water poured over him. He slipped onto the wet deck, then regained his footing. He struggled to steady himself on the buffeting boat. Kneeling on one knee, he aimed at the jetliner again.

The chopper fired a warning machine gun burst over the boat's bow as it came into Vladimir's view. He ducked down instinctively, sighting the boat on another buoy. He veered away sharply, skipping the boat into a furious wide turn, spewing up thick sheets of bubbling white foam.

As he sped past a blue buoy, which he had marked as an alternate shooting point, he cut back the throttle. He yanked on the helm again. The bow came around 180 degrees, its stern facing the Rockaway peninsula, and the jet aircraft trying to escape in the distance.

Vladimir cut the throttle and reversed his engines. The cabin cruiser came to a churning stop.

He bent down and unzipped the leather case that contained a short barreled submachine gun. He swung the stock to his shoulder and unleashed a hail of fire at the oncoming chopper.

Abdallah fell back into the well of the boat, as it lurched to a stop. He crashed into Drachev, knocking him off balance. The wiry KGB agent tumbled backwards and cracked his temple against a steel cleat on the stern rail. He lay sprawled on the deck, stunned.

Abdallah crawled to his feet and shouldered the Stinger missile. He aimed it in the direction above the falling red flares, pointing it ahead of the fleeing jetliner. His finger tightened on the firing trigger.

The Huey One overflew its target as the small boat reversed its direction and wallowed in the choppy waters. Forgetting all caution, LaSalle shoved the throttle to the stops. He dumped the chopper onto its side and whipped it around to get into a better firing position. The chopper screamed down and leveled off.

Maccabee opened fire. He squeezed the trigger of the M-60 machine gun, holding it steady. He watched the flame lick-out. One red tracer in every five rounds sped toward the target.

"We've got them now!" he yelled.

His body tensed, absorbing the chattering, jackhammer recoil that surged through his veins. The M-60 and he became one. His adrenaline pumped rapidly. Sweat poured down his brow and into his eyes. His tongue felt thick, his mouth dry. "Pour it on!" he shouted above the din.

He walked the machine gun spray across the stern of the boat. He saw a gunner aiming the Stinger missile.

Maccabee traversed the machine gun and continued firing. The shower of bullets ripped into and across the boat, riddling the gunner's body. The terrorist's arms jerked grotesquely into the air, his hand clawing at his chest. He spun against the stern rail, a blood-soaked pulp. He toppled over the side.

The Stinger plunged into a watery grave with him.

"Chill out!" Maccabee shouted to himself, trying to control his fury. He couldn't slow down. He poured a steady stream of bullets into the boat's stern. Two terrorists pop their heads up over the gunwale, then crumbled together in a heap.

He spotted another terrorist atop the boat's bridge firing a submachine gun at him. He swung the M-60, spitting-out another deadly stream of bullets.

The terrorist disappeared in a sheet of exploding red flame as Freddy's grenade hit its target. Two more grenades plopped into the boat's stern in rapid succession, erupting in showering explosions. The fuel tanks blew up, blasting flaming debris in all directions.

Maccabee let go of the trigger, his fury spent. He inhaled, deeply, regaining his composure. He reached for the transmit button on his radio headset. He spoke into the mike in a modulated, matter-of-fact tone. "JFK control, this is army chopper Seven Seven One. Enemy target engaged and destroyed. Four terrorists wasted. One Stinger destroyed. No friendly casualties."

He paused, briefly. "We're headin' home."

A familiar husky voice cut through the crackling static. It was General Kelley. "Flight One Two Oh is outward bound." The general paused, his words reverberating with deep sincerity. "Dave, I only have two words for you and your team." He paused, emphasizing each word. "Well done!" The gruff voice paused again. "A heartfelt, well done!"

In the cockpit of the Pan Am clipper North Sea, Captain George Bradcliff, a 52-year-old senior pilot, thrust his four throttles to high cruise power, accelerating his air speed. His co-pilot glanced up from the instrument panel. "When are you going to throttle back?" he asked. "The noise abatement sensors are going to play havoc."

"Not this trip," Bradcliff replied. He kept the throttles spooled to full thrust. The big 747 jetliner thundered upwards at 4,000 feet, climbing over the inlet that separated Brooklyn from the Rockaways. Tuned to the JFK control tower's emergency frequency, he breathed a sigh of relief, when he heard the Stinger was neutralized. A lieutenant commander in the Navy Reserve, Bradcliff was the only person on Flight

120, who had been secretly briefed about the pending terrorist threat. He inhaled deeply, realizing the threat had been real.

He looked out the port window as a Phantom II raced past. His co-pilot looked up from the instruments in time to see a second Phantom zoom by on the starboard side. "What the hell was that?"

A voice crackled across their radio frequency. "Pan Am, One Two Oh, this is Fury Six Oh Two, wishing you a happy bon voyage. *Auf wiedersehen!*"

The Captain pressed his mike to his lips. "Roger, Fury Six Oh Two. Thanks for the assist. Glad I missed the fireworks." He grinned at his co-pilot, knowing he had a lot of explaining to do. He thought about all the extra FAA paperwork he'd have to complete. "I bet every noise abatement sensor buzzed its head off," he chuckled, "plus all the phone calls that lit up JFK's switchboard." He laughed again. "When you think about the alternatives, this is one time I'm looking forward to three hours of extra paperwork."

In the rear cabin of the North Sea, Wally Livingston dropped the paperback book he was reading. He stared out the window past a sleeping Brockmann, aghast. He had never seen a jet fighter fly by so close in mid-air. It frightened him. The jet vanished as fast as it had come. He stared out the window into the empty space. His gaze drifted down to the flickering lights of New York City in the distance.

He thought about Kurt Goetz, how he had been killed by the Arab terrorist, how he had sacrificed his life for the guy sleeping next to him. He had nothing but respect and admiration for Goetz. Would he have done the same thing under the same circumstances? He didn't think so.

There should have been another way. Why didn't the air marshals spot the terrorist when she walked into the terminal? Her looks fit the profile. They should have arrested her the minute she stepped out of the taxi. Why was the entrance to the passenger terminal left unguarded.

`Why? Why? Why?

None of it made sense. The attack. Kurt's sacrifice. How the troops had been isolated, then shunted aboard the Pan Am jetliner. Who's going to tell Kurt's wife? Who's going to arrange the funeral?

He worried some more. Everyone was jabbering, rumors ran amuck. Big Ed Contino was on the ground. Maccabee, Morgan and O'Brien were in the air. Even Mac's sidekick, Freddy. He didn't know what to believe.

"What is going on?"

He worried about Liu Ann. What will she think when she hears about Kurt's death? He checked his watch. "I'll phone her as soon as I land in Frankfurt." He thought about Kurt's wife, Erika. He felt sorry for her. He wondered how she would manage her travel agency without Kurt around to advise her. How would Liu Anne manage our import business if I cashed it in?

The thought unnerved him.

His thoughts turned to the unit's training mission in Germany. Despite Kurt's death, the CIMIC troops aboard the plane would do what was expected of them during the NATO exercise. They weren't war lovers. If anything, they appreciated the stand down, glad world tensions had been reduced, glad the Russians had finally become friendly. These were his comrades. Everyday people. People who were proud to serve. Citizen soldiers ... who believed in the virtues of peace through strength.

What he didn't know would boggle his mind later. Aside from Kurt's treason and self-sacrifice, every trooper and civilian on Flight 120 had come within fifteen seconds of making their final sacrifice.

Everyone ... including himself.

As the jetliner climbed into the heavens, Livingston looked down into the sea of darkness. He saw a ship steaming out of New York Harbor. Beyond it, stood the symbol of hope. The eternal lady of freedom. The liberty patch symbol that reservists of the 77th ARCOM wore proudly on their sleeves.

The Statue of Liberty.

20

Gretchen Lundstrom dashed into the Pan Am Clipper Club, searching for Dmitri Kolchak. She looked infuriated and short on patience. She flashed her press and Clipper Club membership cards as she hurried past the reception desk into the main sitting room. Having been to the club many times, she was familiar with its surroundings.

She strode past a short, dark haired woman with Mongolian features, who sat by the near wall, scanning a newspaper. She didn't pay any attention to her. Gretchen felt like she had walked into another world, a secure haven insulated from the terror that had occurred one level below. She spotted Kolchak in the far corner by the window that looked out onto the bay runway.

She walked briskly towards him, passing two young men in conservative gray business suits drinking at the bar. They turned their heads to acknowledge the trim figure in the black jumpsuit striding past them. They continued talking. They also kept a watchful eye on the two Soviet spies in the lounge.

Gretchen was determined to make Kolchak tell the truth. She ignored everyone else in the lounge.

Tanya Szabo recognized Gretchen Lundstrom from the photo that appeared in her newspaper column. The KGB agent's dark eyes followed her warily. "What is she doing here?" she murmured. "We don't need complications." Szabo checked her watch, annoyed that Kolchak's rendezvous with the Spetsnaz had been delayed. She stood and sidled over to a cane-backed settee so she could observe Lundstrom better. She wondered if she would have to silence the famous columnist, too.

Kolchak had lost all glimmer of hope. He sat at the corner table, trying to drown his misery in vodka. He ground a cigarette butt into the ashtray and lit another. The mission had failed. He had failed. The Pan Am jetliner had flown away safely. He couldn't understand what had gone wrong. He saw two air force jet fighters chase after the jetliner, dropping red flares in their wake. If his men had fired Stinger and it hit flare, he should have seen explosion in the sky. Why hadn't they fired?

It was Spetsnaz' fault. He is to blame. Why didn't he identify aircraft? Kolchak knew Moscow would not tolerate failure. He patted his P-38 automatic in his shoulder holster. He'd settle accounts with Spetsnaz at their rendezvous. He thought about his *kombinatsia* and phone calls he had to make. I pick up pieces and make things right. Other military units fly overseas. I organize new terrorist team and start again. My *kombinatsia* has not failed. Only delayed. I do it again, only better. He checked his wristwatch. 6:33. Why hasn't Spetsnaz called?

The monotone sound of the paging system interrupted his thoughts. "Telephone call for Mr. Victor J. Evans, please report to the information desk at the International Airlines Arrivals building. Your party is waiting."

"Finally," he muttered with bitter rancor. "Spetsnaz', your time has come." He needed one last vodka to fortify his courage. He looked up to signal the cocktail waitress, when Gretchen descended upon him.

"What's going on, Dmitri," she snapped, angrily. "You're up to no good, I just know it!" She sat alongside him, crossing her long slender legs, balancing her purse with the Beretta automatic inside it on her lap. Her four-inch spike-heel pumps brushed sharply against his shins. She stared into his eyes, challenging him. "The police wouldn't let me up here. They herded all of the press into an isolated area away from where the terrorist attack occurred. They're not telling us a damn thing. How many people were killed? How many were injured? Their names? The terrorists ... who were they? How did they get here? Nothing ..."

She paused, distraught, her anger increasing. "And you ... you knew beforehand. You knew about the PLO attack."

She caught her breath, then continued her tirade, not letting him interrupt. "You warned me about a highjacker, when you knew a terrible act of terrorism was going to be committed." She brushed the long blond tresses back from her face. "Do you know how many people could have been killed?"

She leaned closer to him, the Germanic inflection in her voice rising abrasively. "What kind of man are you?"

Kolchak's Slavic face blanched to a chalky white. "Do not make scene," he said in a low commanding tone. He bent forward, pursing his lips. He collected his thoughts, then continued the big lie. "My warning about highjacker is true. I was not informed about Arab fanatics. Highjacker has not struck yet."

Gretchen listened to him with disbelief in her eyes. "I thought you said he was highjacking an airplane at La Guardia?"

"I was mistaken," he answered, glibly.

"It's not tomorrow," she concluded. "It's tonight, isn't it?"

Kolchak nodded, relishing how he planned to liquidate the Spetsnaz. He whispered, "Yes, tonight. At Lufthansa Airlines."

Gretchen anger flared, uncontrollably. "Lufthansa, the German airline!" she screeched, her voice rising to a frenzy.

She rose, losing control. She clutched her purse with her left hand, spitting-out her next words in a scathing burst of venom. "Russian pig!"

Her right hand shot out simultaneously. She slapped Kolchak hard across his cheek before he knew what had happened. The hollow smacking sound echoed across the room.

The KGB controller rose quickly to his feet, shocked, angered and embarrassed at this sudden loss of face. He eyed Tanya Szabo who advanced stealthily towards them from across the room. He rubbed the redness of his cheek, trying to regain his composure. His voice quivered, then steadied. "I will forgive this ... this insult, since you think I try to hurt Germany. It is not true. I admire your allegiance to your fatherland ... and to your adopted country. I do not want to hurt anyone."

He smirked. "You want to meet highjacker. Okay, I take you to highjacker. Then you see that I tell the truth. I give you exclusive."

Before Gretchen could answer, Szabo sneaked up behind her. The KGB agent grabbed her by the left hand and twisted it violently in a come-along grip, making her drop her purse. "Don't cry out," she hissed, viciously, "if you know what is good for you." She kicked Gretchen's purse under a couch.

Gretchen became frightened, but knew better than to struggle. She decided to play along with Kolchak and the sinister-looking woman behind her. How far would they go? Was there really a highjacker?

She felt secure that her cover had not been penetrated. Kolchak wouldn't dare hurt a member of the press. She was still in a public place. She could always scream for help if she needed to.

Szabo propelled an outwardly reluctant Gretchen toward the front desk. Kolchak walked one step ahead, blocking the bartender's view.

As they walked past the bar, one FBI agent nudged the other, trying to blatantly ignore what was happening. As the trio passed the reception desk, the two FBI agents jumped off their bar stools and scurried after them.

Kolchak swung open the heavy pine doors of the Clipper Club and led the way into the empty vestibule by the VIP elevator. He walked to the heavy glass door that led to the rooftop parking, which had been locked for several years because of the terrorist threat. Without hesitating, he pulled out a passkey from his pocket, inserted it into the door's lock and twisted it.

Minutes later, they forced Gretchen into the rear of the KGB black Chevy van. Szabo wheeled the vehicle onto the down ramp and into the street below.

Maccabee leaned out from the open hatch of Huey One as it veered across Jamaica Bay toward the bay runway at JFK. He could see the clear outline of the Pan Am passenger terminal building growing larger as they approached. The chopper descended to a hundred feet over the tarmac and hovered over a turnaround, awaiting final clearance to land.

He listened to Freddy shouting into his mike over the staccato sound of the rotor blades, talking to Major Morgan in Huey Two. His burly sidekick jerked the mike away from his face and threw his arm around Maccabee's shoulder, shouting into his ear. "She flew into dah kill zone right after we left. Dey hovered over dah area fer about ten minutes, searchin' for bodies. Wouldn't yah know, dat lady found one!" He rubbed the back of his head, amazed. "She radioed dah Coast Guard cutter and dey fished dah body out. She just landed at Floyd Bennett Field. Wants to see if she can identify dah body and anythin' else dey found."

Maccabee nodded. He adjusted his mike and called the tower. He was patched into Big Ed Contino instantly. "I'm coming in. Anything new?"

Big Ed's voice resounded across the air waves. "The airport is crawling with the press. It's like a zoo. They're acting like animals. TV crews climbing all over the place. Photographers. Reporters. Everyone's screaming to know what happened. They're turning it into a major media event." He chuckled. "If they only knew."

A look of consternation crept across Maccabee's face. "Is Kolchak still in the Clipper Club? That's the guy I want to get my hands on, that Soviet bastard damn near wiped out our troops."

"Rog', on that. There's a tough-looking Russian female up there, who looks more Asian than European. We think she's KGB. We're watching both of them, hoping they'll lead us to the Spetsnaz commander."

Maccabee frowned.

More static. Then Contino's afterthought. "By the way, your girlfriend flew in by chopper minutes after the terrorist attack. She's been flashing her press card all over the place. She's up there talking to Kolchak right now. There are more spooks up there than Clipper Club members."

Maccabee shook his head, alarmed. "Kolchak's dangerous! Doesn't she know that?" *Damn it, even if she did take me for a sucker, somebody has to watch out for her.* He wanted to grab her and shake some common sense into her. *She's walking right into a cross-fire. Doesn't she know better?*

There was a momentary silence. Big Ed's voice came on. "Wait one."

The Huey One suddenly lurched forward, yawing in a straight line toward the Pan Am terminal's East Wing. Maccabee grabbed a stanchion for balance. He slipped off the headset, keeping one earphone fastened to his ear.

Contino's voice came back on the air. "They're on the move!" He spoke excitedly. "Don't want to worry you old buddy, but it looks like your girlfriend is leaving the club under duress. She may be a hostage."

"Under duress? What do you mean?"

"They forced her into a black Chevy van. Has USSR diplomatic plates. The FBI is tailing them. They parked in the short term parking lot in front of the International Airlines Arrivals building, and they're heading for the lobby entrance."

Maccabee switched the intercom to LaSalle in the cockpit. "Did you hear that?"

"Aye aye, skipper," LaSalle barked back. "JFK control, this is army chopper Seven Seven One. Request change in landing instructions. Request permission to land at the International Airlines Arrivals building?"

Contino responded instantly. "Permission granted. You are cleared for immediate landing at Gate 44, IAB, West Wing."

"Rog', out." The chopper altered its course, hovered, then darted toward the landing site. As its skids crunched down onto the cement hardstand in front of the U-shaped building, Maccabee and Freddy jumped to the ground. They ducked their heads under the twirling rotor blades, shielding their eyes from the blinding dust.

As soon as Maccabee ran clear of the chopper's blades, he looked up at LaSalle in the cockpit window. He snapped a fast thumbs up signal, then a sharp salute.

LaSalle nodded, returning the salute. The chopper lifted off the pad, dipped its nose and roared across the runway, heading north to Stewart Field and home.

Maccabee and Freddy rushed inside an employee's door beneath a loading bridge and up an empty stairwell. They raced into the long sheeprun corridor, running at full speed. They charged past a few Italian stragglers with takeon luggage who were bringing up the rear guard of a departing Alitalia flight.

"I'm getting too old for this kind of stuff," Maccabee shouted to Freddy, as he puffed heavily. He tried to catch his second wind. "I thought we left this kind of action behind us in 'Nam."

The husky NCO laughed, setting a fast pace. He ran interference for his boss, who charged closely behind him like he was following a blocker on a football field. They bumped into four Japanese tourists, barging past them. Freddy shouted over his shoulder as they ran down the long corridor, which measured over a city block. "We really blew 'em away. Don't know how anything wuz left floatin'. Man, I'm still on a high. I ain't felt dis good since we left Da Nang." He rammed his fist high in the air, scurrying forward. "We may be a couple ole war horses, but we still gotta lot of fight left in us."

"Yeah," Maccabee answered, his chest heaving with each long stride. "It was close. Too damn close."

Freddy pivoted, running backwards at full tilt, like a drill sergeant on a parade field. "Dah troops are on deir way safely. Not a hair hurt. Only dah mole, and he had it comin'. I feel good. Come on, don't let dah killin' get yah down. We did what we hadda do." He pivoted forward again to avoid crashing into an elderly couple with suitcases, not missing a stride.

"It's not over, not yet," Maccabee shouted, following the path that Freddy opened for him. His breath became easier, his strides more relaxed. They slowed down as they neared the baggage claims area, jogging past a cluster of people, who were claiming their luggage near a conveyor belt.

Freddy did an about-face again, running in reverse, eye-balling his boss. "Tell me yah didn't getta thrill mowin' down dose terrorists wid dah machine gun. Now be honest wid me."

Maccabee laughed. "Yeah, it felt good wiping out those bastards. The cold steel vibrating in my hands, the red tracers spitting out death ..."

Maccabee stopped abruptly. His green eyes blazed with alarm. His mouth gaped open. A shocking realization struck home. Deep within his subconscious ... the shadowy image that had been eluding him ... it suddenly bubbled to the surface, growing clearer.

Freddy jammed on his brakes. "What's the matter, boss?"

"Those words ..."

"What words?"

"Mine. What I just said. They're not my words."

"Not yours?"

"No, I heard them some place before."

The words jarred his memory. The image exploded into a clear picture. Yakov! Cousin Yakov had told him at Jackie's seder about his combat experience in Afghanistan. He had flown in a Soviet gunship. He had used the same precise words "... red tracers spitting out death."

It was Yakov, after all. Long lost cousin Yakov. How blind could he be? Yakov was the bastard we've been hunting.

Freddy was his usual flippant self. "No-o-o problem!" he surmised. "So yah plagiarized somebody. Who's gonna sue yah?"

Maccabee's face contorted in anger. "C'mon," he said, shoving Freddy forwards. He began to jog, picking up speed. "I know who the Spetsnaz is!"

Freddy jogged alongside, his head bobbing. "How do yah know?"

Maccabee threw him a nasty sideward glance. "I just know." He increased the pace, looking this way and that. "I need to find a phone."

A security guard near the U.S. Customs' inspection area ran toward them, waving his arms for them to stop. He had a walkie-talkie glued to his ear. Freddy took the lead. He flashed his CI ID card as he vaulted over two rows of suitcases. "Army intelligence!" he shouted.

He sprinted toward the exit door on the lower level. He dashed past a final customs' checkpoint with Maccabee two steps behind. Another uniformed customs agent shouted a warning to stop. They ignored him. They scampered through the exit and out a narrow passage that looked like a cattle chute. They elbowed their way past a stream of chattering passengers, who were being greeted by a boisterous crowd of well-wishing friends and family. They walked deliberately onto the crowded main concourse with two armed customs agents in pursuit.

Maccabee scanned the string of airline offices on the corridor to his left. He spotted a row of open pay phones on the far side, about one hundred yards away. He darted in that direction, reaching into his pocket for his telephone calling card. "Take care of the guards. I have to call my sister."

On the empty balcony overlooking Maccabee and the bustling crowds in the lobby, the Spetsnaz stood by an open pay phone with the receiver to his ear, listening to it ring. He had a few minutes to spare before his fateful meeting with Kolchak. A sudden inspiration seized him. He felt obligated to make one last call. He held his breath, hoping cousin Jackie would be at home.

The phone rang ... once, twice ...

Petrovich was confident that Kolchak wouldn't recognize him, since the KGB rendezvous plan required him to wear a Lufthansa workmen's uniform prior to his final change of clothes. During the half hour that had elapsed since Pan Am Flight 120 had taken off, he had slipped into an employee's rest room. Using a corner toilet stall, he had slipped out of his wetsuit and Lufthansa uniform and buried them at the bottom of an oil soaked trash bin. Changing into a dark business suit, he had donned a gray wig that added twenty years to his appearance. Black horn-rimmed eye glasses added to his disguise.

He clutched his canvas totebag, knowing that another change of clothes was inside. He had planned his escape carefully, following GRU orders, not KGB. Kolchak had provided him with a Lufthansa ticket to Frankfurt under the alias of Horst Gunther. He smirked, anticipating a KGB betrayal.

He patted the money belt that fit snugly around his midsection. Inside was a GRU-forged Swiss passport, complete with his photo and another identity. Herr Carl Schachter, professor, University of Geneva. He also carried a gold American Express card with a credit limit of $10,000.

Yet a strange feeling engulfed him. A nagging premonition warned him that he might not elude his pursuers, that this time his luck had finally run out. He sulked momentarily, then cast aside any vacillation. He readied himself mentally for his encounter with the KGB controller.

The phone was picked up on its fourth ring. A cheerful voice answered. "Hello, this is Jackie Ackerman speaking."

"This is cousin Yakov."

"Hi, cousin, it's good to hear your voice. I really enjoyed having you visit with my family. When am I going to see you again?"

Petrovich maintained his crafty subterfuge, trusting no one. "I fly to Frankfurt tonight. Urgent business."

"Frankfurt?" Jackie repeated, disappointedly. "I thought you had another week here. I wanted so much to see you again."

"I am sorry, but I must go. I want to say good-bye."

"When will you return to the United States?" she asked, eagerly.

"I may never return."

"Never?" She paused briefly. "How will I find you?"

"I do not control my fate. Please say good-bye, my beautiful cousin, to your husband and sons. And to my cousin Dave."

"What's wrong, Yakov? You sound troubled. Please tell me."

The Spetsnaz stared at the receiver, saying nothing.

"Yakov, you must write to us, stay in touch."

"I will try. Good-bye, my cousin." He hung up.

Petrovich walked back to a cocktail lounge and sat behind a round white patio table that looked down onto the main lobby entrance. A large beach umbrella hid him from view, especially from anyone looking up from below.

He ordered a stein of Heineken beer from a fat waitress with red-tinted hair. He began thumbing through a copy of the *Post*. The Spetsnaz riveted his eyes on the lobby below, waiting to lure Kolchak into his trap.

"Dmitri, you're hurting me!" Gretchen cried, as the KGB controller squeezed her arm, hustling her forward at a fast trot. Szabo had parked the van in a parking lot directly in front of the International Airlines Arrivals building. "My high heels," she shouted, "I can't keep up with your long strides."

She half-ran, half-trotted and was half-dragged as Kolchak crossed one road, then the second that separated the parking lot from the passenger terminal's main entrance. Szabo ran alongside her, clutching her other arm roughly. Gretchen felt like she was pinioned between them like a prisoner. The pain was excruciating. She wanted them to release her arms.

A taxi screeched to a stop, almost hitting them as they rushed onto the crosswalk. Kolchak waved his fist at the cabby, dashing onto the sidewalk. "Keep up!" he shouted to Gretchen, pulling her along. "Take your shoes off if it will help!"

"No, I won't!" Gretchen answered, defiantly, chafing at the indignity of being forced to run on shoes that were four-inches off the ground. "Slow down, another minute or so won't matter." She pulled back stubbornly, forcing them to stop at the lobby entrance. "Please, I need to collect my wits." She tugged her arm loose from Kolchak's grasp, wincing in pain. "How will I know the highjacker when I see him?"

Kolchak licked his lips, sneering at her. "I point him out to you." He moved forward and started to grab her arm again.

Gretchen jerked back out of his reach, spinning on the balls of her feet, breaking Szabo's grip. She held both hands up defensively, stepping backwards. "Let's walk inside like mature adults. Stop manhandling me." She added a threat that snared their instant attention. "If you don't, I'll scream!"

Kolchak took one step forward menacingly, then stopped. "Have it your way," he warned. "I want no trouble from you. I must find terrorist before it is too late."

"Who is he?" Gretchen demanded, adamantly.

Kolchak lit a Carlton with his lighter. He blew smoke deliberately into Gretchen's face. "I told you. He is Horst Gunther ..."

Gretchen interrupted, choking. "Stop lying. I know he is not a Stasi double agent. I checked the West German embassy. Tell me the truth."

Kolchak's evil eyes narrowed. He shrugged, still twisting the truth. He sidled up to her, confessing in a conspiratorial whisper. His face was inches away. "He is renegade Spetsnaz by name of Petrovich, Soviet commando, who went crazy in Afghanistan. He is sadistic killer bent on avenging son's death. He has committed great crimes against Soviet state. He must be captured and returned to Moscow, where KGB firing squad awaits him."

Gretchen stepped back, gasping for fresh air. Kolchak's breath reeked from stale tobacco, and it nauseated her. "What does he look like?"

The KGB controller walked through the glass doors into the spacious lobby. Gretchen followed closely behind with Szabo at her side. "He wears Lufthansa workman's uniform. In mid-forties. Blond hair, Slavic face, muscular with big shoulders and bull neck. Has ticket to Frankfurt under name Horst Gunther. He plans to sneak onto Lufthansa flight tonight."

Kolchak turned and grabbed Gretchen by the arm, pulling her forward. He stepped out in long strides. He tightened his grip as she began to struggle and fall behind. "We must hurry," he urged. "I must see Spetsnaz before he sees me. He must be stopped!"

Maccabee relaxed when the busy signal to Jackie's phone stopped buzzing. He drummed his fingers impatiently on the side of the pay phone, until he heard his sister's familiar voice.

As she began to talk, he interrupted. "It's me, Jackie. Dave." His voice had a note of urgency in it. "Have you heard by any chance from cousin Yakov since we had dinner at your home? I need to find him."

She echoed his serious tone. "What's wrong, Dave? What's going on?"

"A helluva lot, sis," he said, anxiously. "More than I have time to tell you." His voice became demanding. "Has Petrovich called?"

"Yes," she answered, worried. "I just hung up. He just called and sounded troubled. Dave, you called him by his last name, referring to him like a stranger, like somebody you don't like. What's happening?"

"What did he tell you? What did he say? C'mon, sis, tell me quick, before he gets away."

"He said he's flying to Frankfurt tonight," she said, astonished. "What do you mean by 'before he gets away?' He said we may never see him again. Dave, I don't understand what's going on."

"Did he tell you what airline he's flying on?"

She hesitated, then answered. "I think he said Lufthansa. Yes, Lufthansa, that's the one. Tonight. He didn't say what time."

"Thanks sis, I'll call you later and explain."

"You'd better. Is there anything I can do to help?"

"Yeah, if he calls again, try to stall him and find out where he is, his specific location. Call me at Ed Contino's office at the Port of Authority at JFK. It's a national emergency, sis. Be careful and don't tell him anything I've said. Watch your back, too."

"David!" she reprimanded, "that's your cousin you're talking about." She paused, her cheerfulness returning. "He said to say good-bye to you, to cousin Dave."

"Yeah, I bet!" He heard another rebuke as he hung up.

The Spetsnaz watched Kolchak and two women walk through the glass doors into the lobby. He huddled behind the beach umbrella in the cocktail lounge above them, hidden from view. He saw the blond struggle on her high spike-heels, trying to keep up with Kolchak, who strode forward pulling her along roughly by the arm. He recognized the stocky brunette with the pasty Mongolian face from GRU briefings. Lieutenant Tanya Szabo, a skilled KGB assassin.

They walked across fifty feet of open space, stopping at a passageway that led to a string of airline offices. They stood in a semi-circle, their backs to the wall. Kolchak eyed the nearby crowds, his eyes shifting back and forth.

The Spetsnaz thought Kolchak looked out of place amidst the clamor of smiling faces. Parents talked animatedly with their children. Toddlers scurried about, clutching colorful balloons. Skycaps pushed dollies overloaded with heavy luggage. Couples strolled aimlessly about with bored looks on their faces. College students sprawled out against their rucksacks, taking catnaps.

Petrovich noticed three young men in dark business suits rush into the lobby and scatter. One man in gray pinstripes rushed up the escalator toward the Citibank branch office. The other two in solid colored suits took up positions along the opposite lobby wall and entrance. They tried to act nonchalant, yet their eyes never wavered from Kolchak, keeping him under constant surveillance.

He spotted an agent with his back against the entrance wall whisper into a tiny device on his lapel. He noticed a blond pigtailed teenager listening to a small radio. He guessed by the way she was pointing it, there was a high speed camera inside. She was photographing everyone who came within ten feet of the KGB controller.

The Spetsnaz rose slowly from behind the beach umbrella. He tossed a ten dollar bill onto the table. The waitress could keep the change. He wouldn't need it. He grabbed his canvas totebag and edged his way back across the balcony ledge toward the main corridor, unseen to those below. The man in the pinstripes on the far side of the balcony, maintained his vigil, looking down into the lobby. The Spetsnaz made his way back to the row of pay phones, where he had called cousin Jackie.

He dialed the information desk on the lower level of the main lobby. "Please page Mr. Victor J. Evans."

Kolchak heard the page instantly. He inhaled deeply on the cigarette he was smoking and ground it out on the floor. He was tired of playing games. His eyes darted left and right. Where is the Spetsnaz?

He whispered a few words of instruction to Szabo, who grasped Gretchen in another handlock. She pressed against the stately blond as if they were engaged in a serious conversation.

"I'm not going to run away," Gretchen pleaded, trying to relieve the pressure on her arm. "I'm after a story, an exclusive. Remember."

Her protests went unheeded.

Kolchak hurried across the open floor in a straight diagonal line, bumping into a Hindu woman dressed in an embroidered sari. He knocked several bundles of clothes out of her hands. They fell to the floor. He bent over and picked them up, apologizing as he did it. He wondered if she understood what he had said. He hurried on.

A frumpy clerk at the information desk looked up from her crossword puzzle as he approached.

"You have call for Victor Evans?" he asked, curtly.

"Yeah," she said, pointing to the black phone on the far edge of the counter. "You can take it over there."

Kolchak picked up the receiver and heard the Spetsnaz' unmistakable, raspy voice.

"Imbecile! Do not turn around. You are being followed. Have you no brains in your head? You will lead police to me."

A cold sweat broke out on Kolchak's forehead. His breathing became rapid. His pulse quickened at an alarming rate. He wanted to see where the Spetsnaz was calling from. The police ... why are they following me?

He began to panic. His hand holding the phone trembled. He stole a furtive look out of the side of his eyes. "Are you positive?"

The Spetsnaz' harsh, abrasive tone terrified him. "Idiot! Do not question what I say. Who are two women with you?"

Kolchak gulped, trying to think fast. "What women?"

"Two women leaning against far wall."

"Girlfriends," he suggested, lamely. "They came to see you off, to bid you farewell and a pleasant journey home." He thought he heard a snicker on the other end of the line.

"You will do exactly as I say. I have secret document to give you. You will take escalator to upper level. Go to gift shop and browse. I meet you inside and hand you document. Do not show any sign of recognition. No sign. Absolute!"

21

Maccabee spotted Freddy about ten yards ahead, shielding him from two uniformed customs guards, who had pursued them.

His burly sidekick argued with the two officers, who holstered their .38s. "Call dah tower, call dah tower!" he shouted, holding up his CI card. "Our general is up dere. He'll tell yah it's okay. Christ! Yer holdin' us up, man. Dere's a killer loose. Yah heard me, call dah tower. Do it!"

Maccabee rushed over, showing his ID card. He glared at the senior customs agent, who had his ear peeled to a walkie talkie, listening with a disgruntled look.

"I'm Colonel Maccabee, Army Intelligence. We're on a high priority mission, cleared by the Pentagon. We can't stand here arguing with you."

The customs guard nodded as a curt order crackled over his two-way radio. "You guys can go," he said, ominously, "but don't pull that shit on me again. You guys should know better than to run through a security check. We could've shot you and got a medal for it."

"Yeah," Maccabee answered, knowing that he was in the wrong. "You better get back to your stations. We didn't mean to pull security away from the main lobby. You may be needed again before the night is over."

The customs agent frowned, not comprehending. He looked at his younger cohort, who shrugged. They turned and ambled back toward the customs gate.

Maccabee grabbed Freddy by the scruff of his collar and propelled him down the long corridor toward the lobby. "Let's go," he urged, breaking into a fast jog. "I have to find the Spetz. I'm probably the only one who knows what he looks like."

Maccabee set the pace with Freddy running abreast. They lumbered into a fast shuffling gait, the kind the Green Berets use when they have to run twenty miles or more without stopping.

Freddy looked confused as he darted around a wave of people coming from the opposite direction. "How do yah know dis Spetsnaz?"

"He's my cousin," Maccabee said in a solemn tone. "That's how I know."

Freddy's mouth gaped open in disbelief. "Come on, boss. Yah gotta be kiddin'?"

"Nope. I'm telling it to you straight." Maccabee declared, still upset with himself. He couldn't understand the mental block that kept him from associating Yakov Petrovich with the Spetsnaz terrorists. Yakov had served in Afghanistan and Iraq. How could I have forgotten?

Maccabee continued jogging, recriminations surging through his brain.

Freddy chuckled. "You taught me dere's always more den one solution to any problem, always a middle ground. Right?"

"Right"

"No-o-o problem. Right?"

"If you say so."

"Well, yah gotta real-l-l problem." His eyes flicked in bemusement, still not believing. "No kiddin', he's really yer cousin?"

"Yeah, my grandma and his grandpa were sister and brother. Helners. Grandma came over from the old country. Her brother stayed behind." He told how the Nazis killed Yakov's mother and wiped out her family at Auschwitz, how his partisan father became a Soviet general. "That's how we're related."

"Whew-w, youze guys are two of a kind," Freddy exclaimed, dodging a skycap pushing an overflowing baggage dolly. "Yah both end up in special forces wid generals fer fathers. Yer cousin's dah enemy ... wow-w!" He jogged slower to avoid running into a ticket agent. "What's dis guy Helner look like?"

"His name is Petrovich. Looks Slavic with blond hair, prominent cheek bones, green eyes like mine. He's about 45, built like a block of granite. Carries himself like a soldier, ramrod stiff."

"Whadda yah think he's wearin'?"

"I don't know. Your guess is as good as mine."

They slowed to a walk as they approached a crowd of arriving passengers pouring out of a custom's checkpoint that looked like a cattle chute. The chattering herd flooded onto the main concourse, greeted by their families and friends. They shouldered their way past them into the main lobby.

"How we gonna find dis guy wid all deese people around?"

Maccabee shook his head, scanning the lobby's entrance. "If we can find Kolchak and Gretchen, maybe they'll lead us to him."

Kolchak walked back to the far wall in the lobby, which led to the East Wing of the building, where Gretchen and Szabo were waiting. His face had drained to a livid white. His eyes glowed yellow like a vicious animal primed to stalk its prey. "He's here," he said, sneaking a glance at the overhanging balcony. He looked for the Spetsnaz, but didn't see him.

He barked at Szabo, "Let her go."

The KGB assassin released her handlock on Gretchen and stepped aside.

Kolchak turned to Gretchen and said, "Come with me. You are uninvited guest. Expediency must take precedence over courtesy."

Gretchen rubbed the soreness on her hand. "You don't have to be so rough," she complained, bitterly.

He ignored her comment. "I meet Horst Gunther in gift shop on balcony in five minutes. You will recognize him immediately. He will be wearing Lufthansa workmen's uniform." He spun around, scanning the balcony again to see if anybody was watching. The few people leaning over the rail were minding their own business.

He turned to Szabo and snapped out short instructions in Russian. Szabo nodded and headed for the wide staircase that led to the upper level.

"I give her two minute head start," Kolchak said. "Then we take escalator to upper level."

"Good," Gretchen answered. She watched Szabo start up the stairs, holding onto the banister on the right side of the staircase. Traffic flowed up on the right side, down

214

on the left, like a two-way highway. Szabo walked upstairs in her correct lane. It won't be long now, Gretchen thought, before I meet the terrorist, face-to-face. She didn't know how long she could continue her sham. If I only had my Beretta. I feel so vulnerable.

Szabo started up the stairs slowly, measuring each step deliberately. She opened the flap of her brown leather purse, which hung loosely off her right shoulder. She reached inside and fingered the P-38 automatic hidden there.

The stocky Mongolian climbed nine steps and stopped. She stepped aside to let two college students with orange rucksacks strapped to their shoulders pass. They didn't seem to be in a hurry.

She looked into her purse again, searching for a deep pocket. She unzipped it and grasped a black fountain pen, KGB issue. She cupped her hand around its thick barrel, knowing its hollow insides were fitted with a plunger that functioned like a hypodermic needle. It contained a lethal dose of poisonous strychnine.

She pressed a button with her thumb. A thin steel two-inch needle popped out. She slid the barrel back into the recess of the pocket, hiding it from view.

Szabo shuffled upward again, grim-faced. She planned to meander into the gift store and shop for a souvenir. Kolchak will divert the Spetsnaz' attention. Then she'd strike like a viper and jab the poisonous needle into his body. The Spetsnaz will be dead in seconds.

She climbed the long flight of stairs slowly. She didn't want to get too far ahead of the crafty KGB controller or let him out of her sight.

Kolchak dragged Gretchen forward by the arm, off-balance. He strode forward with long strides, pulling her along awkwardly. She tried to run on the balls of her feet. For every long step he took, she had to take three.

He forced her to cross the lobby, then did a ninety degree turn toward the escalator. It was his last chance to spot anyone watching him.

He looked to his left, then right. He lit a Carlton, his eyes darting everywhere. He saw a baldheaded janitor in a gray workmen's uniform, mopping the same spot on the floor, looking up with quick glimpses. Their eyes locked momentarily. He turned away, busying himself. "Ah-ha, FBI," Kolchak muttered to himself.

He glanced up at the balcony and saw a young man in a gray pinstriped suit leaning over the rail, watching him. "The Spetznaz is right," he conceded. He didn't see two other FBI agents on the lobby floor or the blond pigtailed teenager with a small radio, who was photographing every move he made.

"What's this important document Spetsnaz must show me?" Kolchak murmured. "Does he think he can hoodwink me into giving him another chance? He has ruined my *kombinatsia*. I will not forgive him. If it is last thing I do, I will liquidate him." He reveled in vile contemplation. "If FBI wasn't following me, I'd make him die slowly, make him beg for death."

He tightened his grip on a P-38 in his overcoat pocket. He scowled, tugging hard on Gretchen's arm, almost wrenching it loose from her shoulders.

"Dmitri! I can't keep up," she screamed as she stumbled forward on her four-inch spike high-heels. Her normal sensuous walk had been replaced by a gawky, teetering motion. She leaned back on her heels, trying to balance her hips. It didn't work.

He tugged harder on her arm as they neared the escalator. She felt like she was running on her tip toes. "I'm going to twist my ankle," she pleaded. "Please let go of my arm."

Kolchak looked up the staircase and spotted Szabo half way up. She had stopped and was waiting for him to start up. He turned on Gretchen and growled, "Hurry! We have no time to lose. Spetsnaz is waiting ..." He signaled Szabo with a flip of his hand to stop dawdling, and to move ahead.

He dragged Gretchen onto the narrow escalator, protesting. She scrambled onto the flat grated steel step behind him. She jostled for a foothold, as the first moving step ascended to its full eight-inches of height.

"Oh, no-o-o!" she shrieked. The heel of her left shoe struck the sharp edge of the rising steel step and snapped off at the sole. "My I. Miller shoes!" she screeched. "My beautiful, expensive shoes. You've ruined them."

She lurched backwards, off-balance. She slipped downwards, one step, two steps ... She broke his grip. She clutched at the escalator's moving railing, trying to regain her balance. Her left foot felt four inches shorter than her right.

"Damn fool!" Kolchak shouted. He stepped down, grasping her arm in a vice-like grip to keep her from falling. "Stop fighting me," he barked, "and take your damn shoes off!"

Gretchen struggled to pry loose.

She lunged backwards in desperation, freeing herself from his grip. She held onto the railing with one hand as the escalator slowly wound its way upward. She stepped out of the broken shoe, then the good one. She straightened up, holding both shoes in her right hand. She stood on the cold metal steps in her stocking feet.

Kolchak stepped down one step towards her with a wild-eyed look. He grabbed frantically at her arm again.

"That's it," she screamed, hysterically. "No more!"

She pulled away. He wouldn't stop. She dropped the broken left shoe. It landed on her stocking foot. "Ow-w-w!" she cried.

Kolchak grasped her left arm, twisting it with savage ferocity.

He pulled her up onto the next step close to him.

Gretchen struck back, unleashing her pent-up anger. She whacked hard with all of her strength, her right hand using the only weapon at her disposal. Her right shoe -- with its four-inch spike-heel.

The blow landed on its mark, stunning him. The spike-heel ripped a one-inch gash above Kolchak's left eye. Blood flowed into his eye and down his cheek.

He lunged forward, swinging his fist at Gretchen.

"Leave me alone!" she screamed, as she ducked. She stepped down two extra steps for safety. She gripped her spike-heel and cocked her arm, ready to bash him again if he came closer.

Kolchak wiped the blood away from his damaged eye with the back of his hand. His vision blurred. He didn't know how badly he was hurt.

"I must meet Spetsnaz and settle accounts. I must stop bitch's meddling."

216

He reached into his pocket and pulled out his P-38.

The escalator continued its slow upward climb towards the balcony.

The Spetsnaz readied his ambush on the upper level.

His eyes fastened on a fat, homeless, old lady with sagging breasts, who looked like an old fat milk cow gone dry. Her shabby, sooty clothes were in tatters. Her craggy face and stringy disheveled hair of tinted orange and gray were repulsive. She sat alone in a deserted row of plastic seats, guarding her belongings. Three shopping bags of grimy, putrid clothing overflowed on three seats next to her. She mumbled gibberish as he approached.

The Spetsnaz pulled out a ten dollar bill from his wallet, and flashed it in front of her ugly face. He could smell cheap wine on her foul breath. "Want to make easy ten dollars?"

The bag lady looked at him with a sullen expression. "Whatta I gotta do?" she croaked in a gravely voice.

"Don't want wife to catch me with girlfriend," he smiled. "I want you to walk downstairs with me to lobby entrance. You get ten dollars now, ten more dollars at door. That's all you do."

She labored onto her feet, scratching her flabby behind. "Yeah," she said, snatching the ten dollar bill out of his hand. She held it up to the light, then nodded her head, stuffing it into a grimy apron pocket.

She picked up two shopping bags and belched, "Let's go, I ain't got all day."

Petrovich swung his canvas totebag over his right shoulder and picked up the third shopping bag with his right hand. He choked on its rancid odor. He escorted the bag lady by the crook of her arm towards the staircase.

Petrovich trudged forward with his shoulders slumped like an old man. His clothes were in disarray, his shaggy gray hair a mess. He adjusted his horn-rimmed eye glasses as they waddled past the FBI agent at the balcony railing, who ignored them.

The Spetsnaz let the bag lady start down the concrete stairs ahead of him. Her enormous bulk filled the space of two people walking abreast.

Petrovich fidgeted with a thick gold-plated ring that was fixed to the wedding finger on his left hand. A unicorn protruded from its base, a horse head with a single horn on its forehead. He clenched his fist, squeezing a bead-like cone. A sharp one-inch barbed needle with poisonous strophantine and curare poked out from the unicorn's horn.

He kept a sharp eye on Szabo climbing up the stairs toward him. He also watched Kolchak struggle with the blond woman on the escalator.

He followed the bag lady down the steps, letting her enormous bulk hide him from view. He switched the shopping bag to his right hand and let it dangle at his side. He clenched his left fist, poised to strike.

Szabo stopped climbing the stairs when Gretchen screamed. She tensed as she saw Gretchen swing her shoe and hit Kolchak in the face, bloodying him.

She heard him cry out in pain. She took a step downward, instinctively. Then

217

stood fixed in place. She thought about leaping onto the aluminum barrier that separated the staircase from the escalator. She could scamper down its diagonal surface and help Kolchak subdue the journalist. They couldn't lose any more time. The Spetsnaz was waiting. They had to take him by surprise.

She watched Kolchak grapple with Gretchen, her attention diverted. She didn't see the bag lady approaching.

The bag lady waddled down the middle of the stairs, swinging both shopping bags that were filled with grimy clothes. She lumbered down the middle of the stairs like nobody was in front of her. She thumped a shopping bag crudely into Szabo, hardly giving her a glance. She brushed past her, flinging the smaller Szabo back against the stairwell wall.

The KGB assassin flattened herself against the railing, leaning over the wooden banister, trying to get out of the bag lady's way. She whirled around sideways and saw Kolchak reach for his P-38.

She sensed a new threat. She glanced back. A shaggy gray haired man in horn-rimmed glasses and slumped shoulders tramped behind the fat lady, treading closely on her heels. He shuffled towards her, swinging a gritty shopping bag in his hand.

She leaned over the railing, trying to get out of his clumsy way, trying to avoid the rancid, stinking odor. She didn't recognize his silhouette until it was too late.

Petrovich stumbled bodily into the KGB assassin, smothering her short stocky frame with his immense bulk. He jabbed the poisonous unicorn horn viciously into her thigh. She jerked backwards, crying out in pain, as he stuck the needle into her. It snapped in two. Only half of its deadly venom spurt into her veins. She slumped sideways, sprawling into a heap on the cold concrete step. She wanted to shout, but words eluded her.

The Spetsnaz plunged down the stairs, taking two at a time. He dumped the shopping bag, spilling its grimy clothes onto the steps behind him.

He elbowed the bag lady out of his way, knocking her to her knees, screaming. She dropped her two shopping bags and grabbed for the railing to keep from falling. Her shopping bags tumbled down the stairs, spewing its filthy contents in all directions.

Petrovich scurried down the stairs past Kolchak, who still struggled with the blond on the moving escalator. The bag lady chased after him, shoveling her grimy clothes back into a shopping bag. She yelled after him, "Hey yah horse's ass, look whatcha did. Yah still owe me ten more bucks!"

Petrovich ignored her. He looked back over his shoulder and saw Szabo slump against the staircase, her horrified unforgiving Mongolian eyes following him. He bounded down the steps and hurdled over the banister when he hit the lobby floor.

All bedlam broke loose at once.

Maccabee dashed past a mob scene of incoming tourists, when he heard Gretchen's scream. He bumped into a bearhugging couple, who were kissing each other by the

218

roped-off arrivals' area. He charged into the lobby's midway as Gretchen hit Kolchak in the face with her spike-heel. He rushed toward the escalator, yanking out the .45 tucked into the back of his waistband.

He saw a kaleidoscope of violence, all happening at once.

Gretchen struggling to get loose.

Kolchak with blood running down his face.

Kolchak swinging a fist at her.

Gretchen ducking and trying to get away.

A gun!

Kolchak has a gun! He's raising it in my direction ...

Maccabee braked, swinging into a full-bodied combat shooting stance. He crouched with shoulders squared, arms fully extended, his elbows locked. Both hands gripped the butt of his .45. He pointed the automatic at Kolchak's chest shouting, "Freeze!"

Gretchen spun around on her stocking feet. She saw him. A stunned look of surprise flooded across her face. "Dave!" she cried.

Maccabee shouted again. "Gretchen drop! Hit the deck! He has a gun."

Two images burst into his peripheral vision.

A contorted face popped up midway on the staircase. Female. Mongolian. She was hurt. Her hands groped for a finger grip on the wooden railing.

Above her at the top of the stairs, a guy in a gray pinstriped suit. He was yelling something.

"FBI. Drop your gun!"

Kolchak doesn't hear. He's pointing his gun at me ...

On the staircase, Szabo pulled her tortured body up to the railing. Her throat muscles contracted. She couldn't call out. Her legs became weak and unstable. She couldn't hang on. She slipped. The weight of her body dragged her down. She draped her body over several steps, clinging for support.

She strained to reach her purse. Her hand clawed out for her P-38, finally grasping it. She laid on her back like a helpless turtle, her face upward.

She saw an upside-down view of a man in a gray pinstriped suit at the top of the stairs.

He was yelling, "FBI."

As the icy Mongolian winter clouded her vision, she rolled painfully onto her side, sliding down another step. She aimed at the FBI agent on the top step and fired.

She twisted her body, trying to find Petrovich's broad shouldered silhouette. Despair flooded through her. She felt cheated, destroyed. In that last horror-stricken moment, she knew what had transpired.

The Spetsnaz had struck first!

She saw the fuzzy shapes of Kolchak and Gretchen fighting on the escalator. As paralysis overwhelmed her, the KGB assassin pointed her P-38 and squeezed the trigger one last time.

Kolchak panicked. Blood streamed down his face into his eyes. He saw Szabo fall. He saw a fat bag lady raising a commotion, chasing a shaggy gray haired man in glasses down the stairs. He became confused. Disoriented.

The Spetsnaz, where is he?

He couldn't get his hands on Gretchen. She kept backing down the escalator, evading his grip.

Blood blinded his left eye. He blinked, feeling dizzy, trying to focus his other eye.

Szabo's head rose up over the banister, then disappeared.

The guy in the gray pinstriped suit yelled, "FBI! Drop your gun." Who was he shouting at?

Szabo's gun flashed.

The FBI agent sprawled backwards, hit, disappearing from sight.

The escalator neared the top of its rise, the balcony landing a few steps ahead. He looked down at the lobby below. He saw a fuzzy silhouette of a broad shouldered, shaggy, gray haired man in horn-rimmed glasses, watching him from the foot of the staircase. He had a sneer on his face.

The Spetsnaz!

He saw a ruddy-faced figure in a safari jacket dart across the lobby towards the escalator, shouting at him to "Freeze!"

Everyone was shouting.

He steadied himself with one hand on the escalator's railing, which continued to climb upwards. He turned sideways in an offhand shooting position, extending his right hand. He pointed his P-38 down toward the broad shouldered silhouette standing on the lobby floor, near the entrance. The man was reaching for ...

Maccabee vaulted over the wooden banister onto the moving escalator. He extended both hands, aiming the Colt .45 at the KGB controller's chest. He wanted to fire, but couldn't. If Gretchen would get out of the way and give me a clear shot.

"Get down, Gretchen!" he shouted, never taking his gun sight off the Russian. "You're in the line of fire."

Why won't she listen, and do as I say?

"Drop your gun, Kolchak. Do it ... Now!"

Gretchen sidestepped away from Kolchak's reach, retreating down the escalator one step at a time. Dmitri was acting irrational. She had to keep a safe distance where he couldn't grab her.

Despite the danger, she couldn't quit. Not now. She was determined to get to the bottom of Kolchak's conspiracy, no matter what.

She had to meet the Spetsnaz.

Now Dave is here.

He'll ruin everything.

Szabo's gun flashed a second time. It's stray bullet honed in on its nearest victim.

Gretchen heard the shot, its significance not registering. She felt a sudden, sharp impact of the bullet tear into her flesh. Her body jerked backwards, spinning her around. The spike-heel shoe flew out of her hand.

" Davey," she cried-out. "I'm hit!"

She felt herself falling. Where did the shot come from? Who shot me? She clutched her left shoulder, growing faint. She reached out to break her fall. She collapsed onto the moving steps, hurt and bleeding.

Kolchak heard the shot. He saw Gretchen's body stiffen, spin around and crumple in front of him. Nothing made sense anymore. The Spetsnaz! I must kill the Spetsnaz. He wavered momentarily, then aimed. His finger gripped the trigger, applying steady pressure ...

On seeing Gretchen hit, Maccabee didn't hesitate. He squeezed off two fast shots with his .45. Kolchak's body jerked high in the air, then spun against the escalator's railing. His gun squirted out of his hand, unfired.

The escalator carried Kolchak's and Gretchen's sprawled bodies onto the top of the balcony landing, where they tumbled together, prostrate.

Maccabee bounded up the escalator's moving steps, taking them three at a time. Freddy was right behind. They leaped over the two bodies and pulled them away from the escalator and onto the balcony floor. Maccabee cradled Gretchen in his arms, clasping her tenderly.

She looked up at him, crying softly. "Thank goodness, you're here."

He looked down at her. Blood seeped from her shoulder wound. Maccabee shouted at Freddy. "Medic! Get a medic! We have to stop this flow of blood." He reached into his hip pocket and pulled out a handkerchief. He pressed it against her throbbing open wound. "Hang on," he whispered. "You're going to be okay."

"Are you sure?" she asked, timidly. "You're not kidding me, are you?"

"No way," he replied, forcing a thin smile.

She raised her head with an anxious look on her face. "Dave, I haven't been totally honest with you. I haven't told you everything about me."

"I know," Maccabee answered as he stole a glance at Freddy.

His sidekick knelt on one knee, ready to administer first aid to Kolchak who was barely alive. "Yah hit him good boss, nailed him smack in dah center of dah chest. He ain't gonna make it."

"Let the bastard be," Maccabee shouted. "Damn it! Get a medic for Gretchen!" He looked up into the face of the blond pigtailed FBI agent, who had tears streaming down her eyes. She had just seen her dead partner. She disappeared, running towards another FBI agent with a walkie talkie.

Gretchen whispered, "I should have told you."

"Save your strength," Dave urged. "I understand. I know who you really are and whose payroll you're on."

"Please don't hold it against me," she moaned, trying to make him understand. "New loyalties don't wipe out old loyalties." She looked up with pleading blue eyes. "I

221

love you, David Maccabee. I really do."

He looked down at her with compassion, his true feelings jumbled. "Does it hurt?" he asked in a concerned tone.

"Just a little," she sighed. She raised her head and saw the blood seeping down the length of her jumpsuit. "My six hundred dollar Ann Klein original!" she cried. "I'll never be able to replace it."

Maccabee stifled a laugh. Three white clad paramedics with stethoscopes around their necks surrounded them. They examined Gretchen quickly, stemmed the flow of blood and slipped her onto a wheeled stretcher. Maccabee held her hand gently, as Freddy knelt alongside him.

Gretchen grasped Maccabee's hand. "I know who Petrovich is. He's a Soviet Spetsnaz using a German alias of Horst Gunther. Kolchak said he's flying on Lufthansa tonight. He's wearing a Lufthansa workman's uniform. We were going to meet him at the gift store."

Maccabee turned and barked a quick order at Freddy. "You heard her. Now we know what Petrovich is wearing. Warn security. Seal off every departure gate before it's too late. Then catch up with me."

"No-o-o problem," Freddy answered, rising. He swiveled his head around, spotted the FBI agent with a walkie talkie, and hustled in his direction.

Turning back toward Gretchen, Maccabee held her hand gently. "Thanks for the info. The Spetsnaz is my problem, not yours. I'll find him. Take care of yourself. I'll fill you in later, when I get back. There are a few things I've been hiding from you, too. We both have a little explaining to do."

Gretchen nodded, smiling demurely. "I love you, Dave. Please ... please, tell me. I need to hear you say the words."

He looked down at her as the paramedics began to wheel her stretcher away. "I guess the feeling's still there," he whispered. He bent over impulsively and planted a light kiss on her lips. He smiled, squeezing her hand affectionately. "I love you, too."

He watched the paramedics wheel her down the main concourse. He glanced at Kolchak, who lay dying on another stretcher. Two paramedics hovered over him, pressing a sterile dressing onto his chest wounds.

Kolchak's tormented eyes saw shapes of people encircling him. He heard a voice. "Federal officers, FBI. Please stand aside." He saw the baldheaded janitor with a badge pinned to his gray workman's uniform peering down at him. He wanted to confess, to tell him about the Spetsnaz. They had to find him, liquidate him. He began to choke uncontrollably. He spat out his last words in Russian in a croaking splutter. "Voy-ska-a spets-s-s ...s."

The FBI agent pressed his ear to the Russian's lips. "Louder," he urged. The KGB controller arched his back, convulsed, and laid still.

Maccabee knelt at his side. He checked the man's wrist for a pulse. A paramedic pressed a stethoscope to his heart. He shook his head.

Maccabee rose, stiff-lipped. He said to the FBI agent with no sign of remorse, "The Russian spy is dead."

Big Ed Contino tapped Maccabee on the shoulder, pulling him aside. They walked to an isolated row of seats on the balcony. He faced Maccabee and spoke in a low, guarded tone. "We just received an urgent message from the White House, Eyes Only. Gorby called on the Hot Line to warn about the Stinger attack. He just discovered the plot. It was an unauthorized, maverick operation from start to finish. Looks as if the old guard was trying to overthrow the government. Gorby nipped the coup d'etat in the bud. Every KGB and GRU officer involved in the plot has been arrested. He says that all guilty parties will be punished severely."

"He sure took his damn time telling us," Maccabee snapped. "When did you get the message?"

"About fifteen minutes after you blew the Stinger away," Contino answered. "Doesn't make much difference. We still had to hunt them down." He shrugged. "They sent us a description of the Spetsnaz commander. They faxed the photograph to the Soviet Embassy. We'll have a copy circulated to all the airlines within thirty minutes." He pulled out his notepad and started to read. "His name is Colonel Yakov Petrovich. Want to hear his physical description?"

Maccabee shook his head. "No, I've met him."

"You've what?" Contino exclaimed. "Why keep it a big secret?"

"It's no secret," Maccabee growled. "I didn't know who he was."

"He's tough. Listen to Moscow's assessment of him." Contino read from his notepad again, pausing after each statement to emphasize its importance. "Petrovich is stubborn as ox. He will not surrender. He will not stop fighting until he is terminated. He is dangerous killer. Beware!"

"I'm going after him," Maccabee said, flatly. "Killer, beware ... I'm bringing you in, one way or the other."

As he shook hands with Contino for luck, Maccabee didn't see his erstwhile robust cousin standing outside the lobby entrance, paying off the feisty bag lady with a twenty dollar bill.

Petrovich looked up at the balcony and saw cousin Dave talking to a tall dark haired official. He grinned, begrudgingly, a sense of pride engulfing him. He murmured to himself. "Good shooting, my cousin. Kolchak needed killing. He was bad man. Assassin. Scum. You save me job of killing him. You good soldier, my cousin. You do good in any army. If circumstances different, you make good Spetsnaz."

He inhaled deeply, absorbing the fresh night air. He wanted to treasure these last moments of freedom.

22

Maccabee knew he was on a collision course with Yakov. He had to find his cousin and neutralize him before he did any more damage. He hurried down the stairs toward the main entrance in the lobby.

Dashing through the glass doors, he eyed the bag lady squatting on the sidewalk, rummaging through a grimy shopping bag. He stopped and asked, "Did you see a husky guy about my height with a Russian accent? He's wearing a Lufthansa workman's uniform. Has blond hair and green eyes like me?"

The bag lady looked up from her scroungy belongings with disdain. She bellowed, "What's it worth to yah?"

Maccabee reached into his wallet for a five dollar bill. He thrust it in front of her craggy face. "What did you see?"

She shook her head, wrinkling her face into a sourpuss. "Dah other guy gimme two sawbucks. I don't take no less!"

Maccabee retrieved the five and handed her a twenty dollar bill. "Okay, tell me what you know?"

She snatched the money and jammed it into her apron pocket. "He ain't blond, mistah, and he wasn't wearin' no uniform. He's got gray hair, wears glasses with thick black rims, hadda neat black business suit. Dah clumsy oaf dumped all my stuff down dah staircase and ..."

Maccabee suddenly recalled the scene vividly. "Didn't I see you chase a gray haired man down the stairs during the shooting? When the female Russian spy was killed, that was you. When all the shooting started?"

She wiped her fat lips with the back of her hand. "Yeah, dat wuz me. And dat wuz dah guy. I couldn't get outta dere fast enough."

The realization hit Maccabee hard. The Spetz! The Spetsnaz had been on the staircase. Yakov had killed the female KGB agent. "The gray haired man with you, which way did he go?"

The bag lady pointed east. "He said somethin' about Lufthansa." Maccabee's eyes swept the length of the empty sidewalk. Dusk was closing in, its cloak of shadows obscuring the Lufthansa sign located about a block away. He took off at a full sprint. He could hear her gravely voice behind him. "Hey, mistah, I ain't through talkin' to yah."

The Spetsnaz dashed through the doors into the Lufthansa German Airlines passenger office and came to an abrupt stop.

"Walk natural," he told himself, "not too fast, not too slow. Don't call attention to yourself." An attractive blond ticket agent looked up from behind the baggage counter.

She smiled, then continued talking with another ticket agent sitting next to her. He spotted the up escalator off to his left and rode it to the upper level and the main concourse. He walked briskly, reversing his direction, doubling back in the direction that he had come.

He spotted the sign that he was seeking. Men's Rest Room. He went inside. It was empty. He walked into a corner toilet stall and latched the door. He took off his horn rimmed glasses and gray wig, and slipped out of his business jacket. He switched them quickly for a frumpy brown tweed sports jacket and white turtleneck sweater that were in his canvas totebag.

He rushed to the wash basin and splashed cold water onto his face. Reaching into a tiny cosmetic case, he inserted a soft contact lens into each of his eyes. Two unyielding azure blue eyes stared back. That's better.

He slipped on a wig of tousled dark brown hair, then pasted a down-turned mustache and trimmed vandyke beard onto his face. He perched a pair of wire-rimmed half-eye glasses onto the bridge of his nose. A different face stared back in the mirror. "College professor, yes-s?"

He slipped his P-38 into a compact hip holster on his left side. He rolled his business jacket, shirt, tie and gray wig into a bundle and buried them at the bottom of a towel bin. The unicorn ring came next. He slipped it off of his finger, turned a bead counter-clockwise and watched it self-destruct.

Two more items. He slipped his new passport and American Express credit card into his inside jacket pocket. Grabbing his canvas totebag, he rushed onto the main concourse, slipping into the passenger mainstream enroute to their departure gates.

Maccabee raced into the Lufthansa baggage check-in counter. Two blond female ticket agents were sitting behind the counter, talking to each other. He flashed his ID card. He gave two descriptions of Petrovich; first, the old man, then the real one. He asked if either one had checked in?

The first agent said no to both descriptions.

The second agent remembered seeing a gray haired man in eye glasses hustle up the escalator about ten minutes earlier. She pointed toward an exit that Lufthansa shared with Air Lingus.

That's all Maccabee had to hear.

He sprinted toward the exit, veering sharply to ride up the escalator. He stopped at the escalator's landing, marking time, as Freddy whirled through the glass doors, puffing heavily.

"I've passed dah word to all dah airlines, boss," Freddy gasped, braking to a stop. "Security will interrogate everyone inna Lufthansa uniform."

"He's switched clothes," Maccabee barked, describing what the bag lady had told him. He gazed out the door, watching a yellow cab drive around the outside perimeter toward the TWA passenger building. He grabbed Freddy by the arm and pivoted him toward the outside door. "You go that way," he said, pointing toward the TWA red and white sign in the near distance. "I'll go this way." He nodded towards the escalator. "If you don't spot the Spetsnaz, catch up with me. Be careful. He's like a lethal weapon waiting to explode."

Freddy snorted, slyly. He patted his .38 and darted out the building.

Maccabee started up the escalator. He glanced back over his shoulder to the adjacent office of Irish Airline. He saw the green shamrock on the wall and smiled. "I could sure use the luck of the Irish right now."

He dashed onto the main concourse, looking in all directions.

The Spetsnaz poked his head into the KLM passenger lounge. He hesitated, changed his mind and backtracked. "Can't trust the Dutch," he murmured, not wanting to rely on a NATO country for his escape. He quickened his pace, hurrying down the East Wing past Icelandic, Varig, Japan, AeroMexico and Iberia airlines. He became one of the endless swarm of faceless people wandering through the corridors. He stopped to tie his shoelace, peering back. Nobody was following him.

The concourse doglegged to the left, then to the right. He slowed his pace as he walked into the central hub of the International Airlines Arrivals building. He passed an alcove of duty free shops and fancy boutiques that looked familiar. He recognized the gift shop that he had told Kolchak about. He noticed two detectives in plainclothes talking to a uniformed policeman on the balcony that overlooked the lobby. The dead bodies had been removed.

He looked straight ahead, keeping to the center of the main corridor. He controlled his anxiety, modulating his breathing. He walked past the observation deck, a restaurant and a long hallway of administrative offices.

The concourse doglegged to the right, then left, spilling out onto the West Wing of the mile-long building. He spotted the Swissair sign, where he planned to stop. "I have failed in America," he murmured. "Maybe it was meant to be." He shrugged, accepting his fate. "Maybe Gorbachev is best thing for Russia, for whole world."

As he continued walking, he knew he would be targeted for retribution. When KGB learns about Kolchak's and Szabo's killing, my life will be worthless. I must get away from KGB vengeance, get to West Germany where my underground network exists. They will be surprised to see me after all these years. He sneered, then laughed. "Time is coming for wake-up call."

Instinct warned him that Swissair was a risky choice. He sauntered past a group of food concessions and small boutiques on his left. He needed to put more distance between himself and the killing scene.

He passed Alitalia, SAS and El Al airlines, seeing the red, white and blue flag of Air France at the far end of the building. He walked ahead briskly, contemplating a new plan.

He entered the Air France waiting lounge, which was empty. He circled around a cluster of cocktail tables with embroidered white tablecloths and trotted down the center staircase to the ground floor. He drew on his reservoir of hidden strength that always supported him when he needed it.

Yakov Helner Petrovich walked up to the reservation counter and forced a guileless smile. "My name is Carl Schachter. I am professor at Geneva University. I have been directed to fly to Paris tonight to attend important seminar that starts Monday morning." He handed the ticket agent, a motherly type in her late forties, his forged GRU passport and American Express credit card.

She keyed the computer, looked up from the screen and smiled. "I can give you a first class seat on our 10:00 flight. All economy seats are booked."

"Good," he said, inhaling deeply. He let his breath out slowly. He felt secure in his disguise. No more obstacles. Nobody will stop me now.

She wrote the ticket, stamped it and stapled it to a boarding pass. She handed them to him, asking, "Do you have any luggage to check through?"

"No, only totebag I carry on plane. My trunk will be shipped tomorrow."

She said, graciously, "You can wait in the lounge upstairs. It's empty now, but it will fill up with passengers in about half an hour. Bon voyage, monsieur. Have a pleasant flight, and thank you for traveling Air France."

He thanked her, checking his watch. He had ninety minutes to wait before boarding time. He headed back toward the escalator and the lounge. It was time to get a bite to eat. He also needed to hide his P-38 before going through the final security check.

Maccabee rushed into one European flag carrier after another, dashing from the upper level waiting lounge down to the passenger agent counter and baggage weigh-in scales on the street level and back up again. He skipped the Hispanic and Far Eastern flag carriers, concentrating on the European ones.

He tried to empathize with Yakov. What would I do if I was in a similar situation? He knew the Russian mind was structured like a straight-jacket with little room for flexibility. They followed a prescribed, predictable doctrine. They had tunnel vision, a myopia that forces them to steamroll ahead, blindly. To charge over a cliff obediently, if necessary, without ever asking questions.

Yet, Yakov was trained in a different mold. He is resourceful, shows initiative, and is unpredictable.

There must be a pattern to his movements ...

Maccabee raced down the east wing and into the connecting section that separated it from the West Wing.

He stopped, momentarily to collect his thoughts.

Petrovich had to be the forward observer, who directed the Stinger missile boat toward the correct runway. Even with tight security, he penetrated our defenses and signaled the boat successfully. Another few seconds, and it would have been a disaster. He shuddered.

And when push came to shove, he outsmarted Kolchak and wasted his number one assassin. A female killer, no less. He lured them into a perfect ambush, and used me to help him execute it.

He's like a chameleon, constantly changing colors. The KGB looks for a blond Russian in a Lufthansa worksuit, he shows up in a gray wig and glasses, disguised as a businessman. They plan to liquidate him at a gift shop, he meets them enroute. Now, he's on the move, tricks us on Lufthansa, and goes in the opposite direction. Where will he show up next?

If he assumes his own identity to fool us, we'll nail him at the gate. If he changes colors again, what disguise this time?

Stroke, counter-stroke ...

That's why I'm chasing him down this damn corridor. He's playing with me like a kid, hide 'n seek, leading me on.

Stroke, counter-stroke ...

There is a pattern. If he runs one way, I chase after him. He does a one-eighty flip-flop and passes me going in the opposite direction. I need to leapfrog ahead, to beat him at his own game.

Maccabee popped his head into the Swissair passenger lounge. Petrovich wasn't there. He chased downstairs. No Yakov. He rode the escalator back up to the main concourse. He saw a Port Authority guard driving a white golf cart. He flagged him down, flashed his ID card, used Contino's name, and climbed aboard. "What airline is located at the end of this building?" It looked a city block away.

"Air France," the driver answered.

"Then Air France, it is," Maccabee snapped. "How fast does this baby go?"

The Spetsnaz rode the escalator up to the top landing and strode across the open floor of the empty Air France lounge. He dallied at a glass enclosed counter showcase of imported French cognac. He leaned over the counter, reading the labels. He pursed his lips. It won't be long now before I enjoy its sharp aroma and flavor. A little bit longer and ...

Maccabee burst through the heavy glass door into the passenger lounge. He charged across the room, not seeing Petrovich, who had his back toward him. Maccabee hurried toward the down staircase, which ran adjacent to the up escalator in the center of the room. He caught a glimpse of a shadowy movement out of the corner of his eye. He did a double take. Somebody else was in the lounge with him.

Petrovich straightened up, looking over his shoulder. He recognized Dave instantly. His first instinct was to greet his cousin. He knew he shouldn't. He masked any sign of recognition. He gathered up his burly frame and trudged warily toward the glass door that led out onto the concourse.

"Wait a minute," Maccabee called out, loudly. He strode forward.

"Who me?" Petrovich asked in a puzzled tone, pressing both hands to his chest like there was some mistake.

"Yeah, you." Maccabee squinted as he advanced toward the stranger, getting a better look. The man was big and husky and moved on the balls of his feet like an athlete. His hair color was wrong. The blue eyes, mustache and vandyke didn't fit. The specs. He looked scholarly, yet ...

Petrovich picked his way past several small cocktail tables. He made a wry face, shunning any attempt at conversation.

"Do I know you?" Maccabee asked, casting aside caution. He wasn't certain, but he had to take a closer look. He edged closer, wondering if he had made a mistake.

"You speak to me?" Petrovich said in a gruff Russian accent that he couldn't suppress. He swung around and faced his cousin, standing his ground.

Maccabee nodded, stepping forward with an outstretched hand. He said, "My name is ..." then tripped over his own feet. He stumbled deliberately into the muscular stranger, who didn't relinquish an inch of ground.

"It's you!" Maccabee sprang back, putting about six feet of safe distance between himself and his adversary. His voice cracked, "Yakov!"

Petrovich laughed, hoarsely. "I can't pull wool over your eyes, my cousin. You are too smart. My disguise does not fool you." He removed his specs and pocketed them.

Maccabee shook his head. "I've been looking for you. It's open season on you, Yakov. Even your own people are looking. You're a hunted man."

Petrovich grimaced, reciting a Russian proverb. "A bear is lucky in not meeting hunter, but sometimes hunter is lucky in not meeting bear."

Maccabee thrust his forefinger angrily into Petrovich's chest. "You had us fooled, you had me fooled. You sat at my sister's table and prayed to God for freedom, while all the time you planned to slaughter three hundred and fifty innocent human beings." He clenched his fist and cocked it, stepping forward one step. "What kind of animal are you?"

Petrovich stepped back one step, maintaining the six feet of empty space between them. He raised both his hands, palms-out, in a defensive gesture. "I am not savage beast. I am soldier. I am Spetsnaz!"

Maccabee dropped his fist to his side, unflexing. He remained silent.

"I am obedient officer. I follow orders like you. I ..."

Maccabee cut in. "I'd never obey a criminal order. That's where I'd draw the line."

Petrovich smirked. "When you were Green Beret in Vietnam, you did not kill innocent civilians in crossfire or by accident, yes? You know it happens. It happened in Vietnam, it happened in Afghanistan, it happens in every war. A soldier must accomplish his mission."

"This isn't war," Maccabee interrupted. "This was a barbaric act of terrorism."

Petrovich protested, clutching both hands to his chest. "I did not want it to happen, believe me my cousin. I hoped to last minute that mission is canceled. I have no use for KGB or PLO. I was selected because of my son's death, because I sought to avenge his death, because I hated everything American. I did not know what life was like here in America ..."

Maccabee was adamant. "But you learned, you now know the difference."

Petrovich nodded, grimly. "My country is morally corrupt. We have never known freedom. Changes are coming, but it is too late for me. There is no way out ..."

Maccabee stepped forward, searching for an answer. "You could have defected. I could have helped you. With all the information rattling around in your head, you can cop a plea. You'll be a valuable asset to the CIA."

Petrovich stiffened. His chin jutted-out, defiantly. "Betray Spetsnaz honor? Never! I would not. You would not." He lowered his head, exhaling dejectedly. "I am glad mission failed. I am doomed man."

He looked up under glowering hooded eyes. "And now, my cousin, it is me and you who remain. What now?"

"I'm taking you in," Maccabee answered flatly, as he glared at his cousin. He reached behind his back in one rapid motion and whipped out his .45. He pointed it with his right hand at Yakov's chest.

The Spetsnaz stepped back. He raised his arms shoulder high. "I am unarmed," he lied. He watched Maccabee move closer, measuring the distance between them.

"Turn around," Maccabee snapped. "Lean against the wall, so I can frisk you."

He started to reach for Petrovich's shoulder to shove him forward, but the speed in which the big man moved surprised him.

Petrovich started to turn toward the wall, then spun around. He pivoted on his left foot. His right foot kicked-out in a vicious karate back-kick, catching the .45 with his heel. The gun flew across the room.

Before Maccabee could react, Petrovich pivoted again. His left foot lashed-out with lightning speed, catching Maccabee with a brutal roundhouse kick. It smashed into his cheekbone, sending him sprawling across the floor. He slammed into several chairs and cocktail tables, knocking them over.

Petrovich pulled out his P-38 and pointed it at Maccabee, who scrambled slowly to his feet. "You Americans are courageous fools," he mocked, waving Maccabee back with his automatic. He moved cautiously across the room, keeping a steady aim. He picked-up the .45 lying on the floor and stuffed it into his waistband. "You are too trusting, my cousin."

He motioned Maccabee to move toward the down staircase. "I make bargain with you. Your life in return for my escape." He pursed his dry lips, his eyes glinting coldly. "You have not found me. Go to Pan Am and wait. In two hours I will be secure aboard Air France aircraft and on my way to safety."

Maccabee rubbed his swollen cheek, gaining respect for his cousin's prowess in karate. He kept his palms open, waist high, hoping he'd have an opportunity to strike back. How do you stop a Brahma bull?

He eyed his robust cousin with wary eyes. "You haven't a chance. Your mission's been scrubbed. Gorbachev has arrested every GRU and KGB officer involved in the plot. Moscow faxed your photo to Washington and New York. They're looking for you at every airline departure gate. My sidekick saw to that. You'll never make it."

"Comrade General Secretary did this? I do not believe you."

"My information is reliable. Straight from the White House. You're a hunted man. No matter where you go, someone out there's waiting to kill you ... to earn a rep'. You don't have a chance."

"They do not know how I now look."

"But I do."

Petrovich's finger tightened on the trigger. "You will tell them?"

"If they don't get you at this end, they'll get you when you land."

"You do this to your own cousin?"

"It is better to surrender to me than to ..."

Petrovich broke in, angrily. "No! I will not be imprisoned like caged animal. I follow orders. I am Spetsnaz. I will fight and die like soldier."

Maccabee glanced over his shoulder, apprehensively. Where in hell is Freddy? Maccabee inched forward, his eyes never wavering. He started to grin in a disarming way, then shot his right foot out, kicking at Petrovich's gun hand.

The Spetsnaz saw it coming. He rolled backward, spinning. He kicked out viciously with his left foot, smashing it into Maccabee's knee. He holstered his P-38 so he could have two free hands. He crushed his brawny weight into Maccabee.

The two men crashed onto the floor with Petrovich straddling Maccabee's chest.

They slid into another cocktail table, toppling it over. Maccabee 's head slammed against the back wall, stunning him.

He tried to roll and buck his cousin off, but the big man pressed his weight down harder. Maccabee felt his iron grip clutching the lapels of his safari jacket, pinning him to the carpeted floor. He arched his back and kicked out with both feet, trying to throw him off. It didn't work.

Petrovich dug his shoulder into Maccabee's chest, burying his head under Maccabee's shoulder, where he couldn't get to him. He clenched his fists into two hard knots and pressed them inward and down against the two jugular veins in Maccabee's neck.

Maccabee fought back, but felt his strength weakening. His vision blurred. He began to black out.

Darkness overcame him.

The vice-like grip on his throat loosened. The tons of weight on his chest lifted. He blinked his eyes. His vision returned slowly. He saw a fuzzy image of Petrovich kneeling at his side, glaring down at him. He clutched at the sore muscles in his throat.

He heard gruff words emitting from his cousin's thick lips. "I will not kill my own blood. You are cousin. Family. You are not enemy. Someday, my cousin, our countries will learn to trust each other. We will live in peace."

Maccabee struggled into a sitting position. He choked, then swallowed hard. He wet his lips and took several deep breaths. Petrovich knelt at his side. He held his hand out and pulled Maccabee to his feet.

Maccabee steadied himself, trying to regain his balance. He lowered his head, shaking it back and forth vigorously. His vision cleared.

Petrovich grinned. He twisted his head to see how badly his cousin was hurt. "You see good in minute."

Without saying a word, Maccabee's right fist shot out, smashing into Petrovich's jaw. Yakov reeled backwards in surprise. Maccabee followed up with a right cross, swinging from the shoulder with all his strength.

Petrovich ducked under the second punch, kicking Maccabee's right foot out from under him with a sweep of his foot. As he blocked Maccabee's punch, he threw a sharp karate chop into his rib cage. He moved in close, pivoting, grabbing his extended arm.

Maccabee was flipped onto his back without realizing it. The big man's burly arm locked around his neck from behind, choking him in a stranglehold. He could feel the fat of Petrovich's palm pressing against the back of his head. One snap, and he knew it would be over.

"Give up!" Petrovich ordered, "or I break neck."

Maccabee couldn't wrench loose. He gagged, his vision blurring again. He slapped his free hand weakly against Petrovich's burly arm, twice in submission. "Okay," Maccabee spat-out. "I quit. You're too much for me."

Petrovich loosened his grip. "Don't you know when to stop fighting?"

Maccabee forced his arm away. He sat up, rubbing his neck. He climbed up on all fours, crawling back to his feet. His vision cleared. He eyed his burly cousin, then straightened up a chair that had been overturned and straddled it.

Petrovich rubbed his jaw where Maccabee had slugged him. "You hit hard, my

231

cousin. We make good team some day, you and me, yes-s?"

"No way," Maccabee uttered, unyielding. He tried to catch his breath. "You don't have a fighting chance, Yakov. You can't go back to Russia, they'll arrest you or execute you, maybe both."

The Spetsnaz nodded. "I am alone, man without a country. I cannot go home, I cannot stay here."

"Why?"

"I have broken law, I killed KGB assassin before she killed me."

"That's justified manslaughter. I doubt if the FBI would allow the case to come to court." Maccabee hesitated, then asked the painful question he'd been harboring. "Were you involved in General Palmer's assassination or Sergeant Washington's murder?"

"No. That was KGB dirty business. I am not assassin. I swim into New York Sunday night. Kolchak take me to safehouse Monday noon. I had been awake for thirty nine straight hours. I sleep around clock until Wednesday morning. I read about general's death. I am sorry. It was bad way to die."

"And Sergeant Washington?"

"KGB operation, not GRU. I had no part in it."

Maccabee squinched his neck muscles, trying to unlimber. "Did you know anything about the mole in the 38th CA Command, about Major Kurt Goetz or his German-born wife, Erika?"

He blanched. "A mole? I do not understand."

"Kolchak had a spy hidden under deep cover in our unit. A mole."

"Ah-h, a mole," he laughed, comprehending. "I have network of deep cover agents in West Germany. No, I know nothing about mole in 38th."

"Yet, you have no sense of guilt about blowing three hundred and fifty innocent people in a civilian airliner out of the sky?"

Petrovich nodded. "I am Spetsnaz commander. Target was identified seventy-two hours before attack. There was no time for conscience, only execution. If I had been on boat, I would have pulled trigger. Victory is more important than survival. I would not have failed. So, you see my naive cousin, I am part of conspiracy to embarrass America, to catch America asleep during weak moment while it pursues policy of peace."

"Now you're an outcast."

The Spetsnaz nodded, recognizing his intolerable plight. "I am now renegade. My life is over ... forfeit."

"There has to be an alternative, a way for you to redeem yourself. A way to save your life."

They stared at each other, saying nothing.

Petrovich laid his forged passport and Air France ticket onto the table. "You would identify me, my cousin, when I deplane in Paris?"

"Yes," Maccabee nodded. "It's my sworn duty."

Petrovich smiled, stoically. "You see, we are alike. You and me. We follow orders to bitter end."

He rose to his full height, shoving the chair aside. He grabbed Maccabee's .45 out of his waistband and snapped back the receiver to see that the chamber was empty. He

232

ejected the magazine clip and slipped it into his pocket. He handed the .45 to Maccabee, butt first. "Time for shooting each other is over. Come, let us walk together on concourse before I am discovered. I must find way to escape."

Maccabee hesitated. A new idea surged through his mind. "I may have a solution to your dilemma."

"I will not defect to United States," Petrovich protested, angrily. "Never!"

"Who said defect?" Maccabee replied. He grasped his unwilling cousin lightly by the arm. "Someone out there needs your help. I think there's a way to put your years of experience to good use. Come, follow me."

Maccabee led Petrovich out onto the main concourse. He looked down the long corridor that led back to the balcony overlooking the lobby of the International Airlines Arrivals building. He didn't see any sign of danger.

They strolled past Sabena and Air India Airlines. Maccabee noticed a few passengers standing in line at a hot dog stand among the food concessions. Petrovich drifted over to a nearby garbage bin and buried his canvas totebag, false passport and credit card underneath the trash. As they approached the next airline, Maccabee stopped. He took Petrovich by the elbow and led him to the bomb-proof steel door. He rapped sharply on it.

Maccabee stepped aside to let Petrovich fill the entranceway.

His cousin studied him thoughtfully, then gazed at the sign on the locked door. He laughed aloud, his self-confidence returning. A genuine smile spread across his broad bullish face. "It is good idea. It will work."

A young security guard with dark Yemenite features, wearing a white open collar shirt and blue slacks, opened the heavy door, exposing a snub-nosed .38 in his hip holster. He poked his head out. "Yes-s?"

Petrovich shoved the door open wider and stepped inside. Maccabee marched closely behind him. A heavy blue haze of cigarette smoke, and the clamor of boisterous, chattering vacationers all talking at once engulfed them.

Petrovich spoke to the guard in a gruff military manner. "Take me to Mossad. I seek asylum. I am Soviet GRU Spetsnaz Commander, Colonel Yakov Helner Petrovich. I am Ukranian Jew. I seek right of return to Israel. My life is in immediate danger."

Within seconds, they were confronted by two armed El Al security guards in their early twenties, who held Uzi submachine guns trained on them. They were instantly surrounded by three Israeli intelligence officers.

The senior officer named Schmulig, a native-born Israeli paratrooper in his forties with blond curly hair and blue eyes, scrutinized the Russian carefully, asking abruptly, "You have papers?" He switched his penetrating gaze to Maccabee. "You look American. You are with him?"

Maccabee nodded. He flashed his army ID. "He speaks the truth. He doesn't have papers, but I'll vouch for him. If you contact Colonel Ed Contino at JFK security, he'll verify what I've said."

Schmulig signaled a young security guard, a Sephardic Jew with dark hair who stood next to him, to use his two-way radio. The guard spoke in Hebrew to his

233

superiors, who were watching them on video monitors. Schmulig asked bluntly, "If he is Soviet defector, why don't you grant him asylum in United States? Why Israel?"

Petrovich brushed forward, aggressively. "I answer for myself." He opened his sports jacket, exposing his holstered P-38. The Israeli guards snatched the gun from his holster. They manhandled him, pushing him against the wall, face first. They frisked him from head to toe, finding the magazine clip to Maccabee's .45 in his pocket. He turned his head and scowled. He spoke directly to Schmulig. "I cannot stay in America. I kill KGB assassin here at airport one hour ago. I am man without country. KGB will hunt me down in U.S. and murder me. Only Israel can provide sanctuary."

The Israeli security guards isolated Petrovich, moving him away quickly from the cluster of curious tourists. They also disarmed a cooperative Maccabee and relieved him of his .45.

"That magazine clip belongs to me," Maccabee said, pointing to it. "I'd like it back." He stood near the doorway, observing silently.

Petrovich nodded his approval to the Israeli security guards, who ushered him toward a staircase that led to their security office on the third floor. "Very professional," he murmured. He turned to Schmulig and demanded in a brusque tone, "I must speak to Mossad officer of equal rank. I have secret military intelligence to share with him."

He stopped and walked back several steps towards his cousin. The armed security guards opened up an aisle for the burly commando to pass through. He clasped Maccabee's hand firmly in his. "Perhaps, we meet again, my cousin." He smiled, warmly. "As we said at cousin Jackie's, next year in Jerusalem."

Maccabee grinned. His square jaw jutted out. He gripped his cousin's right hand and squeezed it with firm resolution. Both men stared into each other's eyes, neither seeking to gain advantage, their strength binding them together as allies instead of adversaries.

Petrovich slapped Maccabee vigorously on the shoulder. He started up the stairs. Stopping, he turned back and shouted in a gruff Russian accent that everyone could hear, "As we Israelis say ... Shalom!"

He winked, waved his hand in farewell, and was gone.

Maccabee stared ahead, saying a silent prayer. He thanked God that Grandma Clara Helner had migrated to America when she had, that his side of the Helner family had been spared the agony of the holocaust. He fought back the tears that began to well up in his eyes. Since Yakov wouldn't defect to the United States, at least there's a chance for his redemption in Israel. He watched his cousin disappear.

No one heard Maccabee whisper, "That could have been me."

The End

234